Praise for the novels of Lisa Plumley

HOLIDAY AFFAIR

"Secrets and subte... this well-crafted, heart... th of engaging characte... rable children, and great... ying, cocoa-worthy holi...

—...*urnal*

"Lisa Plumley's latest holiday novel delivers. It has warm gooey holiday moments complete with happy children, Christmas traditions such as caroling and decorating Christmas cookies, and, oh yeah, hot and steamy romance. Loaded with fun pop-culture references and witty dialogue, *Holiday Affair* delivers on entertainment!"

—*The Romance Reader* (5 Hearts!)

"A delightful story with utterly charming characters. It brings to life the sounds, smells, and tastes of Christmas as it brings together more than just the two main characters for a joyous holiday season."

—*Romantic Times BOOK Reviews* (4½ stars)

MY FAVORITE WITCH

"In keeping with Plumley's tradition of lively romantic comedy (*Home for the Holidays*), her first foray into the paranormal-witch-world subgenre is quirky, sexy, creative, and hilarious."

—*Library Journal*

"Humorous adventures and unexpected romance with a sprinkling of heartwarming moments will keep the reader well entertained in this delightful tale, skillfully crafted by the clever Plumley."

—*Booklist*

HOME FOR THE HOLIDAYS

"Lisa Plumley once again gifts readers with a Yuletide story sure to put you in a holiday mood. This is vintage Plumley. She's created a cast of characters that are a bit eccentric, quirky, and likeable, and spun a story that will make you smile."

—Lezlie Patterson, *McClatchy-Tribune News Service*

"A delightful secondary romance adds to the fun in this upbeat romp that is touching, hilarious, and lightly dusted with seasonal charm."

—*Library Journal*

LET'S MISBEHAVE

"Once again, Plumley shows her fine flair for comedy as Marisol learns that there is life beyond Rodeo Drive, and the Connelly triplets discover that they can't scare away every nanny. Full of witty dialogue and hilarious situations, this romp with a heart is certain to please readers."

—*Booklist* (starred review; named one of the Top Ten Romances of 2007)

"Plumley not only delivers a fun-filled premise, clever dialogue, and a delightfully sexy sports-loving hero, she brings to life a memorable, hilarious, and utterly unique heroine readers will adore. This is pure romantic fantasy and an absolutely entertaining novel from start to finish."

—*Romantic Times BOOK Reviews* (4½ stars; Top Pick!)

"*Let's Misbehave* is funny, romantic, heartwarming, and sexy. It's fantastic!"

—*Joyfully Reviewed*

MAD ABOUT MAX

"A cool cast of secondary characters adds much to the story as clever Plumley, who is already known for her entertaining romantic comedies, presents another winner in this humorous and engaging tale about a man who literally loses his shirt, but finds his heart."

—*Booklist* (starred review)

"*Mad About Max* kept me laughing from beginning to end. What great characters! Very highly recommended, especially for fans of romantic comedy."

—*Romance Junkies*

JOSIE DAY IS COMING HOME

"Turning not-so-perfect, unlikely characters into romance heroes and heroines is Lisa Plumley's forte, and she once again delivers a zany cast who will make you laugh!"

—*The State* newspaper

"In this heartwarming, often humorous story, the feisty Josie proves that you can go home again—if you've got the right stuff. And once again, the talented Plumley, whose books include *Perfect Switch*, proves that when it comes to writing romantic comedy, few do it better."

—*Booklist*

Also by Lisa Plumley

MAKING OVER MIKE

FALLING FOR APRIL

RECONSIDERING RILEY

PERFECT TOGETHER

PERFECT SWITCH

JOSIE DAY IS COMING HOME

ONCE UPON A CHRISTMAS

MAD ABOUT MAX

SANTA BABY
(anthology with Lisa Jackson,
Elaine Coffman, and Kylie Adams)

I SHAVED MY LEGS FOR THIS?!
(anthology with Theresa Alan,
Holly Chamberlin, and Marcia Evanick)

LET'S MISBEHAVE

HOME FOR THE HOLIDAYS

MY FAVORITE WITCH

HOLIDAY AFFAIR

Published by Kensington Publishing Corporation

Melt Into You

LISA PLUMLEY

ZEBRA BOOKS
KENSINGTON PUBLISHING CORP.
http://www.kensingtonbooks.com

ZEBRA BOOKS are published by

Kensington Publishing Corp.
119 West 40th Street
New York, NY 10018

All Kensington titles, imprints, and distributed lines are available at special quantity discounts for bulk purchases for sales
promotion, premiums, fund-raising, educational, or institu-
tional use.

Special book excerpts or customized printings can also be created to fit specific needs. For details, write or phone the office
of the Kensington Special Sales Manager: Attn.: Special Sales
Department. Kensington Publishing Corp., 119 West 40th
Street, New York, NY 10018. Phone: 1-800-221-2647.

Zebra and the Z logo Reg. U.S. Pat. & TM Off.

ISBN-13: 978-1-4201-2211-4
ISBN-10: 1-4201-2211-8

First Printing: May 2012

10 9 8 7 6 5 4 3 2 1

Printed in the United States of America

To Peter Senftleben,
with thanks for all his enthusiasm,
encouragement, and insightful editing!

And to John Plumley,
with all my love, now and forever.

Chapter 1

September 2002
La Jolla, California

Damon Torrance believed in a lot of things.

He believed in perfect surf, unassailable integrity, and the ultimate Baja fish taco. He believed in making connections, making things happen, and making a never-fail margarita (it was all about the blue agave tequila). He believed that nudity was better than wearing . . . anything at all, no matter how pricey the clothes were or where you happened to be going.

He believed that rules were made to be broken and that whoever had said virtue was its own reward probably hadn't tried hard enough to be bad first. He believed that person shouldn't have made that decision so damn hastily. Or so publicly. Because that idiot had ruined it for everyone else who just wanted to have a good time.

When it came right down to it, more than anything else, Damon believed that life was too short to waste time with anything less than hundred-percent pleasure. Plain and simple.

That's why, when he found himself spending a week with

an attractive, capable, flirtatious, and ultra-available journalist (she made it bluntly, sexily, one-step-short-of-manhandling-him obvious that she was single) who was writing a profile of him and his family's company, Torrance Chocolates, for *Oceanside Living* magazine's "Getting to Know . . ." feature, Damon took the only reasonable action.

He let her seduce him. On his desk. In full view of the glittering Pacific Ocean outside. Right between his stapler and his office phone, with his brand-new, full-size desk calendar for a cushion. Not that Kimberly (the journalist) bothered to scout a prime location before she smiled, dropped her notepad, and lunged at him.

It would have been rude to say no, Damon reasoned. So he met her kiss with a sliding, seductive, nice-to-meet-you lip-lock of his own . . . and before he knew it, they were "Getting to Know . . ." each other pretty damn well. Kimberly's warmth was a sharp contrast to the brisk ocean breeze coming in off the Pacific. Her perfume added synthetic flowers and spice to the sugary smells of the confectionary shop downstairs. Her breath panted over him. Her I'm-a-professional suit jacket hit the floor. So did his I'm-supposed-to-be-working shirt. They kissed a little more. Then they kissed again, more passionately.

A discordant electronic jangle startled them both.

Kimberly quit kissing him. She frowned. "What was that?"

"Who cares?" Right on cue, it happened again. At the sound, Damon glanced sideways. "Oh. It's my father's BlackBerry."

At her mystified expression, Damon nodded at the device.

"It's used to get e-mails and appointments on the go. I gave it to my dad as a birthday present, but he didn't take to the technology the way I hoped he would. That's why it's in here and not with him." Damon smiled at her. Confidingly, he added, "I think he's afraid he's going to drop 'that expensive gadget' into a vat of bittersweet chocolate ganache or something."

It was semi-likely. Jimmy Torrance spent most of his time and all his creativity on the family business. That's how he'd turned a tiny seaside sweetshop into one of San Diego's favorite "hidden treasures" for thirty years running. That's how he'd earned himself the very office that he shared with Damon today.

"Aw. You gave your dad a birthday present?" Kimberly cooed, running her fingers over his bare chest. "That's *so* sweet!"

"It's not that unusual, actually. He *is* my dad, after all. I give my mom something on her birthday every year, too."

Kimberly shook her head, seeming inordinately impressed with his filial devotion. "I knew you were more than just a studly corporate hotshot." More stroking. "You're a nice guy, too! I have to say, when I heard I'd be profiling the company's head of Internet development, I was expecting to meet someone a lot more . . ." Here, she broke off. She gave him a thorough once-over. She shrugged. "Well . . . geekier."

Damon grinned. "You can't judge a book by its cover. Any second now, I might start talking about byte serving, hypertext transfer protocol, and compression scheme negotiation."

"I have a better idea." Kimberly slid her hands lower. She cupped his ass, then hauled him nearer. "Don't talk at all."

"Yes, ma'am." Agreeably, Damon concentrated on using his mouth for more diverting activities than talking. But even as he did, his dad's BlackBerry chimed again. Damon began remembering something—something he ought to have remembered earlier.

At the same time, a familiar voice floated down the corridor outside his office. "Damon? Well, I guess you'd say he's a genius," his father was telling someone proudly. "His official promotion was a long time coming. He resisted it, but—"

Whatever else Jimmy said was lost to Damon. He was too busy simultaneously enjoying the naughty way Kimberly was nibbling on his ear and trying to remember what his father had said earlier.

All that came to mind was his father saying, as he'd done a million times a day since Damon had been old enough to outwit his first babysitter and go looking for adventure, "You've got to *focus*, Damon. Focus! Try to behave for once. All right?"

But all those requests were bona fide lost causes, and they both knew it. Who did his father think he'd been raising all this time? One of the Backstreet Boys? A new Disney teenybopper idol?

Hell, no. There was no fun to be had in being *good*. Damon knew that. There was no glory to be found in staying focused, either. All that mattered was looking ahead . . . and maybe finding out if Kimberly's freckles meandered all the way to her cleavage. Curiously, Damon started unbuttoning her shirt.

The voices outside grew louder. His father—and his unknown guest—were coming closer. Probably to this office. Damon swore.

With a mighty effort, he wrenched himself away from Kimberly. He peeked down at his desk calendar. It was rumpled. It had slid pretty far sideways. But Damon could still make out something handwritten on the square representing today's date.

There, right next to Kimberly's delectable bare thigh, were the words *administrative assistant* and the time, *9:30*.

Having deciphered his father's unmistakable scrawl, Damon blinked in surprise. "You can *write* on these things?"

Kimberly laughed. "That's what they're for, silly."

"Oh. I thought it was decorative. But in my own defense, I don't spend much time in the office." Momentarily distracted again, Damon lowered his gaze to the cleavage he'd revealed, framed now by Kimberly's silky unbuttoned shirt. He looked at the high, *high* slit on her *Ally McBeal*-style miniskirt (damn, he loved that trend), then stroked his fingers over her knee. "It made a really fine landing pad, though. You were clever enough to discover that for us."

"It was my pleasure. *Believe me*." Kimberly gave him another sultry look. She seemed to specialize in them. "Now . . . where were we?"

"Right about . . . here." Damon squeezed her thigh. Another kiss kept him pinned atop her, even as he heard footsteps coming nearer. Just then, he didn't care. Life was all about enjoyment.

". . . and this is where you'll be spending most of your time," Jimmy Torrance said as he opened the office door. "I'm afraid you might be stuck inside a lot, but the view is awfully nice."

"Oh, yes, it *is* nice," his father's female guest said in an appreciative tone. Her footsteps preceded his into the office. "I love the ocean!" There was a pause. Then, in a wry voice, she added, "Will the guy who's humping like a bunny on the desk be here every day? Or is that a one-time-only thing?"

No one ever answered her question. Natasha Jennings would have been lying if she'd said she wasn't disappointed by that.

In the few minutes it took for Jimmy Torrance to hastily cross the room, shut off his dinging BlackBerry on the other unoccupied desk, and confer with the desktop Casanova and his nearly naked female partner, though, she did learn several interesting facts about her new workplace.

First of all, she learned that either today was Nooky Monday or Torrance Chocolates was a *lot* more freewheeling than she'd anticipated. Second, she learned that it was both busier and much more charming—given its location inside a two-story former surf shop in La Jolla—than she'd foreseen based on her initial interview. Third, she learned that although her official job title was *administrative assistant*, they might as well have had *miracle worker* printed on her business cards.

Because so far, all she'd done was tour the shop, the chocolate-making kitchen downstairs, and the several makeshift offices upstairs, and already Natasha could see that Torrance Chocolates needed help. They had plenty of drive, heart, and inspiration, that was true; but their transition from mom-and-pop shop to burgeoning corporate power player was clearly overwhelming them. At the moment, they were short of staff, space, and direction. To manage those things, they needed *her*.

Jimmy Torrance and the rest of his staff might not know it yet, but the smartest thing they'd ever done was choose Natasha from among the dozens of (curiously bodacious-looking) applicants she'd seen during the open interviews last month.

In fact, it occurred to her, most of those applicants had looked a lot like the woman who'd been doing the horizontal desktop tango a minute ago. They'd been made up, perfumed, and dressed to attract. They'd worn super-high stilettos and trendily flat-ironed hair. Most inexplicably, they'd been unable to say the name of their potential future boss, Damon Torrance, without giggling and trading giddy, girlish glances with each other.

All in all, the experience had been a lot like interviewing for a job as head groupie for a rock band. Which, in retrospect, made Natasha wonder why Jimmy Torrance *had* chosen her. Because while she did have her share of vanity—and her very own flat iron, lip gloss, and high heels—what she didn't have was the kind of va-va-voom necessary to hold the attention of a rock star . . . or the corporate equivalent of one.

Not that she cared about that too much, Natasha reminded herself. She didn't need nonstop reinforcement of her own attractiveness. Especially not now and especially not at work.

As the daughter of parents who'd both held down more than one job on several occasions—just to make ends meet—Natasha understood the value of hard work. She'd made it through high school and graduated from community college and then UCSD, all while working full-time to pay her tuition.

This was her chance to kick off her career, and Natasha wanted to succeed. Admittedly, she was starting at the bottom, but still . . . she was only twenty-four. She was here. She was *in* at a growing company. Unlike her competition, she hadn't had to outfit herself in sexed-up "office attire" like a hot-to-trot fugitive Victoria's Secret model to make it happen, either.

Speaking of hot-to-trot . . .

Natasha gave the office-hopping Lothario a second look. He was probably only a couple of years older than she was, but he'd made her first day at Torrance Chocolates memorable, that's for sure. She wondered if he made the rounds of *all* the offices and *all* the different desks, or if he'd come in here solely for the spectacular view—which, in hindsight, had only been improved by the addition of *him*, looking all shirtless and muscular and dark-haired and intense, doing his thing in the middle of it.

Either way, she doubted this particular incident was his first time getting lucky at work. Whoever he was, he had that aura about him—a quality that made people want to be close to him. Looking at him more carefully now only confirmed Natasha's initial impression: this was a man for whom things came easily, whether those things were women, good times, or success.

Speaking of success . . .

Where was her über-impressive new wunderkind boss? She wasn't going to be working as a direct report to Jimmy Torrance, Natasha remembered as she watched Mr. Desktop considerately shield his paramour from view so she could get dressed. She was going to work for Jimmy's son, the famously titillating Damon Torrance, who'd been curiously absent from the hiring process.

He's pretty easygoing about these things, Jimmy had explained with a nonchalant wave. *He'll be happy with my choice*.

Natasha hoped Jimmy was right. As she watched the now-dressed woman scoop up a notepad, a pen, and several glossy issues of *Oceanside Living* from the credenza, she further hoped that whoever worked in this office wasn't too attached to their desktop calendar. Because although Mr. Desktop hastily gave it a sideways shove to straighten it, the calendar looked wrecked. The only way to extract any useful information from it would be to read and interpret the butt prints. Everybody knew that, in the Internet age, butt-based cryptanalysis was a dying art.

Finally, the door shut behind the woman. Silence descended on the office, emphasized by the low crash of the surf outside.

Jimmy cleared his throat. The mystery man didn't speak, leaving Natasha plenty of time to notice that in addition to behaving in an undeniably chivalrous manner toward the woman, he'd also tried to compose himself by dragging on his shirt. But that effort was largely ineffective. He'd buttoned his shirt crookedly, he still seemed . . . *distracted* somehow (probably by thoughts of all the workplace exhibitionist sex he was missing out on), and his dark wavy hair, while doing a very good job of framing his handsome, sharp-nosed, stubble-jawed face, looked all bedhead-y and messy, too. It was way too easy to imagine him actually lolling around sexily *in* bed, Natasha thought, which definitely spoiled the whole "I'm hard at work" effect.

Evidently he hadn't gotten the memo that, these days, all the cool guys gunked up their hair with gel. Even her husband, Paul, who'd been a hard-core flannel-and-grunge guy when they'd met, now looked like a runaway member of 'N Sync. It could have been worse, though. He could have developed a thing for those velour tracksuits or the loud shirts worn by TV poker players.

Natasha was sick to death of poker. If she never saw another green baize table with sunglasses-wearing card players around it—on TV, in a movie, or at a party—it would be too soon. In fact, she didn't even know why poker was so popular. *American Idol* she understood. Kelly Clarkson really *was* talented; she'd deserved her win. As current pop culture phenomena went, even the merging of J.Lo and Ben Affleck into "Bennifer" was easier to tolerate. As a matter of fact, Natasha was kind of rooting for them both. At heart, she was a die-hard romantic. She *wanted* true love to conquer all. So when it came right down to it . . .

Suddenly, she realized that Mr. Desktop was watching her. There was no question: He'd caught her daydreaming on the job. It was a good thing *he* wasn't her boss, Natasha told herself with a stalwart lift of her chin, because she didn't think she wanted a supervisor who could read her so easily. She definitely didn't want one who looked quite so . . . *fascinating* while he did it.

No wonder he'd successfully seduced a woman on a desktop. In broad daylight. With strangers wandering the halls outside. Mr. Desktop had some kind of remarkable give-it-to-me mojo—some kind of you-know-you-want-to appeal that would have softened even the hardest of hearts. Or opened even the most tightly crossed legs. Not that *she* wanted to open *her* legs, but still . . .

Vividly, Natasha imagined *herself* on that desk, crumpling the calendar with her own nearly naked booty, having her shirt unbuttoned and her neck kissed, with her breasts heaving and her thighs parting as she pulled Mr. Desktop closer and closer. . . .

Too late, she understood. "*You're* Damon Torrance."

Chapter 2

Damon's eyes gleamed, brown and full of mischief. "Guilty. And *you're* my new assistant." He held out his hand. "I'm sorry about . . . before. It was all my fault. Sometimes I get carried away." His smile looked unrepentant, full of blatant resolve to besmirch that very same desk ten minutes from now if he had the chance. Probably he would. Contritely, he put his free hand over his heart. "I promise I'll try to reform while you're here."

He made it sound so temporary. "While I'm here?"

He seemed abashed. "Your predecessors haven't lasted long."

"Oh." Wondering why that was, Natasha accepted his handshake. As she did, an unmistakable jolt crackled through her. It felt real. Electric. Her knees weakened. She wanted to stare. She *did* stare. Damon Torrance was different when his focus was centered on you, she realized. His eyes, his face, his shoulders, his mouth . . . even his nice white teeth all seemed ridiculously interesting. "Why is that?" she asked, striving not to steer his hand to her breast. Oh God. Had she really just thought that? What was the *matter* with her? She slapped on a casually inquisitive look. "Is the work difficult?"

"Not really." Damon shrugged. "I don't think so."

She couldn't quit gawking. Reluctantly, Natasha slipped her hand from his grasp. Sex appeal rolled from him in dizzy waves. It broke along the shore of her determination not to be wooed, then crested again. It was a good thing she'd armored herself with a prim suit, worn her hair in a strict ponytail, and gotten used to tamping down her more . . . *inventive* side while at work.

Well, technically she'd gotten used to tamping down her inventive side everyplace these days, in every circumstance—mostly to make way for *Paul's* inventive side to flourish, since he needed it to make a living and she didn't—but still . . . she'd been smart to play it cool for her first day at work.

"The truth is, my assistants all leave because I sleep with them," Damon explained, appearing unbothered by admitting it. "Sometimes they fall in love with me. Sometimes I fall in love with them. It never lasts. I'm kind of fickle." Another grin. This one seemed thoughtful . . . and maybe 10 percent devilish, besides. "But that won't be a problem with you, Natasha." He turned. "Right, Dad?"

Jimmy Torrance frowned. "I hope not, son." Astutely, he glanced at Natasha. "He's right. He *is* fickle. This thing with the journalist was just the latest in a long line of—"

"Come on. I already explained that. All my fault." Damon held up his palm, good-naturedly diverting the conversation. "Anyway, I won't be having those problems with Natasha."

"You won't be?" Perversely, she felt stung. She also felt idiotically enamored of the way he said her name. *Natasha. Nataaasha.* She could have listened to him say it all day. All night. Over and over and—Just in time, she got a grip on herself. She shook her head. "No," Natasha announced in her most forceful, definitive tone. "You won't be." A beat. "You won't be having any problems wanting to sleep with me because . . . ?"

"Because you're married." Damon raised his eyebrows,

appearing surprised to have to explain himself. "A man's got to have his principles. Mine involve Pop-Tarts, kung fu, and not screwing around with married women."

At her undoubtedly openmouthed expression, he laughed.

"Especially *happily* married women," Damon added, "which *you* qualify as, if that enormous hickey on your neck is anything to go by." He leaned nearer. With a conspiratorial whisper—and a cheerful wink—he added, "Makeup never works to hide them. Especially on blondes, like you." He nodded at her shoulder-length blond hair, then gave the rest of her a swift, masculine, thrillingly appreciative perusal. Natasha had the unmistakable impression he'd seen *all* of her . . . and approved wholeheartedly, too. Damon's gaze whipped back to her hickey. "Just hold your head high and forget about it. That's all you can do."

That sounded like the voice of experience talking. Aghast, Natasha flung her palm over her neck. She'd forgotten about her hickey—and for one brief nanosecond, she'd forgotten about being married, too. But now that Damon had pointed it out, her marriage came rushing back to her. So did her ability to use her brainpower for more than swooning over her new boss.

Of course she didn't want Damon to want to sleep with her. *She* had principles, too! While they didn't involve junk food or martial arts, they did involve avoiding infidelity.

No matter what.

"Wait a minute. I didn't tell you Natasha was married." With endearing old-school politeness, Jimmy swerved his gaze away from her telltale hickey. "I didn't even give you her personnel file—not that you would have read it if I had."

"You didn't have to tell me. I guessed." Damon gave her a speculative look. "You're a newlywed, right? Just back from your honeymoon? I'd say you went to . . . someplace sunny. Acapulco? No, wait." He snapped his fingers. "Cancun, right along the coast."

This time, Natasha *knew* she was staring openmouthed. "I haven't even unpacked yet. How did you . . . ?"

"Your wedding ring. And your glow. You're glowing."

At that, she beamed. She probably *was* glowing. Because of *Paul*, Natasha reminded herself. Because of her *husband*.

"My husband is an artist. A painter," she felt compelled to say. "He's very talented. He was especially inspired by Mexico."

"Mmm." Obviously, Damon was too busy practicing his Twenty Questions-style guessing game to give too much thought to trivialities like husbands. Or their unique artistic inspirations. "The pattern of your sunburn was a dead give-away." Damon nodded at the neckline of her suit. "If you weren't so buttoned up, it would be even more obvious."

It was a good thing she was "buttoned up." Otherwise, Damon's apparent X-ray vision would have left her feeling even more exposed than she already did. As though the imprint of her teeny honeymoon bikini was imprinted on her skin—and technically it was, only in reverse—Natasha crossed her arms over her chest.

"Besides, you didn't have to give me Natasha's personnel file, Dad," Damon went on blithely . . . the same way he appeared to do everything. "Brittney in HR was *dying* to do me a favor."

Jimmy sniffed. "I'll just bet she was." He shook his finger at his son. "This is why I hired a new assistant for you!"

"Right. And your insistence on doing that is why I went along with it." Damon tossed his father a plaintive look—one the elder Torrance seemed to miss. "I want to make you proud, Dad."

"That's easy. *Don't* sleep with this one! Hear me?"

"I hear you." All the same, Damon appeared wounded. "Don't I get any credit for doing my due diligence this time? I read the personnel file! It was boring!" He stared out the window, possibly hungering for a turn in the lineup of surfers. "That's more than I did when the last four assistants came on board."

"Four?" Natasha blurted. "You slept with *four* of them?"

Her new boss was a man slut. This job was going to be tricky. She was going to have her hands full of him. *With* him!

Damon had the grace to appear embarrassed. "Except for one instance, it wasn't my idea, I swear." He gave her a humble look. "Was I supposed to say no? Feelings would have been hurt."

"Right." She scoffed. "Women just leap into your arms."

Unfazed, Damon and Jimmy gazed at her. They both nodded.

"Yeah. Pretty much," Damon said, rubbing his stubbled jaw.

"Since he was a teenager," Jimmy agreed with a long-suffering sigh. "It's the damnedest thing. But when *you* interviewed with me, Natasha, and said you were about to get married, I knew—"

"You knew you'd found your son's kryptonite. Me."

It was all right there in Damon Torrance's philosophies for living: Pop-Tarts, kung fu, and not screwing around with married women. Simultaneously relieved and incredulous, Natasha frowned.

"My qualifications for this job go way beyond being married," she argued. "I'm smart, I'm capable, I'm passionate—"

"I'm listening," Damon said, perking up.

"—and I'm not going to put up with any bullshit. Get it?"

Both men widened their eyes. It was almost as though they'd never heard a blue-eyed, blond-haired, bubbly California girl talk frankly before. Jimmy rallied first. Soberly, he nodded.

"Based on my research"—and Natasha had, indeed, done plenty of research, because while you could take the girl out of UCSD, you couldn't take the UCSD out of the girl— "I think you're headed for the top of your field, Damon. And

I intend to go straight to the top with you. If that's not what you want, tell me right now, because I don't have time to waste. I've done a lot of work to get my foot in the door at a good company. Now that I'm here, I plan to take full advantage of it."

She might have downgraded her ambitions to the assistant level in order to help support her husband, Natasha knew, but she'd be damned if she'd tamp them down completely.

Gratifyingly, this time Damon was the one staring at her.

Solemnly, he took her hand in his. "You're not kryptonite. You're incredible. You're like . . ." Seeming at a loss for words, he swore. "You're like a badass cheerleader who makes straight A's. Like a fast-talking Goody Two-shoes who just shot her first *Playboy* centerfold. Like the world's sexiest, strictest, most nurturing CPA-turned-supermodel." Seeming on the verge of coming up with several more unlikely alter egos for her, Damon stopped. He smiled. "You're unique, is what I'm trying so say. I *do* want what you want. In fact, I think I just fell in love you."

For a heartbeat, Natasha was almost sucked in by that. His deep brown eyes lured her. His happy-go-lucky grin beckoned her. Even his body, all tall and strong and masculine as he stood there before her, seemed somehow magnetized to pull her nearer.

She wondered, incredibly and nonsensically, what it would be like to be truly loved by a man like Damon Torrance. Then she gave herself a mental pinch and came to her senses for good.

"Don't tell me that again." Natasha pulled away. Doing so required far more effort than she would have liked or intended ever to admit. This . . . *attraction* she felt toward Damon would have to be squashed, plain and simple. It was wrong and foolhardy and just . . . *wrong*. She loved Paul! She truly did. "Don't tell me you love me. Don't flirt. Don't inform me of your sexual conquests or expect me to bail you out of them. I'm your assistant, not your nanny. If you remember that, we'll get along fine."

"You're my assistant, not my nanny," Damon repeated.

Even as he dutifully said those words, though, he just kept on grinning at her. It was as though she were a ray of sunshine warming him, an adorable puppy cheering him, a plate of Pop-Tarts . . . well, she didn't know *what* the Pop-Tarts were for, only that he seemed to have an ideology constructed around them.

Someday, she'd have to ask him about that.

"Right. And if you don't remember that—if you try to take advantage of me—I won't hesitate to take my talents elsewhere. Got it?" Natasha held out her hand. "Do we have a deal?"

Curiously, Damon considered her. "Do you always set up so many boundaries before doing things?"

"Usually they're necessary."

To her relief, Damon didn't ask *why* they were necessary.

Instead, he made a rueful face. "Why do I feel, all of a sudden, that *you're* the one who's hiring *me*?"

At the other desk, Jimmy laughed. "You'd better agree, son. If you try to stall, she'll talk you into a ten percent raise."

"Good idea." Natasha nodded. "But now that I've sized up the job, I'd say fifteen percent sounds more appropriate."

"Done." Jimmy agreed. "It'll be worth every penny just to see how this turns out—for however long it lasts, at least."

Natasha couldn't let his skepticism affect her. Now that she knew *they* needed her as much as *she* needed them, she had a little bit of leverage. It felt unfamiliar—but kind of good, too. Despite its newness, she couldn't help liking it.

And Paul had said she *wouldn't* be good at business. . . .

Damon gave her a forthright look. "Do you mean it?" he asked soberly. "Do you really think you can handle me?"

At that moment, Natasha could think of several scintillating ways to *handle him*. But since she was trying to focus on staying true to her wedding vows—and since Damon actually seemed concerned and hopeful and boyishly earnest—she turned her thoughts in a less bawdy direction. She nodded.

"Together, I think we can take on the world and win."

With that, Damon clasped her hand. Natasha felt another inner tremor rock her from her heels on up. As she and her new boss sealed their reckless deal, she hoped with all her might that the words she'd just said would be prophetic.

Together, I think we can take on the world and win.

She didn't know what that would look like or how it would feel. But now that she'd met Damon Torrance in person, Natasha had the sudden, unmistakable sensation that for the first time in her life, winning big was possible. She would have been a fool to let that go . . . no matter how stupidly giddy she felt when Damon smiled at her. She could handle that. Easy-peasy.

All she had to do was get started.

Oh, and stay married.

That way, she'd qualify as Damon's kryptonite for the long haul. After all, that's what seemed to have nabbed her the job over all the competition in the first place.

But since Natasha intended to do both those things anyway—get started *and* stay married—there was no problem here.

No problem at all . . .

Chapter 3

June 2007
Maranello, Italy

With his heart pounding, Damon gripped the wheel of the vintage Ferrari he was driving. He rounded the next corner at the Fiorano Circuit, feeling more alive than he had in months.

The car's engine roared. The chassis rumbled, transmitting barely contained power to Damon's entire body. The smells of petrol, motor oil, and burnt rubber filled the air. Gleefully, he inhaled all of it. His hands were full. But he wanted more.

When it came to shaking out the cobwebs, there was nothing like having a private racetrack at your disposal. For too long now, Damon realized as he took a curve, he'd been cooped up indoors. He'd been doing TV interviews. He'd been making press appearances. He'd been working hard to bring Torrance Chocolates to the whole sugar-crazed world, one truffle at a time.

It was working like gangbusters, too. Businesswise, things had never been better. The same was true for him personally.

   Good luck and good things seemed to stick to him like glue, Damon had noticed. Not that he tried very hard to ditch his own personal lucky star . . . and the friends, women, money, and (to be brutally honest) charmed life that went along with it.

   Officially speaking, Damon had come to Italy to use that magic of his to partner with Bandini Espresso. His mission was to persuade Bandini to join him in Torrance Chocolates' existing global chain of almost a thousand high-end chocolate boutiques and luxury cafés. If he succeeded in bringing Bandini on board, both companies would expand their product lineups, their customer bases, and their potential avenues for future growth and partnerships. The truth was, Damon wanted that partnership the same way he'd wanted to drive the Ferrari: without reservations.

   But that didn't mean he couldn't have a little fun while he was at it. So when Giada Bandini had invited him to take a spin around the Fiorano Circuit—where the Ferrari company tested new models and developed its cars for the legendary Suderia Ferrari Marlboro racing team—he'd agreed immediately. After all, he didn't want to become one of those "all work, no play" guys.

   Besides, Damon had already paid his dues. Just like he'd told Oprah last month during her latest "Favorite Things" episode featuring his company's cafés, he'd practically grown up behind the counter at Torrance Chocolates. He'd swept floors. He'd cashiered. At their original boardwalk location, he'd discovered a knack for relating to customers. Then, five years ago, he'd taken the company online . . . and everything had changed.

   Being one of the first companies to offer Internet ordering had put Torrance Chocolates on the map. The "Web" had sparked interest; that interest had led to calls for an IPO and more orders than they could handle. They'd ridden the dot-com bubble to the top. When that bubble had burst, they'd survived and even thrived. Now, five years later, the company was a runaway success—and because he'd helped make it happen, Damon had all the attendant perks and privileges and bonuses *he* could handle.

Nah. That was a lie, Damon decided as he brought the Ferrari to a squealing stop. He could handle all this and more.

More, more, more. More than ever, that was his credo.

"*Damn!* That was one fine ride." Wearing a nonstop grin, Damon caressed the roadster's steering wheel. His ears still rang with the aftereffects of speed and horsepower. The old-model Ferrari had a candy-apple-red body that hugged the road, abundant curves, and an open top that let its driver feel the *Italiana* wind racing past every pore. After driving the car once around the course, Damon felt completely fired up. On edge. Ready for action of any kind. "I want to go again."

"Screw that. It's my turn." To his left in the car's passenger seat, his friend Jason Huerta gave his shoulder a shove. "Move it, Herbie. I'm not letting you hog all the fun."

"I don't think you have much choice about that."

"Oh yeah?"

"Yeah. I'm bigger and stronger than you are. Also, I have the keys. And *my* wife isn't on her way over here—"

"You don't have a wife, Bozo."

"—but *yours* is." Squinting against the sunshine, Damon peered at the crowd of spectators milling at the track's edge. Farther in the distance stood a group of flag-toting *Tifosi*—ardent racing fans—but he was more concerned with the petite, blond-haired woman who had separated herself from the throng and was currently headed toward the car with a purposeful stride. Damon aimed his chin in her direction. "It looks as though Amy might have something to say about you having 'your turn.'"

Jason looked, too. At the sight of his wife, he gave a sappy grin. Then, already climbing out of the low-slung roadster, he waved at Amy. "Well . . . she might have a point if she did," he told Damon as he exited the car. "I spent the morning in business meetings with the Bandini execs and the afternoon playing racecar driver with you. This *is* supposed to be a romantic first-anniversary trip for Amy, after all."

"So? Maranello is romantic!" Damon gestured at the grass surrounding the track, the jumpsuit-wearing mechanics, the asphalt and spare tires. "*Speed* is romantic. Really romantic!"

Sadly, Jason shook his head. "You're woefully misinformed about romance, bro. Sure, *speed* is sexy. But *slow* is romantic."

"Sexy. Romantic. What's the difference?"

"About half an hour, multiple orgasms, and a lifetime of togetherness." With that laughing pronouncement, Amy arrived. She grabbed Jason the moment his feet hit the racetrack. "I got an amazing picture of you, babe! Are you having fun?"

Despite Damon's dire warning, Amy didn't *seem* like a woman who was about to quash her husband's turn at Ferrari driving.

Pointing out as much with a meaningful over-the-shoulder glance at Damon, Jason nodded. "Hell, yeah! I'm driving next!"

The two of them embraced. Then they proceeded to full-on kissing, snuggling, whispering, and generally excluding everyone else. It was kind of their thing. Nonstop love-a-rama, 24/7.

For one wistful instant, Damon gazed longingly at them. It didn't take a genius-level intellect or twenty-twenty vision to see that what Jason and Amy had together was special. Really special.

Damon had known Jason since . . . forever. They'd shared skateboards and video games. They'd bonded over Transformers toys in grade school—and they kept a few (strictly as collectible items) even now. But even the choicest, rarest, most valuable Optimus Prime 'bot had never made Jason one-tenth as happy as Amy did.

Hell, even *calculating* the trade-in value of Optimus Prime hadn't made Jason happier than Amy did, and he was a genuine numbers nerd. He actually *liked* spreadsheets and formulas and profit/loss ratios. He thought it was fun to estimate his taxes. He understood every variable in his car lease, his insurance coverage, and the mortgage he and Amy had taken out on their tiny two-bedroom house in San Diego's up-and-coming University Heights neighborhood. If it could be calculated, Jason loved it.

For his and Amy's wedding, Damon had treated them both to a trip to Hawaii, leis and all. Afterward, he'd promoted Jason to CFO of Torrance Chocolates. The promotion had been completely deserved. But it hadn't done what Damon had hoped. It hadn't brought his longtime friend back to him for the same full-time camaraderie and spur-of-the-moment carousing they used to share.

"It's not as though you two have been apart for years or anything," Damon grumbled from his position in the Ferrari's driver's seat. With deliberate effort, he tore away his gaze. "It's only been a few minutes since we roared down the track."

"Actually, your time was 1:47:00. A new course record." Giada Bandini strolled up with a stopwatch in her hand. Next to her curvaceous body, the technical-looking instrument seemed twice as austere and about ten times less interesting. Giada was a brilliant and gifted businesswoman. She also would have looked right at home in a Botticelli painting. Flirtatiously, she swept her fingertips along Damon's arm. Sexily, she smiled. "Not bad for an amateur. But if you want to improve your standings, I think I can show you a trick or two."

Giada gave him a suggestive glance, making her meaning plain. Damon didn't need the clarification. He and Giada had spent the morning and part of the afternoon trading repartee, getting to know one another, and recognizing their equivalent interest in coming together . . . on personal *and* business levels.

"I already sent my associates back to the office," Giada went on. "So for the rest of the day . . . I'm all yours."

And I'm yours, Damon wanted to say, just the way his libido demanded. But this time, uncharacteristically, he hesitated.

He glanced at Jason and Amy again, watching as the two of them teased each other. They were bantering about who'd been the better—and worse—driver during their vacation so far. Somehow they seemed absolutely enthralled by one another while doing it.

All at once, a powerful wave of loneliness hit Damon. In that moment, *he* wanted what Jason had. He wanted a woman who loved him. He wanted a woman who would be there for him—even if he didn't have the best racetrack time, the biggest house, and the fastest growing company in California. He wanted a woman he could love back—a woman he could partner with and confide in.

Into the brooding silence that followed that unwelcome revelation, Giada leaned nearer. "I like it fast *and* slow," she confessed. Her breath tickled his ear. "With me, you can have it all—sexy *and* romantic. You don't have to choose either one."

Her words—and her deliberately provocative, Italian-accented tone—conjured up a whole series of illicit images . . .

images that had the expected effect on him. Damon tried to resist. Giada's gaze wandered to his lap, then lingered.

She licked her lips, and Damon gave in. What the hell was going on with him, anyway? Giada was propositioning him, and he was *deliberating* whether to say yes? When a woman like Giada came knocking, no man turned her down. Not even Damon Torrance.

He had to be crazy. Maybe he'd had too much delicious Bandini espresso. Maybe he hadn't had enough. Either way . . .

"Hey, you lovebirds! Break it up." Another of Giada's guests on the Fiorano Circuit, So Cal media mogul Wes Brinkman, strolled up with a bottle of Cuvée Femme in one arm and a particularly luscious lady racing fan in the other. In a clear signal to party, Wes raised the champagne. "I hear we've got a new business partnership to celebrate. To Bandini! And to Torrance Chocolates!" Wes winked. "Long may they prosper."

Damon didn't know Wes very well; they'd just met today. But since Damon recognized a kindred spirit when he saw one—and so did Wes—they'd hit it off immediately. They both liked fast vintage cars, good times, and playing to win. They both appreciated the complexities of women, the mysteries inherent in their smiles, and all the diverse pleasures they offered.

Even before today, though, Damon *had* heard of B-Man Media, Wes's much-buzzed-about mass media company. Everyone had. Wes was a few years further along in his career than Damon was. Wes was older and probably wiser. He'd had an undeniable head start in his career by inheriting a family fortune first.

But Wes's very presence there at the Fiorano Circuit—with a woman on his arm and a bottle in his hand and a twinkle in his eyes—assured Damon that it *was* possible to succeed at work and have fun while doing it. If he'd been looking for a role model to reassure him that the path he was on was the right one—that work and play could coexist— Wes would have fit the bill nicely.

And if Wes seemed vaguely rough around the edges sometimes . . . well, the pursuit of pleasure took its toll eventually. Everyone knew that. Besides, Wes *was* headed toward forty. Nobody stayed invulnerable to excess forever. But living like Keith Richards was better than living like Ward Cleaver, wasn't it?

You only get one shot at living, Damon reminded himself. That meant you'd better make it good while you had the chance.

Pulling himself back to the conversation, Damon eyed Giada. "We have a deal?"

"Of course!" With a gentle tug, she urged him out of the Ferrari. "Your initial pitch was very impressive. It was evident you knew what you were talking about when it came to e-tailing, customer engagement, merchandizing, emotional branding, top-of-mind awareness, menu engineering . . . all those little details we corporate types love so much." Casually, she ticked off those elements of their previous discussions. "I knew I'd say yes, Damon. I could have told you that over the phone, of course." Playfully, she smiled. "But where's the fun in that?"

Belatedly realizing the truth, Damon regarded her. "You lured me to Italy under false pretenses."

Giada shrugged. "You didn't mind."

She was right. "I'd do it again in a heartbeat." With a grin, Damon nodded. "I prefer doing business in person."

"Proximity definitely has its benefits." Without an ounce of coyness, Giada grabbed his necktie. She eyed him up and down, then gave him another yank—this time, in the direction of the buildings ringing the racetrack. "We'll catch up with you later," she told the others with a toss of her hair. "Right now, Damon and I have a union to broker."

Wes gave a knowing chuckle. "Take your time!"

"Take *lots* of time," Amy advised loudly. "Remember—"

"Remember our flight leaves at ten," Jason interrupted, perennially attentive and numbers-minded. "Don't be late."

Giada laughed. "You might have to hold the plane."

Damon hoped so. Because all at once, as he let himself be tugged along by his necktie, headed for a sexual tryst he knew would be mind-bending, with a woman whose voluptuous hips, winsome smile, and ingenious mind had already entranced him, he began wondering . . . could Giada be *the one* for him?

He could love her, Damon decided as he felt her hip bump enticingly against his. She could love him, he imagined as Giada tossed him a sizzling look. They could make this work.

The longer he thought about it, the more real it felt.

Taking charge—of *this*, of today, of his destiny for all the days to come—Damon pulled Giada into the shadows along the exterior wall of the mechanics' shop. With the whirr of power tools and the smell of hot metal filling the air, he kissed her.

It felt good, so he did it again. Against the hard brick wall of the shop, he lost himself in another kiss. When it was over—eventually—Giada grinned up at him. "That's more like it. For a minute there, I thought you were going to turn me down."

"Not a chance," Damon told her. He kissed her harder.

Sure, Damon decided as Giada moaned in his arms. This felt like love. It did. If it wasn't love quite yet, it would be by the time the night was through. He'd make sure of it.

Because nobody took away what Damon Torrance wanted. Right now, what Damon wanted was *love*. Sweet, commanding, necessary love. Love like Jason and Amy had. Love that meant adoring looks and holding hands and teasing banter and warm, soft hugs and—

Oh yeah. *And* being dragged into a nearby office for a more private make-out session at Giada's insistence.

Because, Damon told himself further, a man's definition of true love had to be flexible. Right now, his definition included whispered terms of endearment in a language he didn't entirely understand, a stand-up quickie in a sunlit, out-of-the-way vacant office . . . and a woman who screamed when she came.

Hey, everyone said love was a many splendored thing. Who the hell was Damon to argue? If *this* was love, he was in.

Chapter 4

Natasha's first clue that her day might not go well was when she felt her battered Civic swerve sharply sideways. A weird clunking sound came next. Then, as she cautiously pulled into the breakdown lane on I-5, she felt her car dip ominously.

A minute later, staring at the blown-out treads on her left front tire, Natasha frowned. This was why everyone urged her to spend some money on a new car. Given her escalating salary at Torrance Chocolates, she could—technically—afford to buy herself something a little flashier, or at least a lot more reliable.

But as Natasha popped open the trunk and wrestled out her trusty jack from beneath her three-year-old son's beach towels, playground ball, spare bottles of water, and sandcastle-building toys, she knew she wouldn't do it. Not only was she reluctant to spend money unnecessarily—especially now—but she also knew she felt too sentimental about her car to give it up.

With grumpy forbearance, she eyed her Civic. The paint

was scratched on the driver's side rear door. That had happened on the day she'd started working with Damon and Jimmy. Damon had generously given her some additional up-front vacation days ("The honeymoon should last at least as long as the sunburn," he'd insisted with a grin while shooing her out of the office), and Natasha had been so eager to meet up with Paul afterward and share her good news that she'd almost taken out one of the support beams of their apartment complex's covered parking structure.

Instead, she'd merely splintered the support beam. A little. Which, as Natasha had later explained to her landlord (and mother-in-law), Carol Jennings, had been a blessing in disguise. Because the termite infestation that had been discovered during the beam's repair would have cost *thousands* more to deal with if it hadn't been uncovered until later.

Fortunately for Natasha, Carol had seen things her way. From that day on, they'd gotten along famously, too—which was saying something, given everything that had happened since then.

After getting out her spare tire, Natasha ran her fingers over a crunched-in spot on the bumper. It was only noticeable if you looked closely, so she'd assured herself it didn't need fixing. That particular ding had happened on the day she'd come home early from a business trip—just over four years into her marriage—to find her husband naked with a model in his artist's studio, indulging his "creativity" in new and unexpected ways.

Natasha had been so shaken by Paul's infidelity—especially in light of the way *she'd* selflessly set aside her own attraction to Damon and devoted herself to her family—that she'd backed out too fast from her parking space and collided with the car adjacently parked by Paul's favorite "muse."

Natasha had offered to pay for the damage, of course.

But Paul's luscious, doe-eyed, twentysomething Mexican muse—freshly in town from Cancun, where she and Paul had met *during Natasha and Paul's honeymoon*—had refused to accept (also, of course). But Natasha still thought the incident qualified as poetic justice. She also figured it was smart to remember life-altering events like that one, which was another good reason not to have the dent fixed.

Sometimes people needed reminders to stay strong. *She* needed a reminder that her own judgment could be flawed. She'd trusted Paul. He'd betrayed her by scampering off to be with his alluring "muse" full-time (strictly for the sake of his art), leaving Natasha to raise their toddler, Milo, on her own (with a little help from hands-on Super Grandma, Carol), and Natasha had realized, too late, that her heart could feel as broken as her poor beat-up car did. If she ever felt *sure* she could trust herself again, she'd promised herself after that, she would fix that dent. In the meantime . . . she was getting by okay.

Like her life, her Civic was imperfect. But she'd worked a lot of hours—at a variety of part-time retail wage-slave jobs—to pay for that car, Natasha reminded herself as she crouched beside it to work the jack. She'd been *proud* to put down her own money on it. She'd been proud to slip behind the wheel, inhale that new-car smell, and know *she'd* accomplished buying it all by herself.

No one in her family had ever owned anything but used cars; Natasha had blazed the new-car trail. Her parents, who still lived in the nearby working-class community of El Cajon, had been beside themselves with pride. They'd even taken snapshots of her striking a cheesy pose beside her Civic like an auto show model. Just the memory of those pictures made her smile.

As much as her beleaguered marriage did, her Civic proved that Natasha didn't give up on things easily. Her car had taken her to classes at UCSD, to friends' houses, and to the mall, she reflected as she finished changing the tire while cars whizzed past a few feet away. It had taken her on road trips, on beach runs, and all the way to her life-changing interview with Jimmy Torrance. Today, she remembered wryly, it was supposed to have taken her to the launch of the hot new Apple gadget, the iPhone.

Damon was *dying* for an iPhone. But since he was in Italy working on the Bandini Espresso deal, and the gadget was only available in the U.S. for now, Natasha had volunteered to stay behind—which she tried to do as often as possible, for Milo's sake—and score one for him. As she gave the last lug nut a final spin, then jacked down her Civic, she kind of regretted doing so. Most likely, Damon was enjoying himself right now. He usually was. And she . . . well, she just needed to get on with it.

Natasha's second clue that her day might be less than spectacular occurred when she finally arrived at the Fashion Valley Mall, made her way toward the Apple Store, and realized, with a sinking heart, that she could barely *see* the Apple Store.

The whole mall was thronged with lined-up customers, gadget devotees, gawkers, and even local media. She spotted a B-Man Media crew getting the scoop on the regular networks. She saw bystanders filming with camcorders. She heard . . . was that *cheering*?

It was. Following the sound, Natasha looked across the open-air mall. To the delighted shouts of the people waiting—some of whom looked as though they might have *slept* in line last night in sleeping bags, like those *Star Wars* fans on the news—dozens of Apple employees marched over to open the store.

It was mayhem—*ridiculous* mayhem. Being there was like being a wallflower at the prom, standing on the sidelines, then seeing the king and queen and their court making their grand entrances. No one else mattered. With their clean-cut looks, minimalist T-shirts and pants, and ID badges, the Apple Store employees had the only keys to the candy store. All eyes were locked on them.

People surged forward. Suddenly in real danger of being trampled, Natasha stepped back. Damon had warned her that it might be tricky getting one of the launch-day iPhones, but this was absurd.

"I thought you were kidding," Natasha murmured as she was pushed back a little farther. Far, *far* beyond her position, the store's doors opened at last. The crowd literally went wild.

Oh boy. If she was supposed to cope with this, she needed coffee first. She, unlike Damon, wasn't typically surrounded by eager yes-men—not to mention willing yes-women— who wanted to serve coffee to her in fine china with biscotti on the side.

Groaning in resignation, Natasha beelined toward Starbucks. By the time she got a little more caffeinated, things would probably have settled down somewhat. If not, then at least she'd be better able to cope with it than she was right now.

But then, digging in her laptop bag for cash to pay the barista, Natasha encountered the bundle of mail she'd stuffed inside to sort through. She had, at a minimum, expected to kill some time at the Apple Store. As a single mother, she'd mastered the art of being prepared, too. But as she browsed through her bills, junky postcards, and magazine subscription offers while waiting for her extra-hot, no-foam, triple soy latte, she spotted one particular envelope . . . and her whole body went still.

Staring at the letterhead on the envelope, Natasha felt the world around her receding. The other customers turned invisible. The hubbub in the mall went mute. The cutesy slang employed by the baristas fell away, replaced by an indecipherable hum. Everything blurred into nothingness as Natasha's third clue that her day wasn't going to go well invaded her consciousness.

No, Natasha realized as her fingers started to shake. It didn't just invade her consciousness. It didn't simply make the world seem unreal and far away and inconsequential. This time, her burgeoning bad day reared back, gave her a nasty smile, then kicked her in the teeth. Because inside that envelope could be only one thing: Natasha's official, fully finalized, now-it's-really-happening set of divorce papers.

Numbly, she clutched them. Somehow she'd expected this to feel different. She'd expected . . . something other than this.

"Triple latte?" the barista said. "Is this one yours?"

Startled, Natasha glanced at the friendly redheaded woman across the bar. *Nothing* was hers anymore, she thought in a daze. Not the future she'd expected, not the predictable day she'd had planned . . . nothing. She shook herself. "Um, yes. I guess so."

"I have an extra shot back here if you want it." Sympathetically, the barista nodded toward her espresso machine. "You look as though you could use it. Tough day already?"

Trying to rally, Natasha raised her envelope. "I just got my divorce papers. We've been separated for a while now, but . . . I guess everything's finally finalized. It's really official."

"Oh. Wow." The barista peered at her. Decisively, she took back her latte, added an extra shot of inky, crema-topped coffee, then replaced the lid. She nudged it toward Natasha, then shook her head. "Sorry. Not exactly your lucky day, huh?"

Natasha gave a helpless laugh. If Damon had been born under a lucky star, *she'd* been born under a gloomy, gray, rain-spitting, thunder-crackling, cartoony cloud of misfortune. Her "lucky" lottery-ticket numbers never won. Her Civic broke down at the worst possible times. Her excursions to the beach brought rain, her surfing forays meant wipeouts (no matter how many lessons she took), and her bad-hair days were legendary. It probably wasn't possible that she was genuinely unlucky and doomed to haplessness. But sometimes it sure felt that way.

The best part of her life was Milo. Her son, as adorable as he was, didn't officially qualify as a lucky charm.

"If one lucky day is all we get, I think I missed mine," Natasha said wryly. "It must have sneaked past when I wasn't looking."

"Well, maybe it'll come around again. You never know." The barista grinned encouragingly. She nodded at Natasha's envelope. "Besides, you're probably better off without the bastard anyway. Right?"

Better off without Paul? Truthfully, Natasha had never thought of it that way before. She'd spent so long putting his needs first, tending to their relationship the way her neighbor, Kurt, looked after his prizewinning begonias, making sure her husband felt valued and respected and loved. Even after they'd separated, she'd considered Paul's feelings and needs.

In fact, Natasha reflected, she'd done more caretaking of Paul than his own mother had lately. Carol, after years of giving her "artsy" son a pass for his misbehavior, had quit making excuses for him. In the interest of making sure she could see Milo—and help Natasha with babysitting—Carol had given her a standout deal on rent and a lot of support, too. They'd worked out a really friendly, mutually caring relationship.

Staring again at her divorce papers, Natasha reconsidered. *Better off without Paul?* Could it be true?

"Maybe I am!" Natasha said with a sudden burst of defiance.

This wasn't the fifties. She wasn't a hopeless housewife with no job, no future, and no prospects for fun. She could date again. She could find someone new. She could be happy!

It wasn't as if her divorce finalization had come as a

surprise. Technically speaking, Natasha had known those papers were on their way. She just hadn't wanted to think about them.

She'd had a lot of good reasons *not* to think about them.

But now . . . "Thanks for the coffee. And the pep talk!" Mustering a smile, Natasha stuffed away her divorce papers. She dropped a generous tip in the jar, then used her amped-up latte to salute the barista. "Today, that was just what I needed."

As if punctuating her statement, her cell phone rang. At the sound of her saucy new Beyoncé ringtone, Natasha smiled a little more widely. Paul *wasn't* "Irreplaceable." Not to her. Not anymore. Just like Beyoncé had in the video, *she* could move on.

But first . . . "Hello?"

"Tasha?" Amy Huerta's panicky-sounding voice crackled over the connection. "Thank God you're there! I'm freaking out."

"Amy?" Instantly concerned, Natasha cradled her cell phone. Balancing all her things, she moved to a quieter corner of the coffee shop. She set down her belongings. "What's the matter?"

"It's Jason. And Damon." Amy gulped back a sob. "And Wes and Giada and the *Tifosi* girl! It would have been me, too, if I hadn't been in the bathroom when it happened, but I was, so—"

"Amy, slow down." Reflexively, Natasha drew in a deep breath. "Everything's going to be all right. What happened?"

Amy inhaled, too. "They're all in jail. Everyone's in jail, Tasha! You've got to get them out. Please!" Wherever Amy was, a loud buzz came over the line. Then voices. A door slammed. "Wes's assistant tried to pull some strings, but he only made it worse. Even Giada's best people couldn't help—"

"Bandini is involved in this?"

"—and the *Tifosi* girl is too drunk to be any use—"

Natasha frowned. "What's a *Tifosi?*"

"A Ferrari racing team fan." Amy sounded a little calmer now. "We were celebrating the close of the partnership deal—"

"It went through? That's great!"

"—at a local nightclub, and, um, things got out of hand." More clanging came from Amy's end of the conversation. And more talking. "I didn't know what else to do except call you."

"Don't worry. I'll take care of it," Natasha assured her. She'd liked Amy from the moment they'd met, a few years into Natasha's tenure at Torrance Chocolates. Amy had come in to visit Jason—another of Natasha's favorite people—and Natasha had given her a personal tasting tour of the chocolate selections while they'd waited for her then-fiancé to arrive. "Just sit tight."

"The police haven't been very cooperative—especially since Wes threw that punch," Amy said. "The language barrier isn't exactly facilitating things, either. Are you sure you can help?"

"I'm sure." With a welcome sense of being useful and needed, Natasha set down her latte. She pulled out her trusty PDA full of important contacts. Like Damon, she had a thing for technology. Unlike him, she didn't usually indulge her whims for the latest gadget. "I bail out Damon all the time. Believe me, this is not the diciest situation I've ever scraped him out of."

Chapter 5

Thirty-nine and a half laborious hours later, Natasha stood expectantly in the baggage claim area of San Diego International Airport. Harried travelers rushed past. Prerecorded announcements droned over the sound system. The greasy smells of stale pizza and french fries lingered in the air. But as Natasha stood waiting, none of that mattered . . . and the reason was Damon.

Natasha wasn't sure why, but being around him just made her feel better. It always had. Damon was like the fun-loving yin to her more studious yang. They were two halves of a better whole. Because where she was practical, Damon was *fun*. Where she was organized, he was spontaneous. Where she was dependable, he was . . .

Well, he was *late*, actually. Standing on tiptoe to catch a glimpse of her sexy, trouble-attracting boss and his undoubtedly weary travel companions, Natasha felt her heartbeat kick up a notch with anticipation. Or maybe with concern. Sure. It was probably concern. Because he'd been through a lot in Italy.

She'd been through a lot here. After all, bailing him out hadn't been easy. But she'd done it. She was proud of that.

At long last, Damon came into view—broad shouldered,

slim hipped, and smudgy under the eyes. He wore perfectly fitting jeans, a white shirt, and an expensively distressed jacket. None of those items could have looked any better than they did on him. Just glimpsing him made Natasha's breath catch in her throat. She felt *so* relieved he was okay— so relieved he was *home*.

Once again, he'd been lucky. Excessive partying hadn't caught up to Damon in the same way it would have to anyone else.

He spotted her. As a greeting, Natasha held up the coveted iPhone she'd practically had to kick and claw to get. Damon's face brightened. Then she held up *another* iPhone—this one a gift to herself, from Damon, as a thank-you for rescuing him.

Instantly, Damon recognized as much. Because despite his playboy image, he was much cleverer than he let on. He was also capable of intuiting a lot; he'd always had a talent for that. His knowing smile beamed at her to prove it. Then, moving a little faster, Damon reached her. He dropped his carry-on bag on the airport floor, then pulled her into an embrace.

Tears actually sprang to her eyes. Feeling him all warm and real and safe against her, Natasha laughed. Damon squeezed her.

"I was worried you wouldn't be here," he said as he pulled back. "You told me you'd leave if I pushed you too far. I was afraid I'd finally made you bail me out one too many times."

"Nah." *Wow*, he looked wonderful. His eyes were all smoky brown, his jaw was all shadowy with beard stubble, and his hair defied gravity in places. But his sought-after smile was just for *her*, and that was all Natasha needed. "That's what the second iPhone was for. It's a bribe from you to me. So . . . thanks!"

Damon laughed. She loved that sound. When she had to go without it for too long—because he was traveling or she was busy or they were being pulled in separate directions by their separate lives—Natasha got undeniably cranky. She might not be Damon's girlfriend, and he was *definitely* not the kind of man she needed in her life right now, but they cared about one another. They connected on a deeper level. What she and Damon shared couldn't be replicated.

It couldn't quite be quantified or defined, either, Natasha mused as she inhaled the familiar piney aroma of his fancy shaving soap and smiled all over again. She and Damon had forged a close-knit working relationship—a relationship she believed they both treasured. They'd never tried taking that relationship to another, more personal, much *sexier* level. But as Damon hugged her again, then reared back to drink in the sight of her, Natasha began wondering, for the first time in years . . .

Did Damon ever think of *her* as anything other than his trusty gal Friday? Did he even know she had a finalized divorce to cope with, a cutie-pie son to raise, and a broken-down car?

She'd always been scrupulous about keeping her private life separate from her work life. At first, it had been a matter of simple self-preservation: Natasha didn't trust Damon enough to let loose about anything that really mattered. Later, she'd kept her boundaries in place as a matter of routine. But now, *here* . . .

Well, *now*, in that moment, with Damon's touch still making her feel vaguely tingly all over, Natasha couldn't help wondering . . . could there ever be something *more* between them?

Damon's voice, husky and assured, broke into her thoughts.

"Natasha, I want you to meet someone." Wearing a uniquely vivid smile, he urged forward a curvaceous woman with dark hair, glasses, and a fashionable ensemble that fit her statuesque figure to a tee. He touched her arm. "This is Giada Bandini."

"Oh, hello, Ms. Bandini!" Surprised to see the espresso company exec, Natasha held out her hand. "I didn't expect you."

"There's something else you didn't expect." Like a kid with a secret, Damon grinned. He hugged Ms. Bandini closer. "Giada and I got married! We eloped in Milan. Isn't that fantastic?"

Married? When said by Damon, the word didn't compute.

"You're joking." Natasha gawked at him. She'd thought he'd looked so happy because he was glad to see *her*—not because he'd impetuously gotten married. This couldn't be happening. "You can't have gotten married. This is . . . it's a joke, right?"

"Nope." Exuberantly, Damon kissed Giada. "I know it sounds crazy, but I'm finally in love. Real, true, forever love."

Love. Natasha couldn't argue with that. She wanted Damon to be happy. She did. She cared about him. Of course. But . . . this?

It was too soon. It was too reckless, even for Damon.

"So, are we going to ditch this place or what?" he asked.

Natasha blinked at him. "What?"

"I'm dying for a hot shower, a gigantic sandwich"— Damon held apart his hands to show its approximate monster dimensions—"and about fifteen hours of uninterrupted sleep." With cheerful relish, he rubbed together his palms. "I can only get two out of three of those things here at the airport."

"At least legally." Unexpectedly sidetracked by the idea of Damon indulging himself in a steamy, soapy, naked, *non*-airport-provided shower, Natasha looked away. That would be . . . so *hot*.

Then she gave herself a very necessary mental shake.

"I have a car waiting." Airily, she waved her hand. Now that she'd opened this Pandora's box of imagining Damon nude, sudsy, and ready for commitment—albeit to another woman—it was going to be difficult to slam shut again.

"There's champagne there, already chilling. We can use it to toast your marriage!"

The words were difficult to force out. Especially since Natasha's overactive mind was suddenly preoccupied with cranking out fresh fantasy scenarios. Oblivious to the fact that circumstances had irrevocably changed, her imagination conjured up several ways she and Damon could have been together if he'd decided to commit to *her* instead. With Natasha sprawled across the waiting car's expansive backseat, Damon's hands holding her steady as he loved her with his lips and tongue. With Natasha on top of him, her skirt hiked up around her thighs as he entered her. With Natasha moaning as she took Damon in her mouth, making him beg her for more, *more* . . .

Oh God. What was *wrong* with her?

"Excellent! I enjoy champagne," Giada announced, sashaying toward the exit. "This time, we must try not to get arrested."

Wrenched from her problematic fantasies, Natasha stared. "*That's* why you got arrested? Because you were celebrating your wedding?"

Damon looked abashed. "Well, that *and* the merger. We were celebrating both. Torrance Chocolates and Bandini Espresso are definitely long-term partners now." While Giada sauntered onward, Damon held Natasha back. He gave her a concerned look. "Hey—are you sure you're all right? You look . . . different."

She probably looked lusty, Natasha knew. "I'm fine."

"Did something happen while I was gone?"

I got divorced and realized I want you. "Nope."

Damon didn't appear convinced. "Come on. I know you better than that." He frowned. "Is everything all right . . . at home?"

His tentative tone snapped her out of her reverie the way nothing else could have. Damon was usually so certain about things. But not about *her*, Natasha reminded herself. Because Damon didn't really know *her*—not all of her. Thanks to the wall she'd created between her work life and her home life, as far as Damon was concerned she was just another tool to help him achieve his stated goal of world chocolate domination.

Damon still wasn't finished trying to make his father proud of him. To Damon, Natasha was just a means to that end.

"'Is everything all right . . . at home?'" she repeated. While the airport hubbub swirled around them, she gave him a deliberately cynical look. "Tell you what: I'll forfeit my entire year's salary, right now, if you can tell me one single detail of my home life. For instance . . . what street do I live on?"

For a minute, she thought he might actually do it. He had read her personnel file once, after all. He had a very good memory when he bothered to use it for anything other than identifying his favorite brand of tequila. Then Damon gave her a characteristically teasing grin. "Don't *you* know what street you live on? That must make it tough for you to find your way home."

Natasha's heart broke a little. Patiently, she waited.

"All right. Uncle." Damon raised both hands in surrender, not even pretending he might be able to guess about her personal life. "You're fine. I get it. I'll quit bugging you."

"Yes, you will." *No. Please keep trying.* "Thanks."

"But I still think something's going on with you." With more perceptiveness than he deserved to possess, Damon peered at her. "Sooner or later, I'll figure out what it is."

God, she hoped not. "Maybe. You'll probably forget to try."

"Now I'm doubly determined." His grin dazzled her, just the way it always did. But now his was a married grin. An off-limits grin. A grin she had to resist. Damon jostled her shoulder in a brotherly fashion. "I just want you to be happy, Natasha."

Hearing the affectionate way he said her name, she held her breath. Briefly, she closed her eyes. Damon didn't mean that to sound as tender as it did. He couldn't help it. He was . . . *him*.

"I want *you* to be happy like I'm happy." In a jolly way, Damon nodded toward Giada. His new wife was waiting outside with a smoldering Italian cigarette in one hand, looking regal and sophisticated. "It turns out, all I ever wanted was true love."

"You and me both." Spying Jason and Amy and the rest of Damon's weary entourage emerging from the crowd at the baggage carousel with their luggage, Natasha straightened. "Sometimes it's not so easy to find, though."

Her newly finalized divorce papers proved that much.

"We should have found true love together," Damon joked. "That would have been the practical thing to do."

At his blithe tone, Natasha's heart splintered a little more. She hadn't realized exactly how deep her feelings for him went. Now that she was beginning to have an inkling of the way she might feel, it was too late to do anything about it.

"Practical? Ha!" With effort, Natasha met Damon's gaze directly. "I know you way too well to think *you* could ever be practical. That's *my* world, and we both know it. You just visit it from time to time to impress the board of directors."

Damon laughed. "You're right. You *do* know me too well. But hey . . . it's nice living here in Sexy Fun Town. Why would I ever want to leave?" He glanced at Giada. "And speaking of sexy fun . . . I've neglected my wife for too long already." He paused, shook his head, then gave Natasha a look filled with pure incredulity. "My *wife*. Can you believe I just said that? Isn't that something?"

Then, without waiting for Natasha to answer, Damon ruffled her hair the way a big brother would do to a pesky tomboy sister. He picked up his carry-on bag, assembled his usual mixture of machismo, magnetism, and carefree swagger, then took himself off to the cloud of smoke that encircled his new wife.

Wistfully, Natasha watched as Damon and Giada reunited. They looked happy enough. A little jet-lagged maybe. But happy.

If *she* was going to be happy, too, she'd just have to move on. She would have to lock away those irresponsibly spicy feelings for Damon, forget about imagining what it would be like to see him naked, and get back to the business of taking them both to the top—one delicious, chocolate-centric deal at a time.

She could do that. Easy-peasy.

But Natasha sure wished, as she went to greet Amy and the others and shepherd them to the waiting car, that she could have spent a little time with Damon in Sexy Fun Town first.

She'd never heard him describe his life that way before, but it sounded pretty accurate. It sounded like an awfully entertaining place to visit, too. . . .

Chapter 6

Present day
Las Vegas, Nevada

Sin City had definitely earned its nickname—and Damon treasured that quality about it. In Las Vegas, whatever you wanted, you could have. Whatever you needed could be arranged. Whatever kinky, surreal, or extraordinary activity you felt like experimenting with . . . you could. Openly and without recrimination.

What happened in Vegas stayed in Vegas. The end.

At least that's the way Damon's imagined version of Las Vegas operated. In reality, people barged into your hotel suite at ungodly hours—before it was even dark outside!—pestering you to do things you didn't want to do, like conduct business, stand upright, or get dressed. He *really* didn't want to get dressed.

Across his suite, a muted whir sounded. The luxurious, extra-thick draperies that hid his view of The Strip began to part. A sudden and ruthless shaft of sunlight seared its way in.

"Argh! Argh!" Flinging his naked arm over his face, Damon rolled over in bed. A ladies' high-heeled sandal stabbed him in the back. He pitched it out. He felt for the empty liquor bottle that poked at him next, then threw away that annoyance, too. He burrowed beneath the covers. "For God's sake, shut the curtains! Are you trying to kill me? I only went to bed an hour ago."

"That's why coffee was invented," his tormentor said.

Grouchily, Damon peeked out from under the covers. His pal Jason Huerta stood far across the penthouse suite's expansive square footage with the room's remote control in hand, clearly prepared to push more buttons. There were more draperies to be drawn back. State-of-the-art sound systems to be engaged. Enormous 3-D TVs to be turned on. Knowing Jason's diabolical nature, he'd activate all three at once, just because he could.

"You know I don't drink coffee anymore," Damon reminded his so-called friend. "I never touch the stuff. Not since—"

Not since Giada. He should have known that impulsively getting married was the king of bad ideas. So what if she'd been smart, vivacious, and intriguingly open-minded? She hadn't been right for him. He hadn't been right for her. They'd ended things amicably—and relatively quickly—but still Damon regretted it.

Marriage, it turned out, had not come easily to him. Everything else had, for as long as he could remember. That's how Damon had known that marriage wasn't meant for him.

"Since Giada?" Jason asked, echoing his thoughts. "That ended years ago. Don't tell me you're still hung up on her."

"I'm not still hung up on her." Damon slapped the nightstand, looking for a bottle that wasn't empty. He found one. He took a swig. Vodka. Ugh. "I'm just saying I no longer enjoy waking up to a tasty cup of espresso." Illustratively, he took another, more vigorous drink. "See? I've moved on."

"You might not have noticed, but that's vodka."

"Hey, it's made from potatoes or something, right?" Damon raised the bottle in a wiseass salute. "I'm practically having a plate of hash browns." He frowned. "Why are you here, anyway?"

"Natasha called me." Jason stabbed at the remote. The rest of the draperies cruelly parted, allowing more desert sunshine inside the room. "She said you needed a shower, a wake-up call, and maybe a babysitter—and today it wasn't going to be her."

Petulantly, Damon scowled. "Why not?"

Silence. That was the thing about expensive penthouse hotel suites, Damon thought as he hugged the vodka to his chest. They could shut out the whole world . . . whether you wanted them to or not. This morning, that silence made him feel impossibly alone.

"She couldn't wrestle you into the shower. You were too drunk to cooperate." Jason came nearer. In his collared shirt and dark denim jeans, he looked every inch the responsible number cruncher and father of two (with one more on the way) that he was. He also looked worried. "Natasha said she had to settle for spritzing you from afar with the shower nozzle."

"Aha." Damon patted himself. "That explains the dampness. For a minute, I thought I had something to be worried about."

"You do." Soberly, Jason took away the vodka bottle. His gaze met Damon's, incongruously reminding him of similar but happier circumstances during their bachelor days. "Also," his friend went on, "I think she can't stand seeing you this way anymore. You've been on a real bender, bro. For a while now—"

"Bender?" Damon scoffed. "What do you know about a bender? To you, staying up past ten o'clock is a wild night. You haven't been anyplace fun in ages—despite multiple invitations." From *him*, in fact, and others. "You wouldn't know a good time if it danced a tango and then bit you on the ass. So before you start telling me to rein it in, *bro*, you might want to wait for a topic you actually know something about first."

"I'm married. I have kids. I have responsibilities," Jason said. "So, yeah . . . I don't stay out late. But that doesn't mean I can't see the truth. What you're doing to yourself isn't good."

"Right." Irately, Damon eyed the vodka bottle. He didn't really want more of it. Despite Jason's worrywart routine and Natasha's supposed frustration with him, he knew his limits. He knew he'd neared them. "Because if someone said *you* could date supermodels, go skydiving with basketball stars, run your own company, make a bazillion dollars, have superhot sex every day—"

"I *do* have superhot sex every day," Jason interrupted smugly—and implausibly. "Marriage is awesome. *Amy* is awesome."

"—go where you wanted, do what you wanted, win at every blackjack table in this damn city," Damon forged on, remembering his unending lucky streak at the casino downstairs, "and have everything you touch turn to freaking *gold*, you would say no?"

Jason nodded. "I would say no. I'm happy as I am."

Disbelievingly, Damon stared at him. "The hell you are."

"It's true. You don't get it. Maybe you never will."

Damon swore. "I can't believe this. If Natasha really sent you in here—to do this, today—she has a mile-wide mean streak."

"What Natasha has is a mile-wide streak of soft-heartedness and compassion for *you*, dumbass." Jason gave him an atypically flinty look. "In fact, I'm glad she called me. I say it's about time she wised up and quit taking your shit."

Damon went still. It was possible his heart actually stopped. He clutched his covers. "She didn't leave, did she?"

He'd lived with that doomsday scenario hanging over him for years now. For one impossibly brutal moment, Jason was quiet, allowing Damon to speculate that it had finally come to pass.

Then, "No. She went shopping. She promised to bring home a souvenir for her mother-in-law. And of course she wants to bring home something neat for—" Abruptly, Jason stopped talking. A canny look spread over his face. "Tell you what: I'll forfeit all the new computers for the accounting department, right now, if you can tell me who else Natasha's shopping for."

Damon nearly exploded with exasperation. "Why the hell does everyone keep quizzing me about Natasha's personal life?"

Jason looked even more self-satisfied. "You give up, then?"

"No. I just feel like taking that shower now, that's all."

With dignity, Damon flung back the covers. He couldn't help noticing that he seemed to be wearing . . . a fringed suede loincloth?

Damon gawked down at himself. "What the hell?"

"Your partner in crime last night was a member of one of those French acrobatic troupes." Jason took pains to put on a straight face. "She probably got you to wear it . . . Tarzan."

Irritably, Damon flipped him his middle finger.

"Natasha must have gotten an eyeful when she was here," Jason mused further. "Maybe that's why she called me. She didn't want to come eye-to-eye with your loin-cloth-wearing wild side."

Could that be? Damon wondered suddenly. Could Natasha really have gotten so fed up with him that she couldn't stand to see him nearly naked? They'd been through a lot together. They were close. No one in the world understood him like she did.

He didn't want to lose her. Natasha kept his life running smoothly. She calmed him and nurtured him and organized him.

Without her, he would be . . . well, Damon couldn't imagine it.

"*Everyone* wants to come eye-to-eye with my wild side," he told Jason confidently, hiding the fact that he'd been spooked by the very idea of going so far that he might alienate Natasha. "Today, I'm going to prove it!"

"No, today you're conducting a workshop presentation on varietal chocolates from around the world," Jason disagreed in his usual pragmatic, reality-bound, buzzkill kind of way. They'd come to Las Vegas for the annual chocolate-industry convention. Evidently, there were expectations—at least on Jason's part—that they'd actually work while they were there, not just gamble and drink and get lucky. "There's a limited amount of wildness you can display during a workshop, He-Man. Although the lady chef from B-Man Media who's joining you to do the chocolate fondue demonstration is pretty cute. Maybe she likes loincloths."

"Har, har." Damon headed for the shower. It was easy to find his way; the bathroom was nonstop marble and gold fixtures. It was nearly as blinding as the sunshine outside. "And she *will* like loincloths . . . if I'm wearing one." Not that he planned to.

"Whatever. Just sober up and get dressed before everyone starts wondering if all the wild stories about you are true."

"They *are* true." Damon stripped. He wrenched on the shower's hot water. It cascaded down right on cue, exactly the way things tended to happen in his world: perfectly, easily, and without too much effort on his part. "I don't care who knows it."

"Your dad cares who knows it." Jason's voice pursued him;

fortunately, the man himself didn't. "Your mom does, too. If you don't watch it, dude, Jimmy and Debbie will decide they need more than a flashy face to head up Torrance Chocolates."

Damon paused. Then he shrugged. "I bring a lot of publicity and relationship building to the company," he argued while soaping himself up. "I'm valuable with the online stuff, too."

Although to be fair, Damon realized belatedly, he'd delegated most of his day-to-day responsibilities to his staff. It had been years since he'd done more than represent Torrance Chocolates on TV, in negotiations, and—once—in a movie cameo.

"I know you're committed to a life of decadence. But your dad's looking to retire soon, and he needs someone who can fill his shoes at the company—management-wise *and* creatively. If I were you, I'd get busy showing the old man you can dish up a new product or an original truffle flavor or something. Stat."

Stat? That sounded dire . . . as if time were running out.

But if Damon really was supposed to create something in order to save his job and impress his parents, time might as well be running out. He wasn't good at creativity. Or at real chocolatiering. He never had been. That's how he'd known, right from the start, that those parts of the business weren't for him. It was just like his marriage: despite his best efforts, he'd tried and he'd failed. So he'd (wisely) never tried again.

His natural talents just didn't lean toward creating things. He'd always figured he was good enough at everything else to make up for that . . . even if his dad hadn't always agreed.

Remembering that, Damon frowned. Then he made himself rinse off, just as though he didn't have a care in the world. "If you were me," he called to Jason cheerfully as he stepped out and grabbed a towel to wrap around himself, "you'd buy yourself a new Porsche, fill every room of your house with gold-plated calculators, then get personal with every pretty girl in sight."

"Nope." Jason rounded the corner. Upon seeing that the steam-filled bathroom wasn't featuring a full-on shower-time peep show, he leaned in the doorway. He crossed his arms. "If *I* were *you*," he argued, "I'd take another look at Natasha. Then I'd beg her to forgive me for being such an ass, and I'd try my damnedest to make things right somehow." He gave Damon a meaningful grin. "*Then* I'd buy myself a new Porsche."

"You know, you probably could afford a Porsche right now. It's not as though we're skinflints at Torrance Chocolates."

"I know. But our portfolio took a hit in the economic downturn, and Amy's been concerned about retirement. So—"

"Retirement?" Damon wiped condensation off the colossal, gilded-edge mirror. His reflection stared back, bleary-eyed and bleak. Damn. He really needed some sleep. "You're thirty-six."

"It's never too soon to plan. Compound interest being what it is, the bulk of the dividends won't be fully realized until—"

Damon groaned. "Cut the financial talk, Egghead." He made a time-out T with his hands. "You're making me reconsider my stance on coffee."

"Good. You should reconsider your stance on a lot of things."

Hell. "Who are you, Jiminy Cricket?" In the mirror, Damon met his friend's gaze. "Did I drunk-dial you and ask for a lecture? Is annoying, know-it-all ass-hattery on sale today?"

"All I'm saying is, your workshop today is the perfect opportunity for you to show what you can do," Jason told him, not the least bit daunted by his outburst. "Creatively, I mean.

Your dad is here. Your mom is here. Every media outlet in the world is here. They're all watching you—so don't blow it."

Don't blow it. At that, Damon swallowed hard.

Why had Jason had to tell him that? That was like hearing his dad tell him to behave himself and focus. Damon knew he couldn't do either of those things—at least not for long.

Being told he had to do something—anything—called up every rebellious instinct he'd ever had . . . and then some.

All of a sudden, all Damon wanted to do was screw up on a massive scale. At least then the pressure would be off him.

Fighting against that urge, he picked up his razor. "What's the lady chef's name? I'll start with her and work from there."

Jason gave him a skeptical look. "I'm not sure it's wise for you to begin with the female component of this mission."

"It's a *mission* now?" Damon swore. "Just tell me her name."

"Her name is Tamala. She trained at Le Cordon Bleu in Paris. She has a popular cooking show on B-Man Media. Her specialties include cocoa painting and nougat modeling, as well as sugar cages and other pulled, poured, and blown sugar work."

Damon stopped in mid razor stroke. "Is it just me, or does all that sound incredibly erotic? I've got to meet this girl."

"Can you focus? *Ever*? Just for five minutes?"

"I *am* focusing." Feeling harassed, Damon finished shaving. "I'm researching. I'm going to knock this workshop out of the park today. In fact, I might ask Wes to send over an exclusive camera crew from B-Man Media, just to document my triumph."

Jason looked dubious. "That might be overkill."

Damon only gave him an offhanded grin. "Too much is never enough. That's my motto. That, and *more, more, more!*"

"Subtle." Jason shook his head. "Just remember: I'll be

flying back home before your workshop starts, so if things go belly-up, I won't be there to hold your hand."

"Thanks, but you know you're not my type."

This time, Jason flipped him his middle finger. Then he laughed. "I mean it, dude. Good luck today. Need anything else?"

Just Natasha. Who *was* she shopping for, anyway?

Damon shook his head. Then, "Hey. Natasha's out shopping for me, isn't she?" he guessed. "She wants to surprise me."

Jason rolled his eyes. "You should be so lucky."

"You don't have to be a dick about it." Damon frowned. "'You should be so lucky.' What does that mean, anyway?"

"If you were paying attention, you'd know." His buddy set down his allocated keycard to the hotel suite. He gave Damon a smart-alecky farewell salute. "Knock 'em dead today."

"I always do," Damon said, waving Jason out. But just at that moment, he felt a lot less certain than he sounded.

He'd never had to impress someone on demand. Not officially, anyway. Not onstage in a workshop. How was he supposed to score a big *creative* win on the spur of the moment?

Natasha had picked a hell of a day to abandon him, Damon brooded as he went to pick out a suit. If there was ever a time he shouldn't be left on his own to sink or swim, it was right now. When Natasha came back, he fully intended to tell her so.

But first, he had a sexy lady chef to meet. It would probably be a good idea, Damon told himself, to go find Tamala and see if they could strike up a useful rapport before the workshop started. You know, just to kick off things on the right foot. Professionally speaking. And maybe to find out exactly what cocoa painting, nougat modeling, and sugar cages involved.

Yeah. That was exactly what he should do, Damon decided.

When Natasha realized the thrilling educational experience she'd missed out on—because she could, after all, have been included in this potential professional ménage à trois, too—she'd regret leaving him on his own twice as hard.

With that heartening thought in mind, Damon dragged on his clothes, then went on the hunt for Tamala. He felt better already. He felt ready to take on the world. He felt . . . invincible.

That was *always* a good sign . . . wasn't it?

Chapter 7

Present day
Las Vegas, Nevada

The thing about Sin City, Natasha reflected as she waited in the noisy, crowded, smoky din of the casino down The Strip from the chocolate-convention hotel, was that it removed you from your life. Piece by piece, the things that ordinarily kept you grounded fell away. Before you knew it, you were living in a neon-lit, adults-only, twenty-four-hour wonderland, without so much as a clock on the wall to tell you night from day.

Here in Las Vegas, responsibilities were optional. Conventional morals didn't apply. Indulgence was not only tolerated, but encouraged. Here in Las Vegas, there was nothing to stop a person from going all-out crazy for a night or a weekend . . .

Or maybe for longer. Which was the hook, in the end, that made Natasha say yes when a supply rep from a luxury chocolate packager asked her to dinner. She hadn't been on a date for a while. She knew Scott from other industry events; he was a nice man. He didn't make the earth move with his presence alone, but short of Damon, who did? So when he'd asked, she'd said yes.

Now, waiting for Scott outside the chic, five-star restaurant they'd agreed upon, Natasha felt glad she'd taken a chance. Sure, this was a business trip—but Damon enjoyed himself all the time while he was away for work. There was no reason she couldn't do the same. In fact, it had felt pretty good this morning to call Jason for Damon-wrangling duty and slip away to the casino shops for a few hours. Now that she'd tasted a little freedom from her self-imposed obligations to her boss, Natasha wanted a little more. Preferably tonight. *Privately*. But first . . .

The cell phone in her hand finally connected. Cradling it to her ear, Natasha found a slightly quieter corner. She smiled as she spoke, growing more engrossed the longer she talked. Her conversation *also* had the power to make reality shift—but this time, it was the unwanted reality of tipsy, glassy-eyed gamblers and raucous clumps of college-age tourists that slipped away.

"Did everything go all right today?" Natasha asked her mother-in-law ten minutes later. "With the birthday party?"

"Everything was fine," Carol assured her warmly. They'd grown even closer in the years since Paul had moved to Mexico to be with his "muse" full-time—since Carol had practically taken to arm-wrestling Natasha's parents in the who-can-spoil-Milo-the-most sweepstakes. "Everyone had a very nice time."

"Good. I'd hoped so. What about the cake?"

"It was practically hypoallergenic. Tasted like it, too."

"No nuts? No milk? No gluten? Are you sure?" Worriedly, Natasha scanned her memory for specific recollections of other parties given by the same hosts. "You know even the smallest amount can trigger a reaction, so it's very important to—"

"I'm sure," Carol said. "Look, you just think about having a nice time in Vegas. Are you doing anything fun tonight?"

Natasha squinted at the casino-goers, deliberating whether to share the news of her impromptu date. "I have a date."

"Is this a 'date' like the 'date' you had to work overtime filing overdue tax papers for your boss?" Carol asked with a hefty dose of cynicism in her voice. "At least that time, that nice Jason Huerta helped you. Or is this a 'date' to bail out Demon Damon from jail again? Wasn't he extradited last time?"

Demon Damon. "I asked you not to call him that anymore."

But her mother-in-law was on a roll. "I've got it! This is a 'date' to let yourself be worked to the bone by a self-centered, unappreciative jerk who can't see all you do for him!"

"You don't know Damon," Natasha argued for the umpteenth time. "You've never even met him. You don't understand."

"I understand that you deserve better!" Carol said loyally. Then she sighed. "I'm sorry. Maybe I don't know Damon, but I *do* know when you're being taken advantage of, and it bothers me! I know your job is lucrative, but haven't you saved up enough money to quit yet? You've been piling up savings—again, with Jason Huerta's help—for years. By now you *must* be able to—"

"It's not about the money." In fact, Natasha *had* amassed a substantial savings portfolio over the years. At this point, she had a very reliable safety net in place; the resulting security and peace of mind were worth a lot to her. "I like my job! Some parts obviously excluded, of course," she amended as the memory of spritzing a nearly nude, mostly drunk, fringed-suede-loincloth-wearing Damon with the shower nozzle came rushing back to her. That had *almost* been the last straw. Seriously. He couldn't have bothered to put on some pants? It was almost as if he was *daring* her to get fully fed up with him. "And you know I didn't set aside all that money just to pay for daily expenses. Some of it is meant to finance my—"

On the verge of explaining herself yet again, Natasha spied a blond, suit-wearing man headed toward her across the casino.

Scott. He smiled and waved when he saw her. He was stuck behind a woman driving a motorized scooter. Patiently and kindly, he allowed her to pass. She nearly mowed him down in her zeal to get to the next bank of gleaming slot machines.

At that only-in-Vegas sight, Natasha couldn't help smiling. She'd tried her luck with those machines, too. She'd lost, of course. At least she hadn't gambled much—only a few dollars.

"I'm sorry, Carol. I've got to run. My date is here."

"Your date? Humph. If you want to keep calling it a date, you can. What *I* call it is wasting your time on a dyed-in-the-wool playboy. Demon Damon is never going to change!"

"My *date's* name is Scott," Natasha specified with a smile, shifting her gaze to the man himself as he came nearer. He really seemed nice. Funny and sweet. "And the one thing we absolutely *won't* be talking about tonight is Damon." She took care of a few details. Then, "I'll see you tomorrow. Love you!"

Breezily, Natasha hung up the phone. Expectantly, she turned to Scott, enjoying the grown-up, cleaned-up, laid-back surfer boy vibe he gave off. Smiling, she hugged him hello.

Up close, Scott looked even better than she remembered. He was clean shaven, nattily dressed, and intriguingly muscular. His brilliant blue eyes sparkled at her. His smile beamed.

This was going to go well tonight. She just knew it.

As if agreeing with her, Scott took her elbow. They

headed inside the restaurant—one Natasha had purposely chosen because of its distance from the hotel that was hosting the chocolate conference—then sat at a cozy table in the bar. Scott ordered a drink; Natasha did, too. She'd only begun sipping it, enjoying the convivial atmosphere between her and Scott, when he leaned forward. He touched her forearm. His eyes danced even bluer.

She had a sudden yearning to kiss him, right then and there. It was Vegas. Who would care? Besides, she felt *so* lonely tonight. Phone calls weren't the same as real connectedness.

Scott drew in a breath. "So, what's the story with Damon?" he asked. "All anyone could talk about today was his varietals workshop. I figured I could get the inside scoop from you."

Great. Scott was a Damon groupie, Natasha realized. He must have asked her to dinner hoping to garner some tips on how to succeed in business. And pleasure. And everything in between.

This had happened to her before. It was never fun.

But just in case she was wrong, Natasha smiled.

"Look, I said yes to dinner tonight because I wanted to get to know *you*, Scott." Across the table, she took his hand. "So if you don't mind, I'd rather not talk about my boss. Okay?"

Scott seemed confused. "Really? But today, Damon was so—"

"I was out shopping most of the day," Natasha interrupted with a lighthearted wave. She sipped more of her drink. It tasted delicious. It tasted like the teensy dose of freedom she'd had this afternoon, after she'd unloaded Damon's care and feeding to Jason, for once. "I played hooky from the conference. Sometimes I just feel . . . naughty, like that." With sham innocence, she raised her eyebrows. She slipped off her slingback shoe, then playfully nudged Scott's muscular, trouser-covered calf with her bare toes. "Don't you feel naughty sometimes, too, Scott? I mean, here we are, all alone together in Sin City—"

Now he appeared flustered. "But it was *Damon Torrance* today. The superstar stud of our industry! How can you ignore—"

"Easy." Her nonchalant wave turned downright glib. "I'm used to him. In fact, I'm *over* him. And do you know why?" Here, Natasha nailed Scott with a straightforward look. "Because Damon Torrance doesn't appreciate me, and I want a man who does."

Just then, Natasha could think of several ways the right man could *appreciate* her properly. Starting with a kiss . . .

Incredibly, Scott shook his head. "You probably just don't comprehend the full magnitude of Damon's business genius."

She stared. "You're *defending* him?" *And calling me stupid?*

"Of course." Scott slipped his hand from hers. He hoisted his drink. "Damon's a legend. Not just in our little bittersweet corner of the world, either." He gave her a semi-smarmy grin. "Did you see what I did just there? 'Bittersweet.' Get it?" With a sudden frown, Scott leaned nearer. "Hey, do you think he'd mind me calling him Damon? Because until we've been introduced—"

"I'm not going to introduce you to Damon."

"Well, not *tonight*, of course!" Scott gave an uneasy chuckle. Hastily, he grabbed her hand. His fingers, wet and sticky from his drink, kneaded hers. "Tonight is all about us!"

"No. I'm not introducing you to Damon. Ever."

Now Scott appeared wounded. "Why not?"

"Maybe you can mull over that question yourself." Natasha snatched away her hand. With dignity, she rose. No one in the dark, crowded bar noticed. "While you're dining *alone*."

"Wait." Scott gawked. "You're offended? Oh, come on!"

She ignored him. It was hard to behave with poise when you were fishing surreptitiously, foot first, beneath the table for your slingback. Where was her damn shoe? She couldn't *believe* she'd come on to him. Of all the people, in all the world . . .

"I mean," Scott went on in a more conciliatory tone, "you're a very cute girl. You are! But your real value lies in being close to Damon Torrance, not in being . . . well, just yourself. You must know that. It doesn't mean we can't be friends—"

"'Friends'?" Indignantly, Natasha arched her brows. "I was planning to invite you back to my room tonight, if things went well!" Because of Milo, it was tricky for her to arrange grown-up "sleepovers" at home. Also, Carol lived right next door in the adjacent duplex apartment; not much sneaked by her—including manly overnight guests doing the walk of sexy conquest. Irately, Natasha regrouped. "But now *that's* out—"

"It doesn't have to be out." With a suddenly ingratiating demeanor, Scott leaned back in his chair. He smiled, spread his knees, then rested his drink-holding hand near his crotch. He waggled his eyebrows. "I'm still up for it if you are."

Oh God. "No, I'm not 'up for it,' you moron!"

Exasperatedly, Natasha gave up on discreetly retrieving her shoe. She dropped to the floor, grabbed her slingback, then stuffed it on her foot. When she rose, Scott was still giving her the come-hither routine. "Moron" was too good for him.

"I was letting you know what you'll be missing tonight," Natasha told him haughtily, "now that you blew it with me."

"Oh." Scott's brows knit. "I get it." Then he brightened. "So now that we're *not* having dinner—or anything else— together, how about that introduction to Damon? Because if your objection was mixing business with pleasure, well . . . there's no problem now!"

Natasha grit her teeth. Usually, she tried to be nice. She truly did. But between Damon's inconsiderate drunkenness this morning—she hadn't mentioned to Jason that she hadn't merely tried to sober up Damon; she'd also walked in on him engaging in some (fairly limber) shenanigans with the French acrobat—and Scott's rude behavior tonight, she was ready to blow a gasket.

Maybe that's why, when her iPhone rang, she took one look at the absurdly handsome photo of her grinning boss on its screen and felt like drop-kicking the device back to San Diego.

"You want to talk to Damon?" Natasha asked Scott archly.

Like an overeager puppy, he nodded. "Yes! I do!"

"Then here." She grabbed her iPhone and hurled it at him. It smacked his chest. "Here's Damon now. Knock yourself out."

Triumphantly, Natasha swiveled on her heel, then stalked away. Unfortunately, she wasn't as lucky as Scott had been. Because *her* grand exit was interrupted by the speedster driving the scooter. Before Natasha knew what was happening, she was on the floor. Dazedly, she raised her head. "Hey! Hit and run!"

The woman tactlessly zoomed toward the next bank of slot machines. A crowd formed as Natasha got awkwardly to her feet. As soon as the onlookers realized she was neither injured nor likely to chase down the scooter driver and exact revenge by assaulting the woman with a bucket of quarters, they lost interest. Chattering and smoking and drinking those foot-long cocktails served in Las Vegas, the bystanders meandered away.

Although Natasha felt embarrassed—and her knee hurt a little—she did realize one saving grace. Scott hadn't noticed.

In the distance, he merely jabbered away. "Natasha?" she heard him say into her phone. "Yeah, she's right here." A pause. "No, she gave me her phone." Another pause. "Me? I'm Scott—"

Natasha stalked nearer. She snatched away her phone.

With relish, she ended the call. "Whoops. I forgot my phone. I guess you'll have to make a first impression later."

Scott appeared stricken. His mouth froze in an O shape.

"Oh, wait. I forgot. You only get one chance to make a first impression. I hope you didn't intend to ever do business with Torrance Chocolates, Scott." Natasha leaned nearer, making sure he discerned exactly how flattering her first-date dress was. The minute his gaze slipped to her cleavage, she smiled. "Didn't anyone ever tell you? You should never piss off the gatekeeper. And at Torrance Chocolates, *I'm* the gatekeeper."

Scott swallowed hard. He seemed taken aback to be hearing such blunt language from her—a usually sunny girl from So Cal.

"I'm . . . sorry?" he ventured. His gaze wandered to her iPhone. Not surprisingly, it rang again. Damon was persistent that way, especially when he wanted something. "I'm really, *really* sorry!"

"Too late." Musingly, Natasha regarded her iPhone. She showed its screen to Scott. "Oh, look. It's the superstar stud of our industry, calling *me*." On behalf of beleaguered personal assistants everywhere, Natasha smiled. Scott's fingers jerked with a reflexive urge to take her phone. "I'd better get this."

Then, casually raising the phone to her ear, Natasha sauntered away—and this time, fate was with her. She didn't even get smacked by a runaway tourist for her trouble. "Hello?"

* * *

"Natasha? Thank God you're there," Damon said.

Striding through the casino, Natasha made a disgruntled face. Why did her phone calls so often begin with that phrase?

"Yes, I'm right here, as usual," she said curtly. "I'm the Red Cross of personal peccadilloes. The 'fixer' of front-page predicaments. The person who can be counted on for the inside exclusive on the latest business deals *and* for fresh coffee—"

"Hey. You know I don't drink that stuff anymore."

Right. He'd interrupted her rant to obliquely remind her of his ill-fated marriage to Giada—the same marriage that had wrecked her hopes for a little something personal between *them*.

Since then, Natasha hadn't even bothered telling Damon about her divorce. He hadn't asked. She hadn't volunteered, partly for fear of seeing their working relationship change because of it. After all, she still had her reputation as Damon's professional kryptonite to consider. She didn't *think* Jimmy Torrance would give her the boot for being single, but . . .

"Maybe you should." *Drink some coffee, I mean. Buckets and buckets of coffee.* "I hear it's useful for sobering up."

Damon let that slide. "Who was that with your phone?"

"My date." She kind of reveled in saying it. "Scott."

There was a disgruntled silence. "He sounded like a dweeb. You can do better." A pause. "So, the reason I'm calling is—"

So much for inciting a little curiosity about her personal life. Natasha exhaled. "Look, Damon. I'm busy. I only answered my phone in the first place so I could storm off in a huff."

Predictably, Damon didn't ask why she needed a huff.

"—because I need you," he went on. "I'm in a bit of—"

"Trouble?" she guessed, marching through the thronged casino at double speed. She reached the taxi stand outside, then got in line. "What else is new? Can't you handle it yourself? I'm tired. The good news is, the taxi line is so long that I'll probably have time for a nap before I snag a ride, but—"

"I'm in *serious* trouble. I'm in my suite. I can't move."

Natasha scoffed. "You dialed your phone, didn't you?"

"All right. Fine. Specifically, I can only move my left foot from the ankle down. And my head. A little. The thing is—"

"Does that mean you dialed with your foot? Or your head?"

"It's not funny!" For the first time, Damon sounded concerned. "You'll see what I mean when you get here."

She'd already seen more than enough of him for one day.

"Damon, call someone else. Okay?" Feeling besieged, Natasha moved up in line. "I'm really not up for this tonight."

"But . . . there isn't anyone else," Damon said in a low, husky tone. "There isn't *anyone*, Natasha. There's only you."

For the space of a breath, Natasha went still. How many times had she dreamed of hearing him say that? A million? More?

With a tentative smile, Natasha hugged her phone closer, imagining Damon on the other end of the line. She'd been foolish to think she could happily date Scott or anyone else, Natasha realized. Although she'd had her share of short-term affairs since her marriage had ended, none of those relationships had made her want something more. That's how she'd known she was meant for something bigger and better—something *truer*.

"Damon." Touched to realize the risk he was taking with her, Natasha broadened her smile. "Do you really mean that?"

If he did, that was it; she'd be at the hotel in a heartbeat. Even from here, she could see its incandescent, ornate tower of luxurious rooms . . . one of which contained Damon.

He was waiting there for her.

There's only you. Only you.

"Yes, I mean that," Damon told her, sounding endearingly gruff. "You're the only one with a keycard. Jason left his on the foyer table when he left this morning. It's got to be you."

Oh. Deflated, Natasha gripped her phone. The sea of cars and lights and taxis and people turned blurry. Was she actually *crying*? When was she going to learn she couldn't count on Damon?

"Listen. *Please* just come," Damon urged in a surprisingly (for him) no-nonsense tone. "The air-conditioning is on high, and I think I'm getting a serious case of blue balls."

"I'm going to pretend I didn't hear that."

"Why are you being this way?" Damon asked in a genuinely mystified voice. "You know you're going to come. You always do. If you want me to beg, I'll beg. It's that urgent."

Just like that, Natasha made a long-delayed decision.

"You know what, Damon? I *am* going to come over there," she said. "Because I have something important to tell you, and it can't be said over the phone."

"You're really coming?" He sounded hopeful.

"Yes. I'm really coming."

"Good," Damon said. "Bring a Snuggie for my testicles."

Completely against her will, she smiled at that. Such was the power of Damon Torrance's charm. Even ribald humor sounded good coming from him. Everything sounded good coming from him.

"But you'd better brace yourself," Natasha felt compelled to warn him as she moved a pace farther in the taxi line. "What I have to say to you might come as a big surprise."

"I can handle it. Just as long as you bring the ball Snuggie," Damon said. "Maybe a hot toddy, too, if you can swing it. The bar downstairs makes an excellent one." He sounded immeasurably cheered by her imminent arrival. As always, he trusted her to save the day. "Natasha, you're a lifesaver. My balls and I thank you. We can't wait until you get here."

"I know," Natasha said, unable to suppress another smile. "I'm on my way."

And that . . . was that.

For better or worse, the decision was made.

Chapter 8

In his own defense, Damon *did* try to prepare Natasha for the sight she'd see when she came around the private foyer corner, strode through his deluxe penthouse suite, and reached the bedroom. Unfortunately, he wasn't accustomed to being responsible. His version of a warning sounded a lot like . . .

"Natasha? I'm in here! Hurry up! I'm freezing."

Her footsteps sounded across the marble floor, barely overriding the nonstop, too-diligent hum of the air conditioner.

With a malevolent glare, Damon eyed the nearest vent. He wished he could cup his groin for warmth. He had goose bumps on top of goose bumps. He was pretty sure his *hair* had frostbite. After he got out of this, he was sleeping in a sauna tonight.

Natasha's footsteps slowed, then stopped. Damon imagined her capably sizing up the situation. With Natasha's reliable nature, take-charge demeanor, and perky nurturing ability, she could handle it, Damon knew. She could handle anything.

"Is that . . . chocolate I smell?" she asked. "Hot . . . chocolate?"

Damon sniffed. That delectably sweet, alluring fragrance still hung on the air, so familiar to him and—tonight—so condemning. It wasn't surprising, given the circumstances.

"Did you host your workshop in here?" Natasha guessed.

He heard her handbag hit the sitting area table. Her iPhone plunked down, too, reminding Damon of the bewildering surprise he'd felt when a strange *man* had answered Natasha's phone—and so intimately, too. What the hell gave *Scott* the right to do that?

He wondered if Natasha was having an affair with him.

Damon didn't think she was the type to cheat on her marriage vows, but weirder things had happened on business trips. Especially in Las Vegas. The idea felt disconcertingly possible. And disappointing, too. Damon treasured his notion of Natasha's infallibility. He liked her integrity and her poise. Sometimes, he needed her better qualities to stand in for his.

Tonight was one of those times.

"There's not much room for a workshop," Natasha went on in her expert way. "It must have been standing-room only."

She didn't know. She hadn't heard. A sense of overwhelming relief flooded him. Until that moment, Damon hadn't realized exactly how much he hadn't wanted Natasha to see him the way everyone else had seen him today: as a gigantic public failure.

The truth was, his varietal chocolate workshop had been a debacle. The B-Man Media footage of Damon—basically having an on-camera meltdown while semi-drunkenly trying to devise an impressive new flavor of truffle on the fly—had already gone viral. It was on the CNN news crawl. It was the talk of the conference. It was fueling rampant schadenfreude in the chocolate industry. Worst of all, the resulting gossip—or maybe just Damon's incompetence itself—had even made his mother cry!

Damon still couldn't get over that. His mother had *cried*. His father had looked tight-lipped and dissatisfied. No matter what Damon had said—for the first time in his life—it hadn't helped. In fact, the only person who initially *hadn't* seemed to find Damon's colossal screwup reason enough to ridicule, reproach, or simply abandon him was Tamala, the pastry chef—and soon enough, Tamala had shown her true feelings for him, too.

At least she hadn't brought a crème brûlée blowtorch . . .

To be sure his one-person reprieve was real, Damon called out warily to Natasha. "You didn't see the footage online?"

"I told you, I was on a date," she said. "Remember Scott?"

"Remember being married?" Damon couldn't help frowning. He was that disillusioned. "What about . . ." *Hell*. He couldn't remember her husband's name. Pedro? Patrick? Pacey? *Pacey* sounded right. But no—Pacey was on *Dawson's Creek*. Damn it. When it came to Natasha's husband, Damon had some kind of mental block working against his usually excellent powers of recall. ". . . your husband?"

Natasha rounded the corner. She saw him. Her eyes widened.

It wasn't too late to apply some charm. "Um, ta-da!"

"'Ta-da'?" Arching her brows, Natasha examined him—at length, and once by turning her head to view him upside down.

She sighed. The fact that Natasha had been through a lot with him showed, because she was otherwise completely unfazed by his compromising position. "I don't think you have any room to judge me with all these probing questions about my husband, Damon." She pointed at him. "You're tied up, naked, covered in chocolate, and decorated with strategically placed—" She paused. "What *is* that, exactly?"

"Nougat. It's modeled nougat." Helpfully, Damon aimed his chin at his groin, where Tamala had outfitted him with a makeshift confectionary Speedo. At the time, he'd thought it was strange, but he'd been up for it. Now, he frowned. "You might be surprised to learn that nougat is *not* as warm as it looks."

"I see. Anyway," Natasha said, crossing her arms in a "you're headed to the principal's office" fashion, "the point is, you're hardly being . . . restrained yourself at the moment."

"Actually, I'm being *quite* restrained at the moment." Damon tugged at the red velvet souvenir scarves that bound him to the bedroom's chaise. With an exuberance he definitely didn't feel, he gave Natasha a smile. Maybe he could wriggle his way out of this by joking. "You know, in the 'tied up' sense of the word."

"Right. 'Tied up.'" Natasha didn't seem amused.

She also didn't seem, it occurred to him, very interested in the fact that he was essentially naked. Damon didn't get it. Women *liked* seeing him naked. He typically returned the favor.

He knew Natasha had noticed his physique a time or two; he wasn't blind *or* oblivious to a certain . . . underlying sizzle between them. It had been there from the start, from the day they'd met in his office. But she was married. *And* she was his assistant.

Despite his current predicament, Damon *did* try to be good sometimes. He always had his philosophies involving Pop-Tarts, kung fu, and *not* sleeping with married women to fall back on.

Doing anything else—like seducing Natasha into abandoning her wedding vows—would have ultimately made her unhappy. Making Natasha unhappy, on purpose, was where Damon drew the line.

It was a good thing she possessed an oversize quantity of tolerance when it came to his antics, he realized. Because otherwise, he might have found himself making her unhappy a lot.

But Natasha had never given him a single indication that she was bothered by coming to his rescue. She'd always seemed unfailingly patient, tirelessly proficient, and brilliantly ingenious. She'd backed him up time and again. She'd never even revisited her threat to leave him if he took things too far.

But just in case she was toying with the idea . . .

"So . . . this isn't 'it,' is it?" Damon asked, just the way he always did. If he hadn't literally been bound into immobility, he would have given a carefree gesture toward his outrageous position, too. Because even though he desperately needed reassurance from Natasha—tonight more than ever—that didn't mean he had to tip his hand overtly. He was tougher than that. "This isn't the thing that finally makes you leave, is it?"

"This . . ." Dismissively, she gestured at him. ". . . thing?"

"Yes." For the first time today, inexplicably, Damon felt ashamed. He'd survived the workshop meltdown. He'd endured the crushing looks from his parents, colleagues, and friends. He'd even managed to swagger his way through his later encounter with Tamala. But seeing Natasha looking at him that way nearly broke his spirit. Defiantly, he eyed her. "Yes, *this thing*," Damon said again. Then, just to be excruciatingly clear—because that would make Natasha's inevitable reassurance twenty times more valuable, and also because the world loved a man who was willing to risk it all on a dare, and *he* was definitely that man, above all—Damon added, "This thing that involves me being tied up, naked, covered in chocolate, and sporting a nougat thong."

"Right. I get it." A pause. "If you had known it *was* the thing that might make me leave," Natasha asked, gazing at him through dark and unfathomable eyes, "would you still have done it?"

What a ridiculous question. Of course he wouldn't have.

Damon tried to chuckle. "Well, it's not *every* day a man gets invited to become a real-life, chocolate-covered, finger-painting palette in a naughty game of bondage taste testing."

Not that the situation had gone down remotely in that way, he knew. Tamala had invited herself in, gotten him all worked up, taken her time seductively painting him all over with bold Cote d'Ivoire and honeyed Carenero Superior, then snapped a few compromising photos with her cell phone and taken herself away.

Apparently, Tamala had wanted retaliation. Or leverage, in case her association with his workshop threatened her job. Damon wasn't sure exactly what Tamala had wanted. Either way, it didn't matter now. All that mattered was Natasha . . . and making sure she forgave him, released him, and maybe even smiled at him.

Preferably, in that order. His unwanted chocolate coating was beginning to harden. Soon he'd be homemade Magic Shell.

"You ought to try a lick," he joked. "I taste delicious."

Natasha's eyes flickered, but still she didn't move.

Humor was a gamble. Damon knew that. His situation was tenuous. But if anyone could get away with cracking wise at that moment, it was him. He'd always been blessed with an unfair share of charisma—and a lifetime supply of get-out-of-jail-free cards, too. He'd used them time and again, even with Natasha.

Obviously, a crueler woman—a woman like Tamala, who'd exacted her revenge on him with the help of his own dense, clueless, horny, and always affection-craving self—would have walked out on him already. She would have left him (and had) for a hapless member of the housekeeping staff to discover sometime tomorrow. But Natasha would never have been so cruel to a hotel employee. She was too kind. Too considerate. Too giving.

She would, it turned out, be cruel to *him*, though.

"Yes, Damon," Natasha said. She spoke clearly and yet somehow he still couldn't believe it. "This *is* the thing that makes me leave you."

He felt as if he was hearing her from underwater. Maybe he had chocolate couverture in his ears. Just in case, Damon decided to brazen out the conversation. She'd probably been kidding anyway. That was the relationship they had. "Well, you can take that ten pounds of tempered milk chocolate with you, if you want. God knows, it didn't do me a damn bit of good today."

This time, Natasha appeared even stonier. He'd meant she could take the chocolate with her because it hadn't helped him create something amazing to impress the world with. He'd meant it hadn't helped him wow his father or secure his future at Torrance Chocolates. But Natasha didn't know that, because she was the only person on the entire freaking planet who didn't already know about his humiliating workshop-based breakdown.

Vaguely, Damon wondered if this was what hitting bottom felt like. But then he remembered: *he* was *him*. He was fine!

At a loss for another quip, Damon gazed directly at Natasha. *Yes, Damon. This* is *the thing that makes me leave you*, he heard again, if only in his desperate, befuddled mind, and he knew that that couldn't be what Natasha had said, because that would be bad. Bad things never happened to him. He didn't want this to be happening . . . thus, it wouldn't occur. It couldn't occur.

In the silence, Natasha stared at him, almost as if she was waiting for more. Damon could have sworn there were tears in her eyes . . . except that was impossible, too. Natasha had nothing to be upset about. *He* did. He was the one who was tied up, wasn't he?

"Hey, don't cry," Damon joked. "You weren't even there. You'll have to get the workshop director's cut on DVD. It comes with bonus footage of me making an ass of myself in public!"

But Natasha didn't hear his last, despairing joke. Instead, from far across the room, she gave a mystifying, muffled sob.

"I can't stand this anymore, Damon," she said. "You, me, all these . . . situations you get yourself into. I can't do it."

Well. *That* couldn't be good. "I know," Damon began, trying his best to sound contrite while simultaneously racking his brain to remember what Jason had said to him this morning. "I've been on a bender. It's not good. You want to go to bed early!"

"No, I don't want to go to bed early." Her quizzical look was replaced by a mighty sniffle. She sighed. Then, before Damon could guess what was happening, Natasha hurried to the chaise.

She dropped beside it, then began untying the red velvet scarves with hasty, jerky motions. Were her hands . . . *shaking*?

He didn't want her to shake. Not like this. Not because of him. As soon as Natasha had freed his arm, Damon caught hold of her hand. Cradling it, he peered intently into her face.

Immediately, he discerned that those *were* tears. Uh-oh.

"Natasha, I'm sorry! I know things have been a little out of control lately. But it's got nothing to do with you. *You're—*"

Wonderful. Amazing. The only person who really "gets" me, Damon meant to say. But Natasha interrupted him before he could.

"I'll submit my formal resignation to Jimmy tomorrow, after I get back to San Diego." Natasha pulled free the final knots, then plucked off the Liberace-worthy scarves. "You won't have to tell him yourself. If he's disappointed, it'll all be on me."

"No. See?" Feeling truly alarmed now, Damon nudged up her chin. "You're still trying to take the fall for me! You're still trying to protect me." He gave her a fond smile. "That's how I know you're only kidding with this quitting stuff. You don't mean it." *God, he prayed she didn't mean it.* "You could *never* mean it. You and me . . . we're a team. Together we're like—"

"I quit, Damon. Listen to me: I quit," Natasha said. "I'm leaving. I'm finished making excuses, finagling appointments, and juggling pouty ex-girlfriends for you. That's it."

He couldn't comprehend it. "But I need you," Damon protested. He wanted to get to his feet, but he couldn't move. His legs had fallen asleep sometime during his vigil. "Natasha, I . . ." He hesitated, searching for something that might make her stay. There was only one thing that always— *always*—worked in these situations. "I love you! I do. Please don't go."

Disbelievingly, she stared at him. "You love me."

Eagerly, he nodded. Inwardly, he held his breath.

"I told you *never* to tell me you love me."

Vaguely, Damon remembered that. *Don't tell me you love me*, Natasha had stipulated during their initial meeting at Torrance Chocolates. *Don't flirt. Don't inform me of your sexual conquests or expect me to bail you out of them.* Well, three out of four wasn't bad. Until tonight, he'd been batting .750.

"How else can I do it," he asked, "except with words?"

"Easy. Don't do it at all."

"But I can't just let you leave! How will I"—urgently, Damon cast about for something really convincing to tell her, something incontrovertible—"get through my day without you?"

"You'll manage. You're the luckiest man I know."

Just then, Damon didn't *feel* very lucky. Instead, he began to feel angry, unfairly judged . . . and most of all, stuck on the chaise. With a groaning lurch, he managed to get upright.

Next, he made himself stand. The effort almost made him fall over. Pins and needles shot through his legs. For modesty's sake, he cupped his groin—because his nougat covering didn't feel super sturdy—then released a pained, involuntary groan.

Instantly, Natasha was at his side. Her brow furrowed.

"See?" he pointed out, gratified by her response. "You *do* care. You can't be that upset. Besides, it's not as though you haven't seen me naked before. You have, just this morning. It's not as though you haven't bailed me out before. You have, plenty of times, and from worse situations than this."

Not *much* worse, he knew, but still . . .

"No." Natasha clenched her fists. "This is different."

"Why? Because I interrupted your 'date' with Scott?"

At that, Natasha shook her head. Tears still glimmered in her eyes—tears that left Damon awash in commiserative misery.

He'd made her cry. He'd made his mother cry, *and* he'd made Natasha cry, both in the span of a single awful day. The two of them were the kindest, gentlest, most generous women he knew.

If he could hurt them . . . what the hell would he do next?

All of a sudden, Damon didn't really want to find out.

"It wasn't that you were naked and called me to bail you out that upset me, you idiot," Natasha said. "It was that you lied and said you loved me! I'm not one of your good-time girls, Damon. I'm *me*. I deserve better. For you, talk is cheap." Sadly, she shook her head. "But for me, *I love you* means something."

"It means something to me, too!" he insisted. "It means—"

It means I might get my way . . . and make you stay.

Just as he realized that ugly truth, Damon met Natasha's gaze. She'd already known that about him, he understood as he looked into her eyes. She'd known, and she'd stayed anyway.

Until now. How many people would have done that for him?

"Oh." Uncomfortably, Damon rubbed the back of his neck. He shifted his gaze away from hers. "I see what you mean."

All at once, he felt embarrassed for Natasha to see him as he was. He was nearly naked. He was painted with multiple kinds of chocolate. All his enthusiasm for having a good time showed.

So did all his weakness when it came to being a good man.

"I guess I have to let you go, then," Damon said quietly.

"I guess you do," Natasha agreed. She touched his face, then gazed into his eyes one more time. "Take care of yourself."

He *knew* he couldn't do that. He couldn't fathom why Natasha didn't. He quirked his mouth. "I'll try. You do the same, okay?"

"I will." She inhaled, then let her hand drop to her side. At least she was no longer shaking. "Bye, Damon."

He'd never thought he'd hear those words from her. The sound of them made him want to howl with grief. It was probably self-centered grief, Damon acknowledged, but still . . . "Bye, Tasha."

He'd never called her that before. Other people did, but not him. Doing so would have meant thinking of her as a woman, not his assistant, and Damon had needed the distance he'd gained from calling her Natasha. *Natasha*. That semi-formality between them had helped him not be tempted to seduce her into abandoning her marriage vows, the way he'd secretly wanted to do. But now . . .

Well, now Damon didn't need to create any false dis-

tance, because they'd have genuine distance between them.
Forever.

Fifteen seconds after he realized that, Natasha was already gathering her things in the sitting area of his penthouse suite. Her high-heeled footsteps sounded. There was
a final, lingering silence. Damon held his breath. Then, an
instant later, came the muted thump of the suite's door closing behind Natasha.

It had really happened. For the first time in years,
Damon realized, he was truly on his own—and he had no
freaking idea what came next.

Chapter 9

San Diego

As the days piled up since quitting her job at Torrance Chocolates, Natasha gradually realized that her impulsive decision had caused some sort of elemental shift in her world.

It had begun right away. When she had checked out of the hotel that had hosted the chocolate conference, the night after leaving Damon, the perky hotel employee at the front desk had informed Natasha that she was the hotel's "mystery guest" of the week—and had won a week's prepaid stay in the form of a special voucher, for use any time she wanted a getaway. It was the first thing Natasha had ever won. She could hardly believe it.

At first, she *hadn't* believed it. It had occurred to her almost immediately that Damon might be behind her "comped" stay. It wouldn't have been the first time he'd used his money and influence to try to make amends for something he'd done wrong.

But then, when she'd boarded her flight home and found herself seated next to a fascinating neurosurgeon—a man who had been obviously (and flatteringly) interested in getting to know *her* better—she'd begun to suspect something more inexplicable was afoot. Not even Damon Torrance could cajole a man like Lance, the neurosurgeon, into spending more than an hour talking with her . . . and then inviting her to dinner after they landed.

By the time Natasha had agreed to that date, then retrieved her luggage—and her Civic from long-term airport parking—she'd fully expected fate to catch up with her. Surely the universe would teach her a lesson, right? She'd been *too* lucky so far.

She'd even spontaneously tried out a slot machine at McCarran International Airport—and been rewarded with a nearly thousand-dollar jackpot on the spot. There was no *way* Damon could have had anything to do with that. That was just good fortune.

It was, she figured, good fortune that she'd inevitably be made to pay for, one way or another. With that thought in mind, Natasha warily pulled onto the freeway. By accepting a free week's hotel stay, gambling and winning, spending an enjoyable morning being flirted with, and making an actual date for the following week, she knew she must have already used up her meager share of good luck. Half expecting her car to pull its usual unreliable routine, she listened carefully to the engine as she merged into the whizzing San Diego traffic.

Oddly, her Civic practically purred along. No blowouts. No scary "check engine" lights. No weird noises. What's more, other drivers graciously allowed her into their lanes. Once, when she accidentally cut off another driver, the man waved off her mistake with obvious goodwill. *That* made her do a double take.

Polite drivers. Huh. What in the world was going on here?

But the oddities had just kept coming after Natasha arrived home to her duplex apartment. She expected the yard to be overgrown with weeds and in dire need of a trim; as the head of her household, Natasha didn't have the luxury of offloading yard work to a "honey-do list," the way other women sometimes could. Instead, she saw as she wheeled her luggage up the walk, her green grass and borders of geraniums looked like something out of *House Beautiful* magazine. Puzzling over that, Natasha inhaled the welcome, briny scent of ocean air. This couldn't be Carol's work; her mother-in-law was wonderful in many ways, but she hated gardening and was too thrifty to pay to have it done.

"Oh, hey, Natasha." Her neighbor, Kurt, lifted a pair of long-handled gardening shears in a welcoming gesture. He'd obviously been out working in his yard. "You're home."

"Yes, I just got back. I couldn't wait to get here."

"Your yard looks incredible," Kurt said with obvious admiration. His own green thumb was legendary. "New gardeners?"

"I don't know. Carol might have hired someone."

It had seemed like a good guess. But later, Natasha had found out that her mother-in-law didn't know who'd tidied and trimmed their yard, either. "I guess it was garden pixies."

"'Garden pixies'?" Natasha had repeated dubiously. But as her unlikely good fortune had continued to pile up, "garden pixies" had seemed as likely an explanation as anything else.

The next day, Natasha's habitually hopeless weekly purchase of a "lucky" lottery scratch-off ticket had actually won almost fifty dollars. Her favorite boutique in La Jolla had called to say they had received a pair of shoes she'd ordered weeks earlier—and they were now on sale at forty percent off.

Her "good mornings" to her neighbors had been greeted with grins and chatty conversations. Her veterinarian had informed her that her dog, Finn, a golden retriever/bulldog mix, was in perfect health . . . and she wanted to use Finn as a model for the adjacent pet store's upcoming ad for training classes, too.

Finn, while undeniably lovable, was only seven months old. And a rascally mutt. He needed to be *in* a doggie training class;

he in no way exemplified the ideal canine graduate. But Natasha had agreed anyway. Finn would be compensated for his work in the form of free veterinary checkups and dog treats, and maybe he'd pick up a few obedience tips while he was being photographed, too. It was sort of a win-win, even if it *was* unexpected.

Natasha's date with the neurosurgeon, Lance, had gone without a hitch. Her suggestions to Carol regarding the duplex's exterior repainting job were met with enthusiasm *and* agreement. When she went out, men smiled at her and turned flirty; when she saw her friends, they laughed at all her jokes and hugged her warmly and complimented her effusively on every outfit she wore.

Upon learning that Natasha had left Torrance Chocolates, headhunters called her with tantalizing offers of new employment. They wooed her with lavish expense-account meals and promised her unbelievable perks. Her page on LinkToMe, the online corporate networking site, practically brought down the server with constant activity from people trying to reach her.

"Wow." Natasha gaped at her laptop's screen, blinking at the dozens of requests for new associations. "I should have left Torrance Chocolates years ago. Who knew I'd be in so much demand? I was afraid to take that leap and risk giving up my income, but I could accept any one of these new jobs and start tomorrow—with my own office, more authority, and identical pay."

"*I* knew you should have left," Carol told her warmly. "You should have done it as soon as you met Demon Damon. You always deserved better than the crummy way that man treated you."

Demon Damon. Yes, he'd been that, at times. But he'd also been so much more, especially to her. Which only brought Natasha around to the one lingeringly painful truth:

no matter how terrific things had seemed lately, she still missed Damon.

She missed feeling the energy crackling from him as he arrived in the office—usually running late after having had some adventure or other—and greeted her with his special smile. She missed hearing the good humor in his voice as he confided in her about some grandiose plan he was hatching. She missed seeing his winning smile, feeling his casual touch as he held doors open for her and escorted her through, and knowing he was only a phone call away at any moment. She missed *him*. Period.

"You didn't know him," Natasha said in her former boss's defense. She raised her chin. "Damon wasn't that bad."

"Not 'that bad'?" Her mother-in-law stared at her in disbelief. "He made you buy flowers for the women he broke up with. He made *you* come up with the cards. How many of those 'sorry I broke your heart' bouquets did you send, anyway?"

"Too many to count. But at least he sent them!"

Carol gave a dismissive snort. "Yes, he's a real prince."

"If you ever met him—"

"That will never happen," Carol said, "and I'm glad."

But Natasha wasn't glad. Because despite her own recent good fortune, she couldn't help wondering: If *she* was experiencing an unprecedented streak of good luck (and she was), what exactly was happening with Damon these days?

Standing in the middle of his formerly posh living room, Damon gazed with dismay at the wreckage before him. He stood calf deep in murky water. Sandy grit clung to his furniture, revealing the yellowed places where the water had risen during the flood that had made his oceanfront home uninhabitable.

Despairingly, he sloshed through the brackish water to the other side of the room. He retrieved a picture frame that had been floating in the floodwaters. He wiped its cracked glass front with his shirtsleeve, then peered at it. A ruined photo of Jimmy and Debbie Torrance stared reproachfully back at him.

It was almost like looking at his parents' faces in real life. Since the debacle at his varietal chocolates workshop at the conference in Las Vegas—and the subsequent media shit storm—neither of them had forgiven him. There had been recriminations. There had been tears. There had been threats to "go in another direction" with the future of Torrance Chocolates.

In the end, Damon had skated by without being axed outright; he was grateful for that. But he knew it wasn't blind luck that had saved him. He suspected Natasha had had a hand in Jimmy's decision to offer a "cooling off" period instead. She'd always been his dad's favorite; it wouldn't have been the first time she'd given Damon a behind-the-scenes assist. But despite that reprieve, Damon hadn't rested easy in the days since then.

Instead, he'd tried to set things right. He'd tried issuing penitent invitations to dinner, to brunch, to take trips together, to go shopping, to see a show, to attend the theater. . . .

His parents had refused every damn overture. Nothing had worked. Not without Natasha there to help him.

All at once, Damon had utterly lost his mojo. He only had to look at that photograph, search his short-term memory, and wade to the next soggy area of his home to realize it. He was in a seriously bad way. He had no idea where to go from here.

All he knew was that he *had* to keep moving. Doing so *had* to be better than staying where he was, stuck beneath a figurative black cloud of despair and misfortune. Lately, it felt as if the universe wanted to rain on his parade full-time, Damon thought as he rescued another photo and added it to the growing pile in the crook of his arm. Everything he touched turned to shit.

His run of bad luck had started, appropriately enough, in Las Vegas. Damon had awakened the morning after Natasha's defection, still hungover from the night before, to find that during the night, several of his misdeeds had caught up to him.

The housekeeping staff, usually so understanding and forgiving when it came to him and his transgressions, had reported his suite's chocolate-covered wreckage to management. His hotel bill had skyrocketed. He'd been banned from the luxury hotel and all its associated properties for life. The French acrobat he'd entertained the day before had blamed Damon for her being late and losing her job in her troupe's popular show. And the board of directors for the chocolate-industry conference had explained to him in no uncertain terms that he would *not* be welcomed back to present a workshop the following year.

What's more, Damon hadn't even been able to leave Las Vegas properly. When he'd finally, *finally* wrapped up things with the hotel management, the acrobat, and the board, he'd learned that his driver wouldn't be showing up. Ever. He'd decided to remain in Las Vegas and try his luck at being a stand-up comedian.

Without Natasha on hand to wrangle a replacement, Damon had been forced to hitch a ride to the airport on a crowded, non-air-conditioned, vaguely bacon-y smelling van full of tourists. He'd alighted with relief, stretched his stiff arms and shoulders, then subsequently beelined to the nearest coffee stand . . . only to find his wallet and cash missing. Apparently, during the cramped ride, someone had pickpocketed his ID and all his credit cards.

Naturally enough, the theft had led to Damon's being unable to board his scheduled flight. At first, he'd tried to pull some strings. That hadn't worked. The airport security wouldn't budge. Next he'd called Jason and begged his friend to make the round trip between San Diego and Las Vegas. Jason had agreed. But because he'd brought along Amy and their two toddlers, Isobel and Manny, Damon's escape from Las Vegas had turned into a raging diaper-palooza road trip full of crying and gassiness—not to mention multiple reprimands (and then the silent treatment) from Amy, who had clearly sided with Natasha in her decision to leave.

"You deserve this, Damon," Amy told him. "Every painful minute. I know Jason tried to warn you, but you didn't listen."

By the time the Huertas had dumped Damon on his doorstep, he'd been ready to declare celibacy for life. He was *that* sure that babies and toddlers (and self-righteous wives) were *not* for him. As luck would have it, the women in his life had uncannily agreed. For days now, Damon had been receiving breakup phone calls, e-mails, and even texts (*texts!*) explaining that all the fascinating women in his life wanted him to leave them alone.

Their rejections had been unexpected. And humbling, too.

Apparently, Damon had learned, there wasn't enough charisma in the world to convince so many women to give him another shot. After the first dozen "Dear Damon" messages, he simply gave up.

He had other problems to deal with, anyway. Because as he probably should have expected, his virtual mugging on the smelly airport van ride from hell had led to his identity being stolen and several of his bank accounts being cleaned out—a matter that Damon was still trying to sort out with the bank.

Evidently, these days his engaging smile didn't get the same mileage it used to, either. Because when he tried to expedite the process by turning on his usual charm with the bank representative, she'd reacted with hostility, unhelpfulness, and a lawsuit threat. Some of the female employees at work had suddenly become invulnerable to his charms, too. Prompted by rumors of Tamala's "kinky Las Vegas sexcapades" with Damon (although no one had yet seen the photos), they'd banded together to insist that Jimmy host another round of mandatory sexual harassment training at Torrance Chocolates headquarters.

Jimmy had done so. Then he'd tactfully suggested that, as an alternative to being fired outright—as Damon was still in danger of being—he take a temporary leave of absence from work. Looking weary and disappointed, his dad had explained to Damon that he needed to focus on the company's future ("now more than ever," Jimmy had added enigmatically, "for your mother's sake")—and on choosing his eventual successor—and that Damon's "antics" were a distraction from that.

Blindsided and hurt, Damon hadn't been able to do anything except agree. He'd gotten into his car, intending to take a long, head-clearing drive to the mountainous areas near Alpine, east of the city. But even his trusted BMW had failed him.

Damon hadn't found relief and calm during his drive. Instead, he'd wound up stranded with an alarming quantity of smoke coming out of his engine *and* a flat tire. Getting home again had required multiple phone calls, another awkward ride with Jason, and a final damning declaration from his friend.

"Look, I can't keep bailing you out, bro," Jason had told him, looking uncomfortable. "Amy says you're taking advantage of *me* now, instead of Natasha. And she's right." His friend jutted out his chin pugnaciously. "You're going to have to figure out things on your own for a while. It will be good for you."

Good for him. Right. Damon had had his doubts then, and he had his doubts now—now that he'd come inside after being dropped off to discover that his house was ruined and uninhabitable.

One of the contractors he'd called waded toward Damon. His practical waterproof fishing waders kept him a lot dryer than Damon's ensemble of bare feet, bare legs, and rolled-up pants.

"Hmph. It's the damnedest thing." The contractor peered at his clipboard. He gazed at Damon's formerly lavish living room. Then he looked through the window at the serene beach and ocean, scratching his head. "I've never seen anything like it. None of your neighbors were affected at all. No flooding next door or anyplace else along the beach. Near as I can figure, something funny happened with a city water main nearby, and all the water got diverted straight into your house."

A water main. "All these years living next to the ocean, and it's the municipal water system that finally gets me." Damon shook his head at a bundle of sodden, uprooted weeds draped over his state-of-the-art home entertainment system. "The odds of a flood like this happening have got to be astronomical."

"Probably, yeah." The contractor seemed unperturbed by that morose observation. He thrust his clipboard full of paperwork at Damon. "Here's my estimate. It'll take a while to pump out all the water. That's what'll happen first. Then my crew will dry out everything, repair the structural damage inside and out, perform a series of mold treatments throughout the house—" He broke off, dollar signs practically dancing in his eyes. "Well, you can see for yourself there on the estimate sheet."

Damon looked at it. "How long will the work take?"

"Two, three weeks. Maybe more. It's hard to say. Depends

on if you want us to Dumpster the ruined furniture or leave it."

Oh. That meant things were even worse than he'd thought. Of course his furniture was ruined, too. But a two-to-three-week work time was probably just as well. Damon might need that long to sort out his troubles with the bank; otherwise, he wouldn't be able to pay at all. "Fine." He scrawled his signature.

"I hope you've got someplace to stay," the contractor told him as he tucked away his clipboard beneath his arm. "You sure as hell won't be staying here. Even the upstairs needs work."

Upstairs. That's where his bedroom was. Damon hadn't even waded that far yet. At the thought of his own private sanctuary being destroyed, he felt worse than ever. No matter how far in the world he'd roamed, he'd always loved coming home to his own bedroom—and especially to his own familiar, comfortable bed.

"There's always a hotel," the contractor said. "Sometimes the insurance company will pay for something like that."

Given the way his life had gone lately . . . "I doubt it."

"Well, it's a good thing you're *the* Damon Torrance, then." The contractor grinned. "You must have plenty of rich friends who'll help you."

"You'd think so." Since the workshop debacle, though, many of his friends had been strangely "busy" when he'd called. Newly depressed at the remembrance, Damon did his best to rally. He smiled, then shook hands with the contractor. "Thanks for everything. I appreciate your coming out on such short notice."

"Hey, no problem at all. A job this big is going to single-handedly pay for my kids' Christmas this year—and I've got three of the little rug rats. So I'm more than happy to do it."

The contractor beamed at him. Damon felt strangely cheered. Natasha would have loved to know that he was indirectly giving some junior San Diegans a major-league holiday . . . provided he had access to his bank account or credit cards sometime soon.

How was he going to pay for a hotel without them? Damon wondered suddenly. Where was he going to live for the next several weeks? The uncertainty of it all nearly overwhelmed him.

Natasha would have found a way, Damon knew. Because Natasha was clever and resourceful and not easily discouraged. He missed those qualities in her. Hell, he missed *her*. Period.

He didn't want to admit it, but it was the truth. He missed seeing Natasha in the expansive office they shared at Torrance Chocolates' flagship La Jolla headquarters, perkily talking on the phone or diligently typing notes on her computer. She'd always had a smile for him, he remembered, no matter how wired, hungover, or late he'd arrived. He missed hearing Natasha laugh her husky laugh. He missed seeing her take charge of things. He missed feeling her always uplifting presence in his life.

Without Natasha, Damon realized, he was . . .

Not himself. At all. He was listless, unmotivated, and dejected. Worst of all, he was demonstrably *unlucky*.

How was he supposed to psych himself up, Damon wondered with a jab of defensiveness, without the promise of earning Natasha's smile at the end of the day? He'd done so many things, he'd realized too late, partly to earn her approval. Without that dangling carrot to pull him along, life was full of sticks.

"Hey." With evident concern, the contractor squinted at

him. "Are you okay? You look like you're taking this kind of hard. I swear, we'll get this place back to normal. We will."

Damon shook himself. "Thanks. I know you will." He considered his predicament—and the fact that his BMW was currently being held hostage in an auto repair shop in Alpine—then aimed an earnest look at the contractor. "You wouldn't happen to have a spare worker with a truck handy, would you? I obviously can't stay here, and I could really use a ride."

The contractor frowned. For an instant, Damon expected him to refuse. That's just the way his life had gone lately. Then . . .

"Yeah, I'd like to help you with that. But my other guys are all out on jobs, and I can't spare the few I brought with me today. Sorry." The contractor pointed toward the kitchen peninsula, a granite slab that divided the living space. "I think I saw some spare change in that big bowl thing on the counter. You could take a bus."

Damon glanced at the "big bowl thing"—a limited-edition Dale Chihuly sculpture he'd picked up on a trip to Seattle.

"Yeah. All right," he said. "The bus it is, then."

"Have you ever *ridden* a bus before, Mr. Torrance?"

Damon shrugged. "I've seen them. I've seen the stops."

"Okay. That's a start, I guess." The contractor seemed to be stifling a guffaw. He shook Damon's hand again. "Good luck."

Good luck. Ha. For the first time, Damon understood why Natasha had once accused him of sarcasm when he'd said that to her. When good luck felt totally out of reach, hearing someone wish you a dose of it just felt like a cruel taunt.

"I don't have to go very far," Damon said. "I'll be fine."

"I hope that's true, Mr. Torrance." This time, the contractor *did* laugh. So did his workers. "All the same, my professional advice to you is: phone a friend. Get a ride."

Damon wished he could. "If I could, I would," he said.

Then he took himself upstairs, packed a pair of Louis Vuitton overnight bags with as many undamaged belongings as he could cram inside them, and went to find the nearest bus stop.

Chapter 10

Having an unexpected sabbatical from work *sounded* heavenly. At least in theory, it did. Voluntary joblessness left Natasha's days free to spend time with her family and friends, catch up on chores, organize her closets, do some reading, and finally get through the backlog of TV shows on her TiVo. But that vacation mind-set only went so far, Natasha discovered during her first week of freedom. Because after a while, she got bored.

Not just ordinary, garden-variety boredom, either. No, what Natasha experienced was full-on, mind-crushing ennui. Nothing satisfied her. What she needed, she decided, was to feel productive again. She didn't want to make a decision about accepting a new job just yet, but she didn't want to laze around all day, either. What she needed, she decided further, was to apply her newfound good luck to an entirely different arena.

That's why, late in the first week following her walkout on Damon, Natasha gathered her courage, picked up a feather duster, and headed out to the garden shed behind her duplex apartment.

She hadn't been out there in a while. Not since . . . well, not since shortly after she and Paul had moved into the duplex. But with her ex-husband in Mexico and her own life moving forward, Natasha decided it was time to confront the demons of her past.

Standing a few feet in front of the shed, she eyed its old door, ramshackle siding, and pair of grimy windows. Inside, it probably looked just as bad. The place clearly needed some TLC before she could use it again. She'd purposely neglected it, and it showed. Under its eaves, leaning against the siding, were the various yard tools Natasha stored there—a rake, a shovel, a dilapidated rotary push mower, and a pair of gardening gloves.

All those items more properly belonged inside the shed. But keeping them outside suited Natasha just fine. They were mostly protected from the weather, and they were handy when she needed them. Occasionally, Carol pestered her to either clean out the shed so it could be used for its intended purpose or (more frequently) to "open the damn door and do some work in there!"

Unfortunately, Natasha had abandoned the kind of work she did in the garden shed . . . which had nothing to do with gardening.

Today, though, things were going to be different. Today, she was going to take the first step toward the rest of her life. Inhaling deeply, Natasha marched to the shed's front door.

She glanced around her quiet neighborhood, half expecting someone to accuse her of . . . well, she wasn't sure exactly *what* she expected to be accused of. Not deserving a second chance?

Paul had resented the time she'd spent in her improvised garden-shed workspace, Natasha remembered as she wielded her feather duster. He'd teased her. Sometimes he'd sulked. After a while it had just seemed easier to stop going in there.

Eventually—and much too easily—she'd given up on herself.

But all that was changing . . . starting today. Weirdly enough, it was changing because Natasha had finally gotten fed up with Damon enough to leave. He'd accidentally given her the push she needed, just by being his usual bad-to-the-bone self.

"Thanks, Damon!" she muttered under her breath. Then, after squaring her shoulders and taking another tentative glance around, Natasha opened the garden shed door and went inside.

For the fifth time in as many days, Damon headed downstairs from the luxe guest room that Wes Brinkman had offered him. As usual, during the lengthy journey across Wes's palatial house, Damon tripped over a discarded bottle of vodka, navigated past several passed-out, scantily clad guests from the previous evening's party, then made his way to the kitchen. There, Damon found no sign of the housekeeping staff . . . or anyone else. At Wes's (*unflooded*) oceanfront beach house, things were pretty casual.

That was because Wes didn't have someone like Natasha to maintain normalcy and a modicum of order, Damon had decided. But it might also be because Wes, an inveterate partier, didn't want anyone around who might disagree with his hard-living ways.

Damon could identify with that. Sometimes a man didn't want anyone pestering him to wake up, get dressed, and be responsible. He knew he didn't. Not even now. Screw that.

That's why Wes's place was so perfect for him. *Perfect*.

After a brief rummage through the fridge, Damon unearthed an orange juice from behind the ever-present supply of Veuve Clicquot that Wes kept on hand. Carefully, Damon made a notation on the notepad he kept on the counter: *Orange juice, 1 pint*.

Keeping track of the items he used had been Damon's

idea. Wes had given him no end of grief about it. The orange juice was only the latest in a growing series of penciled-in entries designed to help Damon track and repay his debt to Wes—the only one who'd truly come through for him in his hour of need. His notepad also included entries recording five days' lodging, several full meals, and more than one instance of bus fare.

Damon's Chihuly cache of quarters hadn't gone very far; despite not having ransomed his BMW yet, he'd still needed to get places occasionally. Although his parents were still being chilly—to the point that Jimmy and Debbie had refused to put up Damon temporarily in their house in Solana Beach—Damon remained dedicated to his work at Torrance Chocolates . . . and to finding a way to redeem himself in his dad's eyes.

Now, if only he knew how in the hell to do that . . .

"You know, I'm beginning to think you're an impostor." Wes rounded the corner, toting a whiskey bottle and looking sleepy. He wore his suit from the night before—crumpled and worse for the wear—with an unbuttoned shirt and a day's ration of beard stubble. Lip gloss smudged his collar. "The Damon Torrance I know would have been tallying up bottles of champagne, wrecked hotel suites, beautiful women, and business victories. Not O.J."

"The Damon Torrance you *knew* wouldn't have tallied up a damn thing, because he didn't realize what a mess he was."

Wes scoffed. "Are you still beating yourself up about that?" He traversed the length of the counter on unsteady bare feet, slung his arm companionably around Damon's shoulders, then nudged him in the ribs with his whiskey bottle. "Knock it off already, dude. Your prissy secretary was wrong about you! Look around you—you *won*! You're at the top of the heap! You might as well enjoy yourself, because you damn well earned it. That Vegas thing was just a fucking glitch. A speed bump. Nothing more."

To punctuate his point, Wes knocked back some whiskey. He offered the bottle to Damon. Regretfully, Damon shook his head.

Wes met his refusal with an indulgent smile. "Fine. Be that way, you damn spoilsport. But before you wrap yourself around the axle trying to be a 'better person'"—Wes paused to make derisive air quotes with his fingers—"whatever the fuck *that* means, you might want to ask yourself: Where's the payoff?"

Grumpily, Damon drank his orange juice. He remained silent.

"That's what I always ask myself," Wes told him casually. "Where's the payoff? If there isn't one, I don't do it. So where's the payoff, for you, in trying to be so 'good'?"

Damon wasn't sure. All he knew was that he'd scraped the floor in Las Vegas. From here, he could only go up. He hoped.

"Not everything comes with a profit/loss statement."

"Ooh, listen to you! Now I *know* you've been replaced by a pod person." Wes's eyes glimmered with laughter. "Come on! I'm not talking about P and Ls. I'm talking about life! Living *life*! Grabbing life by the balls and seeing where it takes you!"

"Lately? It's been taking me down some pretty dark alleyways." Sardonically, Damon grinned. "It's been grabbing *me* by the balls and punching me." He sighed. "In the balls."

"I know. I know." In a conciliatory gesture, Wes spread his arms—a motion that sent telltale whiffs of liquor, cigar smoke, and ladies' perfume into the air. All the aftereffects of his raucous lifestyle were present and accounted for. "You told me that when you got here. You've had a run of rotten luck lately—"

Darkly, Damon chuckled. "That's putting it mildly."

"—but have you considered *why*?"

"Why what?"

"Why you've been so 'unlucky' lately." Wes examined his bottle, idly rubbing his thumb over its label. "I mean, all these things going wrong at once can't be a coincidence."

"It *has* to be a coincidence." Privately, Damon had begun wondering if he somehow *deserved* all the misfortune he'd been encountering lately. But he didn't want to think about that. So he didn't. "I'm probably overdue for a lifetime's bad luck, that's all," he told Wes. "I've been skating until now—"

"No. What *you've* been doing is being fortunate enough *not* to come across a vengeful woman," Wes disagreed. "Until now."

Mystified, Damon stared at him. In many ways, he and Wes were like brothers. They liked the same things. They reacted in the same ways. They shared philosophies and business goals. That had been true for five years now. He and Wes were simpatico.

But this . . . "I must be too sober. I'm not following you."

"Natasha." Wes nodded. "*She's* your vengeful woman. You crossed her," he theorized, "and now you're paying for it."

Damon burst out laughing. He couldn't help it. "That's impossible. Natasha isn't making me pay for anything. You've met her—she's about as vengeful as a basketful of puppies."

"Sure." Consolingly, Wes made a face. "She probably *seemed* that way at first—until you pushed her too far. But then . . ." Wes gave an awestruck whistle. "Watch out, sucker. I've seen it happen before. You make one tiny misstep, and little miss basket of puppies morphs into a fucking pile of piranhas."

Involuntarily, Damon thought of Wes's cadre of ex-wives. If the divorce settlements—which were legendary—were anything to go by, those women had definitely been out for the kill. Still . . .

"Not Natasha." Damon shook his head more firmly. "No way."

"Yes, way. The quiet ones are always the deadliest after they've been riled up." Wes slugged back more whiskey. He aimed the bottle at Damon's improvised ledger, where he'd written *orange juice* just moments ago. "Look what she's reduced you to. *Bookkeeping*." He made an even more aggrieved face. "Hell."

"Natasha didn't do that," Damon protested. Although it was, he realized, exactly the kind of thing she'd be inclined to do herself for the sake of fairness. "I did it. It was my idea. As far as the rest of my misfortunes go—"

"Who else had the motive to do this to you?" Wes interrupted. "Who else had the requisite access to you to pull it off? Who else could have reported your hotel suite ruined, canceled your driver—all but guaranteeing you'd be mugged on that airport van—and put out the word to all your lady friends that they should end things? I'll tell you who: Natasha."

"Well," Damon mused aloud involuntarily, "Natasha *did* have contact information for all the women I dated. Over the years, we'd streamlined the process of sending 'sorry I broke your heart' bouquets after the inevitable breakups happened."

"'Sorry I broke your heart' bouquets?" Wes goggled at him. "Gag me. Let me guess: that was your secretary's bright idea?"

"Maybe the first one was. . . . I can't remember."

"See? She's corrupted you!" Wes pointed the whiskey bottle in outright indignation. "Plus, she's obviously turned Jason and his wife against you. Who knows *what* she told your parents to make Jimmy and Debbie turn their backs on you, too—"

"Hey." Damon gave his friend a stern look. "Watch it."

"Sorry." Wes really did appear contrite. For him. Which

didn't mean much. "All I'm saying is, it bugs me to see you suffering this way when you don't have to! It seems obvious to me that your pissed-off secretary somehow put your whole life into meltdown mode, and now you're suffering the consequences."

Almost against his will, Damon found himself nodding. It was true that no one else in his life possessed the necessary access to wreak the havoc he'd undergone lately. Only Natasha.

"Worst of all, you've internalized the damage!" Grandiosely, Wes spread his arms. His whiskey sloshed in its bottle. Across the room, a woman wearing a sequined miniskirt and one high-heeled shoe—and nothing else—stirred in her sleep. "That's the real kick in the head! You're suffering, and you think you deserve it. You think you're supposed to fix yourself somehow, starting with a stupid ledger of orange juice entries."

Somewhere between *internalized*, *suffering*, and *fix yourself*, it occurred to Damon that Wes may have had a *lot* of therapy. Maybe too much. Everyone knew Wes had been in and out of rehab. All the same, some of what he was saying made sense.

"I still don't think Natasha would do anything like this on purpose. She couldn't," Damon insisted. "The really weird part is that while I'm here struggling, Natasha is doing *great*. Jason and Amy told me she's happy, she's got tons of new job offers, her clunker of a car is running well, her flowers look better than Martha Stewart's, her mother-in-law is apparently being extra agreeable. . . . Even that bastard Pacey is probably being nice."

At the thought of Natasha's husband, Damon frowned. But Wes wasn't the least bit sidetracked by thoughts of Natasha's spoiled artiste hubby . . . and how lucky the bastard was to be with Natasha, probably right now, this very minute. Damn it.

"It's obvious what's happened here." Wes gazed directly at him. In a solemn tone, he said, "*Natasha* has *your* share of good luck. *She's* got all the good luck *you're* supposed to have."

For a moment, the idea just hung there between them, feeling important and right and inarguable. Maybe it was.

"That's as good an explanation as any." With a nod, Damon slammed down his orange juice. "I need to get it back."

"Yes. You *deserve* to get it back."

"I'm going to get it back. Today." Warming up to the idea, Damon ran his hand through his hair. This was the first break he'd had in days. He meant to run with it. "I bet all I have to do is get Natasha to forgive me, then . . . bam! The universe will right itself again, and I'll have my mojo back."

Wes beamed. "*That* sounds more like the Damon Torrance I know. Go get her, tiger! For you, this should be easy."

"Yeah," Damon agreed. "It *will* be easy! I might be down, but I'm not out. I'm still me! I can get whatever I want."

"Damn straight, you can." Wes saluted with his whiskey.

Feeling fired up, Damon nodded. "I'd know exactly what to do, too. . . ." He paused. "If it weren't for Pacey." *Stupid Pacey*.

If not for Natasha's inconvenient husband, Damon could have taken the easy way out and charmed her into forgiving him. As it was, he'd have to try some other, less intimately enjoyable method of convincing Natasha to give him a second chance.

If only he knew what it was . . .

Well, he'd figure it out when he got there.

"Point me to suburbia!" Damon told his friend exuberantly. "I'm headed to the land of minivans, carpools, and faithful family mutts—and I'm going to conquer it by lunchtime."

Wes peered at the clock. "It's *already* lunchtime."

"I'm going to conquer it by sundown!"

"Okay." Wes pointed at him with his whiskey bottle. "You might want to put on some pants first."

Damon glanced down at his black boxer briefs. Still undaunted, he said, "If I have to, I'll conquer it naked!"

When it came to Natasha, he wished he could. . . .

"Right." Wes nodded toward the back door, where a rack of key rings hung. "Take my car. Keep it as long as you need to."

"Hey, that's decent of you, Wes."

A shrug. "I've got six more parked out there."

"Still, I appreciate it." Damon squared his shoulders, then gave his friend a confident look. "I'm going to do this."

"I hope so, because you can't come back here." Wes flashed a regretful glance in the direction of the topless, miniskirt-wearing woman across the room. Now she'd draped herself across the sofa. "Destiny says you crush her groove by not partying with us. She wants you to leave. I told her I'd make it happen."

Openmouthed, Damon gawked at him. "You're kicking me out?"

"'Fraid so, dude." Wes gave another genial, man-to-man shrug. "I'm sort of a pushover when it comes to women."

That explained Wes's multiple divorces, Damon thought.

"Besides," Wes added, "I'm kind of a dick. You know that."

Agreeably, Damon nodded. "I think we both are."

But maybe not for long, Damon told himself with a new burst of optimism. If all went well today, he could get back Natasha *and* reclaim his good luck in the process . . . and maybe reboot his messed-up life at the same time. Stranger things had happened.

Not to him. But they'd happened. Probably.

"You can always sleep in my car," Wes suggested. With a leer, he added, "The backseat is pretty roomy. I can attest to that fact personally." He pulled out a wad of cash from his suit pocket, then riffled off a few bills. He raised his eyebrows. "And I can front you some walking-around money. How much—"

"No, thanks." Damon held up his hand. "I'm already indebted to you enough. Besides, I'll be fine."

Wes gave him a dubious eyebrow raise.

"Seriously," Damon assured him. "I'll have this mess straightened out by happy hour. It's Natasha. I know her."

He *did* know her. He could do this. Feeling invigorated and self-assured, Damon headed upstairs.

Halfway there, he turned back.

"But I *don't* know where she lives," Damon admitted to Wes. No wonder he'd failed all those quizzes on Natasha's personal life. He was clueless about the important stuff. "Any ideas?"

Chapter 11

When Natasha first heard her doorbell ring, she thought it was probably a UPS delivery arriving. Or maybe her next-door neighbor, Kurt, wanting to borrow her gardening shears. Or maybe someone looking for Carol and ringing the wrong doorbell.

Most of Natasha's friends knew to bypass the weird clang of the 1960s-era doorbell at her front door; they mostly knocked instead. That meant that the only people who actually rang the front doorbell were door-to-door salespeople and well-meaning missionaries offering Bible tracts—and *that* meant Natasha knew she could safely ignore its ding.

Then it came again. *Ding. Ding. Ding*!

Reluctantly, she made her way to the door, careful not to smudge her fresh pedicure as she went. Given her copious spare time these days, Natasha had taken to experimenting with her "look." It was a suggestion Amy Huerta had helpfully made—partly because Amy, at eight months pregnant, could no longer reach her own toes very agilely. She needed help to paint them.

Ordinarily, Amy had giddily confided, Jason helped with that task. But today, she and Natasha were enjoying a spa day at home while Jason used his employee flextime (a longtime perk at Torrance Chocolates) to take the children to the park at Mission Beach.

"Sorry. I'll be right back," Natasha promised Amy.

She trundled awkwardly toward the front door, balanced on her bare heels, mindful of keeping her foam toe separators safely in the air. Her pedicure—based on a new toluene-, DBP-, and formaldehyde-free "green" nail enamel that Amy had insisted on using—flashed its pretty pink shade all the way across her living room. If she made it to the front door and back without a noticeable smear, Natasha knew, it would be a miracle.

As it turned out, the real miracle was waiting at her door.

Because when she opened it, Natasha, wearing a pleasantly neutral expression and expecting to see a delivery person with a clipboard or maybe a hopeful Girl Scout selling delicious cookies, instead gazed across her sunny threshold and saw . . .

"*Damon*?" Boggling, she stared at him. "Is that you?"

He looked *great*, Natasha couldn't help thinking. He looked tall and muscular and handsome and . . . contrite? And, in a charcoal-colored suit and open-collared shirt, Damon looked . . . out of place. He looked incredibly out of place in her modest neighborhood.

Maybe she was imagining him, Natasha thought for one crazy instant. Maybe she'd missed Damon so much that her imagination had conjured him out of thin air—incongruously fancy suit and all. But then Damon smiled, thrust forward a vivid bouquet of cellophane-wrapped yellow daffodils, and spoke to her.

"These are for you," he said. "They're a peace offering."

"Peace offering?" Natasha angled her head in confusion.

In further bafflement, she frowned. "How did you find me, anyway? I know you don't know my address or even my street, so—"

"Will you please take them?" Damon offered them again. "Please? I have a whole speech planned. It starts with flowers."

"Oh. Okay." Stiltedly, Natasha accepted the daffodils.

At least they weren't the same patented, super-expensive, "sorry I broke your heart" bouquet that Natasha had routinely sent to Damon's exes. That wouldn't have been welcome at all.

Even if Natasha's heart really *was* a little broken. At the sight of Damon, in fact, her heart ached with a bittersweet longing that surprised her. She'd thought she was getting over him. She'd thought she was learning *not* to miss him anymore.

Apparently, there really was some truth to that "out of sight, out of mind" adage, at least when it came to her.

Feeling self-conscious and all too aware that she *did* miss Damon—and didn't know how to stop, short of keeping him distinctly "out of sight"—Natasha stuck her nose in the flowers.

That was what people did with flowers, right? But of course, she didn't smell a thing. These days, most flowers only looked nice; they lasted a long time but had no fragrance. They were bred for showy looks, not subtlety. As a peace offering from Damon, that probably made them particularly appropriate.

When Natasha finally raised her head, Damon was watching her. He appeared crestfallen. "You don't like them?"

She nodded. "Of course I do! I love them."

But of course he'd spied the disenchantment on her face, no matter how brief it had been. As usual, Damon Torrance was one step ahead of her.

Feeling foolish for not having remembered the truth about flowers—for having been characteristically naïve and hopeful, even when experience told her not to be—Natasha looked right at him. "I hear you have a speech prepared. Let's have it."

Damon shifted his gaze away from hers. He swallowed hard.

"All right. The thing is, Natasha . . . I'm sorry." His gaze met hers again, suddenly, with an intensity that shook her. "I'm *so* sorry. I treated you badly, and I took advantage of you. I let you down, and I hurt your feelings, and Las Vegas just brought all that home to me. I never meant to do any of that. I've been torn up about it ever since you left—"

"Shouldn't you be at the office right now?" She didn't want to interrupt, but she also didn't want Damon to drive Torrance Chocolates off a cliff just because he felt guilty. "It's the middle of the afternoon on a Friday. You're missing your weekly staff meeting." *And the test varieties of chocolates that are always served during it*, she remembered. *Yum, yum*.

"—and if you would just say you forgive me," Damon forged on doggedly, "it would mean the world to me. I'm really sorry."

Still thinking it was strange that he'd blow off work to visit her—because while Damon *had* been a chronic playboy, he'd never been truly irresponsible when it came to taking care of his family's company—Natasha frowned at him. "Did you *forget* your meeting?" she asked. "Because without me there to remind you—"

"I didn't forget." For an instant, he seemed torn. It was almost as if Damon was considering confiding in her about something—something to do with work. Then, "This is more important. Making sure you know I'm sorry is more important."

"Oh." Natasha looked at him more closely. Same brown wavy hair. Same hard jaw. Same dark, melty eyes that invited a woman to lose herself in them. Same Damon. She couldn't put her finger on it, but . . . "You seem . . . different. Is everything all right?"

Again, Damon appeared conflicted. He opened his mouth as if to speak, inhaled, then shut it again. "Everything *will* be all right, after you say you forgive me." He took her hand. He smiled, and the Damon she remembered—the teasing, confident, super-sexy Damon—returned. "Come on. You know you want to," he coaxed. "It'll feel *great* to have all this settled between us. Don't you remember what it was like during the good times? When we were laughing and traveling and testing new truffles? Nobody ever meant more to me than you, Natasha. Nobody. Remember—"

"I remember," Natasha interrupted before he could go on—before he could stir up any more nostalgia or longing or memories of closeness between them. She pulled her hand from his grasp, then straightened her spine. "Okay. I forgive you."

Damon raised his eyebrows. "Just like that?"

"Sure." Natasha nodded. "Just like that."

The relief in his face was palpable. Had her forgiveness really meant that much to him? Touched by that, Natasha smiled.

Damon did, too. For a long moment, their eyes met . . . and every single bit of connection and yearning she'd ever experienced came flooding right back to her.

So did a few of her more risqué fantasies about him.

Shaking them off, Natasha examined Damon more closely. How many times had she imagined him coming to her this way? Since Las Vegas . . . *several times*. There was no denying that hearing her former boss beg her forgiveness was pretty darn satisfying.

"Thank you," Damon said in an earnest tone. "Really. You don't know what I went through just to get here, and I—"

"Tasha?" Amy called loudly from the other room. "Is everything all right?"

Startled by her friend's voice, Natasha jumped. Hearing Amy reminded her that whatever else happened, Natasha didn't want to let Damon hurt her ever again. She deserved better. Much better.

"Everything's fine, Amy!" she called. Then she turned to Damon again. Still holding her daffodils, she said, "I've really got to get back. As you can hear, I have company. But of course I forgive you, Damon! You're *you*. I can hardly hold it against you when you screw up. That would be like"—Natasha cranked her arm, searching for an appropriate analogy—"like expecting the sun to feel cold or the ocean to stop making waves."

"That's what you think of me?" Damon appeared stricken. His jaw tightened. He looked away. "After all our years together, *that's* your summation of me? That I'm a hopeless screwup?"

"It's not your fault," she assured him kindly. "It's part of your charm. I just don't want to be part of it anymore."

He frowned. "Hell, Natasha. That kind of takes the fun out of your accepting my apology, don't you think so?"

Natasha shrugged. "But I did it. Let's leave it at that."

"Sure. We could do that." Damon's gaze swiveled back to hers. "But I have to confess, I was kind of hoping . . ."

That we could have something more, she imagined him saying next. *That you'd invite me in and we could start again* . . .

"Never mind." Damon thrust his hand through his hair. He aimed a brief, fraught look at her. "All I really need is your forgiveness, and I've got that. So . . . bye, Tasha. Take care."

Then, without waiting for her to reply, Damon left.

It had been a lot more fun to be the one walking away than the one left behind, Natasha couldn't help thinking as she watched him leave. Not even the delectable view of Damon's cute, suit-clad backside could entirely sweeten the experience.

Exactly what, she wondered, had Damon been going through on his own over these past few days? Whatever it was, it probably explained those meaningful pauses he'd thrown into their conversation. If she knew Damon—and she did, pretty well by now—he had a secret. He had a big secret. A secret that *she* didn't care about in the least, Natasha told herself firmly. Then she picked up her toes, swiveled around, and went to rejoin Amy. Her pedicure had survived. This time, so had she.

It took everything Damon had not to look back as he left Natasha's front porch. Keeping his shoulders steady, he strode past the green grass, past the blooming geraniums, and down the sidewalk toward Wes's car. Without the daffodils he'd brought for Natasha (which he'd purchased after selling his six-hundred-dollar necktie to a Gaslamp street peddler at a ninety percent loss), his hands felt empty. So did his heart. Weirdly enough, seeing Natasha had made him feel *more* alone, not less. He hadn't expected that.

When Damon got into Wes's car, the uniformed Torrance Chocolates security guard who'd accompanied him on his mission gave him a skeptical look. Damon guessed he deserved that skepticism—and the supervision that came along with it. After all, he'd decided to get Natasha's address in the most direct way he could think of—by brazening his way into the La Jolla headquarters and raiding the personnel files to find it.

"Well," said Louis, the security guard. "How'd it go?"

"Fine." Damon gestured toward Natasha's well-kept duplex apartment and flower-bordered yard. She'd seemed so different today. So casual. So open. So . . . well, so unexpectedly *sexy* in her bare feet and loose hair, in her jeans and her T-shirt, in her overall warmth and vitality. Pacey, he thought for the millionth time, was an unfairly lucky man. Damon frowned. "As you could see, I didn't have any nefarious intentions."

Louis shrugged. "I didn't really think you did, Mr. T. But rules are rules. At Torrance Chocolates, we take care of our own." Proudly, he patted the ID badge clipped to his uniform's shirt pocket. "Natasha helped get me my job at the company. She's a great girl. You can see why I had to look out for her."

Right. Damon already knew that Natasha had inspired endless devotion from everyone at work. The entire staff, from janitors to board members, adored her. When she'd quit, everyone had unanimously (and accurately) blamed Damon. Animosity had ensued.

Things had gotten bad enough, rapidly enough, that Jimmy had even cited the need to resolve "morale problems" when he'd asked Damon to take his leave of absence from the company.

"For all I knew," Louis went on cheerfully, "you were gonna stalk Natasha or something. Not on *my* watch, you're not."

"You're very dedicated," Damon told him wryly. He clutched the steering wheel, feeling weirdly reluctant to leave. He should have felt great, he knew; he'd successfully gotten Natasha's forgiveness. Any second now, his usual good luck would kick in, and things would be fine again. Somehow, though, Damon *didn't* feel great. "I'll take you back to the office."

"Aw, we don't have to go back right away." Louis gave him a hopeful look. "You're a legend when it comes to knowing how to have a good time, Mr. T. Everybody knows that. Now that I know you don't mean any harm to Natasha, I don't have to keep any eye on you anymore. Jimmy said so." He grinned. "How about we go grab a beer or something? You know, for old times' sake?"

"'For old times' sake'?" Exasperatedly, Damon stared at him. "I haven't *left* the company, Louis. I'm on leave."

"Yeah, well . . . leaving has a way of becoming permanent, doesn't it?" the security guard pointed out. "Especially if the leaving is involuntary, like yours was." Louis brightened. "Say! We guys in security have a bet going about whether you ever come back to work. Do you mind giving me a little inside info?"

"If I had it to give," Damon said, "I would."

Louis gave a disgruntled sound. Trying to ignore the suddenly pervasive feeling that he was disappointing everyone around him, Damon started the car. Frowning, he scanned the quiet street. He didn't like knowing that his absence from Torrance Chocolates was the subject of speculation. He didn't like knowing that everyone thought he was down for the count.

At least Natasha didn't know about his unwanted leave of absence. It had been hard for Damon not to tell her about it. Especially when she'd been grilling him about why he wasn't at work, at his staff meeting, trying to make his parents proud—trying to develop his family's company and do something worthwhile.

Telling Natasha about everything that had happened to him over the past few days—like being temporarily forced out of his job, seeing his house flooded, losing his car, and having his bank accounts frozen and his identity stolen—would have worked instantly to gain her forgiveness, Damon knew. Natasha was empathetic and kind and giving. She would have wanted to help him—if for no other reason than she felt sorry for him.

That's why Damon had kept his struggles a secret from her. It hadn't been easy, especially when she'd asked him directly if everything was all right. He wasn't surprised that Natasha had somehow been able to intuit the truth: that things were awful for him. But he *was* surprised he hadn't caved in and told her exactly how bad they were. Usually he would have felt no compunction about playing the sympathy card, if necessary.

Maybe he *was* becoming a better person, Damon thought.

Mentally congratulating himself on that, he pulled away.

Simultaneously, Louis shook his head. "I'm sorry, dude. It won't be the same around Torrance Chocolates without you."

"Louis, I'm not leaving! I'm coming back. You'll see."

Doubtfully, the security guard gazed outside. Slowly, Natasha's apartment retreated from view. "Not without Natasha, you won't come back. You can't do it without her."

Since that was Damon's most closely held secret fear, Louis's prediction hit him hard. But since Damon couldn't allow anyone else to know that . . . "You just watch me, Louis. I'll be back bigger and better than ever," he assured him. "Bet on it."

Louis cheered up. "Hey, thanks for the tip, Mr. T!"

In that moment, as Damon drove away from Natasha for the first and probably last time, he made a promise to himself.

He *would* be back at Torrance Chocolates. He'd triumph, too. With or without Natasha to help him do it.

But first . . . "Hey," Damon said to Louis after a quick glance at the car's center console, where he'd stowed his remaining loose change, "do you know where I can get lunch for $8.75 or less? I'm starving. If it's cheap enough, I'll even treat."

"Sure." Louis pointed straight ahead, where the freeway exit swerved southward. "I know an awesome food cart down by the Embarcadero. We can both eat cheap, and I'll buy the beer."

"Sounds good to me," Damon told him.

Tasty food, free beer . . . what more could a man ask for?

It looked as though his luck was changing for the better already.

Chapter 12

Just as the sun was beginning to cast long orangey shadows across Natasha's front yard, her doorbell clanged again.

Instantly, she thought it must be Damon. Again. Only this time, she decided as she strode barefoot from her kitchen to her front door, she would not be such an easy mark for his charm. This time, Natasha promised herself, she would be a *lot* tougher.

Her determination lasted about as long as it took to open the door. As soon as she spied Damon standing there, she almost melted on the spot. No sane woman could have blamed her. Not while Damon stood in the waning rays of sunlight, still wearing his suit, with his dark hair tousled and his eyes fixed on hers.

"I can't do it without you," he said. "I thought getting your forgiveness would be enough. But it wasn't."

"Hello to you, too," Natasha joked. "Long time, no see."

Long time, no see? What was she, twelve? So far, she'd demonstrated all the innate coolness of a preteen with a crush.

Which, technically, pretty accurately described her attitude toward Damon. She *did* have a crush on him. She ought to be honest about that—at least with herself. She'd realized

that much during their time apart. Still, Natasha didn't want
to be defined by her feelings for her unattainable, spoiled-
rotten boss. Inwardly, she groaned. But she couldn't seem
to tear away her gaze from the sight of Damon's handsome,
beseeching face.

"I need you, Natasha," he said, and she wasn't entirely sure
she wasn't dreaming. "I'll do anything," Damon promised.
"I swear I will. I'll do *anything* you want. Just name it."

"Okay." She crossed her arms. "Um . . . howl like a
wolf."

He looked puzzled. "Seriously?"

"Absolutely." She nodded at him. "Go ahead."

"All right. It's your kinky party." Obligingly, Damon
tossed back his head. Then he opened his mouth and
howled in the direction of the fuchsia bougainvillea arching
over her porch.

Her neighbors—if they noticed—were unperturbed.

Natasha approved. "Hey, it's fun to be the one giving
orders. It must be awesome being the boss of people."

"It is." Looking adorably disgruntled, Damon raised his
eyebrow. "Are we done yet? Can I come in? I need to—"

Be with you, she imagined him saying, then cut him
short. As much as that idea segued nicely with her fantasies,
it didn't exactly gibe with her need to keep Damon "out of
sight" and hence "out of mind" long enough for her to get
over him.

However, now that he was here, maybe she could have
some fun with him first. In the spirit of getting while the getting was good, she decided to push Damon a little further.

"Now do a little dance," Natasha instructed, just because
she could. Just for the hell of it. Because this opportunity
might not come around again, and she had to make the most
of it. She swiveled her finger in the air. "Include lots of hip
action while you're at it. Pretend you're bringing sexy back."

"Bringing sexy—" At her overt request that he make

like a former boy band member, Damon scowled. "You're enjoying this."

"More than I ever expected," she agreed gleefully. "Go on."

"No." He pouted. "I'm not your dancing monkey."

"Oh, I think you are. You already volunteered."

"I meant I'd *pay* you to come back to work with me," Damon told her. "I meant I'd apologize again or try to make amends."

"Maybe. But what you said was, and I quote: 'I'll do anything. Anything you want. Just name it.' So I'm naming it."

He exhaled. "Fine. I'll do it."

She waited. A long time. "Do you want some music? My iPod is in the other room. I could just grab it and—"

"No." Stubbornly, Damon closed his eyes. He appeared to be getting himself focused. He inhaled deeply, then shook his arms.

Just when Natasha was about to prompt him to start, he did.

By the time he'd finished his impromptu hip thrusts and rhythmic gyrations on her front porch, Natasha was left gawking. She could hardly breathe. She was pretty sure she was blushing.

"I know," Damon said upon seeing her face. "I should be careful where I unleash that kind of raw sex appeal, right?"

He said it self-deprecatingly, with a trace of humility that she'd never quite glimpsed in him before. But with the memory of his mini performance so fresh in her mind, Natasha couldn't focus on Damon's emotional state. She couldn't even form words. All she could do was remember . . . longingly.

How had he made suit pants look so sexy? How had he *moved* that way, so uninhibitedly? So committedly? So affectingly?

All at once, Natasha wanted to lay out a whole itinerary's worth of special requests for Damon—starting with the suggestion that he come inside . . . and ending with a demand that he kiss her (at the very least) or love her (at the very most).

Clearly, Damon's *Dance Dance Revolution* had melted her brain. She didn't have a lick of common sense left.

Now she wanted Damon to *love her*? Oh, boy . . .

"Your neighbors will never look at you the same way again," Damon prophesied. "From here on, you'll be the woman who demands that men gyrate on her front porch before they come in."

Natasha grinned. "If that's some kind of double entendre—"

"It's not. I promise." Damon's serious, slightly panicked look made her wonder exactly what he thought she was proposing. "You're you, and I'm me," he blathered uncharacteristically, "and there's always Pacey to think of. . . ." On that baffling note, he paused. He smiled straight at her. "So can I come inside?"

No, her good intentions nagged. *Out of sight, out of mind.*

"Yes." Natasha stepped aside. "But you'll have to hop."

Damon went still. "You want me to hop in?"

"Like a bunny," she specified. Just to clarify matters, she added, "I'm not through messing with you yet. So . . . hop."

Hop. With his whole future hinging on his ability to make like Bugs Bunny, Damon took a deep breath. He glanced at Natasha. She still looked unbelievably luscious, even while wearing jeans with holes in the knees and a worn-thin T-shirt with nerdy cartoons on it. She confirmed her outrageous request with a grin, then waited for him to deliver on his promise.

I'll do anything you want. Just name it.

"I never pegged you for the dominatrix type," he grumbled.

"I never pegged you for a welsher," Natasha said cheerfully. With offhanded curiosity, she looked him over. "After you've done all this—to *my satisfaction*, of course—"

To her satisfaction. At that, Damon almost groaned. He was *trying* to be good. He was. But with Natasha tossing out naughty jokes, looking fairly adorable, and (after his stupid dance) practically devouring his body with her "I want you" gaze, he was having a hard time with the whole concept of staying honorable. So far, he hated it. It was not a natural fit.

"I can deliver satisfaction," he couldn't resist saying. Hell, machismo was baked into his nature. It was part of him. "Don't worry about that. But as far as the hopping goes, I—"

"—exactly what," Natasha persisted, "do you get in return? Why are you so keen to do what I want? I don't have anything—"

"You have *everything*," Damon told her, and it was true.

She had everything he needed and more. Because this afternoon, contrary to his deeply held hopes, Damon hadn't become magically lucky again. Things were as bad as they'd ever been. That meant he still had more work to do. With Natasha.

Ignoring her perplexed expression, he gestured grandly.

"Stand aside. I'll need lots of room," Damon told Natasha intently. "Because my hopping is going to *blow your mind.*"

Grinning now, Natasha complied. As she did, he couldn't help noticing that her nipples poked against her T-shirt in an especially mind-scrambling way. Galvanized, Damon could think of nothing else. For a split second, his whole being focused on . . .

Hop, you weasel! his inner drill sergeant commanded. *Hop!*

So Damon did. Desperate, confused, and suddenly horny, he hopped like crazy. Two paces in, he crumpled to the ground.

* * *

"Oh my god!" Natasha rushed toward Damon. "Are you okay?"

"Um, I'm fine. Mostly." From his awkward position on her floral welcome mat, he grinned up at her. "It's all fun and games until someone gets hurt, right?" He got to his feet, then gave a short, shuffling, one-footed hop. Still standing conspicuously on his left foot only, Damon spread his arms in triumph. "See? Ta-da! I told you I'd do it. Is your mind appropriately blown?"

"Like never before," Natasha assured him. Geez, he was like a child sometimes. A charismatic, fun-loving, stubborn child.

Why had he actually *hopped* for her? That was a bad idea.

"Here. I'll help you." Worriedly, Natasha wrapped her arms around Damon's taut midsection for support. "Come inside. Be careful, though! Don't trip over the threshold. I've got new weather stripping installed. It's tricky to get over."

"I have a minor sprained ankle, not a concussion." Damon gave her an exasperated-looking grin. "I can comprehend simple instructions. You don't have to be so careful with me."

"Yes, I do! It's because of *me* that you're hurt."

Feeling awful, Natasha navigated them both into her apartment, keenly aware that she'd just injured a man by making him *hop* for her trivial amusement. *Hop*! He'd done it, too.

"Give me one little power trip, and I become a maniac." She eased Damon into position on her sofa. "I'm very sorry, Damon."

"I'm not sorry." His dazed gaze met hers. In the lamplight, he gave her a loopy smile. "You have very nice hands."

Oh God. "You *are* concussed! I'll call a doctor—"

"No, I'm not. It's just that you were holding me—"

"Feeling up your six-pack abs," Natasha agreed. "Right."

"—and I thought your hands felt good. That's all." There was a lapse in their conversation as Damon took in her living room and its furnishings. She'd never been more cognizant of her penchant for overstuffed upholstered furniture, big random throw pillows, and polished wood. Then, "I like your place," Damon announced approvingly. "It's really cozy. Just like you."

"And doesn't every woman want to be 'cozy'?" Natasha joked. "That ranks right behind 'beautiful' and just above 'funny.'" She gave him a sober look. "That wasn't charming at all, Damon. That proves it. I still think you might be concussed."

Maybe *she* was concussed, too. After all, she'd just announced that she'd felt him up. Kind of. Was she crazy?

"I'm not charming anymore," Damon confided. "I'm just me."

"Right. And *you* are charming. Your charm is elemental, like pink bubble gum and blue window cleaner and green guacamole. You can't have one without the other. You can't have *you* without charm. It's just so much a part of you that you don't notice."

"Oh," he assured her wryly, "I notice."

"So I'd say the fact that you're currently being less than perfectly charming means that I've injured you pretty seriously." Natasha piled a few pillows on her coffee table. "Here," she said, grabbing Damon's leg. "Let's get your ankle elevated. I think I have an ice pack around here someplace—"

Belatedly, she realized that bending over to hoist his leg had effectively put her face in his lap. Helplessly staring at his groin, Natasha lapsed into silence. She was pretty sure she could tell which side he dressed on. His pants looked as if they were made of nice, soft, expensive fabric, too. She bet it would feel good to touch them. She bet *he* would feel good to touch.

Wow. Was *that* ever an inappropriate thought.

Feeling her cheeks heat, Natasha turned away. Determinedly, she busied herself by heading to the kitchen for a bag of frozen peas. When she came back, she couldn't help being aware of how surreal it was to have Damon—*Damon*—there in her living room.

He didn't belong there. Yet she wanted him there. The contrast between those realities felt deliciously . . . forbidden.

Completely unable to get a grip on herself, Natasha did her best to breeze back in, all the same. "I couldn't find the ice pack. But these should work just as well. Frozen peas."

Gently, she laid the bag over Damon's ankle. She patted it.

"You do that really well," he said, giving her a semi-sappy, grateful look. "You have a soothing touch."

"Right. Just call me Florence Nightingale."

"Okay, Flo." Damon glanced up at her. "Hey. Where's Pacey?"

"Who's Pacey?"

"Your husband. *Pacey*." He looked around. "Is he here?"

"Why?" Glibly, Natasha asked, "Do you plan to seduce me?"

Damon looked aghast. "No! I told you about my philosophies. Remember? Pop-Tarts, kung fu, and—"

"—not sleeping with married people. I know," Natasha finished, patiently reciting his long-held mantra. "But I—"

I'm not married anymore, she'd been about to say.

But then, looking at Damon sprawled there on her sofa, all sexy and fascinating and handsome and muscular, Natasha had a better idea. A *safer* idea. An idea that would assure that even if she couldn't keep Damon out of sight and out of mind, she could protect herself from her own inescapable feelings. She could avoid having to resist him any more than necessary.

"I should have told you before," she hedged, "that Paul is in Mexico right now. So he's not here. I don't expect him back . . ." *Ever. Thank God.* Vaguely, Natasha waved her arm. "Anyway, the more important thing is . . . how does your ankle feel? Does it hurt?"

"No more than it did when I got here. It's nothing."

"Quit being macho. Of course it—wait. It already hurt when you *got here*?" Maybe she *hadn't* crippled him with her egomaniacal demand that he hop for her. "What happened?"

Damon shrugged. "The same kinds of things that have been happening to me ever since you left me."

"Bad things," Natasha surmised. Because *she'd* been lucky, Damon hadn't been. The natural order of things was totally out of whack. But he didn't confirm her guess. Stoically, he took in her living room's minor clutter, letting his gaze fall on her lamps, her rug, her TV, the Nintendo Wii console attached to it. . . .

Uh-oh. As though wondering why a thirty-four-year-old woman owned a clearly used video game console and several assorted video games, Damon transferred his puzzled gaze to her face.

"Do you babysit for Jason and Amy's kids?" he asked. "I thought toddlers were a little young to play video games, but—"

"—but what do you know about kids, right?" Natasha laughed. "Yes, I babysit sometimes." Technically, it was true. She did babysit Isobel and Manny. Plus, maybe that would make Damon quit wondering about whatever child-friendly items he might spot next. "So, your ankle looks . . ." She squinted. ". . . like maybe it's been put on crooked. I think you should have that looked at."

"It's just a sprain. Some kid on a skateboard collided with me. I was only trying to grab a peaceful nap on a park bench—"

"On a park *bench*?" Natasha gawked, completely diverted

from her own troubles. "Why were you sleeping on a park bench?"

"Because the car wasn't as comfortable as Wes claimed."

Damon appeared very disgruntled by that fact. Confused, Natasha gave him a censorious look. "You're not making sense. Were you drunk? Because you've been known to have a few too many, Damon, and do things you regret later. And *Wes*, well—"

"No." Wearing an earnest expression, Damon laid his hand over his heart. "I haven't had a drink since Las Vegas. Which hasn't been easy, believe me, because I've been hanging out with Wes a lot lately, and that man knows how to have a good time."

"And *you* don't." With a deadpan look, Natasha examined him. "But if you weren't drinking, why the park-bench nap-a-thon?"

"I'm, uh—" Damon looked into the distance. "I'm temporarily homeless at the moment. It's no big deal. All I have to do is—"

"*Homeless*?" Gripped by remorse, Natasha sat beside him. She imagined him wandering the streets, sitting on sidewalks, napping on benches. The weather in California was nice, but that didn't make this okay. "Damon, what's been going on? Tell me."

"I'd rather not."

"No. No way. This is no time to pull that tough-guy routine." She grabbed his hand, pulled it toward her, then squeezed with all the compassion she could. "Are you okay?"

"Well . . ." He aimed his beleaguered gaze at her. Too late, she noticed that his shave job wasn't quite as precise as usual. His eyes weren't quite as merry. His expression wasn't quite as carefree. In fact, Damon looked worried. Careworn. Seeing her examining him, he cracked a smile.

"Aside from the identity theft, the frozen bank accounts, the flooded beach house, the impounded car, and the unwanted sabbatical from Torrance Chocolates . . . I'm awesome." He gave her hand a reassuring squeeze. "How about you? Are you okay?"

Natasha felt too stunned to answer. Slowly, she nodded.

"Good. Anyway, the reason I came back is that I need you to come to work with me again. *Please*," Damon said. "I know I made a mess of things in Las Vegas, but I swear I can do better."

Judging by the heat he was generating in her thighs just by having his hand resting there, joined with hers, Damon could do anything, Natasha thought. Even do better at work.

With effort, she focused on his face. "Are you serious?"

"Yes. I know you don't *want* to work with me, but—"

"No. I mean about your house and bank accounts and car and sabbatical—" None of that sounded right to her. "Did you really leave Torrance Chocolates? I didn't think Jimmy would ever—"

"That's right. You probably still don't know what happened. Jason said you quit following the industry news," Damon mused. He seemed relieved, but she didn't understand why. "But yes, Jimmy *would* and *did*. He asked me to take a leave of absence, and my mom went along with it. Hell, everyone did. Even Louis."

"Louis the security guard? I know him. He's a peach."

"He thinks highly of you, too," Damon said. "He also lives to eat tacos. I had to sell another tie to get enough of them down at the Embarcadero." He shook his head. "So the upshot is, I've been crashing in Wes's guest room, but that's out, thanks to Destiny, which is probably just as well given how I'm trying to be good now, and of course Louis is counting on me to come back to work so he can win the betting pool, and I'm not sure—" Stopping in mid rant, Damon gazed at her. "No, I *know* I can't go another day without you. *Please* come back, Natasha. Help me."

In that moment, Natasha desperately wanted to. "I can't, Damon." Empathetically, she stroked her fingers over his hand. "I had good reasons to quit. Those reasons are still valid."

"But I'll do anything. *Anything*," he pleaded. "Just name it. I mean it. How can I prove to you how much I need you?"

He was off to a pretty good start already, Natasha thought. She'd waited a long time to hear Damon acknowledge how important she was to him—how valuable her work and her presence were.

But she had to be smart. She'd already let Paul derail her plans for herself; she had the abandoned garden shed work space to prove it. Now that she was finally getting back on track again, she didn't want to risk taking a distracting sideways swerve. It was pretty obvious that Damon's place in Sexy Fun Town wasn't really built for two.

Plus, there was more at stake here than her own well-being. She had to think about that. She had to proceed carefully.

She also had to get more of Damon's hands on her thigh, she thought in a dither. She'd *swear* his palm had slid a little higher on her leg, inciting a heat wave that began at their joined hands and then raced toward her groin. Her body actually *pulsed* with enthusiasm, getting warmer and warmer. . . .

Breathlessly, Natasha squeezed together her thighs. If she could just generate a little more pressure, she might feel—

Damon noticed. He whipped away his hand. His gaze met hers. It dipped to her overheated thighs, then hastily lifted again. It seemed obvious to Natasha that he knew exactly the reaction he'd incited in her. Oddly, though, he didn't seem pleased.

"I'm sorry," he said, raising his palms. "I'm taking advantage of your kindness. Again. I didn't mean to do that."

"You couldn't help it," she assured him. *Besides, I wanted you to do it*. "Besides, I wanted you to do it."

Damon stared at her. She stared at him. A stunned silence fell between them. *Oh God*. Had she actually said that out loud?

Usually Natasha was so good at suppressing her wilder impulses. At least she was when Damon was around.

Maybe their separation had weakened her ability to be sensible. Or maybe she simply felt guilty because she'd been enjoying good fortune and Damon . . . hadn't. He'd been struggling. Her resignation from Torrance Chocolates seemed to have had something to do with kicking off that awful cycle.

Damon cleared his throat. "This was a mistake." Gingerly, he lifted his injured ankle from the pillows. "I'd better go."

Desperate to recover from her erotically charged gaffe, Natasha crossed her arms. "You just told me you're temporarily homeless. Exactly where are you going to go?"

"I'll find someplace."

"You will?"

Stoically, he nodded. She'd never seen him be stoic.

She'd thought she'd seen everything Damon had to offer.

Ridiculously irked to realize she hadn't, Natasha nodded, too. "I hear the park benches at the Torrey Pines preserve are scenic," she volunteered. "Some of them have ocean views. From the bluff, you can see for miles on a clear day."

"Right." Damon grimaced. His ankle must have gotten worse. Clenching his jaw, he hobbled forward. "I'll keep that in mind."

"You can take my frozen peas with you. No extra charge."

"That's gracious of you."

"I might have a spare blanket around here someplace, too."

"I think I'd rather just leave."

"When your ankle heals, you can eat the peas!"

Damon cast her a long-suffering look. "Thanks."

Exactly how far was he planning to go with this? Natasha wondered as she watched her lunkhead ex-boss make his way to her front door. Did he honestly believe she was this heartless?

Probably not. But he clearly believed she was truly wounded by his antics in Las Vegas—and in all the places they'd been together. He clearly believed she was holding a grudge.

Damon had come there to try to make amends. Now she was letting him leave—hobbled, homeless, and alone. Resolutely, Natasha tried to hold her ground. For the sake of her future. For her own happiness. But the one-two punch of potential culpability and unrealized lust was just too much for her.

That double whammy made it practically impossible to do the levelheaded thing—especially while her thighs still tingled with the memory of Damon's touch and her heart still overflowed with compassion for the troubles Damon had been dealing with.

At her front door, he stopped. "Maybe I will take that blanket after all. It's January. It's cold out. While I could probably take the other hobos in a battle for blankets, I'd rather arrive with my own gear. Is your offer still good?"

"Don't be stupid," Natasha said. "You're staying here."

Damon raised his chin. "You really *weren't* done messing with me." He swore. "Remind me not to make you mad ever again."

"No!" At his reminder of her earlier teasing boast—*I'm not through messing with you yet*—Natasha stood. She rushed over to him, feeling her heartbeat pick up speed as she got closer. More than likely, her body recognized the idiocy of this decision, even if her overenthusiastic mouth didn't. "I'm not messing with you, Damon. I mean I *was*, a minute ago, but—"

Proudly, he stared at her door. His shoulders were stiff, his arms motionless at his sides. For the first time, Natasha remembered how cocky Damon had always been. How confident. Coming here could not have been easy for him. Especially since he'd come for the express purpose of begging for her help.

"—but now I'm not messing with you anymore," Natasha finished quietly. "Stay. Stay and prove to me you've changed. Maybe I can talk to Jimmy on your behalf. *If* you behave."

Gruffly, Damon asked, "You'd really do that?"

"Of course." Natasha took his elbow, urging him to come back to her sofa. With hardly any persuasion at all, she got him seated again. "I might sound tough, but I'm still me— sentimental and easy to persuade. Plus, you found my Achilles' heel—my secret weakness that renders me unable to resist."

Unwaveringly, Damon's gaze swerved to the junction of her thighs. Unwillingly, Natasha remembered feeling warmer and warmer, wishing his hand would move a little higher, needing . . .

"Your secret weakness?" Inquisitively and a little devilishly, Damon raised his eyebrows. "What's that? *Exactly*?"

"I can't resist any man who's willing to treat Louis to all the food-cart tacos he can eat. That's a brave man, indeed."

At that, Damon grinned more broadly. "You have no idea. I stared down my own mortality at that taco stand. I'll never be the same." Then he sobered. "I mean it. Thank you for helping me, Tasha," he said. "I honestly thought I'd lost you forever."

Surprisingly moved by the emotion in his voice—and by his use of that nickname for her—Natasha fell silent. Then,

"Nope!" she said brightly. "You only lost me long enough to miss me."

"That's too long," Damon told her. "Way too long."

Just like that, as they gazed into each other's eyes, the scales of the universe seemed to right themselves again. With a nearly audible *clink*, balance was restored.

No, wait, Natasha realized as she propped up Damon's leg again and set the frozen peas in position. That wasn't the *clink* of the universe's equilibrium being restored. It was her back door slamming shut. Footsteps came next. Then snuffling. Uh-oh . . .

She'd forgotten all about Milo. And Finn.

"Damon," she said in a warning tone . . . but she was too late.

Before Natasha could explain, they were already there.

Chapter 13

Damon was still gazing into Natasha's eyes, feeling grateful and relieved and incredulous and glad—and also strangely as though everything was going to be all right now, in a universal and fated-to-be sense—when all hell broke loose.

One minute, Damon was wondering if he could really *behave*, as Natasha had so explicitly stipulated he do. The next, he was wondering exactly what would happen if he let his hand wander a little too high on her jeans-clad thigh again, because although the first time had been a bona fide accident, now Damon was dying to repeat the experience and relive Natasha's hot-hot-*hot* reaction. The very *next* minute, he was being slobbered on.

A clumsy, drooling, fluffy black mutt bounded into the living room. Like a beacon, the dog homed in on Damon. It yipped, showed its pink jaws and puppyish teeth, then leaped.

He couldn't defend himself. Natasha had expertly made sure Damon's injured ankle was propped up on her pillows again. The position was enough to leave him vulnerable to attack.

He would have preferred it was Natasha over-affectionately leaping on him. Instead, it was her dog. Her big, muddy-pawed dog.

"Finn! No!" Natasha cried at the oversize puppy. "Get down."

The dog tried to behave. It did. With canine enthusiasm, Finn tromped all over Damon's lap, trying simultaneously to do what Natasha wanted—get down—and do what he wanted—sniff Damon.

Damon could relate. He was often torn between duty and pleasure. He, too, wanted to please Natasha. That's probably why he let the dog's fluffy tail smack him in the head. Next, Finn's muddy paws stomped onward, crushing Damon's 'nads. His Puppy Chow breath panted in Damon's face with goofy canine abandon. For Finn, Damon realized, this encounter was love at first sight.

"I'm sorry," Natasha said as she ineffectually tried to coax away her wriggling dog. "He's not usually so quick to warm up to strangers. Usually Finn is skittish with new people."

"He's not new!" someone piped up. "We met him outside."

With effort, Damon got the dog into a more manageable, less gonad-crushing position. Feeling like a kid, he gave Finn a pat.

He liked dogs. Evidently, this one liked him, too. At the moment, Finn was even being cooperative enough—lulled by Damon's nonstop belly rubs—that Damon could see who'd just spoken.

A child stood there in Natasha's living room, a boy of seven or eight or . . . hell, Damon had no real idea. He could have been a gigantic mutant toddler, for all he knew. The kid was blond, like Natasha. He was sort of angular, like Natasha. He had an open, friendly face, brilliant blue eyes, and a demeanor that suggested he knew all there was to know about the situation.

Again, like Natasha. This must be one of the kids she babysat, Damon realized. It would be just like her to make the boy feel totally at home at her place. Probably all the neighborhood kids hung out at cool Mrs. Jennings's house.

"You met Damon outside?" Natasha asked, sounding baffled.

"Yeah." The kid shrugged. He glanced at Damon. "Hey, guy who rescued my Frisbee from the tree! How's it going?"

"Pretty well." Grinning, Damon adjusted the dog so that Finn's bushy tail wasn't going up his nose. "Did you have fun?"

"I guess so." The kid frowned. "Is your ankle worse?"

"Worse?" Natasha glanced between them. "What do you mean?"

"After he got my Frisbee for me," the kid said with a nod toward Damon, "he kinda fell out of the tree that it was stuck in. A branch broke. But it wasn't too far down to fall."

Natasha speared Damon with a look. "I thought you said it was a kid on a skateboard who collided with your ankle."

"It was." Having gotten Finn settled in for another belly rub, Damon nodded at her. "That hurt my ankle a little. Then I took a header out of that tree and finished it off." He cast her an aggrieved look. "Why did you think I was so reluctant to *hop* in here? I'm not a wuss! A once-sprained ankle wouldn't slow me down, but a *twice-sprained* ankle is another story. I did it, though," Damon pointed out with a fearless nod. "For you."

Natasha appeared gob-smacked.

"Don't worry. The peas will help." Upon offering that preternaturally wise-sounding statement, the kid meandered over to Damon. He sat on the coffee table, planting himself beside Damon's recuperative pile of pillows. He seemed thrilled that Damon was there—and fully prepared to spend the evening grinning at him. Back when Damon had still possessed his usual mojo, this kind of thing had happened to him occasionally. He hit it off with children—probably because he was a kid at heart himself.

"My mom says frozen peas are good for scrapes and stuff," the boy said. "I'd rather eat them, though. Do you like peas?"

Damon enjoyed this kid's friendliness. No wonder Natasha was willing to babysit him. He wasn't a squalling, sticky-fingered poop machine obsessed with goldfish crackers, like the miniature Huertas he'd road-tripped with. "Peas?" Damon mulled over the matter. "I'm more of a green-bean man myself."

"Me too. Green beans are the best! Peas are disgusting."

Damon grinned. "But peas are infinitely better than beets."

"Totally!" the kid agreed sagely. "*Everything's* better than beets." He shifted his gaze to Natasha. "Have I ever had beets, Mom? Because I'm pretty sure I hate them, just like he does."

Illustratively, the kid jabbed his chin in Damon's direction, while Natasha struggled to come up with a beet-friendly argument.

Damon went still. All he could hear was that single innocent word, echoing in Natasha's cozy-feeling living room.

Mom. *Mom.* Natasha was a mom? *His* Natasha was a mother?

How had he not known about this before?

On Damon's lap, the dog whined, echoing the disorientation and shock he felt. When that didn't get results, Finn shoved his wet nose under Damon's hand in an obvious doggie bid for more attention. Belatedly, Damon remembered Natasha telling people at work that she'd gotten a new puppy—a cute, black golden retriever/bulldog mix—but she'd never mentioned having a son.

A son! Damon shifted his astounded gaze to her . . .

. . . and instantly believed it was true. Natasha was warm.

She was nurturing. She was naturally giving and insanely sweet. Of *course* she had a son. No one would have been a better mother.

In fact, Damon realized as he took another look at the living room, *he* was the moron for not having realized it sooner.

There were framed photographs of Natasha and her son on the walls and the end table. Through the passageway to the kitchen, childish finger-painted artwork was visible on the refrigerator, stuck on with a smiley-face magnet. A Nerf football perched in the nearby hallway, poised to trip an unsuspecting guest.

The Nintendo system he'd spotted wasn't for Natasha, Damon realized upon further reflection. She probably didn't care about *Pokémon Red*, *De Blob 3*, or *Mario Sports Mix 2*. The pint-size Converse sneakers near the window would never fit her. Neither would the Nike-logo sweatshirt tossed beside the lamp or the small windbreaker hung neatly on a hook near the front door.

Natasha most likely didn't play with the multicolored Legos stuffed in the plastic bin on the shelf beneath the coffee table; she probably, Damon knew, didn't drink from juice boxes with straws attached—especially if they contained "froot punch." Yet there was one such container visible on the TV.

Natasha's apartment wasn't just cozy, Damon thought. It was downright homey. It was nice. It *felt* like a home, like a place where a family came together—a family that included Natasha, the little blond-haired tyke who was helpfully holding Damon's bag of frozen peas in place . . . and Damon's new arch-nemesis, Pacey.

He never should have intruded here, Damon understood then. No matter how much he needed Natasha, her family needed her more. Even now, her son needed her to explain about beets.

"Well," Natasha was saying diplomatically, "you haven't tried beets yet, Milo. Somehow they slipped under my radar. But next time I buy groceries, I'll be sure to pick up some for us." She smiled warmly at the boy. "We'll try them together."

Her obvious affection and enthusiasm for motherhood only endeared her to Damon more. Feeling flummoxed, he gawked at her.

He didn't get it. He liked single women. *Free* women. Unattached, fun-loving, carefree women who would run off to Rio on a dare—and wear topless thong bikinis when they arrived.

Natasha's motherhood *ought* to have made her less appealing to him, not more, Damon told himself. This whole scenario was not his thing. Hearth, home, maternal instincts. Ugh. And yet . . .

He couldn't take his eyes off Natasha. It was as if her whole body was suffused with love. It flowed from her in waves and wrapped everyone nearby her with joy and comfort.

How had he never felt that love before? Damon wondered in awe and surprise. Maybe all he had to do was get close enough. Maybe it would touch him, too. Maybe it would save him from—

"I think Milo has adopted you," Natasha said, breaking into Damon's thoughts. She smiled as she gestured at her son, who was currently rearranging his posture so that his foot was propped on the sofa cushion opposite him in clear mimicry of Damon. "If you're not careful, he'll rope you into a game of *Donkey Kong.*"

Milo's eyes widened. He brightened. "Can we? Can we, Mom?"

Natasha bit her lip. Her gaze met Damon's. "It's okay with me, as long as Damon agrees. But if he says no, don't push."

At that, Milo turned into a more blatant con artist than Finn the dog. He adopted an expression of pure entreaty, clasped his hands together in an eager pose, then begged outright.

"Do you want to, Damon? Do you? *Puh-leeze*? It'll be fun."

"Sure." Damon shrugged. "Let's fire it up."

As though blasted from a *Damon-said-yes* cannon, Milo jumped down from the coffee table, all thoughts of becoming a miniature Damon impersonator temporarily (and obviously) forgotten. The kid dropped to the floor beside the Nintendo console. He flipped through the abandoned video game cases with evident zeal.

"You'll like *Donkey Kong*," Milo promised Damon as he cracked open one of the cases. He extracted a game, then inserted it into the Wii. "It's the newest one. Jason and Amy got it for me for Christmas. I'll even let you be Diddy, even though you're bigger, like DK. Diddy has all the coolest moves."

Eagerly, Milo dumped a wireless controller into Damon's lap. Damon watched the boy hunker down to set up the game, his little face a study in concentration, even in profile. From his busy hands to his powers of focus, he was a lot like Natasha.

Damon couldn't help loving that about him. Adapting to the moment, Damon blinked. He wiggled into a more combative pose, preparing to make the most of "Diddy's moves." On the sofa beside him, Finn sneezed his displeasure. The dog groaned, then tried falling asleep while drooling as much as possible.

Natasha nudged Damon. "I'm sorry to surprise you this way," she said in a hushed voice. "I try to keep my work life and my home life separate." She glanced at her son with evident fondness as the TV screen flared to life, ready for gaming. "It hasn't been easy. Like any mom, I want to brag about Milo. I want to show his pictures around the office and bring him in for Take Your Child to Work Day—"

"Milo would love that!" Damon said. "Spending the day at a chocolate shop? What kid wouldn't go crazy for that?"

"Well . . ." Natasha bit her lip. She seemed on the verge of commenting on that further, then didn't. "But since I work—*worked*—for *you*, I didn't have a typical workday. One day we'd be in the office brokering a partnership, and the next we'd be doing a ribbon cutting at a new international Torrance Chocolates Café. One week I'd be doing paperwork, and the next I'd be accompanying you to a commercial shoot in L.A. It was—"

"It was not an ideal job for a dedicated parent," Damon understood then. Natasha must have struggled every time she'd had to leave Milo to go on a business trip, while Damon had never thought twice about a jaunt to Tokyo or Paris. "All that travel. All that uncertainty about what I'd be up to next."

"That's for sure!" Natasha laughed. "You're not like Jimmy, spending all your time in the development kitchen dreaming up new chocolates. At least Debbie knows where he is all the time."

"She knows he's not with *her* spending their golden years together the way they'd planned," Damon said, thinking of his mother's ongoing displeasure over his dad's workaholism—and Jimmy's long-delayed retirement. His dad probably would have retired by now, Damon reasoned, if *he'd* stepped up to the plate in a creative (and not just business-networking) sense. "She has her book club and golf team and yoga classes, though."

"That's true," Natasha mused. "Debbie stays busy. I'd probably be doing some of those same things, if not for Milo."

"And Pacey."

A baffled glance. Then, "Oh. Right. Paul."

Why couldn't Damon remember her husband's name?

"Anyway," Natasha said, "that's why I didn't tell you. I figured it was better to keep things separate. Especially because, well, like you always say, I'm *me*, and you're *you*—"

"And I'm not exactly the best influence on an eight-year-old." Damon frowned down at his Wii controller. Just the way he held the thing proved it: he hadn't even employed the built-in safety strap. It hadn't occurred to him. Defiantly, he didn't use it now, either. Screw safety. "I get it. I'll try not to take Milo out boozing and cruising for chicks while I'm here."

Natasha looked upset. "That's not what I meant."

"But it's true, all the same." Feeling painfully aware of that fact, Damon glanced at the boy. "Ready, sport? Let's go."

For a long moment, Natasha just watched Damon. He began to feel sure she was going to tell him to leave before he accidentally corrupted her son. After all, they both knew Damon couldn't help being himself. What was that she'd said earlier?

You're you. I can hardly expect you not to screw up, Natasha had told him nonchalantly. *That would be like expecting the sun to feel cold or the ocean to stop making waves.*

Who did he think he was kidding? He couldn't cope with this. He couldn't behave. He was a globe-trotting playboy with a penchant for supermodels, a taste for tequila, and a love of fast cars. He didn't belong here in suburbia. He didn't belong with Natasha. But if Damon was ever going to get his mojo back . . .

He would just have to try to blend in. Somehow.

The video game blared to life, blasting gorilla sounds and jungle drums. Milo clicked himself and Damon into action.

Just like that, Damon was on his way.

* * *

"I'd better hunt down some dinner," Natasha finally said. She stood, then checked on Damon's frozen peas as if making sure they were still properly healing his ankle. "Who's hungry?"

"Me!" Milo hollered. "I am. I'm hungry."

Damon didn't answer. He was too busying trying to keep from rolling his video game character off a cliff. He was more of an *NBA Jam* kind of guy, he realized as he crazily tipped the controller this way and that to move Diddy, and less of a scrolling jungle adventure game guy. This kids' stuff was hard.

Damon was also distracted by wondering . . . would any of the supermodels he'd dated have taken care of his injured ankle as carefully as Natasha was doing? Would any of his fair-weather friends have put off their party plans to keep Damon company while he recuperated from his sprained ankle, like Milo was doing? Would Wes's rare prized python have cuddled, like Finn?

Already knowing the disappointing answers to those questions and more, Damon sighed. He tried to rally. Then he realized that his Diddy character wasn't moving on-screen because Milo had momentarily paused the *Donkey Kong* game.

The boy glanced cheerfully over his shoulder at Damon. "You have to say you're hungry," he advised in a knowing tone. "Otherwise my mom gets cranky about making dinner."

"I do not get cranky!" Natasha protested . . . crankily.

Damon winked at her. "Everybody likes feeling appreciated," he told Milo. "When you act interested in the dinner your mom's going to make, you're paying attention to her—and appreciating everything she's doing for you. That's lesson number one."

Natasha raised her eyebrows. "*You're* giving lessons?"

"Just that one," Damon promised as he patted Finn. "Unless something else pertinent and necessary occurs to me later."

"God help us," Natasha said with a grin.

"Everybody likes feeling appreciated!" Milo repeated with gusto. "I can remember that. What else, Damon?"

Before Damon could reply, Natasha touched his shoulder.

"I'll be in the kitchen if you need me," she said. "Have fun with the game." She paused. "Use the two button. It helps."

Then, unbelievably, she left Damon alone to deliver potential life lessons to her son. What kind of crazy, upside-down world was this, anyway? Damon wondered. *He* was no sage.

On the other hand . . . "Me! I'm hungry!" Damon yelled.

He might not be wise, he decided, but he *could* be taught.

Chapter 14

By the time her special-order delivery pizza arrived, Natasha had paced the length of her kitchen six times, deliberated changing clothes and putting on some more lip gloss four times, and called Amy for moral support twice. The first time they'd talked, her friend had expressed surprise and encouragement for Natasha's decision to let Damon stay with her for a while.

The second time, Amy had been a little less circumspect.

"Just don't sleep with him!" she'd said bluntly. "You know you'll want to—anyone would—but you can't. You just can't. It would be a disaster. Right? He'd be all, 'But Tasha, I *need* you, baby,' and you'd be like, 'Bring it on, you big stud!'" Amy mimed, panting for extra emphasis, over the phone. "Before you knew it, you'd both be smacked against the refrigerator, ripping off each other's clothes, breathless and squirming and screaming with abandon. 'Yes! Yes!'"

"Umm . . . Amy?" Natasha tried to interrupt without success.

"Then Damon would shove everything off the kitchen table with one mighty sweep of his arm—have you ever noticed his *amazing* biceps?—and you'd both drop right there on the table, all hot and sweaty and desperate for each other—"

"Amy, you've been watching too many Lifetime TV movies."

"—and you'd do it, like, three times in a row, at *least*," Amy continued eagerly, "and when you were done you would have a huge plate of sashimi, a glass of wine, and a nap—on your belly, the way you *like* to sleep, *without* the baby monitor on—"

"Amy, this has segued into *your* pregnant-lady fantasy, I think." Natasha gripped the phone, helpless to hold back a smile. "Not that I'm not intrigued by all the extra-hot tabletop action, but I don't like raw fish. And I'm more of a stout girl than a wine aficionado. And I'm sorry you have to sleep on your side all the time. Sometimes being pregnant sucks, right?"

"You're telling me, sister. What I wouldn't give for some pinot noir." Amy laughed, apparently having snapped herself out of her X-rated fantasy. "So . . . what's Damon wearing right now?"

Or maybe she *hadn't* snapped out of it yet. Willing to humor her friend, Natasha peeked around the kitchen corner. "A suit."

Amy sighed. "*Damn*, that man can wear a suit. Can't he?"

"Did you forget you're married?"

"No." Amy gave a strangled, frustrated sound. "It's just that I'm so *horny* all the time! And even though we've been through this before with Isobel and Manny, Jason is still leery about having sex. It *is* a little tricky finding positions that work when you're eight months pregnant, I'll grant him that. But I'm desperate for a little action! This morning, Jason bent over to put something in the recycling bin, and I almost jumped him."

Still gazing into the living room, where Damon was playing *Donkey Kong* with Milo—and laughing uproariously while he did—Natasha sighed. "I can relate. I don't

know how I'm going to survive the next few days with
Damon—or however long it takes for me to figure out how
to help him get on his feet again."

"That's just like you, wanting to help," Amy said. "I still
can't believe *Damon* is struggling. That's so *unlike* him."

"I know," Natasha agreed. "But the weird thing is, I
really believe he's trying to change. He seems humbled by
all the bad luck he's had. It's almost as if he believes he deserves it."

They both lapsed into silence, thinking about that.

Then . . . "Maybe he does deserve it," Damon said.

Openmouthed, Natasha turned. Damon stood in the
doorway, leaning on it for support, obviously having over-
heard what she'd said. "I've gotta go, Amy," Natasha said
into the phone. "Bye."

She hastily ended her call, then looked at Damon. "I'm
sorry. I didn't mean for you to hear that."

"But it's true. You still meant it." Seeming a bit steadier
on his feet than before, Damon came forward. He angled
his head toward the living room behind him. "We reached a
new level in the game. Milo went to look up something in
the hint guide."

"Right. He pores over those hint guides. I'm pretty sure
the *Pokémon* version taught him how to read." Natasha gave
a self-conscious laugh. She went to the kitchen table, fleet-
ingly considered shoving everything off it—Amy's fantasy-
scenario style—then opened the pizza box instead.
"Hungry?"

Silence. Natasha looked up. "We've been through this
before," she joked. "When I ask that, you're supposed to say—"

"I *do* want to change, you know." Suddenly Damon was
right there beside her. His body heat touched her; his arm
brushed against hers as he moved his hand to stop her from
serving the pizza. "I *do* feel humbled. But if everyone keeps

expecting the worst of me," Damon said in direct reference to her conversation with Amy, "why shouldn't I just go ahead and live up to that?"

"I . . ." *Sort of want you to be bad*, Natasha thought. When Damon stood this close to her, it was all she could think of. She could see the flecks of gold in his eyes. She could see the scar on his chin, minuscule but evident, from the cliff-diving adventure he'd had in Brontallo. She could feel the inescapable pull of his sex appeal, working to awaken every cell in her body. She wanted Damon to be bad, and she wanted to be bad right along with him. Right now. "I . . . don't know," she managed to say.

Seeming dissatisfied by that, Damon briefly closed his eyes. Then he opened them again, fixing his gaze on her as though she was the loveliest sight he'd ever beheld. He lifted his hand to sweep a strand of hair from her face. His fingers lingered on her cheek. Slowly, disappointingly, he made a fist.

"I still *feel* bad," Damon told her. "I still want to do everything that's wrong for me. I want to stay up late. I want to knock back Ketel One straight from the bottle." He let his gaze roam over Natasha's face again. "I want to kiss you."

She couldn't even breathe. With all her energy, she wanted that, too. She could almost feel his mouth on hers.

Helplessly, she looked at Damon's lips. Without even meaning to, Natasha imagined how they'd feel sliding against hers. She imagined how warm his mouth would feel; how wet and gentle and then how hard and wet and how fast and how more, more, *more*. . . . With a start, she lifted her gaze to Damon's eyes, hoping to glimpse some lucidity there, but that didn't help.

She could tell *he* was imagining all the same things she was. Probably more. Probably in more explicit detail, too.

"You want to kiss me, too." At the realization, he

sounded awestruck. Again, Damon closed his eyes, but this time it was a gesture of frustration . . . and need. "Damn, Natasha! How am I supposed to behave if you're going to look at me like that?" He stepped away. "You're one breath away from inviting me in."

Shakily, she said, "I already invited you in."

"I mean . . ." He lowered his voice to a husky, seductive tone. "You know what I mean. I swear, if it wasn't for Pacey—"

"Paul," Natasha corrected automatically, and the sound of her ex-husband's name was like a bucket of ice water on her libido. Okay, it was like one of those NyQuil medicine cups of ice water on her libido, but that was a start. It was quelling.

Damon was just like Paul, she told herself staunchly. He was self-centered and irresponsible. He was inevitably going to break her heart. He was going to take advantage of her. Again.

For Milo's sake and her own, she had to resist him.

"But you know," she heard herself say, "Paul's not here—"

"Maybe not." Damon grinned. With evident regret, he added, "But your husband has permanent residence . . . right here."

Lightly, he touched her breastbone. *In your heart*, came his unspoken words, and Natasha's heartbeat hammered in response, seeming to prove his assertion. She wanted to grab Damon's hand. She wanted to steer his palm lower to her breast. She wanted to push herself against him and give her hardened nipples all the stimulation they'd been asking for ever since she'd first encountered him on her porch. She wanted all that and more.

Damon couldn't have been more wrong about her feelings for her ex. But Natasha couldn't tell him that. She just . . . couldn't.

"And he has everything a man could want," Damon said, still referring to Paul, "here with you. He knows you're his. No woman could ever be more honest or more faithful than you, Tasha."

Caught in her lie, Natasha squirmed. "Um, I try."

"I know you do." Damon smiled in obvious admiration. "That's why I figure it's safe, just this once, to get this thing out of my system. Don't worry. It won't take long."

Before she could guess what he meant to do, Damon caught hold of her chin. He gently tipped up her face to his, cast another dizzyingly infatuated look at her—she *had* to be imagining that—then brought his mouth slowly to hers.

His kiss was the merest kiss, the barest contact, the most innocent and heartfelt kiss anyone had ever shared.

It was *sweet*, Natasha realized in astonishment when it was over with. Damon's kiss was sweet. Which didn't explain why she still felt some sort of electric current running through her body in response. It didn't explain why she still felt like hurling him to the kitchen table and having her way with him.

"Well. That didn't work," Damon announced brightly. He seemed to be experiencing a similarly electric reaction. "It sounded so reasonable and mature, too. I thought if I kissed you, just that one time, I'd be over it." He appeared perplexed. "I'm sorry, Natasha. I've never felt this way before."

"What way?"

Damon frowned. "Insatiable," he said. "Yet protective. It's as if I want to rip off all your clothes . . . then maybe iron them for you. I'm not even sure I could identify an iron. I've never used one. My housekeeper is devoted to them, though." Damon shook his head as though to clear it. "I thought it was ordinary lustfulness making me obsess about kissing you." He gave a helpless shrug, then grinned. "I guess it was . . . *you*."

Staring at him with her hand on her mouth, Natasha couldn't say a thing. Damon seemed so abashed, so confused, so *nice*.

"Stop it, Damon," she made herself say. "I can take a lot of things, but I can't stand your being *nice*. It's too weird."

"I know. I'm sorry. I'm freaking myself out a little."

"There you go again! Cut it out!"

Damon smiled. Given his recent bad luck, his smile should have lacked most or all of its usual appeal. It did not. At all.

"If only I could stop," he said. "But I really like you."

She liked him, too. She liked him in all kinds of ways.

Just looking at him, Natasha felt her belly do somersaults. Her thighs started tingling again. They'd never done that before today, and now they wouldn't quit. Worst of all, her heart sort of . . . *expanded* while she watched Damon looking at her. Was she actually buying into this Mr. Clean routine he was dishing out?

Yes, Natasha realized. Because while maybe she could resist Damon's overt sexual advances, she could *never* resist his hidden sweetness. She hadn't even known he'd possessed sweetness.

Now it seemed like a perfectly natural fit for him.

"You're being wholesome," she accused, trying to glower at him . . . and probably failing. "What is wrong with you?"

"I could be bad instead," Damon offered helpfully. "You know I think being bad is underrated. It's actually a lot of fun." He let his gaze travel suggestively lower, to the tinglier parts of her, south of her neckline. "Would you like that?"

Yes. "I'm going to serve the pizza," Natasha announced.

"You didn't answer me," Damon pushed. He gave her a long, inscrutable, uncomfortably perceptive look. "I know you feel the same thing I do. Is there something you're not telling me about your marriage? About Pacey? Is there something I should know?"

Damn it. She hadn't expected him to pick up on that so soon. "We like our pizza without cheese," she blurted, putting a slice on a plate and then shoving it at him. "Here's yours!"

Amazingly, her diversion worked. In spite of everything that had just happened between them, Damon reacted the same way everyone did when they ate pizza at the Jennings household.

Damon lowered his brows distractedly. He looked at his pizza, then did a double take. "This pizza is naked."

"No, it's not. It's got tomato sauce and veggies and herbs—the works! Plus, this pizzeria's house-made gluten-free crust is really delicious."

"It looks so . . ." Damon squinted. "*Vulnerable*. Why would you . . ." He broke off, seeming perplexed. "This isn't . . . I'm not sure . . ."

Mission accomplished. Natasha couldn't help smiling. For once she'd outwitted Damon Torrance.

With cheese-free pizza, of all things.

Later, she'd brief Damon on all the precautions necessary to manage Milo's food sensitivities. If he was going to stay there awhile, he'd need to know those details. She didn't want him inadvertently offering her son a Twinkie. But until that time came . . .

"Just eat it." Natasha chose a slice for Milo, then plated another slice for herself. "You'll need your strength for when *I* take you on in *Donkey Kong Country* later. Because I *rock* as DK."

Then, as Damon goggled at her, Natasha called Milo to the table. She bit into her perfectly tasty pizza. She grinned anew.

When it came to Damon, she might be at a disadvantage, Natasha told herself. But so far, she was holding her own.

And that was a very good sign.

* * *

It was curiously quiet when Natasha woke up the next morning. There were no cartoons screeching in the living room. There were no video game sound effects blaring. There weren't even any ordinary, everyday sounds like water running for tooth brushing or cereal bowls being filled in the kitchen.

There *were* unusual smells in the air. From her bed, Natasha sniffed. She detected the intoxicating aroma of freshly brewed coffee, the sharp tang of recently cut grass, and—just barely noticeable—the masculine spiciness of Speed Stick deodorant.

Damon. It all came rushing back to her. Seeing him the day before. Turning him away. Seeing him again. Inviting him to stay with her. Fibbing to him about her ex-husband, nearly making out with him in her kitchen, and playing *Donkey Kong* with him.

After that, it had been bedtime. After their usual routine, Natasha had tucked in Milo. Her son had begged Damon to read him *If I Ran the Circus*, his favorite Dr. Seuss book. Damon had complied, complete with goofy gestures and silly baritone voices.

Natasha had stupidly fallen a little bit in love with him.

She'd offered him her bed (*without* her in it). He'd refused. She'd made up the sofa with sheets and a blanket and a pillow, given Damon some pain reliever for his ankle, then taken herself to bed. Doing so hadn't stopped her from contemplating what—if anything—Damon wore to bed. But getting up and sneaking out to find him sprawled unconscious in just a pair of short black boxer briefs had assuaged her curiosity pretty thoroughly.

Remembering that midnight adventure, Natasha pulled up her covers. She rolled over, then moaned. *What* was the matter with her? *Spying* on Damon? He was her houseguest. He was vulnerable and desperate and in trouble. He was alone and trusting and (unexpectedly) kind. He didn't need to be gawked at right now.

But she simply hadn't been able to help it—and the reality had been even better than her fantasies. Those black boxer briefs had fit Damon's backside to perfection, cupping each ass cheek like an affectionate lover's hands. If famous haberdashers in London made bespoke underwear, Natasha knew, it would look like Damon's. If Calvin Klein models looked as good as Damon did in their skivvies, they'd skip the billboards (and their pants).

If all men looked like Damon did in their underwear, clothes would be illegal, and no one would get any work done.

Even as she wistfully contemplated her illicit view of him—even as she hoped, wickedly, that tonight Damon would fall asleep on his back so she could sneak a full-frontal view—Natasha became aware of something else. Something alarming.

It was bright outside. *Really* bright outside.

It was, roughly, 11 a.m.-bright outside.

She'd overslept.

Milo! Panicking at the thought that she'd accidentally left her eight-year-old son to fend for himself for an entire morning, Natasha leaped from her bed. She dragged on her jeans from the day before, halfway tucked in her sleep shirt to more convincingly pretend it was a real T-shirt, then bolted.

If she found Damon teaching Milo to play poker, shoot craps, or pick up women as his second "lesson," all hell was going to break loose between them . . . and that was a promise.

Chapter 15

When the screen door slammed at the back of Natasha's apartment, Damon didn't think much of it.

He'd been outside in her small, grassy yard for a while now. If there was one thing he'd learned about suburbia, it was that the place had its share of unexpected noises. Cars puttered past. Children whooped in their yards. Dog walkers, runners, and groups of stroller-pushing, power-walking mothers passed by.

All of them made noise—a lot more noise than Damon was used to. At his beach house, he'd realized, most of the noise had come from his own parties or, during those rare calm moments, the crashing surf. Crashing surf was one of Damon's favorite things. It had a way of drowning out human voices, car alarms, and inconvenient police requests that Damon "ask the band to quit playing so loudly, sir" during his parties.

It wasn't all sound and fury in Natasha's neighborhood, though. It was activity and people, too. So far, Damon had met Natasha's immediate duplex neighbor, Carol Jennings. He'd met her adjacent next-door neighbor, Kurt. He'd also met a number of the neighborhood kids and more than one dog. All the canines stopped because of Finn, but they hung around to give Damon a thorough sniff, too. That's how he met all the dog walkers . . . and a good portion of the stroller moms, too. Which was peculiar, it occurred to him, since they didn't even have dogs.

Shrugging off that oddity, Damon glanced in the direction of the slamming screen door. At the sight of Natasha charging across the yard toward him, he completely forgot what he was doing. Not that anyone could blame him. Natasha was braless.

"Oh my God!" she cried, clapping her hands to her tousled hair in a way that only made her freewheeling breasts bounce even more temptingly. "What time is it? Have you seen Milo?"

"Milo is fine." Damon examined her, taking in the appealing perkiness of her breasts. Was her white shirt partly *transparent*? he wondered, even more transfixed. He probably shouldn't have kissed her last night, he reflected too late, but he'd honestly been trying to be responsible about it. He had to cut himself some slack. He was a beginner at being good, after all. "Milo is around the side yard, helping Carol pull weeds."

Natasha went still. "You met Carol?"

"Sure." Damon wiped his forearm over his sweaty brow. For January, it was a warm, sunny day. He already regretted wearing a shirt. Technically, it was just a white undershirt, but still . . . now that Natasha was here, he felt overheated. "Nice lady."

"She was nice to you?" Natasha bit her lip, casting a wary glance toward the side yard. The sounds of boyish laughter came from around the corner, followed by a ladylike chuckle. "But she *hates* you! She's never had a kind word to say about you! Ever!" Natasha swiveled her gaze to Damon. "Did you tell her your name? Your *real* name? Does Carol know who you are, or does she think—"

"I told her I'm an IRS auditor," Damon deadpanned. "I told her I'm here to investigate your flagrant tax fraud."

"*What*?" Natasha boggled at him.

"I told her I'm a drifter, just passing through town."

"Are you kidding me?"

"I told her your roto needed rooting, and I'm just the man to do the job."

"My 'roto' needed 'rooting'?" Natasha arched her brow.

"You know, like Roto-Rooter? The drain-cleaning service?" Upon seeing Natasha's harassed expression, Damon quit joking around. "Of course I told Carol my real name! And my occupation. As if anyone would believe *I'm* good with numbers." With a laugh, Damon finally gave in to the urge to strip off his shirt. He tossed it beside the rake he'd used earlier. "I'm better at—"

Catching Natasha gawking, he quit speaking. She was staring at his bare chest as though she'd never seen a real, live man before. Her gaze wandered from his shoulders to his midsection to the low, probably sweat-dappled waistband of his only pair of casual pants. Damon hadn't seen his former assistant look that mesmerized by anything since at least midnight last night, when she'd sneaked into the living room to get an eyeful of him in his skivvies. Good thing, Damon thought, he hadn't slept naked. He usually did. Out of deference for his host family—and respect for the irksome authority of the absent Pacey—he'd worn briefs.

"I'm better at activities involving tactile stimulation," he finished with his most guileless manner, feeling secretly glad to know that Natasha wasn't *quite* as much of a Goody Two-shoes as she seemed. Her minor transgressions made him feel like less of a miscreant. When he'd kissed her last night, she'd responded. When he'd teased her, she'd teased back. When he'd stripped half naked in front of her just now . . . she'd gallivanted out braless. *Win-win.*

"I've met lots of people today," Damon said to distract himself from that very same bralessness—and from the fact that he'd just noticed that Natasha had missed the top button of her jeans in her apparent bed-headed haste to get outside.

He wanted to give her zipper a nudge, too—in the downward direction. Then he could peel off her jeans, kneel on the fresh green grass in front of her, and bury his face at the junction of her thighs. He could kiss her there. They'd both like it, Damon knew. Even if she'd pulled on underthings—and he suddenly, rousingly doubted she had—he could deal with that. Her panties would be light and lacy and even more transparent than her shirt was. Kissing her, even if he did it through her panties, would be . . .

"What kind of people have you met?" Natasha demanded doubtfully. With an unconsciously dampening gesture, she crossed her arms. "What are you doing out here, anyway? Why didn't you wake me up?"

Damon tried to answer. He did. But as soon as he inhaled . . .

"Are you drunk?" she wanted to know. "I realize you told me last night that you've been totally sober, but—" She stopped and gave him a cagey, curmudgeonly look. "Are you being *nice* again?"

"I thought you'd probably want to sleep in," Damon said in his own defense. He gestured toward the side yard, where Milo was hanging out with his perfectly friendly grandma. Natasha had categorized Carol unfairly. He and the elder Jennings had really hit it off this morning. "I didn't know how long you'd been on your own with Milo, with Pacey being in Mexico and everything. I figured you could probably use a break, that's all."

"That's all?" Natasha's voice cracked. She almost broke down completely. "That's . . ." She gaped. "Do you know how long it's been since I got a good night's sleep?" Natasha shook her head in wonderment. "*So* long! I mean, I shouldn't have done it. What if Milo had needed me? But still . . . I could *kiss* you!"

"You already did." Damon didn't get it. She seemed on the verge of bawling with gratitude. Sure, it probably wasn't easy to cope with motherhood alone—even temporarily, like Natasha was doing—but that didn't mean she had to look at him as though he'd invented oxygen, ice cream, and those bunny-ear vibrators. "You did kiss me. Last night. Remember? But if you want another go—"

Playfully, she swatted him—which only smacked the memory of Pacey into his brain again, just where Damon didn't want it to be. If Pacey and Natasha were such a perfect couple, Damon thought with sudden, stubborn defiance, why couldn't he keep track of the guy? Why couldn't he even remember his damn name?

"No, I don't want 'another go' at kissing you," Natasha told him unconvincingly. Seeming incredulous, she shook her head. "I can't believe you got up early and did yard work for me. I always, *always* get up early. Theoretically, Carol could watch Milo for me, since she wakes up at four a.m. or something crazy like that. But because she wakes up so early, she seems to think I'm being criminally bad just by sleeping until six or seven."

"That's not bad. That's just a different perspective." Commiserating with her—even though she seemed distracted—Damon nodded. "It doesn't feel good to be unfairly typecast, does it?"

"Huh?" She blinked, still gazing at him. "Typecast?"

"Nothing." Stifling a grin, he touched Natasha's chin, nudging her face upward. "My eyes are up here, Mrs. Jennings. You're supposed to look at my face when we're talking. My abdominal muscles aren't very good conversationalists."

"Maybe not. But your shoulders are gossipy chatterboxes."

"Oh yeah? What are they telling you?"

Natasha seemed to be contemplating a whole panoply of responses, starting with *that muscles are super hot* and ending with *that we should definitely kiss again sometime soon*. "That you need some sunscreen," she said. "You're turning pink."

With that, she headed back into the house, leaving Damon, as he leaned on her old-timey, push-powered lawnmower, plenty of time to contemplate the fact that from behind, Natasha looked every bit as delectable as she did from the front.

It wasn't just that her derrière was cute (although it was super cute). It wasn't just that she had a way of walking that made Damon want to throw her in the grass and see if she had as much energy for sex as she did for sashaying away (because she did, and he wanted to, a lot). It was that Natasha, for whatever reason, compelled him to look at her—to be close to her.

It wasn't for just any woman that he would have staggered out of bed before noon and started pulling weeds. It was for her. It wasn't just because he was grateful for her help.

He had, Damon realized, effortlessly thought of something Natasha would enjoy—sleeping in—and then delivered it to her.

It might have been the first time ever that he'd been so selfless. Maybe he really *could* get the knack of good behavior.

Feeling proud of himself for that, Damon looked at the lawnmower. He still had more work to do, but it felt like break time to him. After all, he was at risk of getting sunburned, right?

It would only be prudent to go inside for a while. These days, Damon was all about prudence. Moderation and prudence. And maybe, while he was at it, finding out exactly what was up with Natasha and Pacey. He *knew* there was something she wasn't telling him. Something important. He needed to know what it was.

With that thought in mind, Damon glanced around to the corner yard. He caught Carol's eye, then mimed that he was going inside for a minute. She nodded. Beside her, Milo waved.

Damon waved back. That kid was awesome. And that Dr. Seuss book he'd asked Damon to read to him? Incredible. Hilarious.

Damon didn't know what other kid-style stuff he'd been missing out on via relentless bachelorhood, but if there were other kid things that were *that* entertaining, maybe he'd been too quick to dismiss Jason's daddy-first lifestyle. Maybe Jason and Amy did know a few things about being happy.

Of course, Damon did, too. Proving it, he headed indoors.

He found Natasha in her kitschy, pink-tiled bathroom. She riffled through the mirrored medicine cabinet with her back to him, standing on tiptoe to reach the sunscreen on the top shelf.

"I'll get that for you." From behind her, Damon reached up. He closed his hand on the sunscreen tube and found his nose simultaneously buried in Natasha's shiny blond hair. It smelled like grapefruit and looked like silk, and he imagined it spread across his pillow on a drowsy morning after, spilling on his shoulder as he cradled her close. "You need a step stool."

"I need a tall man around," Natasha joked. "Like you."

"Or like Pacey." Damon made himself step back. In the bathroom's close quarters, intimacy was automatic. "Is he tall?"

"Not like you." Natasha turned, trapped between Damon

and the sink. Slowly and contemplatively, she eyed him. "You could reach everything I ever needed to. Or scratch every itch."

"I could." Equally contemplatively, he eyed *her*. In her semi-sheer top and still-unbuttoned jeans, Natasha tempted him in ways he could not believe were accidental. "I already said I'd do anything you want, Tasha. That offer still stands."

She shook out her hair. It fell over her shoulders in loose waves, making him yearn to touch it. One curl in particular pulled his gaze to her breasts again. They seemed to appreciate the attention. Her nipples hardened; her flimsy shirt didn't hide much. Damon could clearly discern everything he wanted to touch. Instead, shaking, he clasped his hands at his sides.

"Well, if I'd known your offer included sleeping in, I wouldn't have been so hasty about making you leave the first time." Natasha flipped open the sunscreen. She squirted some on her palm, then rubbed her hands together. Inquiringly, she raised her eyebrows. "Do you mind? I'll put this on for you."

Did he mind? What was she, crazy? Of course he didn't mind.

Natasha was going to touch him. She was going to put her warm, slippery hands all over his bare skin. She was going to get closer to him while she did it. She was going to—

She was going to be *nice* to him, Damon reminded himself sternly. Natasha was a caring person who didn't want him to be sunburned. That was all. He had to rein in his raging libido.

"I should probably do it myself," he said with effort.

Damn, he thought, impressed with himself. *That was good*.

It sounded pretty convincing to him, too. It sounded as if he *wasn't* dying to know what Natasha's hands would feel like on his shoulders, his chest, sliding over his abs, moving to his . . .

"Don't be silly!" Natasha laughed. "I already have goo all over my hands. Just hold still. This will only take a sec."

Obediently, Damon held still. He gritted his teeth. He looked down at the crown of Natasha's head as she approached him in the bathroom's glaring, pink-hued light with both hands up.

She was . . . *captivating*, he thought in an improbably corny way as he looked at Natasha's pretty face, determined expression, and stubborn chin. She was sweet and generous and way too trusting. She was too good for the likes of Damon Torrance.

But *damn*, how he wanted her. He wanted her, and he wanted to care for her, too. All at once, that bizarre lusty-protective feeling came rushing back at him. Damon didn't know whether to kiss her or fix her a nutritious breakfast; whether to fondle her ass or find her a step stool; whether to stroke her breasts or balance her checkbook. As if anyone *had* checkbooks anymore.

What the hell was wrong with him? Damon wondered. He didn't even like math. Calculators had been invented for a reason. So had computers. Besides, he couldn't cook or find things. He—

He felt Natasha's hands begin spreading creamy, body-temperature sunscreen over his shoulders and jolted with shock.

His eyes fell closed. His breath caught. All he wanted was a *lot* more of this. All day and all night and tomorrow, too.

"So if you were doing yard work," Natasha said in a casual, conversational, just-had-my-coffee tone, "and thanks for that, by the way—I guess your ankle must be feeling better today?"

Wordlessly, Damon nodded. Her fingers kneaded over

his suddenly tense shoulders. They meandered down to his biceps, then to his forearms. Her hands traveled up to his pectoral muscles. He tightened his fists, determined not to touch her.

Maybe talking would help. It seemed to be helping Natasha remain unaffected by their nearness. Damon cleared his throat.

"My ankle is pretty much cured today," he said in a helplessly husky voice. "I've always been a quick healer."

More stroking. "You weren't faking it, were you?"

"Faking my sprained ankle?" He was offended. And way too horny to care. Principles only got in the way of satisfaction.

"Yes. I wouldn't put it past you, you know." Natasha swept her hands to his abdominal muscles. Judging by the attention she lavished there, they seemed to be at special risk for sunburn.

"I wasn't faking it." Damon wasn't faking his overeager erection, either. His body leaped to attention at Natasha's touch, making a mockery of his efforts to resist her . . . and making a tent of his casual pants, too. She *had* to have noticed. People in other zip codes would have noticed. "I've never lied to you."

"Never?" Seeming unperturbed by his raging hard-on, Natasha squirted more sunscreen into her upraised palm. She gestured for him to turn around so she could slather his back. "Not once?"

"I'm a lot of things," Damon said, "but I'm not a liar. I value honesty and trust and . . . other things . . . like that." *God*, it was hard to talk when Natasha was doing that. "Honesty is important."

"Mmm. Okay." Her purr of assent felt like a reward. Her slow, careful, *thorough* sunscreen application felt like torture. Damon would have sworn he felt her breasts bob pertly against his back as she worked. That couldn't be, but

that didn't stop him from imagining her nipples slick with
sunscreen, picturing them both deciding that Natasha had
applied too much sunscreen and the only thing to do was
get naked in the shower together, fantasizing that Natasha
loved it when Damon soaped up his hands and then slid
them leisurely down her sides, spreading foamy, squeaky-
clean sexiness all over her, dipping his fingers to the silky
blond curls between her thighs, making her gasp and moan
the way he wanted to do, bringing them both closer and
closer. . . .

"Oh," Natasha said perkily. "I'm all out of sunscreen."

Thank God, Damon thought. Also, *noooo*! He wanted more.

Standing behind him, Natasha sighed. "I guess I'll just
have to redistribute the sunscreen I already applied, then."

Unbelievably, she reached her arms around him, then
began rubbing her palms over his midsection in an osten-
sible attempt to "redistribute" the sunscreen. "I want to be
thorough!"

Her hands dipped perilously close to his pants waistband.
Desperately, Damon hauled in a ragged breath. He felt himself surge into a state of hardness that rivaled the concrete
block fence outside. Any second now, his zipper would break.

This was, this was . . . there was only one word for it.

"Is this a test?" he demanded suspiciously.

"A test?" Natasha went on diligently applying sunscreen.
She sounded a little out of breath. This time, Damon was
damn certain he could feel her breasts rubbing temptingly
against his back. She was practically Heimliching him!

"Are you testing me to see if I can be good?" Damon
asked curtly. "Because I think I must have passed by now."
He swore, then swiveled around. He wound up face to face
with her. "I surrender. I can't stand it. You have to stop
touching me."

"You . . . don't like it?" Natasha appeared wounded. And
a little flushed. And kind of squirmy. "I was only trying to

help." She raised her shiny, well-moisturized hands. "Was I too rough?"

If only. Damon closed his eyes. "No. I like it rough."

Her eyes widened. Good. Maybe he'd scare *her* into behaving.

Suddenly reminded of his original mission in coming inside, Damon assumed a more deliberate stance. "What would Pacey think if he were here right now? What would he think if he saw us?"

Natasha didn't even have the grace to look sorry. Her upward jutting chin and belligerent expression confused him.

"Paul would probably say he'd rather be in Mexico."

Damon didn't believe her. She *must* have been testing him to see if he was worth intervening for with Jimmy. But he wasn't getting very far by asking her. He'd have to try another tactic.

"Your husband can't be that much of a jerk," Damon said.

"You don't know that," Natasha shot back. She looked at him, still all hot and flushed and breathless and bold. "Maybe I just like men who are bad. Maybe *I* like it rough, too."

This time, Damon's eyes widened. If Natasha was going to meet him halfway in the bad behavior department, how was he supposed to resist her? He could have withstood her innocent sexiness. He'd done *that* for years. But this naughty, playful, challenging side of her? Damon hadn't even known she'd possessed one of those. He hadn't even considered she might *like* mischief.

She might like *him*, Damon realized, just the way he was.

"But I guess you'll never know," Natasha said. "Will you?"

Then she flounced away, leaving Damon alone and covered in SPF 30 and wondering dazedly . . . what the hell was going on here?

And what the hell was he supposed to do next?

Chapter 16

Using way more force than the situation demanded, Natasha yanked open the door of her garden shed. She stepped inside, switched on the lights, then slammed shut the door behind her.

Inside, the place was everything Natasha was *not* just then.

It was tidy. It was clean. It was safe. It was ready for anything. The lingering smells of hot metal and solder reached her, underlaid with the still-raw freshness of cut grass from outside. Sunlight streamed over her gemstones and wire, her templates and sketchbook, her bead boxes and gold leaf and the found objects that would eventually find new life in her art.

Outside, Milo bounced a basketball in Carol's driveway. A hybrid car hummed past. Birds sang. But inside the garden shed, all Natasha could hear was her own unsteady breathing—and, she imagined, her own heartbeat. It felt as if it was still racing after her encounter with Damon in her bathroom.

She touched her chest. Yes, it was.

But what else had she expected? she demanded of herself as she leaned against the closed door in exasperation.

She'd let herself *touch* Damon. Ignoring every sensible, self-protective instinct she had, she'd let herself run her hands all over Damon's brawny, muscular body. She'd touched his chest. His shoulders. His back. His arms. His midsection.

Good God. *His midsection.* Damon, Natasha had learned firsthand today, had abdominal muscles you could bounce a quarter off of. Or, if you felt like it, lick. He had dark, springy chest hair—exactly as much hair as she liked a man to have. He had warm, nice-smelling skin. He had responsive reflexes, an apparent love of closeness, and an unbelievably impressive cock. If he'd thought she hadn't noticed *that* . . .

Well, he was crazy. Because Natasha had noticed. She'd noticed, she'd appreciated, she'd wondered how he would feel in her hand if she stroked him a little lower. Probably he would feel *really* good, she'd decided. He would feel hard and velvety and wonderfully thick . . . and then she'd forced herself to snap out of her sudden erotic reverie and apply sunscreen to his back.

Because while a girl could pretend that applying sunscreen was an innocent activity, there was no *way* she could pass off unzipping a man's pants and grabbing his cock—and maybe sliding her lips along its erect length—as a bit of harmless caretaking. Or even an innocuous getting-to-know-you exercise. Or even, as Damon had so gallingly accused, as some kind of test. As if.

On the other hand, Natasha reflected as the experience came hurtling back to her again in all its heat and nearness and confusing intimacy, she *had* purposely rubbed her breasts on Damon's back like some kind of trashy lap dancer looking for a bigger tip. She hadn't been able to resist. And she *had* fibbed about running out of sunscreen as an excuse to touch him longer.

Even worse, she *had* felt herself growing increasingly

certain, the longer she'd contemplated Damon's getting-up-early, mowing-the-lawn, reading-to-Milo, getting-along-with-Carol, and petting-Finn Mr. Nice Guy routine, that inviting him to stay with her, even temporarily, may have been a huge mistake.

Speaking of huge . . . *wow*. Damon was gifted in every department. From his smile to his charisma to his willingness to help her, Damon was even more affecting than she'd expected. He was considerate and funny and attentive. He was *nice*. No wonder she'd sent so many "sorry I broke your heart" bouquets. Upon closer reflection, Natasha was surprised there hadn't been more.

Although maybe some of those women hadn't *liked it rough*. . . .

With a shiver, Natasha remembered the feel of Damon beneath her hands again and knew she was lost. It wasn't just that he was handsome (he was). It wasn't just that he seemed to have regained all his lost charm and then some (because he had).

It was that Damon made her feel *special*, somehow. He made her feel as though everything bad that had ever happened to her had been a terrible oversight on the part of the universe, and Damon was there specifically to fix it for her with his capable hands, easygoing smile, and inventive intellect.

Because Damon still had all those positive attributes. Natasha could see them. She could feel them. Damon still possessed every ounce of talent he'd ever had. Some of those qualities were aimed directly at *her* right now, but most of them were available to keep building his family's company into a global chocolatiering mega power. If anything, this new, humbler Damon seemed *more* ready to take Torrance Chocolates to the top. He seemed *more* ready to work hard, sacrifice, and take risks.

Whatever had happened to make Jimmy and Debbie

insist on Damon's current leave of absence, Natasha reflected, it had to be a fluke. It had to be a mistake. She was sure of that.

What she wasn't as sure of—yet—was that she could really help Damon. Sure, she could give him a place to live. She could feed him cheese-free, gluten-free, all-veggie pizza. She could play *Donkey Kong* and spy on him in his underwear. She could even rile him up with an impromptu erotic massage, challenge him with an outrageous boast, then bolt away like a scared nitwit at the first sign of reciprocity.

Maybe I just like men who are bad.

Maybe I like it rough, too.

Well, that might be true. Natasha didn't know. If she was smart, she wouldn't try to find out. Instead, she'd focus on trying to help Damon—however she could—and then getting him safely out of her house, out of her life . . . and out of her heart.

First, she needed more information, Natasha decided. Giving her worktable a regretful look, she did the one thing she'd promised herself she wouldn't: She abandoned her plans for herself. Just for the time being, of course. With the need for speed more evident than ever before (lest she rub herself all over Damon even *more* shamelessly next time, leading to events neither one of them would want to control), Natasha jingled her car keys, drew in a fortifying breath, then headed to La Jolla.

Left on his own with Milo and Carol after Natasha's mysterious "errand" took her away for the afternoon—once she'd given him explicit instructions about what Milo did and did not eat, of course, complete with a detailed tip sheet, a website to visit for more information, a YouTube video playlist of songs by "the Raffi of Food Allergies," and a handy iPod app—Damon decided to try some further adventures in being responsible.

Maybe, he thought, he could pick up some tips from Natasha's mother-in-law. Carol seemed to have her life pretty well together, if her successful management of the duplex, thriving social life, and conscientious manner were anything to go by. Or maybe he could glean some insight from Natasha's son.

What was it that people said? "Out of the mouths of babes"? There was always a chance Milo could help him learn more about Natasha, Damon reasoned. That way, he'd be concentrating on seeing Natasha as a *mother* instead of a potential playmate.

That meant that the next time Natasha came at him with some SPF 30 and a sexy smile, he'd be ready. He'd be tough. He'd be fortified with good intentions and innocent motivations.

He *wouldn't* be tempted, Damon reasoned, to rip off Natasha's clothes, kiss her from her collarbones to her ankles, then make passionate love to her wherever they happened to be standing. Like outside the hall closet, where it smelled "springtime fresh" all the time. Or against the rough-sided wall of the outdoor garden shed (which clearly fulfilled some as-yet-unknown, non-gardening function for Natasha), feeling the sunshine and ocean breezes caress their bare skin. Or even in her undoubtedly feminine bedroom (which Damon hadn't yet glimpsed, out of respect for Pacey and for Natasha), with a soft mattress and hard bodies and an urgency that couldn't be denied.

He and Natasha would be doing something useful, like making the bed, Damon imagined. Their eyes would lock across the acres of messy sheets. He'd take her in his arms. He'd kiss her, hot and deep and breathless, and she'd get that big-eyed look of wonder he loved so much, and then he'd realize Natasha looked that way because she'd unzipped his pants and grabbed his cock, and the next thing Damon would do was groan, because she was just that incredible at touching him, and somehow Natasha's clothes would be gone, just like that, and he'd be bending her over the side of the bed, stroking her thighs, making her ready, feeling her tremble and pant and moan in his arms, and suddenly—

"*You* look engrossed in something." Carol stepped into the sunny kitchen with an armful of paperback books and an impish smile. She nodded flirtatiously at Damon, making her stylishly highlighted hair bob up and down. "Would you care to share these deep thoughts of yours, or are they strictly X-rated?"

Damon started. Carol grinned. She'd flirted with him earlier, too. Of course, he'd flirted right back—in the sense that all flirtation was really just connecting with people on an attentive and positive and open-minded level. But this time, Carol wasn't merely flirting, he realized. She was asking him a question.

Deliberating how to answer, Damon propped the heels of his hands on the countertop behind him. He leaned back, then checked on Milo to make sure the boy was still busy eating his lunch. He was.

"I've been wondering . . ." Damon began as he watched Carol sort her paperbacks. "What's Natasha doing in the garden shed?"

Carol shot him a knowing look. "I saw you just now, remember? *That's* not what you were wondering about."

"I never said it was." A grin. "So . . . can you tell me?"

"Natasha probably wouldn't want me to."

"Hmmm. Okay." No one ever got what they wanted by force. Not in Damon's version of Life 101. He could wait until Carol felt ready. So Damon pushed away from the counter. "Are you hungry? I made sandwiches. That's all I know how to make. This gluten-free sprouted bread isn't half bad." He held up the twist-tied package. "Right, Milo? 'Food Allergies Rock'!"

That was the name of one of the songs that now resided, improbably, on Damon's iPhone. At the table, the kid gave him an enthusiastic thumbs-up signal in response. Then, still chewing, Milo went back to reading his heavily illustrated *Donkey Kong* hint guide. He was undoubtedly preparing to show up Damon's paltry Diddy-operating "skills" later.

"Oh, and you're out of sesame-seed butter, by the way," Damon added, really getting into grown-up mode now. "I started a grocery list, because Milo said that's what Natasha does."

At Damon's indication, Carol glanced at the pad of paper.

"Beets. Sesame-seed butter," she read. "Gluten-free bread without high-fructose corn syrup or trans fat in it." She quirked a brow at Damon. "Really?"

"My housekeeper says those things are bad for you," Damon told her. "I can't believe that information stuck with me."

"Me either." In a droll fashion, Carol put her hands on her hips. She gazed at him straight on. "Look, Romeo. I think you're getting ahead of yourself here. The last thing Natasha needs is another full-time man around this place. I can say that with authority, too, because she married *my* son!" Carol gave a good-natured laugh. "Sure, Natasha could probably use a good roll in the hay right about now. Who couldn't? But that's no reason to—"

As Carol chattered on, Damon couldn't help wondering . . .

Exactly how often did Pacey travel? Was he in Mexico—or elsewhere—a lot? Did he leave Natasha alone often? If he did, that would explain a great deal about Natasha's eager and sweet (but bafflingly close to adulterous) response to Damon.

He knew she was an honest woman. He depended on that from Natasha. But lately she'd been giving him a lot of unmistakable go-ahead signals—like kissing him back, rubbing him all over, making provocative comments . . . signals that didn't go along with being devotedly married to Pacey. *Sure, she could probably use a good roll in the hay right about now*, Carol had said. But why?

Maybe, Damon thought, Natasha was simply feeling neglected by her husband—by the *real* "full-time man" around the place.

Did Pacey *not* see to her needs? The idea was unthinkable.

". . . and I know I just told you I wouldn't spill the beans about what my daughter-in-law is doing out there in her garden shed," Carol was saying, "because Natasha really *wouldn't* want me to. But if you're going to go all Mr. Mom on her, making sandwiches and grocery lists and getting goo-goo-eyed over her in her own kitchen, then I guess I'll have to take matters into my own hands this time."

That piqued Damon's interest. "'This time'?"

"I was a little slow to see what was really going on with Natasha and Paul. You now, *before*," Carol admitted, further stoking Damon's suspicions that the two of them had experienced marital problems. "I felt a little guilty about it afterward, to tell the truth. I probably overcompensate with Natasha sometimes to make up for it—God knows, Paul didn't exactly represent the Jennings family like a superstar. But can you blame me for not wanting to believe what he was doing? He's my son! I didn't want to admit he was acting like a jerk. He's an *artist*. Artistic types can be difficult sometimes. But I don't have to tell *you* that, do I? You've known Natasha for ten years now."

Confused, Damon said, "Yes. Ten years." Wow. No wonder he felt close to her. No wonder he trusted her and relied on her. "But what does that have to do with difficult artistic types?"

Carol peered at him. "You really don't know?"

He shook his head.

"I thought Natasha would have told you by now. If not about her garden shed, then at least about . . . Well, it makes sense, I suppose. She *did* take a job with you rather than follow her own dreams. She decided to be practical and supportive, and she put up with a lot of grief from *you* to do it, let me tell you."

Aha, Damon decided upon hearing her aggrieved tone. *This* was the mother-in-law Natasha had expected he'd meet.

"I'm sorry for all that," Damon told Carol. "I'm trying to change." He gestured at the paper. "I made a grocery list!"

"If you're waiting for me to applaud . . . don't." Carol grinned. "But yes, now that I've met you, several things are clearer to me about Natasha's job—and about why she stuck with you."

"I don't know if I should take a bow or apologize."

"It's too soon to decide either way." Calmly, Carol waved off his concern. "Anyway, just like my son, Natasha is an artist. A good one. She does metalworking, mostly jewelry, all of it exquisite and creative and delicate. All of it by hand, in the workshop she set up in the garden shed. She was an art major at UCSD until she met Paul. But not long after he had his first showing—at a gallery near Balboa Park—Natasha switched majors."

"Let me guess: to business administration."

"Right. Not long after *that*, she and Paul got married," Carol said. "Natasha got a job at Torrance Chocolates to help support them both—her feckless artist husband included. Then Milo came along, and . . ." She sighed. "Well, sometimes life steers you in unexpected directions." Carol gave Damon an inquisitive look. "You didn't actually think Natasha's personal dream was to become someone's administrative assistant, did you?"

Damon was ashamed to realize he'd never thought about it before. "I was just grateful for Natasha. Right from the start. I lived in fear of the day she'd leave me. Then it happened."

Carol crossed her arms. "Was it as bad as you thought?"

"It was worse. Much worse."

"Well, that makes sense. You probably deserved it." With an air of conclusiveness, Carol picked up her dog-eared paperbacks. "Natasha always says that only one person is allowed to be irresponsible at any given time. For years, that person was Paul. Then it was *you*. This morning, it was Natasha." Carol nodded at Milo, obviously referring to the fact that Damon had allowed Natasha to sleep in today. "You probably shouldn't let her get used to that treatment, though," Carol told him. "Once someone's accustomed to getting whatever they want, whenever they want it, they find that habit almost impossible to break."

It didn't require a Mensa membership to figure out what she was getting at. Carol didn't believe Damon could change.

Duly chastened—by a woman who knew how to do the job right—Damon grinned. "Natasha said you didn't pull any punches."

"Only when it comes to watching out for the people I love. Natasha is one of the few and the proud." Carol tousled Milo's hair. "And this little monkey is another one. I love them a lot. But *you* . . ." Here, she gave Damon a warning look. "The jury's still out on you, Mr. Torrance. Don't you forget—I'm watching you."

"Hey, look all you want." Damon winked. "I want to be seen."

"I just bet you do." Carol nodded at him, a girlish blush brightening her cheeks. "I don't know if she's realized it yet, but Natasha is playing with fire by having you here."

"Not necessarily. I'm determined to change, remember?" Damon gave her another smile. "Speaking of which . . . I have a project I hope you'll help me with. Are you interested?"

"Am I *interested*? In a potentially devious project?" Carol perked up. "Do the neighborhood cats poop in my azaleas?"

Damon stared blankly. Azaleas were flowers, so . . .

"Poop!" Milo repeated with a chortle, glancing up bright-eyed from his guide. "Poop, poop, poop! You said 'poop,' Grandma!"

This time, Carol's grin matched Damon's. "Yes, dear," she told Damon in a patient, wholly *un*ambiguous tone. "Fill me in on your dastardly plans, and I'll see what I can do to help."

Chapter 17

As was typical for every busy parent on the planet, Natasha realized too late that just because she'd taken on a new project—namely, Damon—her existing responsibilities didn't exactly shuffle aside to make room.

The day didn't offer up a bonus twenty-six-hour cycle just for her. The laundry didn't leap into her Maytag on its own. The traffic didn't part like the Red Sea. The groceries, despite her wishing they would, weren't planning to purchase or cook themselves.

That's why, after a long and illuminating talk with Jimmy at Torrance Chocolates, Natasha found herself parking her Civic on a tree-lined neighborhood street, grabbing a handful of reusable canvas bags from her backseat, and heading toward the parking lot of a nearby school to visit the farmers market.

She wasn't the only one. The festival atmosphere created by the weekly market drew locals and tourists alike. The vendors awaited at their colorful, awning-covered produce stands, which stretched in multiple rows across the temporarily repurposed lot. Banners flapped at the entryway; balloons bobbed on the breeze. Near the entrance that Natasha chose, a cluster of local musicians played an acoustic set, lending even more ambiance to the proceedings.

It might have been more practical to push a cart down the aisles of the neighborhood mega-mart, but it wouldn't have been more fun—and by now, Natasha knew many of the growers and bakers and artisans who brought their wares to the market. She bought as many things as she could there. Because of Milo's needs—

Just as Natasha thought of her son, he seemed to appear.

Squinting into the crowd, Natasha fought for another look. She could have sworn she'd glimpsed a towheaded boy of about Milo's age, walking hand in hand with a dark-haired man . . . and a leashed black dog. It *had* to have been Finn, Damon, and Milo.

But *here*? Why?

Damon was about as likely to hang out at a farmers market as he was to grow his own rutabagas. And Natasha had left Milo in Carol's capable hands—not Damon's. Although she *had* taken pains to give Damon that food-allergy briefing first, just to be safe, she hadn't asked him to babysit. So what was going on?

In the distance, the trio wandered past a stand featuring piles of vibrant citrus. It was *definitely* them, Natasha saw.

As she headed toward them, the woman behind the makeshift counter of the farm stand spotted them, too. She did a double take at Damon, spied Finn, then utterly melted over Milo. The whole scenario was obvious: She thought Damon was a single dad out for a day at the farmers market with his son and puppy.

Natasha couldn't help taking umbrage at that. That was *her* adorable son! That was *her* fluffy black puppy! That was *her*—

Well, Damon wasn't *hers* exactly, Natasha reminded herself with deliberate, painstaking accuracy as she slung her canvas bags over her shoulder and picked up speed. Damon was free to do as he pleased. Technically. But that didn't mean Natasha was going to let some marketplace floozy get all giggly and hot-to-trot with him right under her nose. Especially with Milo standing there.

There was . . . farmers market decorum to think of! There was common decency to be considered, Natasha told herself indignantly. There had to be standards of behavior, or else . . .

Or else frisky farmers market employees would seize on any opportunity to squeeze Damon's biceps like under-ripe melons—and then coo and laugh as though they were heirloom-quality fruit.

At this rate, Natasha realized, that farm-stand employee was going to rub off all the sunscreen *she* had so meticulously applied. That simply couldn't be allowed to happen, she decided as she marched onward through the throngs of people. Otherwise . . .

Otherwise, Damon might need even *more* sunscreen when he got home. *Hmm*. Tentatively, Natasha slowed her pace. That was tempting. After all, Damon would require *her* to apply it, so—

The woman leaned forward to show Damon some grapefruits—in the literal (as in, she sold grapefruits) and the figurative (as in, she flaunted some *Penthouse*-worthy breasts) sense of the word—and Natasha quit thinking altogether. She just marched faster. This had gone just about far enough for her.

People at the farmers market were so *friendly*, Damon mused as, for the fourth time that afternoon, he found himself surrounded by smiling, chattering, down-to-earth fellow marketgoers. They were so talkative and helpful. He'd never been to the farmers market before (his housekeeper did all his shopping during those rare times when he was at home long enough to require groceries). But so far, he liked the place. He liked the stalls and veggies and music. He liked the arrays of freshly baked bread, the samples of jalapeño jelly and locally produced preserves, and the fact that, if you wanted, you could have lunch at a food cart right there, and watch someone fix you a tamale on the spot.

"These are *very* ripe," the woman selling grapefruits told him. She picked up a round, pink-tinged specimen, then held it out to Damon while brashly making eye contact. "Go ahead. Give this one a squeeze. Feel for yourself how juicy it'll be."

Damon smiled. Under other circumstances, he'd have thought the grapefruit seller was flirting with him. But since he'd lost his good-luck streak *and* his mojo, things like that didn't happen to him anymore. Probably she was simply being helpful.

Agreeably, he accepted the grapefruit. Experimentally, he gave it a squeeze. "I'm not sure what I'm looking for," Damon admitted. "It feels heavy for its size. Is that good?"

"That's *very* good." She thrust out her breasts, leaned over to select another grapefruit, then passed it to him. "Try this."

He did. With both hands full, Damon gave a double squeeze.

A woman nearby sighed. Audibly. And sort of dreamily.

Damon glanced at her. She started, then smiled at him. That was when Damon noticed that the crowd had grown a little bigger.

"You should try the oranges," the other woman suggested, inadvertently pushing forward her own, more petite breasts as she chose two oranges for him. "They're not as big, but they're a *lot* sweeter. Some people like them more than grapefruits."

"Oh. Okay." Again, Damon had the sense she was flirting with him, but he knew that couldn't be true. Obligingly, he put down the grapefruits and accepted the woman's oranges. He gave them an experimental squeeze, then lifted them to his nose. He closed his eyes, then inhaled. "Yes, they *do* seem sweeter."

When he opened his eyes again, Damon felt as if the rapt attention of the whole world was focused on him. Smiles abounded. There was another noticeable sigh, then a murmur from two women standing nearby. One woman winked at him, then took a few surreptitious cell phone snapshots of him. Another waved. It was as if they'd guessed he was a newbie here and wanted to make him feel as welcome as possible. That was nice.

"Try the lemons!" someone shouted. "Or the tangelos!"

"Or the limes!" came another voice. "Stroke the limes!"

Well. That sounded kind of weird. Confused, Damon shot an imploring glance at the grapefruit seller. "Maybe if I tasted something?" He gestured at the multiple overstuffed canvas bags—and one cardboard box—at his feet. Near his bounty—which he'd purchased with some of his necktie-selling cash—Finn flopped in the shade. Milo stood happily eating apple slices from a paper cup given him by the previous farm-stand proprietor. "I've already bought a lot more than I came for," Damon explained. "The person who told me about the market"—*Carol*, who'd hijacked Damon's original plan to innocently try grocery shopping at Ralph's—"didn't tell me there would be so many options here."

"There *are* a lot of different options." Another woman sidled up. Smiling, she caressed his oranges. "Take your pick."

Belatedly, it occurred to Damon that there were a disproportionate number of women at the farmers market. Either that, or women really liked citrus. Also, apples, honey, kale, broccoli, and salad greens, which were the other things he and Milo had examined—and eventually purchased—this afternoon.

"Sure," the seller said helpfully. "You can taste anything you like. Anything at all."

Again, there was that kittenish tone. But Damon had to be imagining it. Because *he* didn't attract women in that same effortless way anymore. Besides, *he* hadn't been flirting.

It always took two to flirt. It was a mutually participatory activity. That was part of what made it fun.

In his book, fun couldn't possibly be wrong. *Fun always wins*, he'd told a skeptical Jason more than once. Wes agreed.

"You've *got* to try a pomelo at least once in your life." Another woman chose what looked like a head-size grapefruit from the stand. With a suggestive smile, she offered it to Damon. "Go ahead. Feel it! It's the biggest and the best. You'll see."

"Thanks. I'm . . . going to taste the oranges first." Feeling unusually rattled, Damon accepted a wedge of sliced orange from the seller. While she bent to offer one to Milo, too, Damon did his best to treat her produce with the respect it deserved. That seemed to be the protocol here at the market. He turned the orange wedge this way and that, admiring its color. A trickle of sticky juice flowed over his thumb. "Ooh, looks juicy!"

Automatically, Damon brought the heel of his thumb to his mouth. He eagerly sucked away the juice. "Mmm. Delicious."

The crowd of farmers market shoppers moaned in agreement.

Feeling encouraged—because maybe he was doing this responsible-shopping routine correctly after all—Damon inhaled the orange's fragrance. He nodded in appreciation. He lifted the wedge in the air, frowned in concentration, then licked it.

"Yes!" someone cried. "Lick it again!"

Well, that was weird too. He only wanted to get a fuller sense of the orange's tart-sweet flavor. A chef friend had once told him that a lot of taste buds were concentrated on the tip of the tongue. Hence, the licking. But now that that was finished . . .

With his teeth, Damon peeled the orange's flesh from its rind. Happily, he chomped away. He swallowed. He nodded.

"Yes, really good." Seriously, he glanced down at Milo. "I think we should buy a mixed dozen or two. What do you think?"

The boy pointed. "I think my mom is here."

Damon looked in the direction Milo indicated. Natasha, inexplicably, really *was* there. She was headed toward them.

Helplessly, Damon grinned from ear to ear. He just loved seeing Natasha coming his way. She was beautiful. She was sweet. She was . . . possibly feeling kind of cranky again, if her slight frown and hasty stomping footsteps were any indication.

Well, if he'd ever needed to regain his ability to charm someone, it was right now. Damon hoped against hope that would happen. But the fact that all the women surrounding him took several steps away from him at that very moment gave him pause.

Now, he was not only *not* charming, but also potentially offensive? What the hell? He'd taken a shower after doing the yard work. He'd put on some Speed Stick. He'd tried to be amiable and receptive since he'd been here. He'd succeeded, too! Damon told himself. For fuck's sake, a second ago, the other farmers market customers had practically been moshing with him!

But now their hesitance to actually *touch* him continued.

So did their sudden reluctance to look at him. Damon didn't get it.

Even as Natasha arrived, the grapefruit seller gave him an apologetic shake of her head. "Sorry. I misunderstood."

With that mumbled apology, she got busy bagging up a bunch of assorted citrus. The shoppers nearby, having put several additional feet between themselves and Damon, watched Natasha.

Damon merely opened his arms to greet her. "Tasha!"

If the other shoppers didn't *actually* retreat even farther, Damon would have sworn they receded from his field of vision.

All he could see was Natasha . . . and the fact that, even though she'd put on a different pair of jeans, a *non*transparent shirt, and a lightweight, complicatedly tied scarf as protection against the variable San Diego weather, she still looked good enough to eat. Or hug. Or kiss. Or mop the floors for.

Mop? What in the world was the matter with him, anyway?

Damon knew what a mop looked like, and he *did* know how to use one. He'd mopped at Torrance Chocolates, back in his days working the counter at the original sweetshop. But he'd never before tried to seduce a woman with his mad mopping skills.

On the other hand, he could probably do it. With a burst of unexpected nostalgia, Damon remembered his teenage discovery that he liked helping customers—that he knew what they wanted almost before they did. That people liked him and he liked them and that made good things happen. That revelation had led to his career in marketing Torrance Chocolates. It had changed his life. But Damon didn't care about Torrance Chocolates anymore.

Not now. Not when he could spend time with Milo and

Finn and Natasha. Maybe, it occurred to Damon, he should include cleaning in his secret plan—his secret plan to become as helpful to Natasha as possible and thereby prove to her that he'd really changed. That was the plan he'd confided to Carol. That was the plan that had brought him to the farmers market in the first place.

But all the best plans were made to be cast aside. Right?

After all, he wouldn't be himself if he hewed too closely to the straight and narrow. He had to mix up things sometimes.

"I just had a great idea." Damon pulled Natasha close for a vaguely stiff-feeling hug. Jovially, he released her. "Let's you and I take Milo and Finn for a picnic. I know a perfect spot."

"A picnic?" Natasha arched her brows. "I don't know, Damon. Can you get away? You seem pretty busy here with your harem."

Harem? Perplexed, Damon looked around. One by one, the lingering shoppers seemed to size up Natasha. They stared intently at Damon's face. They glanced back at Natasha, then sighed. One by one, they drifted away. He didn't know why.

Maybe they wanted to give him and Natasha more privacy for the squabble she appeared determined to have with him. Right there. Near the pomelos. With the fragrance of cut oranges in the air and the band playing a reggae version of an eighties tune.

"I'm just shopping." Damon gestured toward his afternoon's haul of produce. "I thought it would help you. I thought you'd be pleased. I thought Milo and Finn would have a good time."

"We did have a good time!" Milo piped up. He waved his sticky, apple-scented fingers like a pocket-size Broadway star doing jazz hands. He clapped his goopy hands on Natasha's sleeve. "Let's do it, Mom! Let's go on a picnic with Damon!"

Damon gazed at her in equally obvious entreaty. He didn't care who knew how much he wanted Natasha to agree. "Come on," he coaxed with a smile. "What's the worst that could happen?"

"What's the worst that could happen?" Natasha repeated incredulously, staring at Damon's happy face. "That's easy."

I could fall in love with you twice as hard, she told herself in silent answer to Damon's question. *I could find it twice as difficult to say no to you than I already do.*

Because her long-standing affection for Damon had already morphed into a new kind of closeness between them . . . a closeness that came packaged with risqué talk, full-body rubs, and a kiss. She probably shouldn't encourage any more tempting behavior.

That would only make it more difficult when, inevitably, Damon went on his way later. Natasha only had to look at the women surrounding him to know that Damon could have his pick of them. Just like Paul, Damon could choose someone else instead of her. He could leave. She *wanted* him to leave. She needed to. She needed to let him go before he broke her heart all over again.

"It's easy?" Damon raised his brows. "Go ahead, then."

Oh yeah. Their conversation. Swerving back to it, Natasha put her hands on her hips. She looked at the bags of veggies and fruit Damon had purchased. She looked at Milo, contented and full of apples beside him. She looked at traitorous Finn, who'd merely thumped his tail at her approach instead of getting up and risking leaving Damon behind. Even her dog liked Damon best.

"If it's so 'easy' to know what could go wrong with having a harmless picnic," Damon prompted more precisely, "then tell me."

"Well . . ." Natasha thought about it. A picnic. That *would* be nice. Damon probably *did* know of a good place to go. "I was planning to get home. I have some work to do in my garden shed."

"Oh." Damon assumed a peculiarly knowing and intent look. "Okay. We'll do the picnic some other time, then."

He whistled. Finn leaped to his paws. Then he . . . *heeled*.

Natasha boggled. "What did you do to Finn?"

"Hmm?" Damon glanced at the puppy. Finn gazed back at him, tongue lolling, in canine adulation. He didn't otherwise budge. Damon shrugged. "I don't know. I guess dogs just want to please us. All we have to do is step back and let them do it."

"When I step back, Finn piddles on the rug." Natasha gawked at her dog. "He hasn't even had any free dog training yet."

"Well, I've noticed he seems to respond well to whistling. Maybe Finn is musical." Damon gave her a teasing look. "Maybe he doesn't like the tune you've chosen to call him with. Maybe it doesn't sound like *fun* to him."

"Oh, please." Exasperated, Natasha folded her arms. "What's really going on here is that your usual mojo is back."

Damon scoffed. "Yep. And I'm using it to influence dogs."

She swept the market with a meaningful look. "And women. Do you realize you'd magnetically pulled every female within a six-block radius? Even cats? They were all at this stand with you."

"That's just the kids-and-dogs effect." Damon laughed. He accepted the sack of mixed citrus fruits from the seller, then tucked it in one of his bags. "Everyone knows women love cute kids and adorable puppies. If you happen to be packing *both*—"

Women fall at your feet, Damon's body language suggested. *It can't be helped*, his eloquent shrug told Natasha next.

"Then you're not aware that five of those women wrote their phone numbers on those oranges and grapefruits with Sharpies?"

"Sharpies?" He laughed more loudly, then gathered up Milo as easily as he had Finn. Both of them fell in line behind Damon, the pied piper of the farmers market. Helplessly, Natasha did, too. Just to keep up. "Who packs Sharpies?"

"Women. Women with purses. Do you know what I have in here?" To prove her point, Natasha patted her purse. "More than you can imagine. I could survive for a week with this stuff."

Damon thought about that. "Do you have a Sharpie?"

"No." Inwardly, Natasha grumbled. "Not exactly. But—"

His dazzling grin flashed. "I rest my case."

"You don't *have* a case! What you have is unbelievably good luck when it comes to women, misbehaving puppies, and children!"

"Well, all the better for you, then." Fondly, Damon put his hand to the small of her back. He guided her toward the exit. People smiled and made way for them. Reggae music played. Balloons drifted past. So did ocean breezes. "You're a woman with a puppy and a child. That makes us a perfect match."

"We're not a match," Natasha insisted. *We could have been, if things had been different, but . . .* "We're all wrong for each other."

Before Natasha could enumerate the ways, one of the farmers market customers ran up to them. She had one of Damon's canvas bags in her hand and an apologetic smile on her face.

"Here," she told Natasha. "Your husband forgot this."

Natasha blanched. "Oh, we're not—" *Married*? Preposterous.

"It's really sweet to see such a loving family spending the day together," the woman gushed as Natasha automatically took the bag. The woman beamed at Milo. And Finn. "Have a nice day!"

As she left, Damon gave Natasha a wiseass look. "See? That's the kids-and-dogs effect in action. I'm right. Total strangers are corroborating my point."

"The fact that total strangers are rushing to your defense only proves *my* point," Natasha shot back. "You're *you* again."

The realization made her inexplicably sad. She'd kind of been hoping, Natasha realized, that only *she* could glimpse everything that was special about Damon. She'd kind of been hoping that his bad-luck streak would persuade him to reserve his most intimate charms for her.

Obviously, whatever time they had together was limited. The clock was ticking. Pretty soon, Damon would go back to his regular life full of beautiful women, fast cars, and charisma.

But until that happened . . .

"You know what?" Natasha said impulsively, glancing up at his rugged profile. "Let's do it. Let's go on that picnic."

"Picnic! Yay!" Milo danced a jig, holding Finn's leash.

"I don't want to keep you from the work you mentioned," Damon insisted, keeping one eye dutifully on Milo as the boy jogged ahead. "I'm not Pacey." On that confusing note, Damon added, "Besides, I think your work is hot. I like knowing you have a secret side. It makes you even more . . . *you*. It makes you incredible."

Even as Damon delivered her another slow, sexy smile to prove it, warning bells went off in Natasha's head. His reaction was the polar opposite of Paul's. Paul had been threatened by her work. He'd been dismissive of it. Could Damon really think—

No. That didn't matter, Natasha decided, on the verge of being lulled by Damon's potential approval of her artwork. That was a road she'd better not step on, much less travel down.

What did Damon know about Paul's shortcomings anyway, that he'd compare himself favorably to her ex-husband? What did Damon know about Natasha's "secret" work in her garden shed?

What, exactly, had Carol been telling him?

"I do have to wonder, though," Damon mused aloud, "why you wouldn't say *we're* a bad match because *you're* with Pacey."

Caught, Natasha stared at him. "I guess . . . I forgot."

"I guess you did. Naughty girl." Damon's smile leaped back in place, as dazzling and intriguing as ever. He touched her hand. "I guess I'm rubbing off on you. We'd better be careful."

Then, as Damon noticed Milo wandering farther ahead with Finn, he hurried to be at Milo's side. The two of them exchanged smiles. As one, they turned and waited for Natasha to meet them.

But just then, as she looked at her son and at Damon— laden willingly with boxes and canvas bags and the additional burden of Milo's personal, Elmo-branded "green" backpack—Natasha didn't want to be careful. She'd had more than enough of being careful.

Damon was right. He *was* rubbing off on her.

She liked it. She liked the feeling of being naughty . . . even if (or maybe because) she wasn't really doing anything wrong. She'd probably been foolish to fib to Damon about her long-ago divorce—to let him believe she was still married to Pacey (er, *Paul*)—but Natasha wasn't sorry, either.

That little white lie was keeping her safe. As long as *that* continued to be true, she could continue to feel free around

Damon. Free and crazily sexy. So, smilingly, Natasha added
a little extra shimmy to her step as she went to meet him.

It was fun. Fun couldn't possibly be wrong . . . could it?

It wasn't until Natasha was seated on a worn-smooth
boulder, looking out from a private spot near the lighthouse
at Point Loma and getting sloppily juice-spattered by the
fresh oranges she and Damon and Milo had been enjoying
as they gazed out over the wave-tossed ocean that she realized something else. . . .

Damon was the one who believed fun couldn't ever be
wrong.

Not her. Not ever her. *Fun always wins* was one of
Damon's mottos. It wasn't hers. It had never been hers. It
couldn't be.

Struck by that realization, Natasha gazed at Damon.

He *did* seem happy with that philosophy. Even after all
he'd been through with his flooded house and on-hold job
and frozen bank accounts . . . and everything else she'd
learned about today during her visit to La Jolla.

Damon seemed . . . *content*, even as he hunched over
with Milo, helping her son segment another organic orange.
For a renowned millionaire playboy with more charisma
than common sense, that quotidian activity couldn't have
been very fascinating or very fun. Yet Damon made it seem
as though it *was* fun. For him.

For that, Natasha cherished him. For as long as this lasted,
she and Milo would have some extraordinary memories.

Also, it occurred to her, if *Damon* was being responsible . . .

That left *her* to enjoy herself! With that thought utmost in
mind, Natasha stood. She washed her hands in a tide pool.

Milo noticed. "Mom!" he said in a scandalized tone,

looking in bafflement at her. "That tide pool is *outdoors*. It's probably dirty. Don't you want some hand sanitizer?"

"Nope." Cheerfully, Natasha wiped her wet—but now refreshingly non-sticky—hands on her jeans. She stretched herself upward—ever conscious of Damon's attentive gaze on her figure—then looked out at the ocean. The sun dipped low; the wind tossed her hair and made her feel reckless. "This has been fun. So . . . who wants to go ride the Giant Dipper at Belmont Park?"

At her mention of the famous wooden roller coaster near Mission Beach, Finn seemed to sense the excitement in the air. He leaped and wagged his tail, abandoning his farmers market doggie treats in the process. Her puppy seemed ready to go.

But Milo only gawked at her. "The roller coaster? This late? It's already sunset. It'll be my bedtime pretty soon." He looked at Damon, then shook his head worriedly. "You'd better handle this. I think my mom is sick or something."

Natasha laughed. "I'm not sick. I just feel like having some more fun today." The dubious look on her son's face made her wonder exactly how dreary she'd become while striving always to be a prepared, loving, responsible, PTO-volunteering, traveling-for-business, guilty-feeling single mother. But not today. Not while Damon was there to pick up the slack.

"It's not that far to Mission Beach, and the park will be open *way* past dark. In fact, it's better at night!" Cheerfully, Natasha eyed them both. "Who's up for more fun today?"

Milo and Damon traded puzzled glances. Natasha could almost see her son's gears turning as he considered staying up late.

Then . . . "I am!" they shouted in unison.

It was all happening just the way Natasha wanted it to.

Satisfied, she smiled. "*That*," she said, "is more like it. Let's go."

Chapter 18

Feeling uniquely invigorated—and a lot more tired than he (as a notorious, party-all-night, nonstop playboy) had a right to be—Damon followed Natasha into her apartment. He stepped very carefully over the threshold, watching as Natasha turned on the lights. She dumped her purse and canvas bags on the sofa. Then, limned by the lamplight, she turned to face Damon. All around her, the whole place seemed to glow with hominess and welcome.

Awed by it, Damon hesitated. He wasn't sure he belonged.

Milo disagreed. Riding gleefully on his shoulders, the boy clutched Damon's head. He gave him a one-handed shoulder whack. "Mush, Damon!" Milo shouted, wiggling with energy. "Mush!"

"There'll be no more mushing tonight." Natasha knelt to unfasten Finn's leash from his collar. She gave the puppy an affectionate pat, then set him loose to scamper to his water bowl in the kitchen. "It's past bedtime for you, Mr. Giant Dipper."

"Aw, Mom! Do I have to go to bed already?"

"I'm afraid so." Natasha glanced at Damon. "Don't

worry. If Damon's up for it, he can give you piggyback rides all day long tomorrow."

"It won't be as much fun then," Milo pouted as Damon carefully hoisted him higher, then set him on his feet again. "Tomorrow there won't be roller coasters and games and all those flashing lights."

The boy's face shone at the memory, sparking a similar sense of instant nostalgia in Damon. It had been fun visiting Belmont Park today. It had been fun riding rides, playing games, walking hand-in-hand through the beachside attractions. Milo had seemed to relish every minute. So had Damon. He'd felt as if he was finally part of something real . . . something lasting and good.

And Natasha . . . well, *she'd* shown Damon a whole other side to her tonight. She'd raced from ride to ride. She'd shrieked with glee on the roller coaster. She'd bought cotton candy and eaten it with sticky-fingered abandon. Then she'd licked her fingers, one by one, and accidentally ignited an entirely different sense of appreciation in Damon. Not that he was *completely* sure her actions had been an accident. Given the provocative way she'd been looking at him as she'd stuck her finger in her mouth . . .

"I'm sure it'll be fun anyway," Natasha said now, all potential flirtatiousness gone. She smiled at her son, then shooed him toward his room. "Put away your stuff first, then—"

"Tooth brushing. I know." With elaborate worldweariness, Milo picked up his jacket and backpack and all the things he—as a naturally curious little boy—had collected today. "I'm going."

With a nod, Natasha accepted that. She bustled around doing little things, straightening her wind-tousled hair and checking her cell phone for messages. Her newfound sense of fun seemed to be slipping away from her with every moment that passed.

Damon didn't like that. But he *did* like knowing, as he did now, that Natasha was an artist. He was glad that Carol had confided in him. Because he believed Natasha could be creative and imaginative. He believed she could bring beauty into the world. He loved the idea of Natasha being utterly engrossed in doing something. Something that was just for her. Something that brought her pleasure and fulfillment and a sense of purpose.

Natasha's purpose in life went beyond making sure Damon arrived at his appointments on time, he realized in that moment. It went beyond bailing him out of jail, out of relationships, and out of responsibilities he should have shouldered himself. Because of him—and also because of Pacey, that selfish bastard—she'd stymied her natural impulses and dimmed her creativity.

Because of him, she'd given up. But not anymore, Damon vowed. Not if he could help it—and he meant to do just that.

Which didn't mean he was going all one-hundred-percent altruistic. It didn't mean Damon didn't wish he could push Natasha's creative impulses to the limit in other, more erotic ways. He did. But until Damon knew what was going on between her and Pacey—

"Bath time next," Natasha told Milo. She brushed off the tight-fitting seat of her jeans, then made a rueful face. "I think we could all use a cleanup. Then, bedtime. It's pretty late—you'll have to have a shorter bedtime story tonight."

"I want Damon to read to me!" Milo said. "Please, Mom?"

"It sounds as though your adoring public wants an encore." Natasha sent Damon a questioning look. "What do you say?"

"I say I hope there's more Dr. Seuss," Damon told them both. Then, smiling, he went to help Milo get settled in.

* * *

With only one bathroom in her apartment, Natasha was used to juggling shower and tooth-brushing times. She was used to taking turns. She was resigned to semipermanently forgoing luxuries like long, indulgent bubble baths. What she *wasn't* used to was the fact that Damon approached his role in Milo's bedtime routine entirely differently from the way she did. As a result, Milo was ready for bed—and his bedtime story—at warp speed.

Standing in Milo's doorway, Natasha stared in disbelief as her son eagerly crawled beneath the covers. Wearing his *Toy Story* pajamas, with his hair still a little damp and his face shining from a good, soapy scrubbing, he looked so much like the tiny toddler she'd chased nonstop around this apartment a few years ago that it made her feel unexpectedly wistful.

Milo had taken to Damon immediately and enthusiastically, it occurred to her. She hoped she wouldn't regret letting them spend so much time together. After Damon left . . .

Well, she wouldn't think about that now.

Milo seemed to have coped with his father's absence pretty well. He couldn't possibly get *too* attached to Damon over the course of a week or two, could he? However long it took Natasha to help Damon, Milo would be fine at the end of it.

She, on the other hand, might have a more difficult time.

Because being with Damon today had been like being with her dream man. All during their impromptu picnic, during the drive to and from rocky Point Loma, and during their time together at Belmont Park, Damon had smoothly segued from sexy companion to jovial jokester; from hand-holding tease to piggyback-ride-offering helper; from bantering, smiling, *admiring* playboy to backpack- and bag-toting, stuffed-animal-winning, generous, *protective* family man in disguise.

With no effort at all, Damon had sparked all Natasha's fantasies—even ones she hadn't known she'd had. He'd been the ultimate seducer *and* the perfect platonic companion, in fast succession and with evident willingness. He'd been . . . remarkable.

He was still doing it, even now, Natasha saw as she drew in a deep breath and prepared to join him and Milo. Seated on the chair beside Milo's bed, Damon was cracking open a copy of *Yertle the Turtle*, making a joke with Milo before reading it . . . and flexing his biceps in a way that made Natasha imagine what *else* Damon could do with all that strength of his. He could do a thousand pushups. He could open stuck pickle jars. He could balance himself atop her, all those muscles flexing and working, and make love to her in her big double bed in the room down the hall.

Feeling a surge of raw lustfulness sweep over her, Natasha grabbed the doorjamb. With effort, she wrenched her gaze away from Damon. She wished she could blot out his voice, too. Maybe then she would quit imagining Damon using that sexy, husky voice of his to whisper sweet nothings in her ear as he slowly undressed her, urgently touched her, kissed her and kissed her—

Suddenly becoming aware of exactly the silence she'd been longing for, Natasha started. When she glanced up, her son and Damon were both staring at her expectantly. She had the sense they'd been doing that for some time now, while she'd been lost in another erotic reverie about her, Damon, nakedness, heat. . . .

"Ready for a good-night hug?" Injecting some deliberately casual cheer into her voice, Natasha bustled into the bedroom and forced herself to switch gears. *Mom Mode: On.* She sat beside a yawning Milo, smiled at him, then swept back his hair. "I hope you had a fun time today, Milo. I know I did."

He nodded, eyes shining. "Today was my favorite day ever!"

"Good." His enthusiasm felt surprisingly bittersweet. It hadn't been *that* uncommon of a day, had it? They were usually happy together. "We have fun together most of the time, right?"

Milo nodded again. "Especially with Damon! He's the best."

Uh-oh. Maybe Milo *could* get attached to Damon in a matter of days. God knew, it hadn't taken long for Natasha to love him.

"Yes, he's pretty awesome," Natasha agreed, resisting an urge to punctuate that statement with a glance at Damon. She gave Milo a hug and a good-night kiss. They exchanged I-love-yous. Then she added, "Even though Damon will only be here for a little while, we can still enjoy our time with him, right?"

"Right." Emphatically, Milo nodded. "Now, story time."

At his imperious tone of command, Natasha laughed. "I hear a 'get lost, Mom' in that remark. I can take a hint."

"No!" Milo protested. "It's just that while you're talking Damon can't be reading. And I like *Yertle the Turtle*."

"Personally," Damon said, "I can't wait to find out why they named him Yertle. There's got to be a story in there." He waited for Natasha to glance at him, then gave her an unswerving look. "I can handle things here if you still want to spend some time out in your workshop. Don't let me stop you."

"You're not even pretending it's a garden shed anymore?"

Damon shrugged. "I told you—honesty is important to me."

Vaguely, Natasha remembered him saying words to that effect. At the time, she'd been slathering Damon with sunscreen. She'd been exploring all the intriguing contours of his muscles. She'd been learning the warmth and texture of his skin. She'd been trying not to drool on his six-pack abs. She hadn't really registered Damon's apparent insistence on honesty . . . which, to be honest *now*, didn't bode well for her: a person who'd fibbed to him a while ago and was still fibbing to him by omission.

Frankly, though, her discomfort over that lie was small potatoes compared with the guilt she felt over leaving Damon to face his biggest career crisis alone. In Las Vegas, Natasha knew now, she'd accidentally chosen the worst possible time to leave Damon to sink or swim without her. Jimmy had shown her the infamous video today. He'd told her what it was like to be there, in Damon's varietal chocolate workshop, while Damon inexplicably stammered and sweated and tossed off rude, off-the-cuff comments while struggling to create a new truffle flavor on the spot.

He'd been drunk, Natasha had recognized instantly as she'd stared in shock and horror and commiseration at the video. He'd been desperate and fearful and overconfident, all at the same time. Because of that, he'd made one mistake after another.

He'd insulted Tamala, the pastry chef who'd unluckily drawn the workshop presentation spot with him. He'd berated attendees. He'd stumbled over the cables and lights set up by Wes Brinkman's company, B-Man Media. Then, while being broadcast worldwide (and later on several dozen attendees' YouTube channels and Twitter feeds), Damon had seized the chocolate he'd ruined, hurled the hot, sludgy mass at a camera, then walked out in a torrent of crass language and one very obscene gesture.

The whole performance had been the complete opposite of what the world expected from ultra-cool, super-smart, charming Damon Torrance. It had been . . . disastrous. It had been a public meltdown of epic, gossip-worthy proportions. The fact that there were rumors of a kinky sex tape featuring Damon, Tamala, and fifteen pounds of melted chocolate only added to the problem.

And what had Natasha done when she'd discovered Damon at the close of that awful day in Vegas? She'd walked out on him.

No wonder Damon had suffered nothing but bad luck since then, Natasha reflected now. She'd practically put the whammy on him herself! She certainly hadn't been sympathetic or even curious about what had happened to him. She'd simply . . . left him.

She'd been selfish in a way that she hadn't intended or even understood. She'd hurt Damon. She'd abandoned him.

She didn't know what it would take for her to forgive herself for that. But as she looked again at Damon generously preparing to read a bedtime story to her son, Natasha figured helping Damon to regain his lost life—and his place at Torrance Chocolates—would be a good start. Even if doing so took him, as it inevitably would, away from *her* and her ordinary life.

It would do both. Natasha had no illusions about that. As soon as Damon could, he'd go back to his regular luxe life.

Which only lent a sense of urgency to her own life right now. Because as long as Natasha had Damon, she meant to make the most of the opportunity. *That* didn't begin in a shed.

"Nope." Nonchalantly, Natasha rose. She stretched again, knowing that her luxuriant movements would draw Damon's eye. "Thanks, but I don't feel much like working. I'd be crazy to give up a freely given offer of me-time." She gazed directly at Damon. "Right now I feel like having a nice, hot bubble bath."

As she'd expected, he perked up. "Oh. Take your time."

"I will." Natasha rubbed her palm over her jeans' back pockets again. "For some reason, I feel really *dirty* tonight."

Damon swallowed hard. He followed her movements

exactly as she'd hoped he would. He clenched his book harder. "Mmmm."

His thoughtful tone didn't fool her. He wasn't new at innuendo; he knew she was teasing him. He knew . . . and liked it.

Natasha liked it, too. It was fun. Feeling liberated by the effects of her lie, she smiled at Damon. As long as he believed she was still married, she could tease him with impunity. She could protest her innocence and use her supposed status as a *non*-divorced woman as a trapdoor if things got out of hand.

"You probably feel dirty because there was gum on the seat of the roller coaster," Milo piped up. "It's on your pants."

"Really?" Spinning like Finn chasing his tail, Natasha tried to look. "There's *gum* on my pants? Where?"

"Right here." Damon's hand suddenly smacked her derrière.

Frozen in shock, Natasha felt herself flush. *Damon had touched her butt*! His hand was *right there*, right now! He—

"Got it." Blithely, Damon deposited a tissue-wrapped lump in the trashcan near Milo's bureau. His eyes sparkled as they met hers. "You might still be feeling . . . dirty, though." He seemed to suppress a laugh. "You probably still want that bath."

"I . . . I do." Filled with stupid gullibility, Natasha stared back at him. She was insane to think she could actually keep up with Damon Torrance in the seduction department. And yet, primed by the intimacy they'd already shared, she couldn't resist pushing him a little farther. "Let me know if you need me," Natasha said in her sultriest voice. "I'll be the one who's all wet and soapy, wearing nothing but a towel in the next room."

Her seductive moment was wrecked by Milo's chortle.

"He *knows* where the bathroom is, Mom!" her son told her. "And *everybody* wears a towel when they're done having a bath." He traded an exasperated, knowing look with Damon. "Sheesh."

"Yeah," Damon agreed, deadpan and handsome. "Sheesh."

Well, in a world where single motherhood and irresistible longing to get lucky lived in the same, recently washed-in-a-tide-pool body, these things happened, Natasha told herself.

"Have fun, you two," she said with a wave as she made her escape. "I'm off for a long-awaited date with Mr. Bubble."

In the end, Damon didn't require an ounce of subterfuge to find out what he wanted to know about Natasha and Pacey. Because in the end, quite by accident, Damon couldn't stop gregarious, four-foot-tall, eight-year-old Milo from spilling the beans about his parents' relationship . . . unintentionally, of course.

Fraught with visions of Natasha naked in the bathtub next door, Damon did his best to lose himself in *Yertle the Turtle*. Helpless to ignore the occasional splashes coming from Natasha's bubble bath, he read the whole book to Milo. He told him good night. He gave the boy a tentative hug, pulled up the covers, scanned the jumbled bedroom for signs of duties he may have missed . . . then spotted Milo's backpack at the foot of the bed.

"You forgot your backpack down here," Damon told the boy as he grabbed it. "I'll put it away for you."

"No, don't!" Instantly alert, Milo sat up. "I put it there so I'd remember to get out the seashells I got at the beach today." He gestured at his backpack. "In the side pocket."

Damon smiled. When he'd been a kid, he'd collected things, too. All sorts of oddities had caught his eye, especially at the beach. He guessed he was still collecting things even now. Except these days Damon accumulated cars and partnership deals instead of seashells and coins and shiny, interesting rocks.

"I'll get them." Damon fished out several chipped shells, one sandy Lego mini-figure that may have been in Milo's backpack already, and a perfect sand dollar. "Wow. This one looks cool."

"I know, right? I'm going to give that one to my dad."

"Oh." Damon went still, his hand still on the sand dollar. He didn't know why he felt gutted by Milo's devotion to his father, but he sort of—undeniably and irrationally—did. "Okay."

"Put it over there, on my bookshelf, with all the rest of them," Milo directed him with clear authority. "That way I won't forget to mail it. My mom will have to pack it up, but I can—"

In the midst of Milo's musings, Damon felt strangely as though he'd misjudged things. How could he be fantasizing about Natasha's sexy bath-time routine while Milo was pining for his dad? While he was choosing spontaneous gifts to surprise his dad?

"—do the wrapping and write a note to my dad myself," Milo was saying in an animated tone. "He'll like that. And—wait, not there," the boy instructed. "Over to the side a little more."

"Beside all these other shells?" Apparently, Milo collected all kinds, Damon realized, looking at the variety on the shelf.

"Uh-huh. Those are all the shells my dad already sent me from Mexico. That sand dollar might as well live there for now."

Damon dutifully put down the shell. "There. All set."

He turned, getting ready to leave so that Milo could go to sleep. But the boy seemed to have found a second wind.

"My dad knows *everything* about seashells," Milo told Damon with a boastful air. "He and Juanita send me new kinds of shells all the time. They live right on the beach in Mexico, so—"

"Wait." Damon stared. "Who's Juanita?"

"She's my dad's girlfriend," Milo blabbed. "She's really nice. She bought me frozen fruit drinks when I visited her and my dad last summer. With strawberries and pineapple. I think I'm going to go back this summer, too. I hope they still have those drinks where they live, because—" Milo broke off, giving Damon a puzzled look. "Are you okay? You look weird all of a sudden."

"I'm fine." *Except for the way "my dad's girlfriend" is reverberating in my head.* Pacey had a *girlfriend*? Openly? What the hell? Did Natasha know about this? How could she *not* know? He frowned. "How much time does your dad spend in Mexico?"

Milo chuckled. "All his life!" he said in a don't-be-ridiculous-voice. "He's lived there since I was little. I don't see him *that* often," the boy added matter-of-factly, "because of my mom and dad getting divorced and him moving away. But I get lots of birthday cards and Christmas presents and e-mails from my dad. And seashells. I like seashells. They're the best."

Divorced. The word practically draped itself in lights and neon letters and danced a tango. Damon couldn't stop hearing it.

"Your mom and dad are divorced?" Damon blurted.

Milo scrunched his nose. "Usually people try to sound more sensitive about it. Like my teacher at school—she can't say 'divorced' without whispering it. My mom says that's because she's trying to be 'considerate' about my feelings and stuff."

"Uh-huh." Damon's mind raced. *Natasha was divorced.* She *didn't* love Paul. She didn't even live with him! Her ex had moved on to be with his new girlfriend, Juanita. And Natasha . . . well, suddenly her behavior made a lot more sense. "Listen, you lie down and go to sleep now. It's late. I'll tuck you in."

Obediently, Milo squirmed under the covers again. Damon yanked them up over him, then gave a firm, absent-minded pat.

"Hey!" Milo protested. "You buried my head under here!"

Exasperatedly, the boy stuck out his head. Damon only gave a preoccupied nod. He headed toward the door—toward Natasha.

"You knocked my cheeky monkey off the bed," Milo said in an aggrieved tone, stopping him. "All my stuffed animals are—"

"Incoming." Damon scooped up the fallen toys. One by one, he rocketed them at a giggling, confused-looking Milo. Together, they arranged them all around him. "There. Now go to sleep."

"But now I'm all untucked again! And my night-light—"

"Is already on. No more stalling." Diligently but distractedly, Damon covered up Milo's head again. He gave another brusque pat to tamp down the covers. "If I see you again before sunrise, there won't be any more piggyback rides."

Milo thrust out his head again. He gave a big-eyed nod, seeming suitably compliant. "Okay. I'll go to sleep."

"Yes, you will. Hurry up."

"It doesn't work that way," the boy grumbled. "You're only good at reading. You're *not* very good at bedtime."

"That doesn't sound like sleeping to me," Damon warned.

With hilarious urgency, Milo started snoring. Holding back a grin—a grin that would have totally wrecked his authoritative presence—Damon tiptoed toward the door. Halfway there, he heard a small, tentative voice say, "Good night, Damon."

Sternly, Damon switched off the lamp. "Good night, kid."

A pause. Then, "I was wrong. You are good at bedtime."

In the glow of the night-light, Damon smiled. He lingered in the doorway, breathing in the snug atmosphere of Milo's seashell-strewn, Lego-filled bedroom. Then he turned away.

He had another bedroom to visit tonight. Now that he knew that Natasha was free . . . there'd be no holding back this time.

Chapter 19

Damp and flushed from her ultra-hot bath, Natasha strolled across her tiny bathroom. She propped her leg on the closed lid of the toilet. Languidly, she applied creamy body lotion to her calves, then her knees, then her thighs and . . .

Her thighs. They were tingling again.

What in the world . . . ? The only time they'd ever done that was when Damon had been kissing her. As far as she knew, Damon was still busy reading *Yertle the Turtle* to Milo. That meant . . .

That meant she probably shouldn't have brought a big bottle of imported dark stout into the bathtub with her, Natasha realized. But where some women liked wine to relax, she liked Guinness. Now she was undoubtedly a little tipsy, drunk on the stout and on the exhilarating freedom to bathe without anyone knocking on the door, talking to her *through* the door, wondering where their lunchbox was, or asking her to bake several dozen cupcakes for a third-grade school fundraiser the next day.

Replete with relaxation, Natasha capped her lotion. She examined her legs, decided they looked especially lithe and appealing tonight, then pulled on a pair of delicate panties and a matching flowery chemise. The silky fabric eased over her bare skin. It skimmed along her curves, then ended at the top of her still-tingling thighs. She didn't wear this chemise often; its skinny spaghetti straps were barely sufficient to keep it on her and provide coverage. That meant that one strenuous move would cause the garment to practically undress her all by itself. It wasn't exactly mom-type sleepwear, either. If Milo needed her for anything tonight, she'd definitely have to cover up more.

But she wasn't planning on any strenuous moves tonight, Natasha reminded herself as she slung on a terry cloth robe to cover herself for the trip to her bedroom. Milo was asleep. All she was planning to do was find out how much teasing Damon could stand before *he* cried uncle and made her quit.

That's all she'd been able to think about—in vivid, arousing detail—during her bubble bath: bringing Damon to the edge. Being in control of *him* for a change.

That would be quite a thrill, Natasha figured as she hefted her Guinness bottle, then impulsively finished drinking it. It would be . . . unprecedented.

But a lot of unprecedented things had been happening to her lately. She was on a hot streak! After all, she'd won a (small) lottery prize, gotten a zillion new job offers, defeated her Civic's usual breakdown-prone behavior, and been on a successful date with a neurosurgeon (whose second-date offer she'd regretfully postponed—probably foolhardily—with a phone call earlier). She'd done all those things. She could do this, too.

If there was ever a time she could finally have the upper hand with Damon Torrance for a change, this was it. Tonight.

It would be safe, too. *Thank you, Pacey*! Natasha thought

with a grin. For once, her all-but-imaginary husband was
proving useful. His illusory presence in her life was just the
life preserver she needed to really enjoy herself with Damon.

Licking her lips over the idea of doing exactly that—and
still savoring the malty flavor of her stout, too—Natasha
opened the bathroom door. She felt relaxed and ready and
dressed for seduction. She also felt kind of charged up and
eager and daring. Going on the Giant Dipper had fired up
all her senses. Somehow, being tossed and thrilled and
raced along on the roller coaster tonight had ignited every
long-buried thrill-seeking impulse she had. She'd read once
that, because of a similar effect, scary movies revved up
women's libidos. If Natasha had remembered that *before*
she'd suggested throwing caution to the wind and going to
Belmont Park with Milo and Damon, then maybe . . .

Nah. She still would have done it, Natasha decided as
she ducked back into the steamy bathroom to retrieve her
big, empty Guinness bottle. She would have done it because
it was fun.

When she turned back, Damon was in the doorway. He
stood there shirtless, holding a change of clothes and a fresh
towel, looking handsome and rugged and badly in need of
a shave to tame his ten-o'clock shadow. While she took in
his appearance, he stared in a strangely revelatory fashion
at her feet.

"You have a toe ring." He pointed. "That's new."

"Actually, it's old. I've had it as long as my belly ring."

"Oh. You have a navel piercing, too?" At her nod, his dark
eyes flared with interest. "Part of your hidden artistic side?"

"Mmm." An airy wave. "I guess you could say that."

"I like your hidden artistic side."

"I think you said that already."

"It's even truer right now." Damon sent his gaze wandering over her bare legs, robe-covered middle, and faintly

water-beaded cleavage. "I'd like to introduce your secret artistic side to my blatant seductive side. I think they'd hit it off."

Natasha smiled. "I think so, too." With a fresh sense of anticipation, she dragged her empty Guinness bottle from Damon's abdominals to his chest, traveling over all the muscles and skin she intended to get to know better with her hands later. She ended just beneath his chin. She used her bottle to nudge his jaw upward, so he was looking at her face. "Enjoy your shower. I'm pretty sure there's only cold water left . . . but you probably could use some of that right about now anyway."

He quirked his brow. "Why? I'm not feeling especially hot."

"Oh, you will be," Natasha promised. "Just watch."

Then she tore herself away, turned with a flourish that she knew darn well made her short robe and chemise twirl enticingly around her thighs, and headed for the kitchen. Given the way she felt, she couldn't help turning the whole endeavor into a sexy, look-at-me, bump-and-grind routine . . . just for Damon's enjoyment.

This time, no pipsqueaky voice wrecked her moment. Milo must be asleep, Natasha realized with new excitement. Hurray!

Then, emboldened by her own seductive courage, Natasha picked up her pace and ventured into the kitchen. What she needed now was just a *teensy* bit more Guinness . . . and maybe a tiny bite of chocolate-caramel truffle, too. That ought to give her enough oomph to follow through on her plan . . . and then some.

When Damon emerged from the shower minutes later, freshly shaved, wearing a pair of low-slung, drawstring-waist casual pants and anticipating some grown-up time with Natasha, the first thing he glimpsed was Natasha, bent over the sofa as she made up the cushions for him with sheets and pillows and a blanket.

It only seemed reasonable to stop and enjoy the view. So Damon did. He watched as Natasha stretched farther, making her short robe ride up the back of her thighs. He watched as she bent to scoop up a fallen pillow, making her nightwear all but indecent. He watched, leaning on the doorjamb, as she flopped in a leggy, freewheeling fashion on the makeshift bed she'd just made, grabbed a bottle of Guinness stout, slugged back the last of it, then sighed with obvious and goofily endearing gusto.

As he watched, Natasha picked up a truffle from a nearby Torrance Chocolates box. Closing her eyes, she inhaled the chocolate's sweet fragrance. She paused, obviously savoring its depth and complexity. She brought it to her mouth, but she didn't eat it yet. Reflexively, Damon felt his own mouth water.

The variety Natasha had selected was one of his favorites; he recognized its distinctive shape. But as Natasha rubbed the truffle sensuously along her lower lip, still delaying its consumption, then flicked her tongue to give it a tiny lick, his response had nothing to do with wanting chocolate and everything to do with wanting her mouth. As Damon watched Natasha give another, surer lick, he suddenly understood the reaction he'd gotten at the farmers market today with his orange wedge.

Natasha might be innocently tasting, but *Damon* was not-so-innocently imagining things she probably didn't intend.

Just when he was about to make his presence known, Natasha finally bit into her truffle. The chocolate's caramel center must have oozed out, because she cried out with delight and dismay, then lapped up the caramel. Resourcefully and eagerly, she used her tongue to push back the rest of the sweet, gooey center, then allowed the bite she'd taken to melt in her mouth.

"Mmmm." With a groan of pleasure, Natasha flung out her arms, being careful not to let the other half of her truffle touch the sheets and blanket. She gave a happy little wiggle—one that made Damon smile. She popped the other bite of chocolate into her mouth, closed her eyes to savor it, then moaned.

In that moment, Damon was gone. He might not be good at keeping track of Natasha's personal life—he still couldn't *believe* he hadn't realized she'd gotten divorced without him noticing—but he *was* good at recognizing pleasure. Just like him, he saw, Natasha was good at taking pleasure. Really good.

It was all over her face as she savored her chocolate.

If Damon had felt guilty about kissing Natasha before, he didn't now. If he'd felt sorry for putting her in the path of temptation by being there when Paul wasn't, he didn't now. If he'd resisted giving in to his curiosity about her warmth, her surprising sex appeal, her arty side and her intelligence and her humor and her supple, fascinating hips . . . he didn't now.

Because now he meant to seduce Natasha guilt free. He meant to take them as far as they could go. If she stopped him . . .

Well, she wouldn't stop him. Damon knew that. Everything about the way Natasha looked at him, talked to him, touched him . . . it all told him that. In his pleasure-packed life, Damon had seduced a lot of women, for a lot of reasons. He'd enjoyed every single minute of it. But *this*, tonight, with Natasha . . .

This *meant* something to him. Damon hoped it would mean something to her, too. Because after having been so

oblivious for so long—after having been so self-absorbed
and so blind to her life for so long—Damon felt compelled
to pay attention now.

With that in mind, he took a leisurely step forward. "If
everyone ate chocolate the way you do," he said with a
smile, "visiting our boutiques would be an X-rated activity."

Caught by surprise, Natasha gave a wide-eyed scramble
to get upright on the sofa. She yanked down her robe, patted
her cleavage, then self-consciously eyed her debauched duo
of Guinness and chocolate. "I eat chocolate like a normal
person!" she protested. "I don't know what you're talking
about."

"I'm talking about savoring. I'm talking about *indulging*."
Damon came closer. He scrutinized the box of truffles, took
his time choosing one, then looked at it. He transferred his
gaze from the chocolate to Natasha's face. "I'm talking about
being so caught up in the pleasure of the moment that you
don't care who's watching you." He raised his brows. "Another one?"

Mutely, she shook her head. While he'd been busy selecting a truffle, Natasha seemed to have noticed that Damon
was almost naked. Except for his loose, hip-riding pants, he
was naked. He'd forgone his usual boxer briefs tonight, deliberately opting to wear as little as possible now that he no
longer had to strive for decorum or show respect for Paul's
primacy here.

Because Paul didn't have primacy here; tonight,
Damon did.

To prove it, he swept his gaze boldly over Natasha's
body. He took in her long, soft-looking legs and her scantily covered thighs. He looked at her hips and her nipped-in
waist. He gazed at her breasts and her shoulders, at her face
and her hair. . . .

He swerved back to her breasts, drawn to the faint shadow

of cleavage there and the unmistakable beading of her nipples displayed by her tiny, lightweight gown. Natasha's robe had fallen open during her truffle-eating escapade, Damon noticed, and the garment beneath it wasn't much more than a silky scrap of floral fabric. Those skinny straps at her shoulders would probably snap if he looked at them too roughly. He approved. He intended to try out his theory at the earliest opportunity.

But first . . .

"If you don't eat it," Damon said as he offered her the chocolate again, along with a smile, "I will. Last chance."

"No, thanks. I'm not hungry anymore." With that said, Natasha seemed to belatedly remember something. She snapped her gaze away from his naked, water-beaded torso, then jerked upright. She draped herself in a suggestive pose. "I mean," she added in a throaty voice, "I'm not hungry . . . for more truffles."

She was one lascivious eyebrow-waggle away from performing a full hip-swinging, eyelash-batting, ribaldry-packed Mae West routine. This, Damon realized, was Natasha actively being sexy for him, just the way she'd done while sashaying away when they'd met at the bathroom door tonight. While he liked that she was taking the initiative, he couldn't help feeling that she'd been even *more* irresistible when she hadn't been trying so hard. Just by being herself, in all her serious and gawky and openhearted and silly glory, Natasha was . . . amazing. And sexy.

"I'm hungry," Natasha purred, "for *you*."

With a wobbly smile, she lurched upright. She teetered. Her robe slipped off one shoulder, revealing pale skin and the utter flimsiness of her gown's strap. Experimentally, Damon scowled at it. Sadly, it didn't cooperatively snap—as he'd imagined it might—beneath the force of his glare alone. He'd have to be more proactive than that. He'd have to kiss Natasha's bare shoulder, slide his fingertips under that strap, lower it until her gown followed its inevitable trajectory and bared her breasts, too. . . .

Damon imagined them, naked and pert, waiting for his hands. He pictured himself touching her, cupping her breasts, slowly rubbing his thumbs over the soft pink crests of her nipples as—

"I want *you*, Damon," Natasha said, tipsily crashing into him. She pushed her hands on his chest to steady herself, peered in confusion at her palms and spread fingers, then did it again. With woozy intensity, she caressed him. "Mmm. You feel good! And tonight, you're safe! I can do *whatever* I want with you."

She was, Damon realized, a little bit drunk on Guinness.

She was also under the impression that he was "safe."

"I've never been accused of being 'safe' before," he said with amusement. He was anything but that—especially now that he knew Natasha was free to be with him. "And as far as doing whatever you want with me goes . . . don't I have any say in that?"

"Sure!" She gazed at his face. "You can say yes. Hey, you shaved." She rubbed her hand on his jaw. "Feels nice. Too much stubble isn't good, you know." She broke off, delivering him another vaudeville-worthy leer. "It chafes your thighs."

"My thighs?"

"*My* thighs. If you had your head between them *before* you shaved, it would feel *so* . . ." On the verge of completing that titillating statement, Natasha spied the chocolate in his hand. He'd forgotten to set it aside. Her eyes brightened with glee. "Hey! That's my other favorite kind of truffle."

She grabbed his hand. She steered it to her mouth. She gobbled the truffle from his fingers with tipsy enthusiasm.

Then, to Damon's open-mouthed astonishment, Natasha

licked the leftover melted chocolate from his fingertips. She moaned with enjoyment, then moved on to lap up another pesky chocolate smudge from a different finger. By the time she popped his whole index finger in her mouth to suck up *all* the sweetness there, Damon suddenly wished chocolate had a much lower melting point.

He also wished Natasha wasn't quite so drunk. He couldn't seduce her properly if she wouldn't even remember it tomorrow.

"Exactly how much Guinness have you had?" he asked.

"Mmm." Her mumbled, incoherent reply vibrated against his finger. He felt that vibration all the way to his groin. There, it awakened his already aroused instincts to take what Natasha was offering and make the most of it. His pants suddenly felt a lot less loose . . . especially once Natasha gave another, "Mm-*mmm*."

Energetically, she swiped his finger clean with her tongue. Damon couldn't help drawing a sensory parallel between the way her mouth felt—and looked—on his finger, and the way it would look if she grabbed his cock, lowered her head, took him in—

"About twice as much as usual," Natasha answered, having casually quit sucking his finger. She gave him a sparkly-eyed look, then daintily dabbed her finger at the corner of her mouth as though she'd just enjoyed a delicacy. She smiled. "Which means two. *Two* big bottles of Guinness." Helpfully, Natasha held up two fingers in a V shape. "But that doesn't mean I'm *drunk*, Damon. I just wanted to cut loose a little. You know—to have fun! To make the most of having you here, before you pick one of those farmers market floozies instead of me." She gave a mighty frown. "You know it's going to happen, because—"

"It's not going to happen."

Damon didn't want to have this conversation. He *really* didn't want to hear Natasha liken him to her bastard ex-husband, Paul, who must have told Natasha he'd chosen Juanita over her.

He also didn't want to be reminded of what a jerk he'd been all these years. That only made Damon remember how he'd neglected Natasha without meaning to. Because after all, she'd had a *baby* without him noticing! In hindsight, he *did* recall a long stint they'd spent working remotely, with Damon traveling to open all those international Torrance Chocolates boutiques and Natasha staying behind to "run things" in San Diego; that partly accounted for his obtuseness, as did the fact that she'd deliberately hidden her private life. But Natasha had also endured the breakup of her marriage without Damon detecting a single ripple in her outwardly composed and cheerful demeanor.

It was almost as though, by shutting off his romantic feelings for Natasha on her first memorable day at Torrance Chocolates, Damon had inadvertently become oblivious to the rest of her, too. There had to be a way to make up for that.

Once he found it, he was going to do it. Immediately.

"—because you've never even looked twice at me until now," Natasha rambled on, "and now you're only doing it because you need me to help you, and that won't last long because I can tell that your good luck is on the rebound already, which means the clock is ticking, and I have to get busy making you do what I want before I lose my chance. *That's* why I had two bottles!"

Only one part of that semi-slurred declaration seemed relevant to Damon just then. Only one part was actionable in that moment. "So what do you want?" he asked, feeling a sizzle of anticipation as he did. "What do you want to make me do?"

"First?" Natasha raised her face to his. "Kiss me."

It sounded like a good idea. And because Damon felt sorry for the way Natasha must have felt when her marriage had broken up, and because he knew damn well that *he* hadn't been there for her when it had happened, and because now he knew that he'd let her down unforgivably then and so many times later, Damon decided to add a little something extra when he agreed to Natasha's demand—when he cupped her jaw in his hand, pulled her closer, then brought his mouth to hers.

He added *love* to the mix when he kissed her again. Because he *did* love Natasha, Damon realized in that crazy, mixed-up moment of kissing and breathing and clinging and hoping. He loved her in the way he used to love parties and tequila. He loved her irrefutably. Irresistibly. Irrationally. And exactly like those intoxicating activities had done, kissing Natasha made him feel drunk with possibility . . . with ravaging hunger for more.

There had never been enough of anything to satisfy him, Damon realized in that moment. Because you could never get enough of the things you didn't truly want and didn't genuinely need. You could never get enough of substitutes for the real things in life. But with Natasha, Damon *did* want. He *did* need.

With Natasha, there was hope for more, he realized as he held her. There was hope for everything—hope that if he kissed her again, if he brought his other hand to her other jaw and held her steady while he opened his mouth still wider to kiss her and kiss her, everything would be all right somehow.

And it was. It was better than all right. Feeling buzzed and urgent and weirdly overheated, Damon kissed her again.

He slid his hands to the back of her head, tangling her silky hair, losing himself in her warm, wet mouth, knowing that this was more than just a kiss. It was a beginning. It was him telling her that he needed her, that he *wanted* her, that he recognized her wicked Mae West and met her with his best Cary Grant, note for note. *Why don't you come up and see me sometime?*

So Damon did. He saw Natasha through all the wonder and solemnity and extra-hot passion she aroused in him. When he finally leaned back, Natasha was gazing at him with stars in her eyes. Or maybe that was all the stout she'd drunk. Either way, she looked pretty and sexy and en-thralled. While Damon was accustomed to pretty women looking at him, and sexy women propositioning him, and all women liking to be with him, what he *wasn't* used to was having all those things at once from Natasha.

The effect almost bowled him over. He'd waited much too long to experience this. Next to this, everything else felt meaningless. All he wanted was Natasha, in his arms, smil-ing at him and touching him and—

"Second," she announced, "undress me."

Damon's whole body leaped with readiness. It wouldn't take much to undress her; already her clothes were threat-ening to fall off. It was almost as though the universe wanted them to be together this way—wanted them to love and be loved, together.

"Third," she demanded impatiently, "make love to me!"

"Any time." Damon smiled. He stroked her cheek. "Any-where." He paused. "But you seem a little tipsy, and I—" *I want to stop being an inconsiderate jerk and become a good man. For you.*

Before he could tell her that—before he could do so much as take a breath and organize his thoughts—Natasha did it for him.

"Right now," she clarified with a nod. "Right here."

To emphasize her point, Natasha rubbed herself against him, full-body style. She clapped her arms around him, then gave his ass a lusty squeeze. "Maybe you're confused," she said, nuzzling his jaw. "If you won't undress *me*, I'll have to undress *you*."

Her fingers grappled with his drawstring pants. Drunkenly, Natasha weaved sideways, squinting at the knot he'd tied. Damon closed his eyes, trying to resist a powerful urge to help her undress him.

The old selfish him would have taken advantage of Natasha, Damon knew, regardless of her drunken state. The old live-for-the-moment him wouldn't have hesitated for a nanosecond.

Now, Damon *was* hesitating. It wasn't that Natasha wasn't willing. She was. It wasn't that *he* wasn't willing. He was! He could barely think straight because so much blood had rushed to his groin, ably proving his readiness. It wasn't that Damon hadn't yet double-checked to make sure Milo was fast asleep.

Because he had. Milo was.

The coast couldn't have been more clear.

But Damon was trying to behave, he reminded himself. He was trying to be good. He was trying, for once, to do the right thing where Natasha was concerned. But all at once, Damon wasn't sure what the right thing was. Love her? Leave her alone? Make her a sandwich? Now more than ever, he wasn't at all lucid.

"I'll have to undress *you*!" Natasha repeated with over-the-top, bawdy zeal. "Just as soon as I figure out this weird zipper." She frowned at his drawstring ties. "Unzip, damn it!"

Her command was about as effective at undressing him as Damon's glower had been at breaking her flimsy strap.

With a gentle smile, Damon took her hand. "You should probably wait until later to make me your love slave," he said. "Because right now, you seem a little intoxicated."

"No, I'm doing it *tonight*," Natasha insisted. "Anyway, you're already my love slave." She sounded proud of that.

"You already did the first thing I asked." Teasingly, Natasha walked her fingers up Damon's chest. She stroked him there. "You kissed me. It's only a matter of time before you do *everything* I want."

"Nope." Damon felt committed. This was important. *Natasha* was important. Starting off on the right foot was important. He could wait until she was a little less likely to forget the whole incredible experience. He hauled in a fortifying breath. "Not tonight. Tonight, I'm putting you straight to bed."

"But *that's* what I *want* you to do!" Wavering in his arms, Natasha beamed at him in overt, tipsy triumph. "See? *I'm* in control of you now. I'm *excellent* at being in charge."

"Of me? Sure," Damon said agreeably. He steered her down the hall toward her bedroom. There, he switched on a lamp. Inside, her bedroom was comfy and serene, decorated in shades of sky and sand. Entering it felt good, like being hugged by Natasha. Damon urged her inside. "Here we go."

Cooperatively, she followed him in. She closed the door.

He'd done it, Damon realized as he heard the bedroom door click shut behind them. He'd beaten back his own egocentric impulses and put Natasha's needs first, for once. Maybe, he told himself, this was merely the beginning of many more giving, grown-up, responsible, and compassionate victories.

Or not. Because, unfortunately, that was the moment Natasha unveiled her secret weapon—the one thing Damon couldn't possibly resist . . . even if he *was* doing his best to rehabilitate himself.

And he *was* doing his best to rehabilitate himself. In fact, Damon still couldn't believe he'd behaved so honorably toward Natasha so far. He felt pretty impressed with his conduct in that regard. She had, after all, been amazingly tempting.

He probably deserved a medal or something. But he wasn't

going to get one. Because what Damon wasn't prepared for—what he couldn't *ever* have been prepared for—was Natasha turning to him, dropping her robe, and pleasantly saying, "That's all right. I didn't want to sleep with you anyway. Good night, Damon."

Chapter 20

As lies went, it was a pretty big whopper—much bigger than Natasha's initial fib that had let Damon believe she was still married.

I didn't want to sleep with you anyway. Good night, Damon.

It was almost worth saying it just to see the stunned expression on Damon's face. Reveling in that—and in the way he looked at her nearly undressed body, too—Natasha realized for the first time that maybe, *maybe*, Damon was right.

Maybe she *was* too drunk for this.

Her irrational glee at his gob-smacked expression hinted at that. So did the unsteady way she kicked away her dropped robe, then flounced across her bedroom in her silky chemise, knowing full well that Damon's gaze was on her the whole time.

Maybe she ought to be more careful, Natasha thought. Maybe she ought to think twice before she continued taunting Damon.

But thinking twice about things was what she'd hoped to *avoid* by knocking back twice as much Guinness as usual. Her tendency toward being careful was what she'd been trying to obliterate all day long, beginning with her spontaneous picnic and roller coaster ride and ending with . . . *this moment*, right now.

So Natasha only brazened right on with another page from Damon's never-fail playboy playbook. She looked him in the eyes and blew him a naughty kiss. *Try to resist me now*, she thought.

Damon frowned. He put his hands on his hips, making his lightweight pants dip dangerously low. He stared in amazement at her. "You don't want to sleep with me."

"Nope." Natasha waved. "I don't think you could handle it."

His eyes narrowed. "Oh, I can handle it."

"I think all that intimacy and closeness would be too much for you." Slowly, she ran her hand along her hip to her waist and then higher, barely skimming the outer curve of her breast. She stopped with her hand resting on her collarbone, then gave Damon a sultry look. "I think *I* would be too much for you."

"I think *I* would be too much for you." Damon crossed his arms, flexing his biceps. "I think you know what I mean."

"You mean you have an enormous penis." At the thought of that, Natasha felt herself actually pulsing with heat and enthusiasm. Her breath sped up; probably her face was flushed, too. All the same, she made herself offer another offhanded wave. "That's the legend, at least. I think you're bluffing."

"I'm not bluffing."

"I've seen you naked, remember? I don't recall—"

"You weren't looking." Damon's gaze traveled over her skimpily clad body, letting Natasha know *he* was looking right now. At her. And liking what he saw. "You were being respectful and responsible. As usual. But tonight . . ." He lifted his gaze to her face. "Tonight, you're different. You're daring."

She had been daring, Natasha realized. All day. But *this*

was the crucial moment. She and Damon were alone in her bedroom. Milo was asleep. Everything was quiet. A whole night stretched before them, potentially filled with . . . well, if she was lucky, with her seductive plans to make Damon Torrance beg. *For her*.

"Unless," Damon went on, "*you're* the one who's bluffing."

"Me? I'm not bluffing." Technically, Natasha knew, she was. She still had the safety net of her supposed marriage to bail her out, if she wanted. "I'm the one who's willing to take a risk. I'm the one who has something to lose by being with you."

She meant her heart. She stood to lose her *heart* if she went too far with Damon. But in hindsight, Natasha realized her statement could easily be misinterpreted as an allusion to her supposedly intact marriage. If that's what Damon thought she'd meant—and he probably did—he didn't even blink. Uh-oh.

She guessed she should have expected that, Natasha realized too late. Damon was notoriously bad. Maybe he wasn't as wedded to his principles—or to his philosophies— as she'd thought.

For the first time, she began to feel a little wary.

"Carol told me that this might happen with you—that you might find it hard to quit getting what you wanted, when you wanted it. She also told me a few things about Paul." Damon gave her an enigmatic look. "Just for the record . . . all you have to lose by being with me is your history of never being *really* satisfied."

For a second, Natasha wondered if Damon somehow knew about her divorce. Had her former mother-in-law shared that piece of information, along with her tell-all about Natasha's artwork?

But then Natasha belatedly caught up with the rest of what Damon had said—*all you have to lose by being with me is your history of never being* really *satisfied*—and she forgot to be concerned. Instead, unwisely, Natasha felt intrigued.

"Wow. That's kind of arrogant, isn't it? No wonder you have such a reputation for—" *For being incredible in bed.* Whoops. That only proved his point. Feeling flustered, Natasha tried again. She smiled. "What makes you think I've never *really* been satisfied, anyway?" she asked. "For all you know, I have smoking hot sex every night of the week! For all you know, I—"

Damon smiled too. "Have you?"

"Have I ever been really satisfied?"

Wearing a fascinated expression, Damon nodded.

"Well, that's—" Natasha tried to think. Despairingly, she gave up the effort. "I'm not sure. But that doesn't mean—"

"If you're not sure, then you haven't been. Believe me."

"Oh. Well. Why don't you come over here and say that?"

As a rejoinder, it was about as witty as anything else heard on a grade-school playground. She was losing her grip.

She was also, it occurred to her, losing a little of her buzz. She was beginning to feel the real danger involved here.

It was a good thing, Natasha decided, that Damon had already pledged not to sleep with her tonight. Otherwise, she couldn't possibly have kept on teasing him so audaciously.

When she glanced up, Damon was near enough to touch.

"If you're not sure," he said again as he stood there, shirtless, just an arm's length away, "then you haven't been. Believe me."

He was doing it. He was literally coming over there, as she'd demanded, and saying that. If he hadn't looked so completely charming and compelling and hot while he did it, Natasha might have been annoyed. Instead, she felt captivated.

"Very funny." She was dying to touch him. But her so-called

seduction wasn't exactly going as planned, and she wasn't sure what to do next. Going with the flow probably *wasn't* it. She'd only lose her head and all her inhibitions. "If I'd known you were mine to command," she mused, "I would have come up with something a lot more interesting for you to do than talk."

"Really?" Damon seemed intrigued. "Go ahead. I'm game."

"All right." Now *this* was more like what Natasha had envisioned a little while ago, when she'd been all soapy and tipsy and hot and wet in her bath. Experimentally, she angled her head to the side, then said, "Take off your pants."

Just as he'd done when standing on her doorstep, Damon didn't hesitate. Instead, he yanked free his drawstring waist tie with a single hasty movement, then hooked both thumbs in his pants waistband. Slowly, he pulled. Natasha glimpsed bare skin, the interesting amalgamation of bone and muscle at his hip, the tantalizing whorl of dark hair leading from his navel to his pelvis, where, breathlessly, Natasha could *almost* glimpse . . .

"No, wait!" she commanded at the last second. Her heartbeat hammered in her chest, letting her know exactly how risky this was. If she lost the upper hand with Damon . . . "I have a better idea." She lifted her gaze to his face. "Lie down on the bed."

He seemed disappointed. "I can do that naked."

Her thighs tingled at the idea. But Natasha wasn't sure she could control herself if he was naked. "Just do it."

Another, more dazzling smile. "What if I don't?"

"Then you'll miss what *I* do next."

Damon nodded. An instant later, he'd pulled his pants back up and was sprawled on her bed.

He made the space his own, turning her jumble of head-board-propped pillows into a wholly masculine lounging space. He bent his arms over that decorative array, used his cupped hands to cradle his head, then gazed straight at her. "Now what?"

"Now I . . ." *What*? her underutilized dictatorial instincts wanted to know. "Look at you," Natasha settled on saying.

It was an obvious choice. Reclining there, all relaxed and bare and muscle-bound, Damon proved an arresting sight.

Natasha began to resent her own insistence that he keep on his pants. Even with them, though, he was impossible not to gawk at. So she did. She started at his head, enjoying the sight of his handsome face and rugged jaw and smiling mouth. She moved to his broad shoulders, slipped her attention to his chest and arms, then took a while to savor the sinewy strength of his forearms. His hands were incredible, too—big and dexterous and tipped with blunt fingers that Natasha knew would please her.

When he'd kissed her, she remembered, she'd felt his hands tangling in her hair and stroking her neck. She'd felt his hands cradling her jaw and encouraging her to open her mouth wider.

What, she wondered, would Damon's talented hands urge her to do next? Maybe touch his burly chest, she decided, swerving her gaze there. Or caress his taut belly. Or tug down his pants, freeing *all* of him to her gaze, letting her see and touch . . .

"So . . ." Damon said. "Do you like what you see?"

The vulnerability in his voice caught Natasha off guard. It roused an answering vulnerability in her—a defenselessness and caring that might take over if she let it. She had to try not to. Otherwise, she would never be able to protect her heart.

Already, her stupid Guinness was failing her. She felt more and more sober with every passing minute . . . and more and more intoxicated by the newfound nearness she and Damon shared.

There was only one way to transcend that.

"I like it very much." To prove it, Natasha trailed her fingers along his foot, up his shin, over his thigh . . . With a naughty grin, she raised her hand at the most crucial moment, just before she encountered the thick solidity and mesmerizing length still hidden by his pants. "Hold still. I'll show you."

Determined to retain the upper hand with him, Natasha got on the bed too. For a moment, she almost lost her seductress's edge. The mattress swayed and dipped beneath her movements. Damon caught her arm and steadied her. Their eyes met. He grinned and so did she, and she wanted to give in to all the yearning and tenderheartedness and caring she'd ever felt.

Just in time, Natasha resisted. "Don't move," she said.

With his dark eyes gleaming, Damon complied. In the low light of her bedroom, he seemed big and dangerous, though, and to be extra safe, Natasha pinned his wrists to the piled-up pillows behind him. Then he only seemed incongruously sweet.

Probably because he gave her a sappy, eager look. For a man being dominated by his former assistant, he appeared more than willing to go along for the ride—wherever it happened to take them.

"I like it when you take charge," Damon rumbled.

"Quiet," Natasha said, and kissed him.

Just like before, their kiss was hot and deep and fast and necessary, and Natasha couldn't help moaning as their tongues met in a way that made her feel completely dizzy. She wanted this. She wanted *all* of this . . . and more. So much more. Forgetting her plans to make Damon beg, Natasha tightened her grip on his wrists, then kissed him again. There was nothing better than this—nothing better than being close, sharing the same breath, learning the sensuous glide of mouths and tongues and bodies. . . .

Bodies. That was a good idea. Their bodies needed to be closer together, too. Still kissing him, Natasha straddled Damon—and this time, Damon moaned too. His hands lifted to hold her hips, to pull her closer, to make her sit more firmly astride him. His body met hers with heat and hardness; his palms slid over her silky chemise, lifting it higher. She gasped and kissed him harder, needing more, knowing that soon, too soon, she would have to stop. She would have to quit teasing him. She would have to give up *without* undressing Damon any further, *without* revealing him, *without* knowing how he'd feel, entirely naked against her, hard and heavy and thrusting and joining. . . .

Dazedly, Natasha raised her head. She wasn't drunk anymore. Not on Guinness, at least. But knowing that she wanted Damon and he wanted her . . . it was heady stuff. It was all she'd ever wanted.

It *had been* all she'd ever wanted . . . until she got here. Now it only felt like a beginning—like the start of something immense.

"Do you want more?" she asked breathlessly. "Tell me."

"Yes," Damon said. "I want . . . everything. I want *you*."

He smiled and pulled her down for another kiss, making a lie of her supposed dominance of the situation, dragging her breasts over his bare chest, making her nipples peak, making her pant faster, making her yearn in a way she'd hoped, foolishly, that she wouldn't. But she couldn't help it.

"I want you, too," she whispered, splaying her hands over his chest. Trying to gain more leverage, she rocked upward, but that only made her doubly aware of her position atop him. She flexed her thighs. "I want you so much. And now—"

"Now you've got me." Damon's smile charmed her. His

hands still played with her chemise, rubbing it over her thighs and her backside, probably revealing her panties. "I'm all yours."

"Ha." Natasha tried to laugh, but Damon truly seemed to mean it. His sincerity puzzled her. "If *that's* true, then—"

"Wait. Before you make me do something silly—before you make me hop or bark or do a striptease—" Urgently, Damon cradled her jaw. "Look at us," he demanded. His gaze traveled over them both. "Look at where we are, together. You must know I'm not joking about any of this. I need you, Natasha. You need me."

Struck by his intensity, she did look at them both.

What she saw humbled her. Damon had let himself be utterly in her control. He'd let himself be held down, jumped on, teased and taunted by a nearly naked woman, kissed and fondled and bossed around . . . and he still looked at her as though she'd hung the moon. He still smiled at her. He still touched her with nothing but tenderness and truth.

Chastened, Natasha drew in a deep breath. Doing her best to ignore the hot, heavy thrumming between her legs and the shaky, needful feeling in her thighs and the achy, intense longing she felt for Damon to stroke her breasts and tongue her nipples and kiss her on the mouth again and again, she gazed straight at him. "There's something I have to tell you," she said.

Damon shook his head. "I already know."

"No, you don't know this. You couldn't." Desperately, Natasha closed her eyes. When she opened them again, Damon was still waiting. She inhaled again, then told him, "I'm not—"

"*Married*," Damon said at the same time she did.

"—anymore. About five years ago, I got—"

"*Divorced*," he said along with her.

Baffled, Natasha gawked at him. "How did you . . . ?"

After an instant, they simultaneously said, "Milo."

Natasha felt like laughing aloud. Of *course* her son had spilled the beans about her divorce from his dad! Milo was eight. He was an open book. He couldn't keep a secret—not for all the Legos in Carlsbad, just an hour's drive up the road.

"I'm *glad* Milo told me," Damon said, trailing his fingers over her cheek. "It means I can be with you. It means I can start making up for all the rotten things I did and just be—"

"Just be *you*," Natasha said, feeling inexplicably freed by knowing there was real honesty between them. She didn't want Damon to change; she knew him for the man he was and loved him anyway. He *had* to know that, especially after all these years. Affectionately, she smiled at him. Flirtatiously, she stroked his arm. Invitingly, she gave a daring wriggle atop him. "Don't be too hasty about disowning your bad side, either. Because right now I could use a little bit of badness from you."

"Just a little bit?" Damon gave her an answering grin. "You're going to get more than just a little bit. I promise."

"Really? Am I?" With mock dubiousness, Natasha raised her brows. This was more like it—this openness between them. "Are you telling me you weren't just boasting before? Because a girl hates to be disappointed when she's in a position like this."

"I wouldn't know about that. I try never to disappoint."

"I'll bet you don't. But maybe you're all talk—"

"*I'm* not all talk. Speaking of this position . . ." Damon grabbed her hips again, holding her tight against him. "I like it. I *love* it. I do. But there's one small thing it's missing."

"Oh yeah?" Natasha seriously doubted it. "What's that?"

"*Me*," Damon said, using her hips to flip them both. Natasha landed on her back, unsure what had just happened, knowing only that Damon seemed dangerously pleased with himself. "It's about time I had a turn calling the shots. Wouldn't you say?"

Then he clasped her hands in his, lowered his head, and took her mouth in a kiss so sweet and heady it stole her breath.

He gave and he took and he savored, and Natasha couldn't help being reminded of Damon's insistence that she was somehow *unusual* in the pleasure she took—in the enjoyment she found in a tasty caramel-chocolate truffle, in the thrill she realized in being in Damon's arms at last . . . in the wholehearted delight she experienced when he kissed her again and held her again and brought his body down on hers again and again and again.

But there was nothing unusual in loving the warm, soft force of his mouth on hers. There was nothing unique in arching higher to press her body against his, feeling their heartbeats thump together, hearing their breath mingle in raspy, urgent unison. There was nothing uncommon, Natasha told herself as she let her hands rove over Damon's hard-muscled back, in wishing he could be everywhere at once, kissing her mouth and her neck and her breasts and her thighs and . . . at the thought, she sighed again.

There was nothing unusual about wanting or liking those things. But there was everything unusual about getting them.

She'd come into her bedroom believing she wanted nothing more than a fun, lighthearted turn on the merry-go-round that was Damon Torrance. She'd told herself that all she needed was to know what it felt like to be desired, to be needed, to be in control of her own sexual destiny for the night. Instead, Natasha realized as Damon gazed into her eyes and smiled, she got so much more. She got love. She got tenderness. She got . . .

Ooh. She got more than she'd ever imagined, she

understood as Damon delivered her a sexy look, then slid his attention to her chemise's strap. Natasha didn't understand the disgruntled way he frowned at it, but she did understand that she loved it when Damon lowered his mouth to her shoulder, kissed her there, slipped his fingers beneath that fragile strap and then lifted it away, sliding it down her arm, pulling down the silky scrap of fabric that covered her, dragging it across her breasts and lower, and . . . before Damon bared her completely, he covered her breast with his hand. Her nipple pouted against his palm, wanting more—and Damon gave it. His caress made her moan; his obvious happiness in her response made her close her eyes and sigh. She hadn't expected this: this reverence and gladness.

With Damon, Natasha realized as slowly, *slowly*, he pulled down her chemise, she felt treasured and beloved. With him, she felt like the most irresistible woman on earth. Because he made her feel that way, she behaved that way. When Damon lowered her chemise all the way, then whisked it off her completely, Natasha arched proudly beneath him, offering herself to him. When he licked her nipples and stroked her breasts and lifted his head to smile at her, she couldn't help smiling, too.

"You're beautiful," he said, and she believed him.

"You're perfect," Damon added, nuzzling a seductive path downward. He offered her another smiling appraisal of her navel piercing, then used his hands to follow the same erotic path his mouth just had traveled. "You're even better than I imagined."

Disbelievingly, Natasha blinked. "You imagined *me*?"

Damon nodded. His dark wavy hair tickled her ribs. "All the time. Just like this. Just like this . . . and more. I tried not to—"

"But you couldn't help it. I know." Thrilled to know that he'd wanted her too, she caressed his arms, loving the way his skin and muscles felt beneath her palms. "Me too. Especially since we've been here together. All I've wanted—"

"Is this," Damon knew, clasping her hips in his hands.

Slowly, he dragged his mouth over her panties' skimpy waistband. He followed the path it outlined across her pelvis. His breath penetrated the insubstantial barrier formed by her panties' sheer floral fabric. Shivering, Natasha bucked upward.

"And this," Damon added huskily, tracing a similar pathway with his fingers. "I've wanted *this*. I've wanted to kiss you, right here." His fingers delved lower, skimming over all the hot, slick, aching places between her thighs. "I've thought about it so often. How you would feel. How you would taste. How you would respond if I touched you, just like this . . ."

He nudged his fingers a little higher, and it was all Natasha could do not to yell out loud. She bit her lip, tossing her head against the piled-up pillows at her back, needing and wanting and knowing that she'd perilously underestimated the effect Damon would have on her if he was ever allowed to do . . . *this*. Because she'd never felt anything like it. Between Damon's dexterous fingers and his unwavering look of awe and delight and his unerring way of almost, *almost* making her come undone with just his heated breath, she could hardly stand it.

Urgently, Natasha levered upward. His touch was so light, so perfect, so completely effective at making her crazy. . . .

"Yes." Again, Damon smiled. His dark gaze roamed over her, taking in . . . everything. "This is a lot like what I imagined. Only better. Because in my dreams, I couldn't do this."

Finally, *finally* he stroked her a little harder. He brought his mouth between her thighs, then delivered her a wild, arousing, completely necessary kiss. He laughed with pleasure, and Natasha begged him not to stop, and somehow she felt her panties being whisked away, and she definitely didn't need them anymore, just like she didn't need her chemise anymore, because without them both, Damon could see her and touch her and . . . *oh, God*, he could torture her with long, slow, maddeningly teasing strokes of his tongue, and he could slide his fingertips over her, and it was all she could do just to get closer and closer to him, to get more and more from him, and all of a sudden . . .

All of a sudden, the whole world fell apart.

Gasping and clutching and moaning, Natasha went still for one wonderful, nonstop, unbelievable moment. When she came down again—when she finally quit pulsing and needing and feeling her ears ring—Damon was there with her, hot and steady and revelatory. He cradled her to him, whispering things she knew were impossible but appealed to her anyway, because in her bedazzled state it sounded as though Damon said he loved her and needed her and wanted to be with her always, and Natasha said some of those same things, too, because for her they were true.

They *were* true, Natasha realized then. She *did* love Damon. She loved him for his smile and his honesty and his wholly unlikely sense of integrity. She loved him for his sex appeal and his humor. She loved him for his talents with chocolate and his endearing swagger and his insistence that the only thing better than having fun was having *more* fun. But most of all, in that moment, Natasha loved Damon for his pure, raw ability to make her feel incredible . . . and she wanted to do the same for him. Desperate and determined, she grabbed at his interfering pants.

"You have *got* to get rid of these," she murmured, wrestling with his loose drawstring tie. "They're so in the way."

But not for long, they weren't. Between Natasha's now-agile fingers and Damon's always-helpful hands, the two of them made fast work of undoing his pants and getting them off him.

Naked without them, Damon moved across the mattress toward her, his face a study in focus and intensity and wanting, and Natasha knew she'd never seen him look more right or more natural or more at ease . . . not once during all the years they'd shared together, laughing and working and finding their way.

"Nakedness suits you," Natasha panted, reaching for him. "I never knew exactly how well. But now I do."

She *really* did. Damon felt hard and heavy and hot in her hand, and even as she stroked him for the first time, she couldn't help shuddering anew. It didn't seem likely that just touching him could make her come again. Yet Natasha felt a new, decadent, undeniable surge of pleasure as she looked at him, thick and erect and velvety, filling her hand in a way that felt erotic and right and vital. She *loved* the way Damon felt.

Licking her lips, Natasha imagined taking him in her mouth, swirling her tongue over the head of his cock, running her lips along the taut, engorged length of him. She imagined herself sucking him inside, stretching her mouth wide to accommodate his size, making him moan, making Damon thrust uncontrollably as she kissed and licked and drove him to the edge and beyond.

"I know what you're thinking," Damon said. "And *yes*. A thousand times, yes. Another time. But right now I want *you*."

His hand dipped between her thighs again, and all at once, Natasha remembered that *she* urgently wanted that, too. She wanted Damon inside her. She wanted him thrusting and taking and giving, wanted to know that he was experiencing the same satisfaction she just had. Wide-eyed, she nodded. "*Yes*. Hurry."

Her breathless agreement was all Damon needed. A

heartbeat later, he'd settled himself above her, and just when Natasha was about to beg him to love her . . . he did. With one incredible motion, Damon entered her, and everything went still. Their breath held in unison. Their eyes met. Their bodies melded. For once, for then and forever, they were together in a way that felt essential and inevitable and wonderful. Just when Natasha was about to whisper again that she loved him, that she needed him, Damon held her hips in his hands and drove himself home, and everything rational flew from her mind. All that existed were need and love and exquisite friction; all that mattered was being and loving and getting more, more, *more* of this.

It felt like forever between them, and to Natasha it felt like she'd waited forever—waited forever to hear Damon cry out her name, for him to shudder and quake and mindlessly thrust inside her . . . for him to cradle her close and kiss her afterward, slowly bringing them both back to the realization that when it came to this, they were as perfect together as they'd imagined.

"Wow." Replete and quivering, Natasha sank into Damon's arms. She wanted to laugh out loud, to cry with joy, to have another round just as soon as she felt ready. "You're . . . amazing."

"Only because of you," Damon said. He kissed her mouth, kissed her forehead, kissed her neck, then sank atop her with his head sharing her fluffy pillow. "Only because you took me back. Only because you believed in me. I never knew— I never even hoped—" Damon broke off. He brushed a long blond tendril from her forehead. His expression seemed inexpressibly gentle. "*You're* what I've been waiting for, Tasha. You're . . . everything."

Natasha laughed. "I bet you say that to all the girls."

She'd been joking. But Damon wasn't. The truth was there in his solemn, hard-set jaw. "I mean it. I know I've done some bad things. I know I've made mistakes. I've been careless—"

"Only in the sense of being an inveterate womanizer." She couldn't stand his seriousness. This had to be what Damon said to every woman he slept with. "I'm fine, Damon. Really, I am. I know what this is." Despite all the sugary words and racing hearts and intimacy they'd just shared, Natasha told herself she *did* know their limits. "I'm a grown-up," she assured Damon. "Soon I'll be ordering a 'sorry I broke your heart bouquet' for myself," she added glibly, "and you'd better believe it's going to be the biggest, priciest, most *outrageous* bouquet of flowers anyone ever saw, because it would be only fair to—"

"Stop." Appearing stricken, Damon kissed her. Hard. When he raised his head, his gaze searched hers. "Can't you tell? Isn't it obvious? I feel like it's written all over me."

Natasha frowned. "What's written all over you?"

"That there was only one reason I ever played around like I did. There was only one reason I was with so many women."

This ought to be good, Natasha thought, trying not to let disillusionment overtake her. They were still in each other's arms! They were still tangled together, sweaty and breathless.

Why in the world would Damon think *now* was the time to say—

"I'd never been involved with anyone who made me want to stop," Damon told her bluntly. "Hell, I'd never been with anyone who even made me think about stopping. Not until now. Not until *you*." Smiling, he kissed her again. "You're the one I'm meant for, Tasha. No one else matters. No one else ever *will* matter, not to me."

Silently, Natasha regarded him. She didn't want to be gullible. She didn't want to believe him. Yet she couldn't seem to quit wondering . . . "Is that really true?"

Damon's smile washed over her, filled with certainty and bravado. "It's more true than anything I've ever said."

Torn, Natasha glanced away. "Well, you've said a lot of things to me over the years. Things are very easy to *say*—"

"They're easy to believe, too, if you let yourself," Damon assured her in his most effortlessly charming manner. "All you have to do is decide to." Teasingly, he slid his palm along her body, skimming over her curves in a way that almost made Natasha lose the ability to think, much less make decisions. "Don't let the fact that I'm touching you right now influence you in any way."

He raised his brows, letting her know damn well that he meant to convince her to believe him by any means possible.

In some ways, Natasha remembered then, Damon Torrance did *not* play by the rules. But he hardly needed to sweeten the deal with more seduction. She was already helpless to resist him.

And there, in the lamplight of her bedroom, atop the rumpled sheets and crushed pillows, with Damon holding her and her body urging her to be with him, Natasha decided not to.

What was the point in resisting Damon, she asked herself recklessly, when there was so much *fun* to be had giving in?

"Don't let the fact that *I'm* touching you right now persuade you to go for round two," Natasha said with a wicked grin. "Not unless you want to. You might not know this about me, but I can be fairly insatiable . . . when the moment is right."

Beneath her hands, Damon groaned. "Is it right now?"

Playfully, she looked at him. "Yep. It just got *really* right." Feeling grateful for his speedy rebound time, Natasha slid down the sheets. She stroked him a little more deliberately, then straddled him again. Ecstasy engulfed her, but somehow she managed to say, "Mmm. More right than you know."

Damon nodded his agreement, his gaze fixed on hers. He lifted his hands to stroke her, looking masculine and intent and entirely overcome. By her! Just before Natasha drove them both to new heights of pleasure, she had a revelation.

Maybe Damon wasn't perfect, but neither was she. As long as she was going to commit to . . . whatever was happening between them, she might as well go all the way. So Natasha opened her eyes, rode Damon till they were both starry-eyed and shaken, and decided to never look back from here.

No matter what happened next.

Chapter 21

When Damon woke up four days after the first incredible night he'd spent with Natasha, he became aware of several things simultaneously. First of all, that something furry was in his face. Second of all, that someone was breathing heavily at the edge of the bed. And third, that his heart felt exactly as full now as it had on the first morning when he'd awakened beside Natasha—when he'd watched her open her sky-blue eyes to blink at him and been blessed by her wide, beautiful, too-generous smile.

"I don't know how I got so lucky," Damon had told her then.

"Because you're *you*," Natasha had answered in an adorably disgruntled tone, snuggling up to him with one long leg over his hip and one arm flung across his chest. "*You* are *always* lucky."

"Not like this," he'd disagreed promptly, and it had been as true the other morning as it was right now. Damon was lucky to be with Natasha. Next to her, everything else fell away.

Except, just then, the mysterious source of the furry heavy breathing Damon was experiencing. That didn't fall away. In fact, the furriness whacked him in the face again. And the heavy breathing became a guffaw. Never a morning person, Damon was slow when it came to opening his eyes, gathering his wits, and solving the mystery that had awakened him. But he did it.

"Look! It's sunrise! Again!" Milo announced in a gleeful tone. "I've been up awhile. Time for another piggyback ride!"

With a groan, Damon turned his head. He glimpsed Natasha's son standing there, eager and alert. At the same time, Finn—who was parked in a furry canine lump on the pillows behind Damon's head—started wagging his tail again. *Thump. Thump.* Aha.

Groggily, Damon blinked. Milo zoomed into slightly improved focus, making it possible to discern his blond, sticking-up hair, impatient, scrubbed-clean face, and colorful pajamas.

If I see you before sunrise, there won't be any more piggyback rides, Damon remembered warning the boy as he'd tucked him in a few nights ago. Who knew kids could be so literal?

"Milo, we need a new system," Damon announced.

Beside him, Natasha rolled over. She saw Milo. Just the way she'd done for the past few days, she sat up and then clutched the covers, staring warily at her son. "Good morning, Milo."

A grin. "Good morning, Mom!"

With perfect timing, Finn thumped his tail again. The puppy liked this now-usual routine, where Damon and Milo had a ritual pre-breakfast piggyback ride, then walked to school with Natasha.

To be fair, Damon liked it, too. What he *didn't* like was the memory that skated over his mind as Natasha ran her hands through her long blond hair, trying to make herself more momlike and less sex-kittenish. As far as Damon was concerned, that was a losing battle. She was both to him: a mom *and* a sex kitten.

She was also the woman who'd said, with heartbreaking

earnestness and completely unconvincing casualness: *Soon I'll be ordering a "sorry I broke your heart" bouquet for myself.*

Natasha had tried to pass off her remark as a joke. At the time, given their general state of nudity and the imminent possibility of round two, Damon hadn't argued the point. But it had wrecked him to know that Natasha still thought of him that way. It had stirred a soul-deep, fervent desire in Damon to prove to Natasha that there *wouldn't* be any god-damn breakup flowers coming her way. Not from him. Not like that. Not ever.

Because he was going to be a different man. For her.

"Since you didn't sleep in your bed on the sofa again," Milo piped up cheerfully, "I turned it into a fort. It's so cool! You've got to see it, Damon." He looked at Natasha. "Mom, can *I* sleep there tonight, if Damon's not going to use it?"

Natasha's guarded gaze slipped to Damon. She bit her lip, giving a fairly convincing appearance of indecision, but he could read her mind like a book. Until now, they'd been pretending to Milo that Damon *might* go back to sleeping on the sofa. But this morning, Natasha seemed to be mulling over the possibility of making their new sleeping arrangements official.

Probably, she was considering it because Damon had been *awesome* at showing her how reliable he could be. He'd washed her car with the garden house outside, then bonded with her next-door neighbor, Kurt, over changing the oil. He'd made a million more sandwiches on gluten-free bread. He'd walked to the grade school with Natasha to pick up Milo, taken all three of them (four, if you counted the ever-present Finn) to the park, and spent a lot of time playing *Pokémon* with Milo while Natasha ran around town "on errands" that Damon assumed pertained to her artwork. He was proud that he'd become so dependable—and he was especially proud that, unlike Paul, *he'd* supported her art.

He wished Natasha would show him some of the jewelry

she'd created. But so far she remained resistant to sharing with him.

Damon guessed that was her right as a sexy, inventive, blow-his-socks-off artistic type with a navel ring and a creative bent . . . and a pronounced tendency to overthink decisions.

"Mo-om!" Milo flopped his arms and small lanky body in exaggerated exasperation, having waited long enough. "Can I?"

"Um, you bet!" Natasha beamed at Milo from across the bed. "I'm pretty sure Damon is going to be sleeping in here with me for a while anyway, so the sofa fort is yours to keep using."

Carefully, she watched her son. But Milo only beamed back.

"Thanks, Mom! Hey, last one to the kitchen table is giving out free piggyback rides to the first one who gets there! Ha!"

Then Milo giggled at Damon and raced away, hair flying and pajamas fluttering, with Finn scampering puppylike at his heels.

"Hm. I guess you're on the hook for a piggyback ride."

Natasha sounded amused. Trying to rouse himself, Damon glanced at her. That roused him, all right, but it didn't exactly fill him with enthusiasm for piggyback rides. Lazily, he stroked her knee, which was all he could reach while she sat there so alertly. "You look really pretty this morning."

"You say that every morning," Natasha informed him.

"It's *true* every morning. You do look pretty." Sleepily, Damon pulled her back under the covers. Natasha landed with a laugh, in a perfect position for him to slide his hand along her thigh, her hip, her breast. . . . "Mmm. You feel really nice, too." He could have lost himself in the soft, nice-smelling, extra-sexy way her skin felt. "What do you say we get Milo shipped off to school and then meet back here for a little together time?"

Devilishly, Damon waggled his eyebrows.

Natasha smiled at him. "You say *that* every morning, too."

"So? I've heard dependability is a desirable character trait." In fact, Damon was counting on it.

"So is a limitless sexual appetite." Natasha imitated his eyebrow waggle. "That means we both win. It's a date."

Damon kissed her. "Now who's repeating themselves?"

It was, to a word, the same thing Natasha said every morning. But as they completed their ritual with a cuddle and a tease and a lingering yearning to stay in bed—only to be yanked out, as usual, by Milo's exasperated hollering from the kitchen—Damon didn't care about repetition. In fact, he liked it.

Anything that brought him Natasha was good. Like helping and shopping and babysitting. Anything that took him away from Natasha was bad. Like working and traveling and trying to be a creative force at Torrance Chocolates (something he obviously was terrible at anyway). And in the middle? Well, Damon had never been much for middles. He'd always been a man of extremes.

Right now, for instance, he was *extremely* interested in making Natasha his. He was interested in erasing her doubts and proving he'd changed. So, although Damon *wanted* to stay in bed, he heeded Milo's holler instead, got up, and got responsible.

Because it was what Natasha would have wanted. More and more these days, it was what Damon wanted, too.

Waking up with Damon was a highlight of Natasha's days.

Each morning, when she opened her eyes and saw her former boss sprawled there in bed beside her, all big and brawny and vulnerable in his slumbering state, she could hardly believe he was really there.

The first morning, she'd given him an experimental poke, just to make sure. Damon had muttered in his sleep, rolled over toward her, then pulled her snugly into his arms. Even asleep, he'd wanted to protect and hold her. Even asleep, he'd tried to please her. Right then, Natasha had simply . . . melted.

She was as helpless to resist Damon as she was to stop eating chocolate. Both gave her far too much pleasure to quit. In excess, of course, each of those things could be dangerous. She knew that. But now that a few days had passed, Natasha figured she'd gotten the whole thing pretty much under control.

She'd also hit upon a plan to make up for the unforgivable way she'd deserted Damon in Las Vegas, leaving him alone to cope with the aftereffects of his chocolate-workshop meltdown. To that end, Natasha had been working and planning and organizing. She hadn't accomplished much in the way of artwork, of course, but she figured her creative work could wait a little longer.

Damon's problems were happening right now—and they were partly her fault. She *had* to do something about them.

But before she took up that task again, there was still time to savor another morning with Damon—still time to relish the sight of him tossing back the covers and standing to stretch, wearing only his tight black boxer briefs. There was still time to watch him stroll across her bedroom, look out the window, stand there in all his glory with the sunlight washing over his corded muscles and his dark, pillow-tossed hair. . . .

An instant later, a beeping cell phone cut off Natasha's reverie. It was Damon's. As he answered it, she padded to the bathroom. When she came back, Damon was staring at his iPhone.

He heard her. He held up his phone, showing her the screen.

"That was my bank," Damon said in an undecipherable tone. "They straightened out my identity theft. All my accounts have been fully restored. Credit cards, lines of credit . . . the works."

It was still happening, Natasha realized. *Damon's usual life was still coming back to him, piece by piece.* Soon he wouldn't need her at all. She'd miss her chance to make amends.

"Great!" With a smile, Natasha went to him. Casually, she kissed him. "Try not to spend it all in one place."

For once, Damon did not smile back. He merely frowned at his phone. "This means I could leave, if you wanted me to."

She blinked, surprised. "Do *you* want to?"

"I'm not here for the free lodging," Damon told her. This time, he *did* smile. "I'm after something a lot better."

"Oh?" Natasha tried not to sound too hopeful. "What's that?"

Damon opened his mouth. But before he could speak, Milo gave another impatient yell from the kitchen. "Damon! Come *on*!"

"Later." Natasha smiled. "Your public awaits."

"I guess so." Damon kissed her. Then, distractedly, he yanked on a pair of jeans and a shirt and went to tend to Milo.

Whatever he'd been about to say remained a mystery. But Natasha thought she knew what it would be.

You. I want to stay because I want you.

If she played her cards right, that's what Damon *would* say to her—and *not* only while they were in bed together.

With that thought in mind, Natasha got dressed and got started with her day's activities. There was still a lot to be done—and (apparently) not much time left to do it in.

When Natasha came home from another day of errand running and then disappeared into her garden-shed workspace,

Damon was ready for her eventual return. He met Natasha at the back door, gave her a kiss hello, then brandished a makeshift blindfold.

"Hi! You can't come in unless you wear this."

She frowned in confusion. "Is that my scarf?"

"No, it's mine," he deadpanned. "See? It matches my eyes."

Natasha laughed. "Whatever you say, guy from Aerosmith."

"You mean Steven Tyler," Damon told her. "We met once. Nice guy. Good dad. And the scarf is yours. You left it on the bed." Grinning, he gestured for her to spin around. "Close your eyes. I'll put it on you. Then I'll show you the surprise."

"Aha. I get it. This is a game." Natasha's eyes lit up. Her gaze traveled over him. "Do you want me to get naked first?"

I wish. "Not right now, sexbot. Milo is home."

"Oh." Looking intrigued all the same, Natasha turned her back to him. Deftly, he tied on the scarf. "Did you have any trouble picking up Milo from school? Usually Carol fills in for me, but she's been strangely 'too busy' for that lately."

"Yeah, there's a lot of 'busyness' going around," Damon said with deliberate blitheness. He knew damn well that her former mother-in-law had been "too busy" on Damon's request—all the better to allow him to demonstrate his new-found sense of maturity. "Also, yes, I picked up Milo without a hitch."

Natasha patted her blindfold. Below it, her mouth curved in a smile. "Thanks for doing that, by the way. It's really nice of you to take care of Milo while I'm . . . working."

"I like doing it." Wondering at the hesitation in her voice just before she said "working," Damon took Natasha's hand. He hoped she knew that (unlike Paul) *he* considered her artwork valuable. He touched her shoulder, too, then began steering her toward the kitchen, where his surprise awaited. "There was a party at school today, and poor Milo didn't get to have any of the goodies. The little guy was pretty bummed about it, but I—"

"What?" Natasha stopped cold. She grabbed for her blindfold, trying to untie it. "I didn't hear about any parties today. Usually I prep Milo for them ahead of time. Is he okay?"

"He's fine." Damon squeezed her hand. He gave her his most comforting smile, even though she couldn't see it. "In fact, he's the impetus for my surprise tonight. So don't wreck it."

"Wreck it?" She gave up on untying her blindfold and pulled it down instead. *Yank.* "I'm not thinking about your surprise right now. I'm thinking about my son! My son who has multiple food sensitivities to deal with. You just told me—"

"That Milo wasn't thrilled about missing out on all the goodies. That's it." Patiently, Damon reversed the downward pull Natasha had given her blindfold. "It's not an emergency or anything. It's just that until today, I hadn't realized how much Milo's food issues affect him. It's not all silly songs and apps and websites and food lists. It's *feelings*, too."

Skeptically, Natasha frowned. "It's also anaphylactic reactions and epinephrine and responsibility," she pointed out. "But none of that is your problem, Damon. You aren't exactly stellar at dealing with real-life issues, you know, so—"

"So I *might* be, if you gave me a chance." Hurt, Damon frowned right back at her. "I called a friend of mine who works at the Allergy, Asthma and Immunology Division of Scripps Clinic today, and I got more information about this. I told Milo that *I'm* giving up peanuts and dairy and eggs and gluten, too! They're not worth it."

"Right. I can guess how long *that* will last."

Her skepticism stung. "You don't think I have what it

takes to make a sacrifice? Even for Milo's sake? You don't think I can do it?"

"I think you can do anything you set your mind to." Again Natasha lowered her blindfold. From above its folds, she gazed patiently at him. "For a while, at least. And I know you mean well, too, but—"

"But you don't think you can count on me."

"Come on, Damon. Don't be like that." A sigh. "I *know* you, remember? You're not exactly Mr. Dependable. You never have been." Natasha touched his arm to reassure him. "And that's okay! You have plenty of other fine qualities." She winked, then tugged on her blindfold once more. "Like planning surprises. So let's go."

Decisively and sightlessly, Natasha turned. She assumed an arms-up position, ostensibly ready for Damon to guide her again.

He couldn't help feeling the moment had passed.

"I mean it, Damon," Natasha coaxed. "If I wanted you to be a different person than you already are, you wouldn't be here. I like you the way you are. So show me your surprise."

Mulishly, Damon hesitated. He still felt hurt that she didn't trust him—even after all the efforts he'd made.

"If I like it, I'll let you blindfold me again later tonight," Natasha promised in a sultry tone. "Or maybe I'll put this on you, instead. Maybe I'll tease you and touch you and—"

"Fine." Giving in to the moment the way he always did—or at least the way he always had—Damon offered up a grin. "But keep the sexy talk down. Milo is waiting for us in the kitchen."

Then he took her hand and led her in.

The first thing Natasha noticed was the aroma of toasted bread. Then the tang of citrus fruit and apples. Then, underlying it all, the sweet, complex fragrance of . . . chocolate?

Behind her, Damon made a show of untying her blind-fold. His hands worked dexterously. His knuckles brushed her hair. So did his breath. Then, with a flourish she could sense (if not see) Damon pulled off her scarf so she could see his surprise.

"Ta-da!" he announced. "I made dinner!"

Blinking at the array of dishes arranged on the table, Natasha frowned in confusion. She zeroed in on one item. "You made *chocolate* for dinner?" She glanced at Damon's grinning face, thinking that she'd probably been correct in doubting his judgment earlier. "Damon, we can't have chocolate for dinner."

"Yes, we can!" Milo disagreed. At the other side of the table, he surveyed the spread with big-eyed enthusiasm. "I'm going to! Damon already said I could. And it's *all* safe for me."

"It is. The chocolate is dairy free," Damon said. "Do you know how unusual that is? It turns out that most chocolate is made into milk chocolate—or dark chocolate with milk solids added, which aren't technically necessary. But this chocolate is bittersweet Venezuelan Carenero Superior with just a little sugar and no milk added. It's *delicious*. You'll see."

Dubiously, Natasha examined the table again. Beside her with one hand on the small of her back, Damon nodded with pride.

"Also, officially we're having dairy-free chocolate *fondue* for dinner." Damon gave her an abashed look. "Chocolate is the only thing I can make besides sandwiches. And we can *too* have chocolate for dinner. Europeans eat chocolate for breakfast."

"*With* bread," Natasha pointed out, still unconvinced by all this. "In croissants or spread on toast or with fruit."

"We've got toast." With great fanfare—and a sweep of his arm—Damon offered up the food he'd prepared. "*Gluten-free* toast. Also, oranges, apples, grapes, bananas . . . you name it." He crossed his arms. "We've got all the components of a nutritious meal."

"*And* chocolate." Stumped by Damon's reasons for doing this, Natasha stared at it. "You really made chocolate for dinner."

"Only a *little* chocolate. It helps the fruit go down."

He seemed so proud and so gleeful that she just couldn't refuse him. Clearly Damon still loved working with chocolate. He just couldn't give it up. How could she deny him that?

After being away from work, Damon was undoubtedly jonesing for a challenge. Stuck at her apartment this way, with no bikini models to woo or business deals to broker, her globe-trotting former boss was probably going out of his skull with boredom.

But Damon gave no sign of crushing ennui as he hugged her to his side, then grinned at Milo. "After school, I told Milo I'd find a way for him to have treats today," Damon explained. "And I did!" Again, he gestured at the table. "Voilà!"

That really *was* sweet. "You did all this for Milo?"

Damon didn't answer; he only pulled out a chair for her. He ushered her to it with another chivalrous sweep of his arm.

His happy face told Natasha all she needed to know.

"I think you need to get out more. You're going stir-crazy," she joked as she took a seat before the elaborate array of food. "The apple wedges are cut with geometric precision. The bread is arranged in a pyramid of perfect cubes. I think you missed your calling as a sous-chef." Natasha peered more closely. "Is this fruit arranged in *alphabetical order*?"

Damon shrugged off her question. He handed plates to her and Milo, then watched them dig in. Then, "Wait! I told everyone at Torrance Chocolates that I'd take a picture to show them."

Cheerfully, Damon whipped out his iPhone. He snapped

photos from several different angles, being sure to highlight the chocolate. Always ready for a turn in the spotlight—especially with his new pal, Damon—Milo hammed it up for the camera.

The two of them were adorable together. But . . .

"You went to *Torrance Chocolates* to get this chocolate?"

"Sure. Milo and I took a field trip together after school." Damon put away his iPhone, then helped himself to a plate. Eagerly, he sat beside Natasha, then started tucking in to fruit and bread. He dunked a banana slice into the chocolate, then savored it. He swallowed. "That was the only way I could make sure there wouldn't be any chance of nut or dairy exposure. The production lines are shared over various runs of flavors, so unless you have a dedicated allergen-free area of the facility—or an inside man to help you—you're kind of screwed. There'll always be a chance of dairy or nut cross-contact."

Natasha knew that all too well. Over the years, she'd had a difficult time finding treats for Milo. "But wasn't that awkward for you? I mean, you didn't take your leave of absence from Torrance Chocolates under the best of circumstances, right?"

So far, Damon had been a little cryptic about what those circumstances had been. Although Natasha wished he would confide fully in her, she was willing to wait for him.

Especially since she knew part of the truth from Jimmy.

"Oh yeah. I forgot all about my leave of absence. I guess I had other priorities in mind." Looking perplexed, Damon considered that. As usual, he seemed oblivious to the fact that his luck was changing for the better, all over again. Evidently, fate loved Damon almost as much as Natasha did. "I guess all I needed was a good enough reason to go back." He glanced at Milo, making that reason plain. "Everybody seemed glad to see me, though. We had a tour. I saw Jason. He said Amy's doing really well. Even my dad came downstairs."

"Oh. That's good." Natasha perked up. "Did the two of you—"

"Talk?" Damon raised his eyebrows. "No. It was a mission to collect some chocolate for Milo, not a Lifetime movie of the week. My dad hasn't magically forgiven me for Las Vegas."

"He will." Regretfully, Natasha squirmed. "Don't worry."

"I'm not worried." If Damon was faking his nonchalance, it didn't show. He dipped an apple slice into his portion of fondue, chomped it, then looked at Milo. "Well, kiddo . . . do you like it?"

"Mmm-hmm." Mouth full, her son nodded. His hands and face were smeared with chocolate. His cheeks bulged. His plate stood heaped with still more "dinner." He'd never looked happier.

"Good." With a sense of satisfaction befitting his apparent status as Milo's hero of the day (or maybe of the week), Damon surveyed the table. "You can't take chocolate fondue to the third-grade school party, though. It's not exactly portable."

"Or tidy." Natasha handed Milo a napkin.

"*Or* a peanut butter cup." Milo's eyes shone as he mentioned his most longed-for packaged treat. "Or a candy bar!"

Damon mulled over that idea. "I could make a candy bar. It's basically a supersize truffle. I could totally make that."

"I know you could." Natasha smiled at him. "But you'd have to develop it, produce it, package it. . . ." She shook her head at the scope of the job. "All the treats for school parties have to be packaged goods so their ingredients are disclosed. The school has a no-peanuts policy, but some of the parents don't take it very seriously. And it doesn't preclude eggs or dairy."

With his brow creased in thought, Damon dipped an orange wedge in chocolate. He offered it to her. "Well, at least Milo's not alone," he said as he watched Natasha savor her "meal." "My buddy at Scripps told me the incidence of food sensitivities is on the rise. If all of *those* kids want candy bars as much as Milo does, someone could make a fortune marketing them."

"That someone could be Torrance Chocolates."

"Could be." Damon shrugged. "But I'm still officially on the outs there. And my dad made it plain that what happens at Torrance Chocolates isn't up to me anymore. By now, he's probably grooming another successor."

Damon glanced at Milo, held out another napkin for him, then burst out laughing. Eyes shining, Damon shook his head. He withdrew the napkin. "Never mind, Milo. After this, I think we're going to have to hose you down to get you clean again."

Conspicuously *not* caring about the mess, her son giggled. Then he dug into more banana slices. Natasha had never seen him eat so much fruit in all her life. Who knew all she'd needed were a few ounces of melted chocolate and some toothpicks?

"I really think you should pursue your candy bar idea, Damon," Natasha told him, struck by the look of regret on his face when he'd mentioned his father's eventual retirement from Torrance Chocolates. "With Torrance Chocolates' resources and global influence, they could be a real trendsetter in this area. This idea could be just the thing you need to get back in."

"Nope." He dipped a grape, then ate it. "Not interested."

"How can you not be interested?" Natasha protested. Damon *had* to be playing it cool, probably to preserve his pride. He had a *lot* of pride—it was an integral part of his overall package. "You were *born* to work at your family's company! You're really good at it."

"I'm good at a lot of things." Damon leaned over, gave her a sappy look, then offered her a chocolaty kiss that Natasha gladly accepted. "Later, I plan to be good at clean-

ing up this mess—as long as the dishwasher is still working.
I have to draw the line somewhere." Damon grinned at her,
then craned his neck to try to see out the kitchen window.
"Hey, do you think Carol is around? I can't see if her car is
parked in her driveway."

"Lately? She's probably not home," Natasha told him.
"Even if she is, I doubt she's available for . . . whatever you
have in mind. Unless it's another game of Uno. That was a hit."

"Uno!" Milo pumped his fist in remembered triumph.
When the four of them had played a game yesterday evening,
he'd emerged the big winner . . . until Finn had chewed a few
of the cards into unrecognizable, soggy blobs and forced
them to shelve the whole endeavor. "I like Uno," Milo said
with a grin. "*And* apples. And bananas and oranges and
grapes, too!"

Natasha smiled at her son. He must have put away a half
pound of grapes alone. Maybe Damon was on to something.

"If Carol is home, I think she'll be available." Damon
wiped his mouth on a napkin, then stood. "I'll go see."

"You're wasting your breath," Natasha warned good-
naturedly. "She'll never say yes. Not on such short notice."

Halfway to the back door, Damon tossed Natasha a
wink. "You might have forgotten, but I can be pretty per-
suasive when I want to be."

"Oh, I haven't forgotten a thing," Natasha assured him
with a wink of her own. "Go on then. Work your magic.
Good luck!"

Even as she said it, she wanted to cringe, remembering
all the times she'd been annoyed at someone for telling her
good luck when all she'd ever had was not-so-good luck.

But Damon was different. All he did was wave as he
swaggered away. "I don't need luck!" he said. "I've got *you*."

He *did* have her, Natasha realized. Just like old times.

His comment was as close to a call for help as she was
ever likely to get from him. Damon did need help. He must

realize that. He always had before. If he was counting on her (and it sounded as though he was) . . . she really *had* to succeed.

She had to hurry up about doing it, too. Before his super-lucky life came knocking on her door and lured away Damon.

This time, maybe for good. Maybe even . . . forever.

Chapter 22

When Damon came back from talking with Carol next door, he felt as though he could take on the world and win.

It was a feeling, frankly, that he'd missed.

"Slap an 'S' on my chest and call me Superman," he told Natasha as he pulled her into his arms for a spur-of-the-moment dance across the living room, where she'd been picking up toys while Milo watched TV. "Carol agreed to babysit tonight."

"Really? But we didn't even have plans." Natasha laughed as Damon tangoed her, then twirled her, then dipped her in his arms. Eyes shining, she clutched his shoulder for balance. "Usually I try to give Carol advance notice for babysitting."

"Not tonight," Damon said. "Tonight, you don't have to." *Because I took care of it.* "Besides, *I* had a turn at being irresponsible today with my chocolate-for-dinner extravaganza. Now it's *your* turn." Swivel-hipped and loving the way she felt against him, he danced her farther across the room. "So . . ." Adroitly, he dipped her again. "What would you like to do?"

Almost hanging upside down in his arms, Natasha

pursed her lips. She worked her mouth from side to side, thinking about it.

"Umm . . ." She scrunched her nose in concentration. "Well . . ."

"Stop. If you're thinking about it that hard, you're not doing it right." Damon swooshed her upright again, making her blond hair fly. He'd obviously been remiss in showing Natasha how to have a good time. All her years of looking out for him had stunted her ability to be freewheeling. "Tell you what. Why don't you go put on something sexy, and we'll see what happens?"

"Sexy as in a bikini or sexy as in a cocktail dress?"

"Whatever feels good to you."

She seemed stymied by that response. "No, seriously. Sexy as in black-tie affair or sexy as in pencil skirt and pumps?"

"Sexy . . . as in *you*." Damon touched her chin, lifted her face to his, then kissed her. "Just follow your instincts."

She frowned. "I don't think I have any sexy instincts."

Damon begged to differ. He shot a cautious glance at a cartoon-enthralled Milo, then lowered his voice. "You have *crazy* hot sexual instincts. Believe me. You're overthinking this."

Natasha gave him a frustrated look. "I can be sexy while *naked*! That's not the problem. But unless I know where we're going, I can't possibly dress for the occasion."

Damon wasn't worried about that. "You'll be fine. Wear some jewelry, too. *Your* jewelry," he specified with a cajoling smile. "Something you created in your workshop. I'd like to see it."

"You won't like it. It's eclectic."

"If you think I don't know what that means, you're wrong. I'm a world-class chocolatier, not a hillbilly."

Her eyes brightened. "Speaking of chocolatiering, I

really think you should reconsider that candy-bar idea of yours. If—"

"If you don't hurry up, I might change my mind." With a grin, Damon swatted her derrière. "The clock's ticking."

"It's not sexy to have a time limit," Natasha grumbled.

"Don't forget the jewelry," Damon reminded her. "Also, coming out here naked will *not* get you off the hook!" he warned.

"As *if* I would do that." She rolled her eyes toward her son. "Milo's right over there, being young and impressionable!"

"Oh yeah." Sometimes, it occurred to Damon, there were inconveniences involved in family living—like a moratorium on consequence-free nudity. He still hadn't caught up to the inhibiting reality of it all. In many ways, this felt like an extended vacation in suburbia. "Well then, I won't come out naked, either."

At his joking tone, Natasha laughed. "Good call, Superman. I'll be out in a minute." Then she vanished into her bedroom.

Left alone in the tidy living room with Milo, the cartoons, and his own empty arms, Damon couldn't help wondering . . .

Could he make that allergen-free candy bar for Milo (and the thousands of other kids who'd want something similar)? Or was Damon just fooling himself? If he could, did he dare try?

Or would he just go down in flames again?

Almost as soon as Damon thought of it, though, his mind skittered away to something else. He just wasn't ready to confront the whole imbroglio at Torrance Chocolates and his future (or lack of a future) at his family's company. Until he felt a lot more invincible than he did right now, hiding out at Natasha's place seemed like an excellent way to handle things.

Especially once she emerged in her sexy clothes.

"All set!" Natasha announced, looking beautiful and kissable and excited. "And I know *just* where to go."

With the surf roaring in her ears and the moon and stars floating overhead and the city lights sparkling on the distant hillsides, Natasha tromped along the waterline near La Jolla. In the dark, the seagulls were quiet. The sandpipers were active. Most of the people had gone home. All that remained were dark skies, crashing waves, miles of sand . . . and Damon, by her side.

Enthralled by him, Natasha shot him another glance. "I can't *believe* you had formalwear in your duffel bags."

Damon shrugged. "A man should always be prepared."

"For a ball? For a reception for foreign dignitaries? For a royal wedding?" With her arm in his, Natasha strolled a little farther. Her long, chiffon-strewn dress flowed behind her, kept out of the sand and surf by the knee-high, waterproof Wellies she kept in her Civic's trunk for occasions like this one. "Did you pack your bags thinking a black-tie soirée might break out?"

"Well, those kinds of things *do* happen in my life," Damon admitted. "At least they used to." He turned his face to the waves, then inhaled. "I wasn't really thinking straight when I packed."

Struck by his sudden melancholy, Natasha wanted to cheer him up. She wanted to help him. It was the least she could do.

That, and follow through with the idea she'd had earlier tonight, when Damon had conveniently given her carte blanche to take them wherever she wanted to go. After a quick consultation with her trusty calendar, Natasha had known exactly what to do.

"Well, you could be a body double for James Bond in that getup." She gave him a teasing grin. "You could stand in for a male model in an Armani ad. You could get *married*. You could—"

"You don't look half bad yourself." Damon's gaze took in her gauzy silk dress, her body *in* her dress, and her practical Hunter boots. "Your Wellies are kind of kinky, though. It's all that vulcanized rubber. I knew a British girl once who—"

"—*officiate* a wedding," Natasha interrupted, "or—"

"—liked to wear them in bed." Damon glanced at her ears. "Your earrings, on the other hand, are *not* your own design."

"Guilty." Natasha touched them. "These are strictly off the shelf. But *you*! In that outfit, you could lead an orchestra or—"

"Was your plan for the evening to harass me? Because if it was, you could have done that in bed. Naked. I would have let you." Damon grinned, then hugged her closer against him. "Over and over again, until we could barely breathe. Or move."

Natasha smiled, too. "We have to get out of bed sometimes."

"We *do* get out of bed sometimes! There was that time in the shower. We got out of bed for that one." Damon's face turned dreamy . . . then downright wicked. "Also, that time in the kitchen after we dropped off Milo at school, and that time outside in the dark in your backyard in the sleeping bag—"

"I remember." Natasha felt herself blush. She was pretty sure Damon had been trying to inveigle an invitation inside her garden-shed workspace to see her artwork. She hadn't been ready to show it to him yet. Instead, she'd distracted him with a kiss . . . and the rest had been history. Hot, racy history that was probably illegal—at least without the sleeping bag and the darkness. "All I mean is, I thought this would be nice, too."

"It is nice." Through his dinner jacket, Damon's warmth touched her. His hair tossed in the sea breeze, setting up an arresting contrast between his aristocratic profile, his down-to-earth demeanor, and his high-octane outfit. He strolled beside her, not the least bit worried about his dress shoes. "I would go anywhere with you. And I'd love it while I was there."

"Me too, with you." Smiling, Natasha turned to him. She swept her arm toward the sea and sand and moonlight, making her *non*-self-created bracelet glimmer with the motion. "Besides, this beach definitely takes the prize for romantic atmosphere. If not for the occasional dog walkers and the houses over there on the bluff, we could be the only two people on earth right now."

Just as she'd expected, Damon glanced around. His gaze lit on one of the seaside houses—a huge modernistic slab of treated wood and sharp angles, perched on the rocky area where the beach met the hill. Its large, fully lit picture windows showed people milling around inside, laughing and drinking and talking. From its interior, music and jovial voices floated on the breeze.

"Looks like fun," Natasha said. "Doesn't it?"

"Hmm." Damon's gaze remained fixed on the immense house. His steps slowed. His face turned pensive. "Nah. Not really."

"Your own house probably looks a lot like that sometimes," Natasha told him. "If you're worried about the repairs, I'm sure they're coming along nicely. You'll be back there in no time."

She wanted him to assure her that he could wait—that he *wasn't* dying to get back to his deluxe, super-lucky life. But he didn't. Instead, he only gazed more moodily at the house.

"They're close to being finished," Damon admitted. "I had a voice mail from the contractor while you were getting dressed."

A chill rushed through Natasha. First Damon's girl-friendly mojo had returned. Then his money. Then he'd been welcomed back at Torrance Chocolates (at least in part). Now his beachside house was almost habitable again. What would happen next?

She rubbed her bare arms, thinking that maybe a romantic moonlit stroll along the beach in fancy clothes was an activity better suited to late June than late January. She'd always wanted to do it, though. The reality had been even nicer than her imagined version . . . because Damon had been there.

Natasha aimed her chin at the party. "Let's crash it."

"Crash the party?" Damon's eyes lit up. Then, "Nah."

"I'm starting to hate hearing that word from you," she said. "What's gotten into you, anyway? You *never* play it safe."

With effort, Damon turned his gaze away from the party's bright lights. Broodingly, he looked at the ocean. "I do now."

"Just because you had one disaster?" Natasha asked. "That's no reason to ignore all your instincts. That's not the Damon Torrance I know." She tugged his arm. "Come on. Let's do it."

"I'm not crashing a party." Damon planted his feet in the sand, his jaw set in a hard line. "We could get arrested. Carol would have to bail us out of jail. Milo would be traumatized."

Natasha scoffed. "Who has party crashers arrested?"

Wryly, Damon pointed both thumbs at himself. "Just once, though. Some kids busted into a shindig at my place. Jason told me there were liability issues—something to do with the pool, the lack of a fence . . . maybe all the liquor."

He shrugged. "Most of the time, I'm pretty live-and-let-live about things."

"Well, *I'm* crashing," Natasha told him. "I'm freezing, my feet are tired, and I'm starving. I could totally go for a plate of hors d'oeuvres." Decisively, she let go of Damon's arm, then sashayed down the beach. Ahead, she spied a sandy stairway that led to higher ground. "You're welcome to tag along, Mr. Buzzkill. Just try not to get us thrown in the clink, okay?"

Then, without looking back, Natasha hoisted her gown's hem, tromped up the stairs, and headed toward the warmth and luxury of the lights spilling from the party up ahead.

It took Damon a while to catch up to Natasha. Partly, that was because he had never been called "Mr. Buzzkill" before, and he was dumbfounded by the experience. Partly, that was because he was frozen in shock when Natasha sashayed away, hips swinging and blond hair bouncing, with the express intention of breaking the rules. Because Natasha *never* broke the rules. That was what made her such a good stand-in conscience for *him* at times.

Also, partly, Damon hesitated because he could have *sworn* he glimpsed a flashbulb go off—and someone scurry away uphill—in the vicinity near Natasha. The idea of someone taking a picture of her without permission made him want to punch a paparazzo (because those "photojournalists" *had*, in the past, pestered Damon a time or two, before and after his meltdown). And partly (and most disconcertingly), Damon had faltered because after so many years of unfettered access to everything he wanted, he had a tricky time figuring out how to actually sneak in to something.

In the end, he decided on the brute-force method. He crept up the same sand-encrusted staircase Natasha had used, waited until the party house's ocean-side terrace was mostly empty, then vaulted himself over the terrace railing. He landed alongside a tall, short-haired brunette. She started as Damon thumped onto the terrace, then watched as he cavalierly brushed off his suit.

"I dropped a contact lens down there." Damon angled his head toward the bluff. He grinned. "Slippery little suckers."

"That's what I hear." The brunette's smile widened. She looked him over, almost as though she could sense Damon's long-absent womanizer mojo. Maybe she could. Damon absolutely sensed a flirtatious vibe coming from her. She noted his empty hands, then offered up a sham pout. "Poor baby. You need a drink."

"I was just about to get one." Rapidly, Damon scanned the house's brightly lit, luxurious layout. "Shall I bring you one?"

"Only if you deliver it yourself," the brunette cooed.

She was *definitely* flirting with him. Hmmm. Could his ridiculous good fortune with women be back? After all, he'd been more than capable of charming Carol, making friends with Natasha's neighbors—the dog walkers and the stroller moms—and chatting up a whole array of female farmers-market attendees.

Making a quick mental tally, Damon realized that it was possible his luck was changing. Already he'd regained his bank accounts. He'd been assured his home repairs were proceeding ahead of schedule. Some of the Torrance Chocolates employees seemed ready to give him a second chance. He'd even managed to get closer to Natasha—and that was the best luck of all.

If his mechanic called to tell him his car was fixed . . .

Just as Damon thought it, his cell phone rang.

"Excuse me," he told the brunette. "I've got to take this." She nodded and then drifted away, leaving Damon feeling more perplexed than ever. Did women want him again or not?

Had his good luck returned or not? And what did that mean?

His ringtone trilled a third time. Annoyed, Damon answered.

The person on the other end of the line didn't waste time. The moment Damon answered, he heard, "Put down the phone and get the hell out of here, jackass. You're ruining everything."

Damon blinked. He recognized that sardonic voice. "*Wes*?"

A sigh. "You were sharper when you were drinking."

It *was* Wes. Somehow, he knew Damon was here.

That meant Wes must be here, too. Frowning, Damon scanned the crowd, looking for his friend. His gaze climbed the well-appointed hillside house, passing over the stylishly dressed women and suit-wearing men and waitstaff in black and white. On second glance, this place did look a little familiar. It was possible Damon had been here before and didn't recall when.

"Did you hear me?" Wes barked. "Get lost. It's not time for anyone to see you yet—especially not here. If you don't—"

But just as his friend reached full ranting velocity, Damon spotted a vivacious blonde in the center of the next room. *Natasha*. She was surrounded by a circle of interested-looking men, all of whom were listening to her tell a story. Apparently, when given half a chance—and a huge cocktail—she was a natural at misbehaving. She seemed to be having a hell of a time.

"I've got someplace to be," Damon told Wes. "Bye."

His friend squawked through the phone. Damon only ended the call, pocketed his phone, then strode through the crowd.

He had a woman to retrieve—a woman with laughing eyes, a killer dress, and a pair of rubber Wellies that made him wish for rain. He didn't intend to screw around while doing it.

Things were going really well for Natasha. She'd successfully infiltrated the party and gotten herself fortified with a few crudités and a mojito. She'd also defrosted her chilly fingers, touched up her lip gloss, and sought out everyone at the party who could possibly be useful to her plan.

Then she spotted Damon, and things got tricky.

". . . so that's why you should never eat fish and chips in Trafalgar Square," Natasha blurted, hastily winding up the anecdote she'd been telling her engrossed listeners. She glanced down at her mojito, downed the whole thing, then laughed. "Whoops! Looks like I need another drink. I'll be right back."

"I'll get it for you," one of the men volunteered.

She gazed at his eager face—and at the faces of the other men who were also offering to fetch her another drink—and wondered where all this male interest had been a month ago. She'd never been this irresistible. Not even to Lance, the neurosurgeon she'd met on the plane from Las Vegas . . . whom she still hadn't gotten back to about their postponed second date.

Again, she looked at her manly entourage. Maybe they were rubber-boot fetishists, and she was their accidental dream girl.

"That's sweet," Natasha said, "but I can handle it."

She swept away, headed in the opposite direction of Damon, trying to stay one step ahead of him for now. If he caught up to her while she was chatting and recognized some of the people at the party, he might start asking questions—

questions Natasha wasn't prepared to answer. Turning, she stepped toward the bar—

—and almost ran into a burly man with an earpiece.

"Evening, miss," he said. "Can I see your invitation?"

Natasha couldn't believe this. "Um, I have one," she said, "but I didn't bring it. I should be on the list, though."

Mr. Muscles consulted his clipboard. "Your name?"

Biting her lip, Natasha hesitated. Damon was closing in. She could see him from the corner of her eye, looking determined and intent and not the least bit disheveled for a guy who'd recently vaulted over a beachfront terrace railing. She'd seen his Olympic move from across the room and had been duly impressed.

If Damon caught up to her—if he recognized their hosts before Natasha had a chance to put everything in motion . . .

"Ohmigod." She pointed. "Is that a real *sea lion* on the beach outside?" She fluttered her arms. "I've never seen one!"

Politely, the security guy turned toward the beach. "It might be, miss. They come ashore sometimes around here—"

Natasha didn't hear the rest. She was busy sprinting away.

It took much less time for Damon to catch up with Natasha the second time than the first time. He watched in bafflement (and a little admiration) as she deftly ditched the party's security personnel, scanned the crowd, then vanished upstairs.

Damon followed in the same direction.

A minute and a half later, Natasha stepped out from around a corner, deftly ending his search by making her location obvious. Almost as if she'd planned things this way, she grabbed Damon by his necktie, then smashed him against the wall.

Music thumped from downstairs. People's voices drifted

around them. Outside, the waves crashed. But the hallway was (temporarily) empty, and Natasha made the most of their privacy.

Her mouth found his in record time. With an erotic little moan, she wound his tie around her fist, brought Damon even closer, then followed up with the rest of her body. Surprised but willing, Damon felt her hips collide with his, even as her lips just went on adding to the hot, disorienting confusion.

He knew he should protest. But having Natasha in his arms felt really good. Having her kissing him and moaning and grinding her pelvis against him—all while she was wearing that sophisticated, soft little *nothing* of an evening dress felt great. Really great. So rather than behave, the way he should have done, all Damon did was delve his hands in her hair and hold on and kiss her back. Again and again and again.

Too soon, Natasha took away her mouth. Her bright, blue-eyed gaze searched his. She smiled. "I've always wanted to have a sexy, illicit liaison at a party I just crashed. You game?"

"Are you serious?" She *couldn't* be serious. She was Natasha. Although, Damon remembered, she *had* been getting into spontaneity lately. But this . . . "There are people downstairs."

"That's part of what makes it fun." Panting with eager licentiousness, Natasha slid her hand lower . . . almost low enough to discover for herself if Damon was interested. Given her kisses, he couldn't help being aroused. "Come on," she urged breathlessly. "There's an empty room right over there. I just discovered it."

"But you're on the run from the security personnel!"

Natasha laughed. "Then we'd better make it quick, hadn't we?"

Chapter 23

Thirty seconds later, Damon was behind the locked door of their hosts' upstairs powder room, lifting Natasha up onto the vanity. She hiked her dress. She spread her knees. She pulled him into the warm apex of her thighs, grabbing his ass to keep him there in a way that brooked no argument—especially from him.

Lustily, he kissed her. Passionately, he stroked her. Eagerly, Natasha urged him on. With her head thrown back and her long hair tossing wildly around her shoulders and her rubber rain boots looking incongruously sporty next to her bare legs and elegant evening gown, she whispered naughty encouragement the likes of which he'd never expected to hear from her.

"I need you, Damon." She unzipped his pants, the sound of his zipper loud in the small room, then delved her hand inside. She found his cock. With evident delight, she freed him, already hard and throbbing. "I need you, right here. Right now."

All around them, their images were reflected in the powder room's lavish mirrored surfaces. Dizzied by their multiple likenesses, Damon nodded. He hooked his thumbs on Natasha's filmy thong panties, then tugged them down. With leggy agility, she kicked them off. He pocketed them in his dinner jacket.

Avidly, Natasha pulled him nearer. But with her nakedly revealed to him that way, there was only one thing Damon wanted to do. With a grin, he dropped to his knees. With both hands on her spread thighs, he lowered his head, then lavished her with kisses. In no time at all, Natasha shuddered into a climax.

Surely her cries were audible in the hallway outside; probably so was the sound of raw, hard thrusting against the vanity as Damon took his own pleasure next. Natasha's heels thumped against the vanity's lower doors; her hands grappled with its slick surface, trying to find stability in a world quaking with passion. Harder, faster, Damon thrust inside her. They both came closer and closer to the edge. He'd never felt anything hotter. He'd never known anyone more remarkable.

Groaning with a nearly instant release, Damon gave another mindless hip swivel, then buried his face in Natasha's sweet-smelling neck. Her body sagged in satisfaction against his. Her knees clutched his hips for balance. Her hands cupped his ass again. Heart pounding, Damon kissed her. He gazed into her eyes.

It had been only minutes since they'd sneaked into the powder room together, but it felt like forever. It felt amazing.

"That was . . . *incredible*," he breathed, still panting.

"*Really* incredible," Natasha agreed, laughing with joy.

Her face was flushed. Her hair was tangled around her shoulders. With her dress still hiked up high and her body still pulsing intimately around him, Natasha was the epitome of the sex goddess he'd always known she could be. Feeling ridiculously glad about that—glad about *her*—Damon kissed her again.

"I hope that met your expectations of a sexy, illicit

liaison at a party you just crashed," Damon said with a smile. "I'm not sure the vanity can hold up to another try."

"Oh *yeah*." Natasha nodded. "You bet it did."

"I still can't believe you did this." Damon shook his head, marveling at her. "It was so adventurous. So risky. So—"

"So sexy?" Natasha raised her eyebrows. "That's true. The tricky part will be sneaking out of here, though. Any ideas?"

"I vote to brazen it out as if we own the place," Damon suggested. "That usually works for me."

Natasha agreed. A few seconds later, they'd had a quick cleanup, straightened their clothing, zipped up everything that needed zipping, and tidied their disheveled hair. They inhaled and linked hands, preparing to reenter the party long enough to sneak outside again. At the last instant, Natasha turned back.

"Hang on. I've got to do one more thing." She searched her evening bag, pulled out a miniature bottle of lavender-scented spray-on hand sanitizer, then squirted it all over the vanity. She wiped down the surface with a towel, tossed the towel in the nearby hamper, then faced Damon with a self-conscious grin. "There. I wouldn't have felt right just leaving it like that."

"No, you wouldn't. And *that* is how I know you're still you," Damon said with an answering smile as he opened the door for a peek outside. "Still the woman I've come to admire and—"

And love, he'd been about to say, but at the unexpected sight that greeted him in the hallway beyond, Damon fell silent.

"Yes?" Natasha prompted teasingly from behind him. "Don't hold back now, Damon. The woman you've come to admire and . . . ?"

"*Love*, I think he was about to say." In the hall, Wes

Brinkman folded his arms over his chest. He studied Damon and Natasha with knowing eyes—and no small measure of aggravation, too. "Isn't that right, Damon? That's what would fit your playbook right about now. After all I've done for you lately, it's really starting to piss me off."

Surprised to find the B-Man Media mogul standing outside in the hallway, Natasha gaped at him. Hanging back behind Damon, she double-checked to make sure her clothes were in order. Yep. Everything was fine. She could safely face the world outside.

Outside, where the party seemed to be continuing downstairs in all its raucous glory. Then she realized what Wes had said.

"*Playbook*?" Natasha asked Damon. "What playbook?"

Damon looked uncomfortable. He raked his hand through his hair, even though he'd already straightened it. He frowned at Wes. "You don't know what you're talking about, Wes."

"Oh, I think I do," Wes said. "I should have seen this improv coming, too. Only I was distracted by a sudden attack of . . . well, I guess you'd say it was *guilt* I felt." Wes chuckled. "Guilt over having booted you out of my place on Destiny's command. I know, I know." Jokingly, Wes held up his hands. "It's unbelievable, but it's true. *I* felt guilty. You're my friend, Damon! And Destiny and I are history. I realized after she left what an unbelievable ass hat I'd been, leaving you to fend for yourself in your hour of need, so—"

"I can't talk now, Wes." Damon took Natasha's arm, trying to usher her into the hallway past Wes. "Come on. Let's go."

But Natasha dug in her heels. Something about Damon's

guilty expression made her stay put. She wanted to know more.

"What playbook?" Natasha asked Wes.

"Well . . . *playbook* is probably overstating things," Wes admitted with another jovial chuckle. "We both know Damon isn't the greatest at executing a plan, right, Natasha?" He glanced at a tense-looking Damon. "No hard feelings, buddy, but it's common knowledge that you suck at follow-through. You're one hundred percent impulse and zero percent long-term strategy. That's why *I* stepped in to make sure your little scheme to take back what's yours from Little Miss Puppies and Rainbows here achieved liftoff."

Wes nodded toward her. Disbelievingly, Natasha arched her brows. "You mean *me*? *I'm* 'Little Miss Puppies and Rainbows'?"

"Hey." Wes shrugged. "They were Damon's words, not mine."

Openmouthed, Natasha looked at Damon. She wanted to know exactly what he was supposed to have been scheming to "take back" from her. But first . . . "You called me that?"

Damon glowered at Wes. "Only the 'puppies' part."

"*What*?"

"I may have likened you to a basketful of puppies," Damon told her in a low voice, "but only in the best possible way!"

Natasha couldn't think of a single "best possible way" those words could be used to refer to her. Especially by Damon.

Before she could find out more, Wes jumped in again.

"Damon doesn't know the half of it, though, does he, princess? He probably thinks you *spontaneously* crashed this party—this party that just *happens* to be full of movers and shakers and industry types you could—and did—schmooze with on Damon's behalf." Wes shook his head at

Damon. "This poor sap might even think you dragged him in there for a quickie just for the fun of it, when we both know the real reason was to avoid—"

"Hey! I *did* crash this party," Natasha objected before Wes could, damningly, go any further. "And as far as our encounter goes—" *No.* She wasn't going to discuss her quickie with Damon with *Wes,* of all people. "As far as my reasons for being here are concerned, at least *I* have what's best for Damon in mind."

"What's *best* for me?" In a tone of disbelief, Damon broke in. He grabbed her arm. "Natasha, what are you talking about?"

She couldn't tell him. Not like this. Instead, Natasha faced Wes. "When who knows what *you* want to accomplish," she said for diversion's sake, "with whatever you've been up to."

"With whatever I've been up to?" Wes mimed in an overly prissy voice, raising his brows. He laughed. "That's easy! It's no secret. I've been photographing you both. And videotaping you, of course." Appearing simultaneously proud and gleeful, Wes beamed at them. "I've been documenting the rehabilitation of America's favorite playboy, the king of chocolate himself, Damon Torrance!" Wes swept his arm toward Damon in a grand gesture. "The traditional media is going to go ape shit when I release the footage. People are going to eat it up! I might even be able to get a whole reality show out of it. *That's* the payoff I'm always looking for, right there," Wes informed Damon. "Even when I'm trying to be altruistic, I make money! And let me tell you, the whole world is going to want to watch Damon woo his true love, the wholesome single mom from suburbia. It's *so* romantic!"

"You *taped* us?" Menacingly, Damon advanced toward

Wes. "You followed us and filmed us and made a *reality show* out of us?"

"I *did*," Wes said, suddenly disgruntled. "I *was*. Until you blundered in here and threatened to screw up the whole thing by crashing a party and getting busy in the bathroom and behaving like . . . well, *not* like America's sweetheart. More like your old self. Which is why I called you and told you to get lost."

Damon fisted his hands. "You *filmed* us?" he repeated.

"Come on." Unconcerned, Wes waved off Damon's aggressive stance. He sighed. "Don't pretend you didn't see my crew. I know you spotted them a time or two. I saw it on the footage. I saw you spot a cameraman less than an hour ago—and ignore him."

Damon fell silent. This time, Natasha guessed, he couldn't even employ his favorite tactic and just brazen out the situation. Because Wes had deliberately called him on it.

It was true, then, Natasha realized with a sinking heart. Damon and Wes must had been conspiring to rehab Damon's damaged public image. And *she'd* inadvertently gone along for the ride.

"But don't worry," Wes assured them both. "We can edit out the sexy stuff." He leered toward the powder room. "As long as you skedaddle right now. After all, there's no point churning through unusable footage. Time is money." Wes rubbed his fingers together, cash-only style. "I have to give my crew full credit, too. They covered your rehabilitation with almost as much zeal as they did your breakdown in Las Vegas. God knows, it couldn't have been as dramatic." He shot a cheerful glance at Natasha. "That's a cute kid you've got, by the way. Milo, right?"

Natasha gasped. She could scarcely wrap her imagination around what Wes was saying. But it sounded, if she wasn't mistaken, as though Damon had set out to remodel his workshop-damaged reputation by the most expedient means possible. . . .

By pretending to date Little Miss Puppies and Rainbows.

By pretending to *love* . . . her. And having Wes document it all.

"Leave the kid out of this." Damon's face looked stony. "In fact, leave *all* of us out of this, Wes. I don't want—"

"Leave you out of it?" Wes laughed with obvious incredulity. "I can't do that. Not now. Come on, buddy. All's well that ends well, right? You got the girl. So what if your tender courtship winds up on TV? People are going to love the farmers market scenes. When you chose Natasha over all those panting, hot-to-trot Stepford Wives, I thought I might cry."

"Fuck off, Wes. You're sick." Damon shook his head, doing an excellent impression of being disillusioned . . . now that he'd been caught in the act. "I thought I could trust you. Hell, at one time, I even thought I was just like you! But—"

"You *are* just like him," Natasha said quietly.

Damon gawked at her. "I used to be. A little. But now—"

"You're *exactly* like him," Natasha forged onward, feeling almost overcome with grief and disappointment . . . feeling herself growing weirdly detached from this horrible revelation *and* the party continuing downstairs. "The only difference between you and Wes," she said, "is that you're less honest about it."

"Honest?" Damon's jaw tightened. "*You're* going to tell me about being honest? The woman who lied about being married?"

"Woohoo!" Wes said with relish. "*That* sounds intriguing! Tell me more. Maybe we'll make it into a bonus webisode."

Ignoring Wes, Natasha jerked up her chin. She stared at Damon instead, finding him suddenly . . . unfamiliar to her.

She couldn't believe she'd been so blind. She couldn't believe she'd bought in. All Damon's flattery, all his kindness, all his consideration had been false. She should have known him better.

She should have. But she hadn't.

And Damon's supposedly instantaneous, white-hot, super-sexy inability to resist her? That must have been a lie, too.

In retrospect, it all made sense.

"It looks that way, Pinocchio," she said. "It looks like I *am* going to tell you about being honest." With deliberate dispassion, Natasha crossed her arms. "But hey . . . I know what it's like. Pretty soon, you get in too deep to come clean, right?"

At least *she'd* told the truth before sleeping with him. Before falling for him. Before making promises to him.

Damon shook his head. In a cold voice, he said, "*I* don't have anything to 'come clean' about. And if you think I do—"

"I think you do. But I've heard just about enough for now." Squaring her shoulders, Natasha gazed directly at Wes. "You didn't have permission to film us, Wes. If you release that footage, I'll sue your ass off. Consider yourself forewarned."

"Ooh!" Wes made playful paws with his hands. He growled, then waved them in the air. "The puppy just grew claws." He guffawed, then elbowed Damon. "No wonder you're hot for her. Under all that composure and practicality, she's a feisty one."

Wasn't anyone taking this seriously? Heartsick, Natasha addressed Damon next. "I have to hand it to you. You really had me going. After all these years . . ." She shook her head. "I guess you never truly know somebody until you let them screw you."

Damon's eyes widened. "It wasn't about that! Natasha—"

"Good luck, Damon," she interrupted. Then she realized the irony of saying that to *him*, of all people, and tried again. "I *did* come to this party to try to help you," Natasha admitted. "I came here to network, like I've been busy doing all week, with the hope that I could get you on your feet again. I didn't tell you because I didn't think you'd come here if I did."

"You would have been right. I wouldn't have. But that's only because—"

"We were both on the guest list," Natasha went on. "The invitations came weeks ago. I got them from your office, with Jason's help, and I accepted them. I'd forgotten all about it until we walked by. But then I realized what a great opportunity this party might be, and it sounded like fun to crash, so I—" She stopped, then shook her head. "It doesn't matter anymore. What matters is, I felt sorry for you—"

"*Sorry*? For *me*?" For the first time, Damon seemed angry.

"—after what happened to you in Las Vegas," Natasha continued with a hitch in her voice. "I felt sorry for abandoning you the way I did. But you know what I just realized? It doesn't matter if I abandon you. And it doesn't matter if I stick by you . . . *again*. Again and again and again, like I always do. Because what matters is that you're no good at sticking by *yourself* when the going gets tough. *That's* what brought you down during your chocolate workshop with Tamala in Las Vegas—"

Damon's eyes widened. "You saw that? But I thought—"

"—*that's* what you're covering up with all your relentless swagger and refusal to grow up—"

He glowered harder. "I can't believe you can't see—"

"—and *that's* what's making me walk away right now."

With tears in her eyes, Natasha approached Damon. She put both hands on his shirt, straightened his tie, then smiled.

"I love you," she said. "That's the whole truth, whether you believe it or not. But I won't stand by and let you hide

away from the life you're meant to live—not even if doing
that would bring me you. I wanted to let you stay forever
and just play house with me, but that would have been
wrong. For both of us. So I worked to make things right, *for
you*, because that's what I'm best at." Natasha inhaled
deeply. She stroked his jaw, wanting more than anything to
throw herself in his arms and pretend this wasn't happening. "Now it's time for you to go back to your real life,
Damon. Go back to your easy, privileged, happy-go-lucky
life. Because that's what you're best at: being careless and
advantaged and lucky. Not being with me or Milo. Not
living in suburbia. Not any of it."

"I'm different now." Damon's eyes bored into her, dark
and full of what she imagined was anguish . . . even though
it couldn't be. At his sides, his fists tightened. That seemed
convincing, too. "I've changed," he said. "You *must* be able
to see that."

Natasha couldn't. Not then. Especially not a minute later
when, from down the hall, a short-haired brunette with
a lithe, lanky figure approached them. Her smile looked
tentative.

"Hey there, sailor," she told Damon, hefting the twin
cocktails in her hands. "I've been looking all over for you."

Natasha scrutinized the woman—and the vaguely shame-
faced way Damon greeted her. The brunette's bright-eyed,
tipsy gaze swept over Damon, Wes, and Natasha in turn. Her
attention swerved back to Damon. A coy smile edged onto
her face.

"Here are those drinks we were talking about," the
brunette told Damon flirtatiously. "You didn't bring them to
me yourself like you promised, you bad boy." She blinked,
belatedly catching the tension in the air. "Oh. Is this a
bad time?"

"Nope." Natasha took Damon's drink, knocked back the

whole thing, then gave back the glass to Damon's apparent next-in-line. "This is a great time—for me to say good-bye."

"Tasha," Damon protested in a beleaguered tone. "Wait."

But even his use of that affectionate nickname for her couldn't stop Natasha now. She felt much too hurt for that.

"No, Damon. I'm not waiting anymore. I've already waited a long time for you." She glanced at the perplexed-looking brunette. "Turns out, it wasn't worth it. You might think a few days in suburbia changed you . . . but all I see is the same old you."

"It wasn't suburbia that changed me!" Damon grabbed her arm. He gave her an almost-convincing pleading look, heedless of the rudely inquisitive way Wes watched them both. "It was *you*."

"Nice try." With a bitter laugh, Natasha finally broke free. "But I'm not dumb enough to believe that one twice."

Then she swiveled around and marched away . . . and this time, Damon didn't try to call her back. He didn't even argue his point again. Evidently, he'd already ceded her victory.

Too bad no victory had ever felt less victorious.

"Well," Wes said behind her, "I guess there's no point letting that last drink go to waste. How about sharing, doll?"

"Um, I brought this drink for Damon," the brunette said tentatively, "but I guess I could share with you, too. Is that okay with you, Damon? We *were* supposed to have drinks together—"

Natasha didn't stick around to hear Damon's response. She only set her Wellies in motion, hit the stairs, and escaped through the party into the formerly romantic night outside. This time, her beachside stroll would be a whole other experience.

But she knew she could handle it. She always had before.

Chapter 24

By the time Damon woke up the day after his unexpected falling-out with Natasha, it was late afternoon. Feeling bleary-eyed, hungover, and strangely hollow inside, he opened his eyes to find himself in a brightly lit bedroom he didn't recognize. Worse, he had no memory of how he'd gotten there.

It was just like old times.

Too heartsick to be alarmed by his unfamiliar surroundings, memory lapse, and pounding headache, Damon rolled over. He tried to go back to sleep, but for once the universe didn't cooperate. The dark, all-encompassing slumber he wanted wouldn't come.

Instead, fragments of the previous night's events paraded through his mind, jumbled and nausea inducing. Damon remembered accepting a drink—no, *several* drinks—from Sloane, the leggy brunette. He remembered meeting Sloane's party-girl friends. He remembered going to an after-hours club with Sloane and her flirtatious all-girl posse, spotting the B-Man Media crew that Wes had assigned to tail him and Natasha, and punching one of the cameramen in the face. He remembered shouting invectives, breaking a few cameras, and getting thrown out of the club.

He remembered feeling that destroying something that belonged to B-Man Media was only poetic justice. Because Damon had lost something. Now they'd lost something. Even Steven.

Except it wasn't even, Damon realized as he dragged his palms over his face, reluctantly growing a little more alert. *He'd* lost Natasha. *He'd* lost his hopes for a different kind of future. Without those, nothing else seemed to matter.

Last night, all Damon had wanted to do was forget. He'd wanted to box up the time he'd spent with Natasha and stash it away where it couldn't torture him anymore. So he'd done his best to revert to his old ways, which—while not perfect— were usually excellent at helping stem the tide of reality.

But for once, drinking and dancing and carousing hadn't worked. *Nothing* had worked. Nothing had made him feel any better. Because last night, as now, all Damon had wanted to do was brood. He'd wanted to rage at . . . someone.

He'd wanted to cry. And he still did.

Because he missed Natasha already. Because he couldn't stop wondering if Milo still wanted a piggyback ride and if Carol had remembered to take her recycling to the curb and if Natasha was really as hurt as she'd looked when she'd said good-bye to him. Because she'd looked wrecked and disillusioned and sad.

She'd looked the way Damon had felt. She'd looked . . . alone.

Hell. A few days in suburbia had totally unmanned him, Damon realized. He was probably better off without it.

He was probably better off without *her*.

As though underscoring that fact, someone shifted in the bed beside him. With a sleepy murmur, Sloane rolled over.

She saw him. She smiled. "Good morning, tiger."

Oh, Christ. What the fuck had he done now? He'd honestly

thought his days of waking up with near strangers were behind him for good. He'd honestly thought he'd changed.

Even if Natasha hadn't agreed.

"Sloane." Damon squeezed shut his eyes in instant remorse. "Tell me this isn't what I think it is."

"Well, I *could* do that," she hedged with a playful grin, "but that wouldn't be any fun, now would it?"

"*Fun*. Right." *My old pal.* Regretfully, Damon stared at the ceiling. Sunshine splashed into the room from its twin mullioned windows. "So, I don't remember much about last night, but—"

"But nothing happened. Between us, I mean," Sloane interrupted, giving his shoulder a nudge. "I was just kidding before. Wes told me it would probably go one of two ways—"

"I don't want to talk about Wes."

"—either you'd take one look at me and decide I was just the girl to drown your sorrows with . . . or you'd take one look at me and decide I could never replace the girl you *really* want." She gave him a compassionate look. "I guess you went for option B."

Nothing had happened. Engulfed with relief, Damon stared at Sloane, being careful not to glance any lower than her neck. Doing anything less wouldn't have been chivalrous. Because it seemed suddenly apparent to him that Sloane was naked. And that he was nearly naked, too, wearing just his boxer briefs.

"I did. *I* chose option B," Damon said. *Unbelievable.* Pride momentarily overwhelmed him . . . but a second later, the reprieve he experienced was followed by another dose of ruthless reality.

If even *he'd* doubted that he'd behaved himself last night—and he had, seriously, doubted it—how could he expect Natasha to believe in him? How could he expect her to believe he'd really reformed? To believe he *hadn't* used her in the process?

The painful truth was that he couldn't. Not yet.

Even Damon had to admit that the evidence against him looked pretty damning. Clueless Wes had seen to that.

"I'm sorry," Damon told Sloane, forcing himself back to the here and now. "It's not you, it's me. You're an interesting girl. Maybe under different circumstances, we could have . . ."

"Hey, it's not too late." Wearing an inviting look, Sloane rolled over to face him. The sheets dipped dangerously low, revealing the pert curve of her breast . . . and more bare skin that Damon made himself not look at. She propped her elbow against the mattress, then cupped her short-haired head in her hand. She gave him a direct, sensual smile. "I hear tomorrow's another day. If you want to give it a go, I'm game."

Rebelliously deciding that he owed it to himself to at least consider Sloane's offer, Damon looked at her. She was attractive. She seemed nice. She seemed eager for an easy, no-strings-attached encounter they would probably both enjoy.

She seemed . . . *not* to be Natasha. Damn it.

As kindly as he could, Damon shook his head. "I can't."

Sloane's raised eyebrows gave him pause.

"I mean, I *can*. I *can* all night long! But right now—"

"You can't. I get it." Sloane touched his beard-stubbled cheek. She heaved a regretful sigh. "If you ever change your mind, I programmed my number into your phone." She winked, then got out of bed, gloriously naked. "Just don't look at the accompanying photo while at work or in public. It looks a lot like . . ." With a seductive twirl, she held out her arms and then struck a pose. "Well, a lot like *this*. Naked, is what I mean."

"I'm hungover, not blind. But . . . I won't be calling."

"Yeah. I figured as much." Sloane shimmied into a pair of jeans. Topless, she took her time selecting a silky shirt from the nearby closet. Aha. This was *her* place, then. Buttoning her shirt, she added, "But a girl's got to try, right?"

"That's always been my motto."

"Good motto." Seeming surprisingly carefree, Sloane stepped into her strappy metallic sandals. With a graceful move, she fastened them on her feet. "I'm still glad I brought you home with me last night. You were in no shape to be alone."

Damon didn't have a ready response to that. He didn't doubt it was true, but given how little he remembered . . .

"Anyway, no hard feelings, Mr. Torrance." Sloane pointed to the doorway. "I'm meeting friends for brunch. Feel free to use the shower while I'm gone. Help yourself to whatever looks good in the kitchen, too." A grin. "I have to warn you, though, the fridge is pretty bare. I hope you like champagne and leftover chicken vindaloo. Just let yourself out when you're done."

"Thanks." She was an unlikely Good Samaritan, but Damon felt grateful for her help all the same. He watched her pick her way daintily through the other items strewn across the bedroom floor—most of them belonging to him. His dinner jacket. His trousers. His shirt and tie and studs. "You're very kind."

"Nah. I just recognize a useful contact when I see one." Sloane grabbed her cross-body purse and keys. "I'd still like to meet with you once you get your new project off the ground."

"My new project?"

"Yes." Sloane peered into the mirror, seemed to decide she looked presentable, then glanced at him via her reflection. "Your line of allergen-free candy bars. You couldn't quit talking about it last night. Anybody who came within earshot got the whole spiel. How it was going to open up a whole new underserved market. How it was going to revitalize gourmet retailing. How it was going to be aimed at kids instead of thrill-seeking foodies who want bacon-matcha truffles and chocolate shiitake ice cream. How it was going to be delicious and accessible and—most of all—safe for people with food sensitivities."

"I said all that?"

"All that and more, Mr. Wizard. You're quite a showman."

Damon made a disgruntled face. "That's me. The P.T. Barnum of chocolate."

"I'll bet you're a *lot* more than that." Giving him a sympathetic look, Sloane sat on the bed. Companionably, she said, "You've got depth, Damon. I can tell. Because *I* don't—I'm a publicist." She sounded surprisingly levelheaded—and admirably self-aware. Damon liked her. "Besides, last night, it sounded as though you had the whole thing already worked out."

"I'm not even close." *I haven't even dared to try*.

"Well, you must have some ideas tucked up in that famous brain of yours," Sloane told him. "Because you know what they say—no one tells the truth like a liquored-up playboy."

Damon laughed. "Nobody says that."

"I do," Sloane told him firmly. "Once your inhibitions are lowered, the truth has a way of sneaking out. That's why I always make it a point to take prospective business partners out for drinks. It gives me a better idea of who they are. And who *you* are"—she gave him a poke to his arm—"is a man with a plan."

"Ha. Somebody should tell my famous brain to share its ideas with the rest of me. Because right now, I'm tapped."

"It'll happen." With a shrug, Sloane stood again. "Which reminds me—my company is one of the ones who've been pursuing your former assistant, Natasha Jennings. Would you feel better if we opted out of the running? If you're planning to go for your new candy bar idea, you might want to hire her back. I wouldn't want to step on anyone's toes."

Damon froze, staring unseeingly at the windows. Of *course* Natasha had other prospects, he realized. He just hadn't thought about it until now. He hadn't wanted to think about it—hadn't wanted to consider Natasha moving on. Now he had no choice.

With effort, Damon shook his head. "There's no need for that. I won't be working with Natasha anymore."

"Are you sure?" Sloane pressed. "Because at the party, Natasha was networking pretty hard on your behalf. At least she was before our awkward encounter upstairs. I'm a little fuzzy on the details after that, but I remember being impressed with her diligence earlier in the evening. I guess she must have learned some of that by watching *you*."

"Nope. I'm only diligent when looking for a good time. Natasha's skills are all her own." Damon couldn't help grinning in remembrance. "She deserves all the credit . . . and then some."

"Aha. I get it." Wearing an annoyingly knowing look, Sloane leaned in the doorway. "*She's* the one. You're hung up on *her*."

Damon swore. "The hell I am."

"I see that look in your eyes. You've got it bad." Sloane's eyes sparkled at him. "Lucky girl, that Natasha."

"*Gone* girl. We split up. And I'm moving on." To prove it, Damon made himself get out of bed. His body teetered sideways. Forcibly, he righted himself. "I just believe in giving credit where credit is due. I'm a good guy in that way."

"Right." Sloane rolled her eyes, then held up her hand in a farewell gesture. "If that's ever really true—if you ever *really* get over her—then call me. In the meantime, there's a bottle of pain reliever and a bottle of Grey Goose in the kitchen cabinet. They live side by side, just like the good buddies they are. Just choose your poison." Sloane set down her business card. "And remember—let me know if I can get in on your new venture."

"If it ever happens," Damon said dubiously, "I will."

Then, left alone at last, he went to face down the Tylenol-versus-vodka challenge, not knowing until he got to the kitchen and opened the cabinet exactly which one he would choose.

Relief from his headache? Hair of the dog that bit him?

Either way, Damon was kind of screwed. He bit off another obscenity, then reached into the cabinet to make his choice.

Natasha was standing in Carol's portion of their duplex apartment building, surrounded by floral-upholstered furniture, tables with ornately carved legs, and various QVC tchotchkes, when she caught her first post-schism glimpse of Damon.

It wasn't a good one. He was on TV, being featured in grainy, poorly lit footage on one of those celebrity gossip shows as he left one of the city's most infamous after-hours clubs. He was still wearing his get-married, impersonate-James-Bond, officiate-a-wedding, conduct-an-orchestra suit from their romantic beachside stroll. He'd loosened his tie. He'd lost one of his gold shirt studs. His hair was all dark and rumpled, as though he'd been dragging his hands through it—or rolling around in bed, getting all sexy and uninhibited with God knows whom.

"It looks like notorious millionaire playboy Damon Torrance is back in action!" the shellacked, rail-thin TV commenter said in a scandalized tone. "Torrance, seen here leaving a popular night spot last night with not one but at least a *dozen* lovely ladies, suffered a breakdown not long ago following a highly publicized failed workshop at a chocolate conference in Sin City. But Damon *seems* to be rebounding nicely! Known for his lady-killer ways and his knack for publicity, the chocolatier—"

Click. The TV went dark. Semi-guiltily, Natasha jumped.

"Look, it's one thing to be in denial," Carol said as she came forward with the remote in her hand. "Which you are, obviously. But actively torturing yourself with that crap on TV? That's not a good idea." She shook her head. "There are some things you don't *ever* need to see. One is a B-list 'star' trying to stay relevant by fox-trotting in the sartorial equivalent of a tacky ice-skating costume." Making a wry face, Carol gestured toward the now-dark television set. "The other is *that.*"

"Maybe." Natasha lifted her chin. "But the camera doesn't lie. It obviously didn't take Damon long to move on."

Which only seemed to prove what Natasha had concluded last night—that Damon had never cared about her. He couldn't have. Not if he was already appearing in nightclubs with an eager entourage of a dozen women. Obviously, he'd only been using her.

Evidently, she'd been blinded by having all his charisma and good looks focused on her.

"It's not taking *you* long to move on, either. Not by the looks of that sharp business suit you have on." Carol dropped the remote in its designated wicker basket on the coffee table, then faced Natasha with her hands on her hips. "Are you still planning to go through with this cockamamie plan of yours?"

"If you mean am I still planning to go on a series of job interviews this week so I can support myself and my son, then the answer is yes. I am. I've put off taking this next step for too long already." Natasha drew in a deep, hopefully fortifying breath. "*If* you're still willing to babysit Milo, that is."

"Of course I am. I'll watch the monkey." Carol peered at her. "You need a little more concealer under your eyes first, though. The tear tracks aren't quite covered up. Come with me."

Tactfully not mentioning that Natasha had earned those tear tracks by sobbing into her lonesome pillow late into the night, wishing things could be different with Damon and wondering if *she'd* somehow caused the whole mess by being lovelorn and naive and inappropriately eager for sexy time with her hunky ex-boss, Carol bustled Natasha into the tiny bathroom. There, her former mother-in-law whipped out her makeup kit, pulled out a miniature pot of concealer and a brush, then went to work.

Natasha stood patiently while she stippled and smeared.

"Man." Eventually, admiringly, Carol stepped back to study her work. "My son isn't the only one in the family with artistic talent. This is an impressive concealer job, I have to say."

"Thank you. I'm glad it was you who spotted those dark circles and not the first interviewer," Natasha confided in a chatty tone as she looked into the mirror. "That would have been a disaster." She tried to chuckle and prove she was good to go. Easy-peasy. To her horror, though, the laugh she intended to give emerged instead as a weird, unconvincing honk. Her chin wobbled, too. Uh-oh. Natasha blinked extra hard, trying to stem the waterworks she felt looming. "After all, there's nothing more awkward than an overly emotional interviewee!"

"You're not overly emotional. Just human," Carol said gently. "And those weren't dark circles, dear. They were tear tracks. You earned them. Let's call a spade a spade."

"No, thanks," Natasha said with strained brightness. She squared her shoulders. "I'd rather not. Um, thanks anyway."

But there were the tears, all the same, threatening to over-take her in spite of her efforts to compose herself. *Stupid tears*. Feeling them flood her eyes, Natasha hauled in a deep breath. She blinked even harder, desperately fanning her face.

"I think my efforts to put on a stiff upper lip are crumbling," Natasha joked in a creaky voice. "I don't seem to be able to help myself. This happened last night, too. Usually I'm so good at taking things in stride, too. When my latest round of bad luck hits, I always shake it off. This . . . I don't understand."

"I know you don't." With an unexpectedly warm and em-pathetic look, Carol moved nearer. "This is new to you."

"No. I refuse to let this happen." Natasha grimaced. It felt like a near approximation of a smile. "See? I'm fine!"

"Oh, honey. No, you're not. You're not fine." With that galling announcement, Carol stepped even closer. Her lightly wrinkled face glowed with compassion and wisdom. Her eyes gleamed with decades of experience and kindhearted-ness. She looked at Natasha and shook her head. "You need a hug."

"A hug? Don't you dare! *You're* not a hugger!"

Carol never had been. Not during all the years they'd known one another. No matter what had happened, Carol had remained fairly impervious. She was a hard-knock woman . . . not unlike herself, it occurred to Natasha. Carol was tough but kind.

Carol was not a person who enfolded someone in her arms, patted that someone on the back, and murmured com-forting words. All the same, Natasha felt all those things happen. It was all she could do not to bawl even louder. Forcibly, she wrenched backward, putting some much-needed distance between them.

"What are you trying to do?" she demanded. "Make sure I bomb *all* my interviews today? You're my landlord! You should be keeping my fiduciary obligations to you upper-most in mind."

Carol actually laughed. "'Fiduciary obligations'? You've really got it bad, don't you? Next you'll be quoting tax code."

If Natasha could have mustered up a paragraph of IRS regulations, she would have, just to prove she didn't want all this sympathy and hugging. Mulishly, she settled for peeling off a length of the pink, gaggingly floral-scented toilet paper that Carol insisted on buying, then used it to dab her eye makeup.

"All right. Have it your way," Carol said with a frown. "If you're late on your payment this month, I'll charge you a big-ass penalty fee. Your bank account will cry uncle. Happy now?"

Natasha sniffled. "A little," she admitted.

"Good. Because I have more tough love on the way, if that's what you're in the mood for." With calm, deliberate gestures, Carol put away her makeup kit. "I think you're making a big mistake. I think you should forgive Damon and just get on with it. Because even if he *did* initially come here with the idea of making over his damaged image, like you told me last night—"

Suddenly, Natasha regretted all her sobbing just now. She also regretted her tearful, post-midnight tell-all session with Carol last night. But she hadn't exactly been thinking straight, Natasha knew now. It had taken her a while to sober up, get the beach sand out of her dress, and wrestle off her Wellies. She'd thought of confiding in Amy but had decided not to. Right now her pregnant friend needed all the angst-free slumber she could get.

"—that doesn't mean Damon didn't eventually fall for you *for real*," Carol pressed on. "That doesn't mean *you* didn't fall for him, too. So he made one mistake. People do that. It's not the end of the world. All you can do now is try to forgive him."

Natasha gazed at her former mother-in-law, feeling the urge to bawl receding more with every moment. She lifted her chin.

"That's a nice speech," Natasha said quietly . . . and sadly. She looked at Carol head-on. "The trouble is, it's not Damon I can't forgive. I *know* he screws up. It's me."

"You?" Carol looked baffled. "But you couldn't have known—"

"Yes, I could have. I'm the *only* one who could have known." Natasha shook her head. "Don't you see? *I* know Damon better than anyone. I should have realized from the start what he was up to. I should have kept myself from falling for it!"

I should have kept myself from falling for him.

"You couldn't have," Carol insisted, coming forward again with a consoling look. "You're being too hard on yourself."

"And *you're* being a pod person. Look at you!" Natasha cast a chary glance at Carol's outstretched arms. She stepped back. "Are you threatening to hug me again? Have you been possessed?"

"You are *always* too hard on yourself!" her former mother-in-law said. "When you and Paul broke up, all those years ago—"

"No. *Please* don't bring Pacey into this."

Carol looked confused. Too late, Natasha realized that she'd adopted Damon's habit of referring to her ex-husband as Pacey—probably because he seemed less and less relevant to her life as time went on. Paradoxically, it occurred to her, Damon had begun calling her ex Paul at some point—maybe because, once they'd gotten together, Damon hadn't needed to distance himself from her (supposedly intact) marriage anymore.

"I mean," she said more clearly, "please don't bring *Paul* into this. He doesn't have anything to do with me and Damon."

"Actually, he has *everything* to do with you and Damon," Carol countered. "I was there, remember? I was there when your marriage broke up. I saw how my son reacted. I saw how you reacted, too. Or more accurately, how you *didn't* react."

Determined to do exactly the same thing right now, Natasha crossed her arms. "I should get going. Traffic is—"

"Going to have to wait awhile," Carol interrupted. "Because I just realized it's about time I called your attention to a few things—like the fact that Damon Torrance had more to do with your marriage falling apart than you think."

"My marriage fell apart because your son cheated on me in his artist's studio with his 'muse' of the moment," Natasha reminded her, "who turned out to be a far better fit for him, by the way, than I ever was. And now I *really* have to leave."

Natasha turned. But Carol grabbed her shoulder, stopping her. This time, she *wasn't* doling out hugs, either. Uh-oh.

"Just tell me," Carol urged softly. "Was there anything going on between you and Damon then? When you first started working together? There were all those late nights. All those 'brainstorming' weekends. All that out-of-town travel—"

"No!" Aghast, Natasha stared at her. "We were launching Torrance Chocolates' boutiques and cafés all over the country. The expansion was difficult. Damon worked himself to the bone. I did, too."

Carol gave her a sharp-eyed look. "And you never once gave in to the temptation to turn that work into something more?"

Natasha couldn't believe Carol was seriously asking her this.

"I was married! For at least part of the time, Damon was married, too. Remember?" At the mostly forgotten memory of Giada Bandini, Natasha frowned. "Damon and I *never* crossed that line." She gave a rueful laugh. "For all I know, Damon never wanted to cross that line. Not with me. Not then, at least."

"Right. Okay. I guess *you* knew that. And *Damon* knew that." Carol shook her head. "But did *Paul* know that? Did he?"

"If he didn't, he should have asked. He should have talked to me. I was right here." Instantly irate, Natasha frowned. "And if you're trying to blame *me* for my marriage ending—"

"I'm not trying to blame anyone," Carol said. "I'm simply telling you what I know is true: All that time, Paul thought you and Damon were having a fling. He was convinced of it. He told me so. He thought he'd already lost you. All he could see was that you were part of a world he never could belong in, and—"

"I was doing it for *him*. For us!" Natasha cried. "I was doing it so he could create. *Both* of us couldn't be feckless artists. It wouldn't have been practical."

"—and that you were slipping away from him. So yes," Carol admitted, "Paul strayed. When he did, you reacted in exactly *this* way. You ignored the heartbreak and got back to work."

"Well, I couldn't exactly crumple," Natasha protested in her own defense, unsure what Carol was getting at. She didn't like thinking about those gray days when her marriage had broken up. She'd put them behind her already. She'd locked the door and thrown away the key. "I had to take care of Milo."

"It went beyond taking care of Milo," Carol insisted. "It went beyond just trying to cope! You had other options. You could have gotten counseling. You could have talked to

Paul. You could have given it another try instead of instantly giving up."

Natasha goggled at her. "I thought you wanted me to be with Damon. Now you're suggesting I should have stuck with Pacey?"

"No, with Paul." Again, there was that befuddled look. In a milder tone, Carol added, "What I'm suggesting is that maybe you should react differently this time. Last time, you put it all behind you immediately and pretended everything was okay. But it wasn't okay then, and it can't be okay now." Her former mother-in-law shook her head. "I *saw* you and Damon together. I saw the way he looked at you—the way you looked at him! Losing that has got to be a tremendous blow for you both. You were—"

"We weren't enough," Natasha interrupted with painful finality. "If I'm ever going to get the kind of job that will let me get past that, I really have to leave now."

Then, before Carol could stop her or hug her or otherwise cause her to lose her composure again, Natasha grabbed her car keys and headed away.

To her surprise, she made it all the way to her car, got herself strapped into her seat belt, and put both hands on the wheel at ten o'clock and two o'clock . . . and *then* she crumpled.

Then she gave in to all the heartache and loss she'd been feeling since last night. *Then* she considered what Carol had said . . . and wondered if some of it was true. And *then*, before Natasha could get too bogged down in pointless *if onlys* and meaningless *what ifs*, she turned the ignition key and got on with her life.

There was simply no way she could do anything else.

Not now, not later . . . and, knowing her luck, probably not ever.

Chapter 25

Five days later
Torrance Chocolates headquarters
La Jolla, California

In retrospect, the thing that struck Damon the most was that all he'd needed to get started was a teensy nudge from someone who believed in him. All he'd needed to start working on his prototype allergen-free candy bars were a few simple words.

You must have some ideas tucked up in that famous brain of yours, Sloane had told him after their night-together-that-wasn't. Then, to put the icing on the cake . . . *It'll happen*.

Damon hoped it *would* happen. With every passing day, he was becoming more and more hopeful that he'd succeed this time.

Because, ironically, what Damon couldn't do for himself, a near stranger had done for him. Sloane had gotten him started, with no untoward pressure and no unmet expectations looming over him. Now, days after he'd first set foot in the previously unexplored and terrifyingly intimidating territory of the Torrance Chocolates development lab, Damon had yet another array of samples for his panel of volunteer taste testers to try.

"All right," Damon told them as he set down a tray filled with bite-size mockups, each carefully portioned in a fluted paper cup and numbered according to its designated batch, "you all know what to do by now. I don't want any sugarcoating. I want honest opinions. If the sample you try is bad, tell me. If it needs more of something or less of something, tell me." He paused, then delivered the panel—composed of longtime Torrance Chocolates employees and one rogue UPS delivery person—a smile. "Of course, if it's fantastic, I want you to tell me that, too."

One of the assembly line packagers raised her hand. "Are all of these allergen-free samples? Because I'm new to this, and I heard that's what you're testing." She made a repulsed face. "I'm *so* not down with gluten-free this and sugar-free that and stuff made with weird chemicals. I like *normal* food. I'm only here because I forgot to pack a lunch, and I'm starving."

The assembled group tittered. Damon nodded.

"I like normal food, too. That's exactly what this is," he told her. "Some of these samples *are* allergen-free chocolates. Others aren't. It's a blind taste test. It's important to me that this new candy-bar line stacks up against anything else out there. There's no point creating something new if it can't compete and doesn't enhance the existing product lineup."

"I think I got one of the allergen-free samples." Another tester, from the HR department, peered dubiously at the sample she'd chosen from the tray. "Can I have another one instead?"

"No. Just go ahead with the one you have, please."

The woman sighed. She took a hesitant, mouse-size nibble.

Damon watched patiently. He shouldn't have felt defeated by the panel members' obvious—and enduring—skepticism, but he did.

This was only the latest of several tests he'd conducted over the past few days. Even though Damon kept hoping and expecting it might be different, it never was. Everyone greeted his painstakingly developed new product samples with wary uncertainty. Everyone expected the chocolates to taste . . .

"Medicinal," the UPS employee chimed in. He frowned as he chewed his chocolate. "Mine tastes medicinal. Ugh."

There was a general murmuring of agreement while everyone else bit and chewed and sniffed and frowned. Even the simple one hundred percent dark chocolate bar wasn't receiving high scores, Damon noticed. Oddly enough, his most difficult challenge—a bar filled with nondairy, coconut milk-based caramel and egg white-free nougat, studded with crispy, chocolate-enrobed, gluten-free French feuilletine and covered in semisweet chocolate—appeared to be leading the pack. Its scores trended even higher than the leading commercial chocolates he'd employed as a baseline.

Frowning, Damon watched as the testers poured themselves palate-cleansing glasses of water from the table's pitchers. Still chattering about the drawbacks of their samples—or bragging that *they'd* luckily gotten "regular" chocolates—they wiped their chocolaty fingers and filled in their scorecards.

Why am I even doing this? Damon wondered. He'd gotten by just fine all these years without trying to *create* something in the chocolate lab. This was his father's territory. Jimmy made concocting delicious new truffles and interesting new chocolate drinks seem like child's play. In fact, when he'd been a child, Damon remembered in that moment, he *had* played in the lab.

He'd enjoyed it, too. He'd forgotten that. But now . . .

You're no good at sticking by yourself when the going gets tough, Damon suddenly remembered Natasha telling him on that fateful night when she'd left him at the party. *I won't stand by and let you hide away from the life you're meant to live.*

Unfortunately, just then, the life he was meant to live seemed to include lots of negative feedback and disappointing results. At the thought of them, Damon just wanted to quit.

But the memory of Natasha's final words to him simply wouldn't let him. He had to keep going. Because maybe things hadn't worked out with Natasha . . . but the way Damon figured it, he still had some unfinished business to take care of at the Jennings household. He still had to create a scrumptious, allergen-free candy bar for Milo. He still had to *win*. For Milo.

With the memory of that Dr. Seuss-loving, piggyback-riding, video-game-playing munchkin in the forefront of his mind, Damon rallied.

He surveyed the grimacing, extra-critical test panel members, then put his palms together in a determined gesture.

"Thanks for your feedback, everyone. It'll be very useful when I get back to tempering the next batch." As the testers scraped back their chairs and prepared to leave, Damon glanced at the clock. "I'll have more samples ready by the close of business today. Everyone who wants to be part of the next phase of Torrance Chocolates, meet me back here at five o'clock."

Pointedly, no one looked at him. But one of the marketing interns stopped by on her way out. She touched Damon's arm.

"It's admirable of you to try this, boss," she said. "But it's been . . . well, I've lost track of how many batches we've tested by now. You might just have to admit it: Maybe you're just a successful, rich, incredibly handsome networking genius who *isn't* very good at the creative side of things.

We all have our niches to fill. Maybe yours isn't going to be filled here."

Her glance took in the chocolate lab, then centered on the testing table at the midpoint of it. On it were the samples tray—now holding only a few tipped-over, forlorn-looking empty paper cups—and the pile of negative hand-written ratings sheets.

"Face it," the intern said. "You're working really hard for not much return. You should probably just call it a day."

Near the Pacific Ocean
San Diego, California

It wasn't easy chasing a toddler who was determined to give the seagulls a run for their money, Natasha learned as she dropped the plastic shovel she'd been using to build a sandcastle with Manny and took off after little Isobel instead.

Those pudgy wee legs could really move. Determinedly, Natasha raced after the giggling little girl, joined her in a delighted game of Let's Wave at the Seagulls, then picked her up and carried her back to their picnic blanket and sun umbrella.

"Whew! And I thought keeping track of *one* child was hard!" Natasha told Amy as she plopped on to the blanket beside her pregnant friend. Together, they watched Manny and Isobel return to patting the damp beach sand into a lumpy fortress. Mostly, their creation involved piles of sand and a gigantic moat, which Manny gleefully filled by plunging a bucket into the surf. "How in the world are you going to manage with *three* children, all under the age of five?"

"Oh, I'll get by okay," Amy assured her, shielding her

eyes from the sun as she studied her children. "It's not just me, all by myself, you know. It's Jason, too. He'll be there."

"Well, you can't count on *him*," Natasha countered automatically. "I mean, he might be working late or auditing someone or fighting crime or improving his golf game or—" She floundered, running out of options. "Or, um, he could be—"

"Running off with his secret mistress? Launching a scheme to take over the world?" Laughing, Amy shook her head. "They're all equally ridiculous, and no, he won't. Jason is a keeper. I keep telling you, not all men are like Paul." Amy looked away. Casually, she said, "For instance, *Damon* isn't like Paul. He's—"

"He's not on the menu of subjects to talk about, remember? Besides," Natasha pointed out justifiably, "Damon hasn't always been your favorite person in the world."

"I know." Amy sighed. She looked back at Natasha. "But you can't just pretend nothing ever happened between you two!"

"Sure, I can." Natasha struck a goofy, ultra-aloof pose. "See? I'm doing it right now."

"Very funny. My point is, now that the initial shock has worn off, maybe you two can talk reasonably. It can't hurt."

"That's what you think. It *can* still hurt. Believe me, I know." Every day it hurt, and it didn't look as if things would improve anytime soon. Every time Natasha picked up a book to read to Milo, every time she walked the familiar path to Milo's school, every time she looked at a tail-wagging Finn or walked in her front door . . . Damon was there. Except he wasn't. In his place was a big, empty hole, and Natasha had no way to fill it again. "Anyway," she said, "I'm too busy to talk to Damon. This is the first break I've had from interviewing all week."

"And you're spending it with us." Happily, Amy smiled

at her. She cradled her expanding belly, absentmindedly stroking it. "How's the job hunting going, anyway? Made any decisions?"

Natasha shook her head. "It's been weird, actually. All the job offers I've had are terrific. They really are. They're all lucrative and plenty tempting. But none of them would give me the same autonomy and freedom I had as Damon's assistant."

"Really? But I thought the demands of working at Torrance Chocolates were what kept you from doing your artwork?"

"Yeah. I thought so, too. But now it looks as though that situation would be even worse elsewhere." Contemplatively, Natasha watched the waves breaking on the beach. She swept her hair from her face, shivering at the sea breeze. "I'm starting to think maybe it wasn't my job at all. Maybe it was me."

"Well, you could always pursue artwork full-time," Amy ventured, pulling Isobel closer to spray her little arms and legs with a fresh dose of sunscreen. She kissed her head, then set her free and started in on Manny. "You gave up art so quickly after you met Paul. You never really had a chance."

"I know. The thing is . . . maybe it's never been what I really wanted to do. Maybe Paul was just my excuse for quitting." Natasha hugged her legs to her chest, then rested her chin on her knees. "It *was* a big relief to switch majors and ditch the weekly critiques I used to get from my fine arts professors."

"Hmmm. Better for the ego that way, that's for sure."

"Exactly!" Natasha laughed. "No fear of failure. If you don't try, you can't lose." Which sounded a lot like Damon, it occurred to her. Except he'd tried *too* hard in Las Vegas.

With Damon, everything tended to be all or nothing.

"So what do you want to do now? Keep job hunting?"

"Maybe." Natasha shrugged. "I might have to. With my luck, all those companies I've met with will withdraw their offers."

"Right. You're *so* unlucky that all the companies that have been pursuing you for weeks now will give up on you just when you decide to say yes." Amy's caring, unexpectedly exasperated gaze met hers. "I really wish you wouldn't do that."

Natasha blinked. "Do what?"

"Use that 'bad luck' excuse of yours to explain away every ordinary, garden-variety event that ever happens to you."

"That's not what I'm doing! I really *am* unlucky."

"Really? Are you?" Skeptically, Amy peered at her. "Are you sure you're not just using that bad-luck stuff as an excuse? You've already excused yourself at least once before, you know, when you convinced yourself *Paul* was the reason you quit art—"

"He *was* the reason!" Natasha said. "Except . . . I just realized he wasn't. Probably." She bit her lip, feeling uncertain. "I don't know what to think anymore. Quitting Torrance Chocolates and leaving Damon has set me kind of adrift, I guess."

"So it's probably better to avoid the whole thing, right?"

"Right," Natasha agreed emphatically, feeling happy that at least *someone* understood her for a change. "Absolutely."

For a second, the only sounds were the gulls, the waves, Manny and Isobel's nonsense chatter . . . and the guilty, confused beating of Natasha's heart. She lifted her head.

"That was a trick question, wasn't it?" she asked.

Amy smiled. "You'd better believe it."

"You wanted me to realize that avoiding the issue isn't the answer." At her friend's answering nod, Natasha sighed. "What is *up* with you people lately, anyway?" she wanted to know. "Have you been taking lessons from Carol or what? All of a sudden, I can't so much as make a sandwich without my former mother-in-law demanding I reexamine my perspective on things."

"Well . . ." Amy offered a nonchalant shrug of her own. "Maybe you should give it a whirl sometime. Maybe it would help."

With a refusal already on her lips, Natasha stopped herself. Instead of saying no, she only gazed out at the ocean. She remembered how beautiful it had looked during her moonlit stroll with Damon. Then, quietly, she said, "Maybe I will."

If nothing else, it was a start. A tiny, barely noticeable start. But it was better than nothing. She was on her way.

"I really thought I was on my way!" Damon told Jason at 5:15 that evening. With a sweeping gesture, he indicated the paper-cupped chocolate samples, the fresh pitchers of water at the testing table . . . the conspicuously *empty* panelists' chairs. "I really thought I was making progress. And now . . . zilch. There's not a soul here. Not even that guy from marketing who always talks in buzzwords and tells me how 'awesome' everything tastes."

"He's been angling for a promotion, bro." Jason crossed his arms. "He thinks if he brownnoses you enough, you'll put in a good word with your dad. And speaking of Jimmy . . ." Damon's buddy looked around quizzically. "Where is he? He's *always* here in the lab."

"I don't know. He hasn't been around all week—which is probably for the best, frankly. I can't create *and* try to make amends with my dad." Despondently, Damon plopped on the rollaway cot he'd had brought into the lab. He fluffed his pillow, then swiveled on his back and brooded at the ceiling.

"Why didn't anyone come to the five o'clock tasting panel? What do I have to do?"

"Wait. Is that cot for you?" Jason asked. "Has it been here all week? Have you been *sleeping* in here?"

"Don't they know I need testers? Don't they know I can't do this without them?" Damon lamented, feeling unfairly put upon. "I'm trying to do a good thing here," he told his buddy. "I should be rewarded for that, shouldn't I? I'm kind of new to this one-hundred-percent-good-deeds stuff, but—"

"You *have* been sleeping in here." Jason crossed his arms, marveling at him. "You are completely gone over Natasha."

Damon scoffed. "She has nothing to do with this. Besides, even if she did . . . so what? Like *you* never threw yourself into work to forget a girl. Remember, back in college? You—"

The chocolate lab doors burst open, interrupting him.

"Hey! Am I late to the party?" Wes Brinkman strode in, full of his usual wiseass joie de vivre. "Where's the candy?"

"Get out of here, Wes. I don't want to talk to you."

"Yeah. Get lost," Jason said, backing him up. With a certain undeniable zeal, he added, "*You* don't get any candy."

Wes laughed. "Nice to see you, too, Huerta. You're just as sanctimonious as I remember. And Damon . . . well, you're still pouting over Natasha, I see. You disappoint me. You and your newfound faithfulness are a disgrace to millionaire playboys everywhere." Wes clucked with dismay. He strode to the sample table, plucked up a miniature, chocolate-covered sunflower-seed-butter cup, then ate it. His eyes lit up. He selected another variety, then eagerly swallowed it, too. He picked up a third, then used it to point to Damon. "They're going to throw you out of the club, you know. You're playing with fire here, with all this . . ." Wes gave a moue of distaste. "Relentless *work*."

"I mean it, Wes." Getting up, Damon flexed his jaw. "You're the last person I want to see right now. After what you did—"

"After what *I* did? Oh no. You can't offload all this on me," Wes insisted, shaking his head. He gobbled up the last chocolate he'd selected. "Why didn't you tell Natasha the truth that night, dumbass? You know damn well you didn't do anything close to what she accused you of." With another head shake, Wes ate more chocolate. "Instead you just stood there and took it."

Damon glared at him. "You wouldn't understand." He could still see the crushed, inconsolable look in her eyes. Stonily, he strode across the room, trying to forget. "I let her down."

"Did you?" Wes seemed intrigued. "I understand it probably looked that way. *I* didn't realize it at the time, of course, because I was completely smashed." He gave a sweeping bow, as though he expected applause. "But you have to admit, if you *had* been trying to win the fair lady's heart for your own nefarious reasons—to rehab your dinged-up public image—you would have done *exactly* what you did. You would have charmed her, wooed her—"

"But I didn't do that." Feeling confused, Damon stared at Wes with his hands clenched at his sides. "I mean, I *did*, but not for the reasons she thought I did. Anyway, the point is—"

"The point is," Wes said grandly, "that *you* need to cut Little Miss Puppies and Rainbows some slack here. Give her a break. It's not easy living with men like us, you know."

Jason boggled. "You're right about that. You're working on my last nerve, B-Man." He stepped threateningly nearer.

Wes only laughed again. "Settle down, Huerta. There's no need to get thuggish. I only came here to tell Damon something." His gaze swiveled to him. "You expected her to believe you'd changed. You wanted her to validate that, even without your explaining it to her." Wes held up his palm. "Don't bother denying it. I could see it in your eyes," he said, forestalling Damon's interruption. "But nobody else can do that for you. Believing you're good enough is *your* work to do."

"Right." Feeling beyond cynical, Damon folded his arms. He gave Wes a hard look. "Did you read that in a fortune cookie? Or was it included in one of your many sets of divorce papers?"

"Neither one." Wes tapped his temple. "It's all up here."

This time, Damon laughed outright. "Get real. You're hardly in a position to hand out relationship advice, Wes."

"Well . . ." Hesitantly, Jason nodded. "He might have a point."

Damon wheeled around to face him, even as Wes went on munching his way through the array of chocolate-testing samples.

"If there's one thing I've learned from being married to Amy," Jason rushed to say, "it's that everybody has their own sore spots to deal with. And sometimes, when your sore spots collide with *her* sore spots . . . well, disaster strikes. Maybe that's what happened with Natasha. Maybe *she* couldn't give you what you needed—and *you* couldn't ask her for it because . . . Hell, I don't know why. I'm no shrink. I'm just a guy with a wife and a couple of kids. All I know is, maybe you're giving up too soon."

"Giving up?" In disbelief, Damon stared at him. "I've been working my ass off all week. I'm not giving up on anything!"

"You're giving up on her." Wes picked up a swirled candy bar with bittersweet chocolate and a cherry center. He ate it, then nodded with approval. "Don't be a dick, Damon. Go get her."

"I *can't* go get her," Damon insisted. "Not yet."

Not until I make things right. Not until I make me *right.*

Being with Natasha meant too much to him. Damon couldn't risk screwing up. Not with her. Not again. He already knew what colossal failure looked like, and he wasn't interested in re-experiencing it.

In frustration, Damon stared at Jason and Wes. They didn't understand. Jason had Amy. They were the perfect couple. And Wes . . . well, Wes had everything *except* a perfect partner. Including a ridiculous amount of sheer, balls-out, well-meant audacity.

Frankly, it was just like old times between them.

In the silence, Jason nodded toward Wes. "The idiot savant of relationship advice is right. It's time. Go get Natasha."

"Hey!" Wes burst out, looking offended. Then he shrugged. "Never mind. I guess that's fair." He picked up a few more cups of chocolate. "These are really tasty, by the way. Yum, yum."

Taken by surprise, Damon blinked at him. "You like them?"

"Are you kidding me? You'd have to tie me to a tree, cover me in honey, and let fire ants bite me on the testicles to get me to quit eating these things," Wes said emphatically. "Even then, I'd probably try dipping the chocolate in the honey."

"Okay." Making a disgusted face, Jason turned to Damon. "Word of advice? *Don't* go with that testimonial in the advertising."

Damon laughed. "I won't. But . . . you *really* like them, Wes? Some of those chocolates are"—he hesitated—"allergen-free."

"So?" Wes licked his fingertips. "Does that mean they're full of bizarre ingredients or something?" A shrug. "I can't pronounce half the things in a chicken nugget, and I eat those."

"Hmmm. Good point." Damon thought about that. "And

no, they don't contain anything bizarre. The trick is thinking about all the things I *can* include instead of the few things I can't."

"Whatever, Martha." Wes went on chomping. "I don't know squat about chocolate making, but I know what I like. These."

"Well, it's unlikely you're being tactful," Damon told him. "After all, you're *you*. If you hated my candy bars, you'd tell me. You're a giant walking ego. You think everyone cares what you think—and needs to know about it, the moment you think it."

"If you're trying to tell me they don't . . . save your breath."

Ignoring that, Damon looked anew at his chocolate samples. "Maybe," he mused aloud, "what I have here is an image problem, not a taste problem."

Doubtfully, Jason picked up a fluted paper cup full of pea-size, candy-coated chocolate pieces. He sniffed at their TC-imprinted exteriors. He rattled the cup. He tasted a chocolate.

"Nah, dude. It's a taste problem," Damon's friend assured him, making a face. "These allergen-free candies are nasty."

"Those are the standard-issue Torrance Chocolates' take on M&M's." Damon crossed his arms. "You eat them by the pound."

"Oh." Awkwardly, Jason tried another one. He nodded. "Yeah. Yeah, now that you mention it, they *are* the same. Delicious!"

"Actually, I was wrong. Those *are* the allergen-free ones."

"Huh?" Jason looked unhappy. He hung open his mouth, looking for a place to spit. He waved his hands in disgust.

"Oh, grow up, Huerta," Wes said. "You're proving Damon's point for him. He was obviously doing blind taste

tests with a group of biased participants as volunteers. They
expected the allergen-free candy bars to taste 'weird,' so
they hated them."

"Right. And they didn't come back for more." From the
open doorway, Jimmy Torrance spoke up. He strolled
inside, hand in hand with his wife, Debbie. "Probably because you made the taste tests voluntary. Always make the
tests mandatory, son."

"That's right," Debbie agreed. "At this point, you'll need
an all-new test group, Damon. Because the idiot savant of
chocolate testing had it correct." She gave a cheerful wave
to Wes. "Hello, Wesley. Thank you for that enormous dona-
tion to my children's aid charity. It's much appreciated."

Red-faced, Wes gave her a "shut up!" wave. "You said
you wouldn't tell anyone about that! I have an image to
consider."

But Damon didn't have time for Wes's not-so-secret altruistic streak. He boggled at his parents. "Mom? Dad?
What are *you* doing here?"

Jimmy sighed. "We tried not to be here, believe me."

At his side, Debbie cuddled up to him. "We were *enjoying* our time together away from this place. *If* you catch
my drift."

Momentarily mystified, Damon looked from his dad to
his mom. They so rarely took time off. Then, "Oh. Gross!
You were—"

"Repairing our relationship," Jimmy said smoothly, patting Debbie's hand. "I neglected it for far too long. I didn't
even know how to find my way back. All I did was work. I
didn't know how to retire. But luckily for me—"

"Luckily for him," Debbie finished with an impish look,
"I took matters into my own hands and kidnapped him! I
took your father to a lovely resort, where we could both be
alone—"

"The seafood platter there is *excellent*," Jimmy put in.

"—then I gave him an ultimatum. 'Choose your marriage or choose to be a full-time chocolatier,' I told him, 'but if you choose the business over me, I'm through.'"

"Obviously," Jimmy said. "I chose her."

"Wow," Wes breathed in awe. "You don't mess around."

"No, she doesn't." Jimmy gave Debbie an adoring smile. "That's just one of the many things I love about her. Somehow, Debbie knew just how to snap me out of it—just how to make me realize that I was about to lose the best part of my life."

"Dad, you have a son, too," Damon complained. "I'm *right here*. What am I? A big pile of stale, leftover chocolate?"

His parents sighed. "You're important, too, son," his mother assured him. "But we're married. It's different." She gave him a piercing look. "I saw you on TV, by the way. On that gossip show. You're cruising for a kidnapping of your own, Mister Smarty-Pants. If you think you're too old for a little parental intervention to cure your bad behavior, you're wrong."

Wes blanched. "I think that's my cue to leave." He seized a few more chocolate samples for the road, then waved. "Later, all."

"Me too," Jason said. "If I get home too late, Amy invariably thinks I've been hit by a bus." Sheepishly, he shrugged. "It's kind of her thing. She's a worrywart."

"Only because she loves you!" Debbie called after him, waving. "Say hello to your lovely wife for us!"

Left alone with his parents, Damon stared at them in continuing disbelief. "Seriously. What are you doing here? Are you going to tell me you had a sudden urge to go all Chocolatier Rambo on a few hundred pounds of Tanzania seventy perecent cacao?"

Jimmy and Debbie shook their heads. "Several of the

longtime employees here called us," Jimmy said. "We didn't get their messages for a few days, because we were . . . preoccupied. But once I turned on my cell phone to find a whole slew of panicked voice mails telling me that *you'd* gone off the deep end again—that you'd been working in the lab night and day, *sleeping* here, running emergency thrice-daily test panels—we were concerned."

"If you *have* lost it again, dear, we're here for you," his mother promised him warmly. "We were distracted by our marital problems for a while there, but now that's all settled. So don't worry about a thing."

"No, I haven't 'lost it' again. I'm fine." Damon gave them a brief recap of his split from Natasha, offered a synopsized version of his ideas for the new candy-bar line, then finished up with a rundown of his nearly 24/7 progress so far. ". . . except for the testing snag I just hit."

Worriedly, his parents listened. Then, his father said, "We think you should make up with Natasha first. Don't wait too long, like we did!"

At their newfound synchronicity, Damon couldn't help smiling. He really was glad they'd worked out their issues.

"I can't think about that now," he said. "First, I have to deal with this testing issue—" *And prove, tangibly, that I've accomplished something for once.* "—then I'll talk to Natasha."

Jimmy nodded. "All right. It sounds as though the boy's decided. Let's get down to brass tacks on this testing issue, Damon. Do you know of another group you could approach?"

"Actually," Damon said, "I do. One just came to mind."

"Good," his father said. "Then the next thing to do is—"

"Wait." Damon put his hand on his dad's arm, recognizing that Jimmy was about to bustle forward and take charge of the chocolate lab. "Are you really going to help me? I thought—"

"You thought your father had given up on you?" Debbie asked.

At his mother's blunt, spot-on assessment, Damon frowned.

"Well," he hedged, "I haven't given either of you much reason to believe I'd amount to anything on the creative side of things. Especially after Las Vegas." At the memory, Damon shuddered. "Knowing how much I messed up, why would you—"

"Because we're your parents, that's why. We'll never give up on you. We might get wrapped up in our own lives some of the time. We're only human. But that doesn't mean we've given up on you. Far from it." Gruffly putting an end to the discussion, his dad picked up a nearby chocolate sample. He chewed. Savored. Swallowed. "I think you need less sugar here."

Damon still couldn't believe Jimmy was going to help him.

"But . . . this is *your* territory, Dad. I've never been good at the creative stuff! What if . . ." Suddenly, Damon could scarcely say it. With effort, he forced himself to. "What if I really try, and I *still* can't do it? What if this is Las Vegas, all over again?" He gestured at the lab. "This is your life! You *are* Torrance Chocolates! How would you feel if your legacy was handed over to a colossal, globe-trotting screwup?"

At that, his father gave him a serious look. Through wise and experienced eyes, Jimmy examined him. He smiled. "You're not a screwup, son. You just need some practice." He shifted his gaze to Debbie. "If I hadn't been hogging all the creative duties to myself, you might have gotten that practice sooner."

Well. That *might* be true, Damon reasoned. Still . . .

"Besides," Jimmy told him, "it's not the result that matters. It's having the courage to try. Without that, you're doomed from the start." He looked around at Damon's cot, his samples, his notes and packaging mockups and everything else. "You're got courage to spare, Damon. You always have. I'm proud of you for that."

Incredibly, Damon felt tears clog his throat. With a burst of self-conscious emotion, he cleared it away. Damn, but this bawling stuff was hitting him hard lately. What the hell?

"Okay." Roughly, Damon attempted a more manly tone. "Okay, good. Thanks, Dad. Just so we're clear on things. Because—"

Because I've been afraid of doing this for years, he realized then, *and now it's finally happening. With you.*

"Because," Damon tried again, smiling, "you're going to want to retire soon and get on with all that resort-going."

"He means whoopee," his mother informed his father shrewdly. "He knows what we were up to at that resort, Jimmy."

"I know that, Debbie." Damon's father clapped Damon on the back. "By the way, son—there's something I've been meaning to tell you. So while we're here clearing the air . . ."

Cautiously, Damon nodded. "Okay. Go ahead."

"Okay." His dad nodded, too. "Ever since you were a little boy, you've had the idea that you were especially 'lucky,'" Jimmy began. "We let it slide because we thought it was cute. But you're a grown man now. You need to face the facts—"

"You're no luckier than anyone else," Debbie broke in urgently. "You're just not. We're sorry, but it's true."

Stricken, Damon gazed at them. "Yes, I am," he insisted. It was a bedrock belief of his life. "I'm *really* lucky."

His parents only laughed, then rolled up their sleeves.

"Whatever you need to tell yourself, son," his dad said.

Then, leaving Damon no choice but to come along for the ride, they all got down to the serious business of turning raw cacao into something even better: artisanal chocolates made with love.

Chapter 26

Natasha was in her garden-shed workspace, putting the finishing touches on a new piece she'd been inspired to design, when the sound of someone rustling around outside caught her attention. Going stock-still, she paused at her worktable and listened. Soon enough, the sounds came again—a scrape and a thump from outside, followed by a very human-sounding grunt.

Alarmed, Natasha put down her artwork. Wiping her hands on her grungy jeans and then straightening her T-shirt, she headed outside to investigate. There, she glimpsed her backyard, her own slice of blue San Diego skyline . . . and her next-door neighbor, Kurt, who was in the throes of what looked like a wrestling match with a potted blossoming Jacaranda tree . . . or at least a very large sapling. Its branches were already covered with slender green leaves and myriad purple blooms, several of which dropped off in a flurry as Kurt maneuvered the potted tree toward—

"Is that a *hole* in my lawn?" Natasha blurted.

Kurt started. Almost dropping his tree, he gave her a guilty look. "Natasha! You're supposed to be at an interview."

"I canceled it." Bewildered, she gestured at what had obviously been a lot of work. "Kurt, what are you doing?"

"Something I agreed to do a couple of weeks ago," her neighbor replied with cheerful determination. "Since no one ever told me there'd been a change of plans, I'm finishing the job."

"You're digging a hole in my yard and secretly planting a *tree*?" Natasha wanted to glower at it to prove her point, but she loved the flowery beauty of Jacaranda trees way too much to pull off a bad attitude about being given one. Not that Kurt knew that. She settled on crossing her arms. "Did Carol put you up to this? Is this supposed to cheer me up or something?"

Kurt shook his head. With another manly grunt, he released the tree from its container. "I promised not to say."

"You have to say," Natasha insisted. "It's *my* yard!"

"It's supposed to be a surprise." Diligently, Kurt loosened the potting soil around the tree's root ball. With an awkward movement, he rolled the tree into position, then started planting it. "But I *will* tell you it wasn't Carol's idea."

"Then whose idea was it? Amy's? Jason's? *Milo's*?"

Her neighbor merely shoveled more dirt. "You weren't this nosy the last time I did some secret yard work for you."

"When did you . . . ?" At Kurt's raised eyebrows, Natasha remembered. "When I got back from Las Vegas! My whole yard looked fantastic." She gave him a sly look. "You acted as if you were as surprised by my 'garden pixies' as everyone else."

"What was I supposed to tell you? That I couldn't take your yard's Godzilla-size weeds anymore?" Kurt wiped his brow. "I was trying to be a good neighbor. It was just a little tidying up."

"Then it *wasn't* part of my lucky streak," Natasha murmured, half to herself. Kurt's semi-puzzled headshake confirmed it.

Hmmm. If *that* experience was being called into question, it suddenly occurred to her, what did that mean for the other

things that had happened to her recently? The things she'd
attributed to good luck? Like her magically well-running
Civic? Her minor lottery win? Her airborne flirtation and
date with Lance the neurosurgeon? Her thousand-dollar jackpot from the airport in Las Vegas? Her newfound ability to
enchant, ensnare, and get lucky with Damon?

Were all those things just easily explained *events*, too?

They could have been, Natasha realized. Her Civic had
been running better lately because she'd become more conscientious about getting routine maintenance done. She'd
been buying weekly scratch-and-win lottery tickets for
years now; she'd been bound to win sometime. She'd been
feeling pumped-up and proud on the plane back from Las
Vegas, psyched over finally standing up for herself with
Damon; no wonder she'd been attractive to Lance. And
the odds of winning an occasional jackpot on a slot machine weren't that bad, especially in a high-traffic area like
the concourse at McCarran International, where many
people pumped in their quarters and hoped to get lucky
before their flights left.

And Damon? Well, Natasha couldn't quite account
for him.

But if her good luck wasn't real, then maybe Amy had a
point about Natasha's enduring bad luck, too. And maybe,
just like Carol had implied, Natasha's habit of die-hard sto-
icism in the face of tough times was just not working for her
anymore.

Maybe it never had worked. Witness her split with Pacey.
Their breakup hadn't been great. Whose was? But theirs
had dragged on longer than necessary because she'd stuck
her head in the sand and refused to admit it was happening.
That's why, in the end, her divorce papers had come as such
a shock.

Maybe she *wasn't* unlucky, Natasha mused. Maybe she
was just ignoring the parts *she'd* played in those sporadic

catastrophes—in all those mishaps, big and small. Everything from her Civic's flat tires to her marriage's failure to her readiness to believe that Damon had colluded with Wes in an effort to rehab his damaged public persona could be explained by Natasha's determination to believe that bad things "just happened" to her.

Because if bad things "just happened" to her, there was no use in reaching for more . . . right? If she was so "unlucky," then she was also safe from recrimination, safe from trying . . .

Safe from leading the life she wanted to live. Whoops.

"Well. The least I can do is help you plant that."

Resolutely, Natasha grabbed a shovel from the cache of yard tools leaning against her shed. Then, before turning around, she gave the other tools a long, second look. She bet they would fit inside the shed *along with* her artwork and supplies.

Maybe she didn't need them to be kept apart anymore. Her artwork was still important to her. Being creative still meant a lot to her. But now, Natasha realized, it was just another part of her life, like riding bikes with Milo or teaching Finn to catch a Frisbee. Her artwork—and the garden-shed workspace where it happened—didn't need to stand for independence or sacrifice or anything else that *might* have been. Now it could simply be what it was: an artistic outlet, a pleasurable activity . . . a hobby.

Finally feeling at peace with that, Natasha scooped up a shovelful of dirt from the mound Kurt had made. She dropped it next to the tree's root ball, then went back for another load.

"If you were this attentive to weed pulling," Kurt cracked with a teasing look, "I'd never need to be a garden pixie."

"I'm really sorry, Kurt. I'll try to do better, I promise."

Her neighbor shrugged. He leaned on his shovel, then

gave her a contemplative look. "You really can't guess who did this?"

Natasha eyed the tree. She shook her head. "I really can't. It must be someone who knows me pretty well, though. My love of Jacaranda trees isn't exactly a secret, but I don't run around shouting from the rooftops about it, either." She mulled over the question of her undisclosed benefactor. "Does this have something to do with Valentine's Day?" she guessed. "Because today's the big day, after all. Milo was all fired up about it before school started. And the women in my running club have joked sometimes about giving each other 'We Hate Valentine's Day' gifts. You know, just so nobody gets too depressed about all the lovey-dovey, hearts-and-flowers, we're-destined-for-eternity couples' talk that happens around this time of year."

"Hm. And I thought *my* friends were jaded. We all get drunk, have a beach bonfire to burn old love letters and Valentine's Day cards, throw darts at our exes' photos, wear black, blast 'Love Stinks' on nonstop repeat, and have an anti-Valentine's Day movie marathon with *Heathers* in top billing." Kurt considered the issue some more. "Oh, and we totally ban all chocolate in heart-shaped boxes . . . until it goes on sale on the fifteenth of February, of course. We're not idiots. We just don't like being coerced into thinking sappy romantic thoughts against our will."

"You seem like an unlikely choice for a secret tree-planting mission to commemorate Valentine's Day," Natasha observed wryly. "I hope your friends don't disown you."

"They'll never know. This is the *backyard*, after all."

"Well, that's true." With vigor, Natasha shoveled another scoop of dirt. "You know, this looks really nice next to my garden shed," she observed. "It even complements the paint job."

"Yes." Kurt nodded. "That's what Damon said. He told me—"

Abruptly, her neighbor clapped shut his mouth. With newfound industriousness, Kurt went back to shoveling.

"*Damon*?" Natasha asked, astounded that her offhanded inveigling had actually worked to root out the truth from Kurt once he'd let down his guard. "*Damon* put you up to this?"

Guiltily, Kurt looked at his shoes. He offered her a tentative grin. "Would you believe . . . garden pixies did it?"

"No. I wouldn't."

"Would you believe . . . Carol did it?"

"No, I wouldn't." Galvanized by the thought that *Damon* had thought of giving her this Jacaranda tree, with all its lovely purple flowers and shady foliage, Natasha stared at it. "This tree," she told Kurt when she'd begun breathing again, "is the polar *opposite* of a 'sorry I broke your heart' bouquet. This tree is a growing, changing, *living* and enduring thing!"

"It might be," Kurt said dubiously, "if we finish planting it. It's been out in the sun awhile now. It might be—"

But Natasha couldn't listen to his attempts to backpedal now. With a new burst of energy, she grabbed Kurt's arm. "Do you know what this *means*?"

He hesitated, biting his lip. "Uh, it means you're going to have to mulch it regularly?"

"Yes! I *am* going to have to mulch it," Natasha agreed excitedly. "In a manner of speaking, of course. In the sense that mulching is a protective, ongoing, nurturing process that—"

"That will have to wait," Carol finished for her, interrupting as she marched into the backyard with something small in her hand. She raised it. "Milo forgot his epinephrine injector. He's waiting for you to bring it to him at school."

"But—" Dismayed, Natasha glanced from her mother-in-law to Kurt to her new Jacaranda tree. That tree all but proved that Damon had loved her *once* (even if he didn't anymore), because something as mundane as a landscaping tree wasn't a showy romantic gesture—it was a *thoughtful* one. It wasn't the kind of thing a disgraced playboy would do to try to look like a dutiful suburban romantic on a webisode of one of Wes's new-media shows.

It was the kind of thing a man who cared about her—who wanted the space beside her garden-shed work area to be pretty and welcoming and nurturing—would do. The kind of thing Damon would do . . . now that he'd been trying so hard to be a better man.

"But I just realized something about Damon," Natasha protested, swerving her gaze back to Carol. "I should try to find him. I should—" She broke off, knowing that in the end, there was really no argument. "I should take this to Milo before he has an emergency," she agreed, striding to her mother-in-law. She took the injector from her. "His teacher keeps a spare EpiPen on hand, but I'd better not take any chances. They're having a Valentine's Day party at school today. There are bound to be goodies."

"Good." Carol nodded. "I'll go with you!"

"But—" Mystified, Natasha looked at her. "Why? If *you* can go to the school, then why do *I* have to go to the school?"

"Me too!" Kurt announced, dropping his shovel. With relish, he rubbed together his dirt-grimed palms. "I'll drive."

Watching them both sprint away, Natasha shook her head. "But I can drive!" She followed them to the driveway. "Why—"

"Don't ask questions!" Carol blurted. "Just come on."

Wondering suspiciously if there was more going on here than an ordinary mission to deliver Milo's epinephrine injector, Natasha followed them. "All right," she said. "But after this," she informed her impromptu entourage, "I'm going to see Damon!"

"Whatever," Carol said with a blithe wave. She traded a glance with Kurt. "If you still want to do that, you can."

Then, on the heels of that cryptic statement, they all piled into the cab of Kurt's vintage flatbed truck and sped away to Milo's elementary school.

With an unexpected stab of nervousness, Damon paced across the room he'd been using to set up his latest taste test. On the twin tables in its center, trays stood ready with chocolate-filled, fluted paper cups. Near the trays, pitchers of water and modest-size glasses awaited. He didn't want his subjects getting filled up on water; he wanted them focused on the samples.

This time, the chocolates provided were *all* allergen-free mockups; no traditional or commercially available samples allowed. That, along with the small water glasses, had been Jimmy's suggestion. Also among his father's bright ideas were improved packaging examples (whipped up in a flash by the innovative Torrance Chocolates design department), evocative and appealing posters highlighting the potential new line, and a bonus: an appearance by the Torrance Chocolates mascot.

Unhappily ensconced in the mascot suit, Jason trudged to Damon's place in the room. He yanked at the collar of his furry suit, looking very much like an unhappy six-foot-tall sea otter who was temporarily holding his oversize head under his arm.

"Do I *have* to do this?" Jason complained, putting his fuzzy hands on his fuzzy hips. "This suit itches like a mother—"

"Aw, come on, honey. I think you look cute!" Amy said before Damon could reply. From her place at the room's window, she looked up from the toys she'd been using to entertain Manny and Isobel. "You look like my big, strong snuggle bunny!"

"Don't you mean your 'big, strong snuggle *otter*'?" Jason frowned. "Shouldn't we get started pretty soon? The faster we kick off this thing, the sooner I can shuck this suit and go back to looking like a man instead of a walking stuffed animal."

"Soon. It's not quite time yet." With another attack of nerves, Damon stalked to the window. He glanced outside. "I'm still waiting." He cast an apprehensive glance at Amy. "Do you think Carol pulled it off? Do you think she'll get her here?"

"Have you *met* Carol?" Amy asked with a grin. "Once her mind's made up, she'd rather eat rocks than take 'no' for an answer. She'll get her here. You can count on it."

The problem was . . . Damon *was* counting on it. He truly was. If this maneuver failed, he didn't know what he'd do next. All the hearts and flowers and love songs and pink balloons and street-corner flower vendors he'd glimpsed on the way here today had only served to underscore the crucial nature of his mission.

Today, he *had* to succeed. He *had* to make up with Natasha.

Whether he'd proved himself to anyone or not.

"I shouldn't have set up things this way." Damon wrung his hands, still pacing. He thought he might actually be sweating. That never happened to him. But then again, now that he knew he *wasn't* really unusually lucky (just a tad overconfident) and never *had* been unusually lucky (just allowed to believe he was), a lot of things might change for him. Now all he had to rely on were his own hard work and innovative nature . . . which was really all he'd had all along, anyway.

"I should have waited until I had workable prototypes

and rave reviews!" Damon said, still pacing. "I should have waited until this was an unequivocal success."

Amy shook her head. "Natasha never wanted you because you were a success. She wanted you because you were *you*."

Damon was afraid to believe her. "That's easy for you to say. You're one half of the ultimate couple. But Natasha—"

"*Is here*," Jason interrupted. He pointed out the window at a parked flatbed truck, indicating the two women and one man who'd just gotten out of it. "Put on your game face, big shot," he told Damon with an uneasy look. "It's go time."

Chapter 27

Inside the bright front office of Milo's elementary school, Natasha signed in on the requisite visitor's sheet. She stated her purpose for coming to the school, exchanged some chitchat with the receptionist, then glimpsed the vice principal.

"Ms. Jennings!" the woman cried, coming forward with a cheerful look. Warmly, she clasped Natasha's hand in hers. "It's so nice to see you again. We've been expecting you."

"Thanks. It's nice to see you, too." In actuality, Natasha had just seen the vice principal—and Milo's teacher, and several others on the staff, along with a multitude of parents—at the latest PTO meeting. Which didn't explain why everyone in the school suddenly beamed at her as though she'd been lost at sea and had just today staggered home. "I'm sorry to interrupt. Milo forgot his epinephrine injector at home, so I brought it."

"Indeed, you did! We've already called Milo to the office."

"Oh, good. Thanks."

"But while you wait, why don't I issue some visitors' passes to you and your guests?" Before Natasha could refuse, the vice principal and her receptionist outfitted everyone with pin-on name tags. "There." The vice principal beamed. "All set."

"But we don't really need passes," Natasha said, eager to cut short this visit so she could get to Damon. He was probably at home at his renovated beach house, contemplating his next power move at work. Or at an all-day margarita bar, considering quitting work altogether. Either way, she didn't care. "I'm not volunteering today, so we won't be staying. Look, there's Milo!"

Spotting her son, Natasha waved. Her towheaded boy pulled open the door connecting the front office with the rest of the school. He trotted in, looking strangely pleased with himself.

"Hi, Mom!" Milo waved, then gave her a hug. When he pulled back, he waved at Carol, too. "Hi, Grandma! You guys are going to have so much fun today!" He spotted Kurt. "Hi, Kurt! I hope you like candy. There's going to be a *lot* of candy at my class's Valentine's Day party. It's just about to start!"

"Oh, Milo . . ." Natasha hesitated. "I wasn't planning to go to your party," she said gently. "I'm not volunteering today."

"It's just a party, Mom. You already have visitor passes."

"Right." Natasha looked to Carol and Kurt for support. Peculiarly enough, they left her hanging.

"I like candy!" Carol said, comically rubbing her belly.

"Me too!" Kurt added, joining in. "Lead me to it."

"But . . ." Simultaneously wanting to settle things with Damon and *not* disappoint her son, Natasha wavered. "I didn't even bring anything to share. Maybe I should go buy some Sweethearts or something—you know, those Necco conversational hearts with the sayings printed on them? You like those, Milo. They're made on dedicated nut-free production lines, so they're safe."

"There's no need for that, Ms. Jennings." The vice principal leaned in to offer a confiding, twinkly-eyed glance.

"We have a special guest here at school today. He's brought special allergen-free candy to share with all the children."

Natasha stared at her, momentarily speechless. All she could think of was that Damon had lost his big chance. If someone else already had devised a full-range line of "safe" candy that appealed to third graders like Milo . . . poor Damon.

"It's true, Mom. Come on!" Milo urged, taking her hand.

That's how, an instant later, Natasha found herself headed down the hallway in her eager son's wake. Any second now, she'd be settling into a pint-size chair, surrounded by hyped-up students. Any second now, she'd be watching those students trade cartoon valentines. Any second now, she'd step into Milo's elementary school classroom—decorated with plastic-lace doilies and a pin-up chart of cursive handwriting instructions—and probably join in cutting out construction paper hearts herself.

Any second now, she'd be . . . seeing *Damon*, standing outside?

Staring in disbelief, Natasha moved faster. At her side, Milo guffawed. He gave Natasha an elaborate poke. "Look, Damon! I did it!" Milo crowed. "I got my mom to come to school, just like I said I would! I told you I could do it!"

Still gaping, Natasha trailed after Milo, who (unbelievably) rushed ahead to hug Damon. Then, after trading a few whispered words with him, Milo nodded. He pulled open the classroom door, gave a very hammy summoning gesture to Carol and Kurt, then winked at Damon. "There you go, pal! Alone at last!"

At his chirpy, theatrical tone, Natasha burst out laughing.

Then the door shut behind Milo and the others, leaving her alone with Damon. Still hardly able to believe he was really there, Natasha came to a stop a few feet from him. She glanced through the classroom door's rectangular slice of window, spied Amy, Isobel, and Manny, myriad third graders, and . . . an otter?

"Is that *Jason*?" she asked. "In the mascot suit?"

Damon hadn't moved. He was still practicing his best one-shouldered, casual lean against the hallway wall— a move he'd perfected years ago, as far as Natasha was concerned. He gazed at her. Somberly, he nodded. "It's Jason. How did you know?"

"Jason has a funny walk," Natasha said matter-of-factly. "It's as if he expects his feet to fall off at any second, so he shuffles around to make sure they won't have very far to drop."

Damon laughed. "That's it exactly." He shook his head, as though marveling at her. "I can't believe you're really here."

"I can't believe *you're* here—along with everyone else who got *me* here, of course." She wanted desperately to move closer. But now that she was here, she felt ridiculously tongue-tied. Also, enlightened about a few things that had happened to her so far today. "Carol, Milo, Kurt, Amy, Jason . . ." Jokingly, Natasha gestured at her family and friends. "I can tell when I've been set up, Damon. Is there anyone you *didn't* draft to help you pull off this little surprise of yours?"

"I couldn't wait any longer," Damon said in a husky voice. His gaze met hers, dark and magnetic. Then he frowned. "But by the time I realized that, I was already committed to this school appearance. I couldn't just skip out on it. I'd met the vice principal and some of the office staff when I used to pick up Milo and walk him home from school, and we hit it off." Damon's shrug suggested that the mostly female school staff had been more than helpful . . . as usual for him. "When I had the idea to try a testing panel composed of the intended target market—kids—this was the first place that came to mind.

And they agreed! It was only serendipity that it was Valentine's Day this week, and—"

"Thanks for the Jacaranda tree, by the way," Natasha broke in, daring to take a tentative step closer. "I love it."

"—and I'm talking too much. I'm sorry. You probably have no idea what's going on. But then, I'm kind of winging this." With a sheepish grin, Damon shoved his hands through his dark, wavy hair. He took a step closer, too. "The truth is, Natasha . . . I've missed you. So much. I'm *so* sorry for everything that happened with Wes. He got it all wrong! You have to believe me."

"I believe you," Natasha said. She took another step.

"It was all just Wes's boneheaded idea of being helpful," Damon went on in a desperate tone. "He's new at it. He screws up a lot. We *do* have that in common. But I didn't know anything about what Wes was doing. I didn't lie to you. I *never* meant to hurt you! Please, *please* believe me about that. I—"

"I believe you." Natasha took his hand. It felt . . . great.

"I—" Damon stared at their joined hands. Evidently without any volition on his part, he'd tightly clasped her hand, too. Looking befuddled but determined, he forged on. "Before we were together—back in Las Vegas—I realized I didn't like my life anymore," he said in that same raspy, emotional tone. "I didn't like how it felt. I didn't like where it was going. I didn't like who *I* was in the middle of it. But I didn't know how to get out of it." Here, Damon gave a rueful grin. "I guess my public on-camera meltdown kind of did that for me, right?"

Compassionately, Natasha squeezed his hand.

"But I *did* know I liked being with you," Damon went on. "I always have. You rescued me. You stood by me. You made me laugh and you kept me on my toes and you weren't fooled by all my bullshit, either. You were tough. But fair. You were—"

"Yeah. I sound like a real peach," Natasha joked.

Damon smiled. "You *were*. You were the best. And that's why, after my workshop debacle, when Tamala came to my hotel suite—"

"I'm not sure I want to hear this."

"—I let her dupe me into that whole chocolate body painting idea. I let her tie me up and make me a molded nougat thong—"

"La la la!" Natasha sang, playfully covering her ears.

"—and I did it *on purpose*," Damon persisted. "I'd blown it with that workshop because the pressure was too much for me. Afterward, I needed a kind word. I needed a hug. I needed—"

"Kinky sex with a diabolical pastry chef? Well, Damon—"

"—I needed *you*," Damon finished urgently, squeezing her hand again. His eyes met hers once more. "I knew that if I was really in trouble—really, *really* in trouble—you would come."

"I came, all right." Racked with remorse, Natasha looked away. "Then I left you there all alone." She transferred her gaze to Damon again, loving the way it felt to be near him, even if it only lasted a little while. "I'm so sorry for that, Damon. I don't cope well with major emotional events. Or with minor emotional setbacks. Or even with unexpected good fortune. I just sort of freeze up and then go into move-ahead mode. I've just realized that—thanks to my family and friends. So that night, at the party, when we had that run-in with Wes—"

"It killed me to watch you walk away from me."

"—it was just the excuse I needed to bail out," Natasha said. "I couldn't believe, after all these years, that you really wanted *me* for *me*, Damon. I couldn't believe I'd finally gotten lucky in the biggest way of all: in love. So I left."

"I didn't follow you. I'm so sorry for that."

"It wouldn't have mattered." Feeling a fresh allotment of

fast-acting tears—the only kind she seemed to produce lately—brimming in her eyes, Natasha decided to make things quick. "I wasn't ready then. But I'm ready now." Suddenly, inspiration struck. Her sometimes faulty memory rebounded. With a new rush of hopefulness, she raised her wrist. "See? This proves it!"

With raised eyebrows, Damon examined her. "Your bare arm?"

"What?" Baffled, Natasha gave her wrist a second look. Whoops. With an equally melodramatic flourish (maybe Milo came by his theatrical bent naturally, it occurred to her), she raised her other wrist. "No, *this*," she said. "My bracelet."

For an instant, the only sounds were their breathing.

Well, that *and* the boisterous noise of twenty-odd sugar-hyped third graders trading valentines just beyond the closed door. But that wasn't as romantic to Natasha as the near silence in her overactive imagination would have been. Or as romantic as the look on Damon's face was as he nodded at her bracelet, then raised his solemn gaze to her face.

"It's eclectic," he said. "I like it."

Natasha couldn't help sighing. "You *remembered*."

"What you said about your jewelry? Of course I remembered." Damon gave her a dazzling smile. "Thanks for showing me."

"Oh. Right. You're welcome." Caught up in the wonder of his familiar, long-lost smile, Natasha stood there bedazzled and mute for a second. Then, "It's for you!" she blurted, wrestling with the clasp on the heavy platinum chain links. "I made it for you. In my art workshop." Finally, she wrestled it off.

With utter earnestness, she fastened it on Damon's wrist. If he didn't like it, if he rejected it, rejected *her*, after all this time, Natasha thought in a dither, she didn't know what she'd do. She felt as if she might die. Or cry. Or scream.

Nodding, Damon admired his gift. "I like it." With a blithe look, he glanced up. "Does this mean we're going steady?"

"No, you dope!" Helplessly, Natasha swatted his arm. This time, the tears she'd held back *did* fall. "It means I love you!"

"Hmmm." Damon's shining eyes met hers. His mouth quirked in another teasing grin. "It's not inscribed any-place."

Did he have to joke about *everything*? "Actually, it is. You have to turn it over." Natasha watched in agonized suspense as Damon read the inscription: THANKS FOR BRINGING BACK THE FUN. LOVE, N. "But the point is," she went on, "I love you, Damon! I've loved you for *so* long. I love your smile and your generosity and your knack for always making me feel sexy. I love your way of reading to Milo. I love that you let Finn sleep on your head. I love that even when everything is going great for you, you don't even realize it, because you're just happy to be alive. I love that you have fun, and I love that you make mistakes—because without that, you'd be pretty insufferable, frankly—and I love that you're *here* right now, with me. I don't care how it happened—"

"It happened because I made it happen," Damon finally said in a fierce, impatient voice. "Give me some credit, will you?"

Then, before Natasha could muster up the credit he'd just demanded she give him—or anything else even remotely laudatory—Damon pulled her in his arms, crushed them both against the waiting wall, and kissed her.

Spellbound and incredulous, Natasha kissed him back. Their mouths met in a way she'd only dreamed about during the long, sleepless nights she'd spent lately, and when their kiss was finally over, when Damon finally lifted his head and smiled at her . . .

When he did that, Natasha only reversed their positions and

kissed him harder. Because Damon wasn't the only one running this relationship. *She* was, too. If he didn't like that . . .

His low, erotic moan suggested he *did* like it. A lot.

Well . . . *good*, Natasha decided. Because she liked it, too.

"If I can get a word in edgewise, I'd like my turn at telling you a few things, too," Damon said breathlessly, still holding her in his arms. "Only *somebody* issued a demand, years and years ago, that I *never* tell her I love her—"

He meant her, Natasha knew. *Don't tell me you love me*, she'd demanded in his office on that long-ago day when they'd first met. *Don't flirt. Don't* . . . Well, the rest didn't matter now.

"Only because I never thought it would be true!" she interrupted hastily. "Only because I couldn't have you."

"You only had to ask." Damon kissed her again. He stroked her cheek, then delved his hand in her hair. "You could have had me at the drop of a hat. All you had to do was say the word."

"The word?" Natasha grinned, feeling happy and fulfilled and more full of hope than she had since . . . forever. "What word?"

"Well, technically, today it's two words." Damon released her. He stepped back, then gestured at the door. "Open sesame."

"What? I don't get it." Natasha scrunched her nose, wondering if all this exposure to Crayolas and glue had affected Damon's brainpower somehow. Then she just decided to take a leap of faith. Why not? It had already brought her this far.

"All right." Natasha faced the closed classroom door. Dutifully, she did as Damon suggested. "Open sesame."

Chapter 28

As leaps of faith went, Damon decided as he opened the classroom door for Natasha, his was a pretty immense one.

Feeling as though he were straddling a chasm between total contentment and utter ruin, Damon held his breath. He glanced at Natasha. He took her hand and led her inside Milo's class.

"They're here! They're here!" the kids shouted.

In chaotic glee, the third graders scrambled around the classroom. Hastily, they grabbed the posters and pictures and big, red, heart-shaped construction-paper valentines they'd made in class. In unison, they hoisted their assorted celebratory items, all in appropriate shades of pink and white and red.

All in the shades of the sappiest love of all.

In obvious confusion, Natasha looked at him. "What's going on?"

"Just hang on." Damon squeezed her hand. "We practiced this part earlier today, but they *are* little kids, after all."

Then, "Happy Valentine's Day!" the children screamed.

They filled the room from wall to wall, gleeful third graders madly waving posters. Someone—possibly the romantic-minded teacher—turned on an upbeat love song. In the center of the room, Milo proudly yanked a string, releasing dozens of red and pink heart-shaped balloons. On both sides of the doorway, two little girls flung out Valentine's Day confetti, literally showering Damon and Natasha with it.

Openmouthed, Natasha touched the confetti in her hair.

"Come see mine next!" With his heart pounding, Damon pulled her to the marker board. He stepped back, then waved. "Ta-da!"

Natasha's brow furrowed. "Spelling words for next week?"

"What?" Terror-stricken, Damon did a double take at the board. Through hazy vision, he saw . . . "It's supposed to be—"

"Gotcha." Natasha grinned. "Payback for that 'are we going steady?' remark a while ago." Then she took a closer look at the image that had been drawn on the board. "Are these two puppies in love? I see hearts shooting everywhere. But those two snuggled-up creatures in the middle are all wobbly."

"They're *us*!" Really panicking now, Damon swept his arm toward the marker picture he'd drawn. "They're *us*, in love! It took me two hours to draw that. I had to start over and over—" Desperately, Damon rushed to the adjacent marker board, almost bulldozing Jason the Otter in the process. He apologized, then kept going. "Look! There's one over here, too. It's a little better." He pointed. "There's you, and me, and Milo, and Finn—"

"*I'm* carrying a Dr. Seuss book!" Milo pointed out gleefully from across the room. "There's still a lot of them you haven't read to me yet, Damon. Like *If I Ran the Zoo*. It's kind of like *If I Ran the Circus*, only with a zoo. It's really good. Maybe it can be the next one you read to me?"

Where everything else had failed, Milo's comment seemed to make Natasha take this seriously. She gazed around the room at all the eager, poster-holding children, at all the balloons, at all the confetti and construction-paper hearts . . . and smiled.

"You arranged all this for me?" Natasha asked.

"Well, most of it," Damon told her honestly. "The party was happening anyway. I just hijacked a part of it." He handed Natasha a hand-scissored, hand-colored, hand-glued valentine. "There's a lot of glitter there," he said. "The construction paper looks cheap. The tacky plastic white doily behind it isn't aesthetically correct. But it's the best I can do, so—"

Natasha lifted her gaze. "It's eclectic. I love it."

Damon couldn't help laughing. Maybe he was becoming hysterical. "Did you just say . . . never mind. Screw your demands."

The teacher gasped. "Mr. Torrance! Language, please."

"Sorry," he told her. Then he took Natasha's hand—the hand that wasn't holding his woebegone excuse for a *non*-verbal love declaration—and stared straight into her eyes. "I love you, Natasha. You're just going to have to get used to hearing me say it. I love you in the morning, when you're all crabby and groggy. I love you during the day, when you won't stop talking and planning and running around. I love you at night, when—"

Here, Damon broke off. He gave the wide-eyed kids and their eavesdropping teacher a cautious look. Then he looked at Jason. "This might be a good time for the candy-bar tasting, Mr. Otter."

Mr. Otter saluted. Then he all but skipped to the other room to fetch the already prepared chocolate samples they'd brought. With that settled—and the children all clamoring in his wake to be the first to try the goodies—Damon turned to Natasha again. With a lump in his throat the size of Wisconsin, he hauled in a deep breath. He gazed into her eyes. He smiled.

"I love you with all my heart, Natasha. I've been waiting

so long for you. All I ever wanted was to be loved—to know what it's like to have someone waiting for me, someone caring for me, someone needing me . . . and *you've* been that for me, all along. I don't know how I've gotten by without you these past few days, because once you kissed me, I couldn't think about anything else. There's only you. Just *you*. You make me want to try harder and be better and give you more and more—"

"All I need is you!" Natasha insisted, and she looked just as beautiful and generous and necessary then as she always did to him. "All I've ever needed is you, with me."

"Well . . ." This was the really hard part, Damon knew. "If you'll have me, you've got me. Please, Natasha. Say I didn't make myself look like a fool for nothing—"

"The drawings aren't that bad. I was only kidding!"

Damon gave her a quizzical look. "I meant with the ring. It's impulsive, I know. If you accept it, it *will* mean we're going steady, in a way, but since you're ignoring it—"

"Ignoring it?" Now it was Natasha's turn to look confused. "I'm not ignoring anything! Not the balloons or the music—"

Patiently, Damon smiled at her. "Look closer at the valentine I just gave you. You know, the crappy-looking one with all the glitter and the plastic lace. Right in the middle—"

"Is a gargantuan diamond engagement ring!" *Really* wide-eyed now, Natasha gawked at it. "I thought that was fake. I've never seen one that big. Not *ever*. I—" She broke off, gazing at him. "I don't know what to say," she breathed. "I'm in shock."

"It's as real as my love for you," Damon assured her. "Only a great deal smaller. They don't make them in infinity size."

At that, Natasha bawled as hard as Damon wanted to.

"Yes!" she cried, prying at the carelessly glued-on gem. "If you're asking me to marry you, Damon, the answer is yes!"

"Don't worry about protecting my sorry attempt at being artistic. You won't hurt my feelings. Rip that sucker apart."

The sound of gleefully rent construction paper filled the room. Eagerly, Natasha plucked free the ring. Her abashed gaze met Damon's, reminding him of everything he loved about her.

"Tiny rips like that are why someone invented tape," she said, clutching the poor, abused valentine in one hand. "I'll take care of it myself," Natasha assured him. "But first . . ."

"But first," Damon repeated solemnly. "I love you, Natasha. Would you please, *please* be with me forever?" Gently, he took the ring, then offered it to her. "Will you please marry me?"

In that slow, single moment when Natasha gazed at him, it felt to Damon as though the whole world stopped moving. No matter what else, he was sure his stupid heart stopped beating.

Then, "Yes! I already said yes! Yes, yes, yes!"

"Good. I say yes, too." With a smooth, certain gesture, Damon slid the ring on Natasha's finger. He lifted her hand, then kissed the back of it. He sighed, then gazed at her. "Now I've guaranteed myself a whole lifetime of good luck."

From across the room, Jimmy Torrance cleared his throat.

"We've already told you, son," he said in the midst of overseeing the chocolate tasting. "That good-luck stuff is an illusion."

"That's what you say, Dad." Damon smiled at Natasha, utterly overcome. "I feel it. It's real. There's no denying it."

"I agree," Natasha said, hugging him close. "Because from here on out, we're making our own good luck . . . together."

"Yay!" Milo shouted. "That means *I'm* lucky too!"

From there on out, the party took on an entirely new energy. Amy gave a few conspicuously sentimental sniffles, then took snapshots of the happy couple with her cell phone. Carol and Kurt both jabbered on about their "vital" roles in bringing together the happy couple. Jason grumpily stomped over for a furry congratulatory handshake. Jimmy made Natasha promise that she'd come over to the Torrance household for dinner very soon—and Natasha made him agree to bring Debbie to the Jenningses' place for a special dinner, too. Reminded of food, Damon glanced around, feeling satisfied and hopeful and free.

"Hey, where's the chocolate?" he asked. "I think the happy couple could use a little pick-me-up."

"Yeah!" Natasha agreed, looking around as well. "I heard there are supposed to be special allergen-free goodies to—" She stopped in surprise, then directed her gaze to Damon. "*You* did it. *You* are the mysterious inventor of the 'safe' candy."

Damon shrugged. "Milo was counting on me."

"I was counting on you, too, son." His father gave Damon a brusque hug. "You did a good job today. After a round of *unbiased* testing, I'd say your new candy bar line is a hit."

"Excellent." Damon looked around at the bedlam surrounding him. Wow, kids were noisy. "But that doesn't explain why we can't find a nosh around here. I'm starving! All this emotion has me hungry enough to gnaw on some tasty number-two pencils."

"Would you settle for some empty testing cups?" The teacher stopped by with one of the Torrance Chocolates trays. She frowned at the empty white paper cups arrayed on it. "I'm afraid all the children *loved* the chocolate. Every bite is gone."

"Well, then. I guess we'll just have to make more." With a heart full of gladness—and a head full of sticky, heart-shaped confetti that *may* have been overkill—Damon pulled

Natasha closer. "What do you say? Will you come back to work with me?"

"As your assistant?" Natasha asked, whipping her admiring gaze from her new engagement ring to his face. She pursed her lips, the telltale sign of overthinking when it came to her. "Well, I don't know. After all that's happened lately—"

"No, you dope! As my *partner*," Damon assured her. "I honestly don't think I can do it without you, Tasha."

Dubiously, she took in the chocolate-fueled mayhem surrounding them. "I'd say you've done pretty well so far."

"Only because I had this little monkey for inspiration." Laughing, Damon pulled Milo nearer. He gave the kid a tickle. "But without both of you by my side, life won't be much fun."

"Aha." With her eyes sparkling, Natasha crossed her arms. She gazed up at him, pretty and sexy and eternally, alluringly wise. "It always comes down to *fun* with you, doesn't it?"

"Sometimes. But if there's one thing I've learned lately, it's that there's enough time for everything—everything at the *right* time." Damon raised his hand in an approximate Boy Scout salute. "From here on out, I promise to have fun *and* work *and* love *and* responsibility, every single day."

Natasha arched her brows. "All at the same time?"

Decisively, Damon nodded. "With you, it will be easy." He reconsidered that. "Well, not easy. But awesome. Mostly. We might have to struggle sometimes. Probably. Because—"

"Yes." Natasha raised on tiptoe and kissed him. "I'll be your partner. I'll be your partner in *everything*."

"—because a smart guy once told me," Damon went on doggedly, casting a grateful glance at his buddy in the furry otter suit, "that sometimes your sore spots come up against each other and cause some problems. But what Jason *didn't* tell me is that your *good* qualities come together, too. When that happens . . .". Happily, Damon hugged Natasha closer. "It's magic."

"It's even better than magic," Natasha told him, hugging him back. "It's *sweet*. For a pair of nonstop chocoholics like us, life just doesn't get any better than that."

"What?" At that, Damon feigned outrage. "Are you saying you're marrying me for the free *chocolate*?"

"No, I'm marrying you for the *sex*," Natasha teased.

Gasping, Damon clapped his hands over Milo's ears. He made sure his feigned outrage got a little more outrageous.

"Uh-oh. Watch your language, you naughty girl."

"You've got that right," Natasha agreed in a low, seductive voice that was aimed at Damon exclusively. "I *am* naughty," she said. "Later on, I'll show you exactly how naughty. In detail."

Then, with a wink to show that she knew damn well that Damon's hands had covered Milo's ears well enough that he hadn't heard her racy remark, Natasha sauntered away to help clean up.

"Well," Damon called after her blusteringly, "I'm marrying you for the true love! So how about that?"

As far as indignant rejoinders went, it was a little weak.

But as far as things that needed to be said went, Damon decided, that one went all the way.

Relieved and giddy, he dropped his hands from Milo's ears.

The boy tugged his sleeve. "If my mom's been naughty," he volunteered, "you should give her a timeout in her room."

"A timeout?" Damon angled his head. "What's that?"

Milo explained about the typical disciplinary action that Natasha employed—something to do with making sure the wayward party stayed in his or her bedroom for a while. With everything else that was going on, Damon was a little hazy on the details.

But he *did* grasp that this so-called "punishment" would

involve keeping Natasha in her bedroom a lot. Maybe all day . . . and all night. Most likely, at Damon's sole discretion.

Overall, the idea had a lot of potential.

"So, Milo . . . can two people be in timeout together?"

The boy shrugged. "I guess so. I don't see why not."

"Me, either," Damon agreed, already making plans as he watched Natasha circulate among the children, talking and coloring and occasionally picking up a fallen balloon. "I might have to give that timeout technique a try. Thanks, Milo!"

"Anytime!" the boy said, then he skipped away.

Satisfied with . . . *everything*, Damon watched him go.

Then he looked at Natasha again. She didn't know it yet, but their life together was going to be amazing. He might not have spent much time in suburbia until now, but Damon figured he was getting the hang of it pretty quickly. This timeout thing was only the beginning.

Feeling unbelievably lucky, Damon went to join the woman he loved. Starting now, he knew as he greeted Natasha and stood by her side, Damon Torrance believed in a lot of things. . . .

And at the very top of the list . . . was true love.

Dear Reader,

Thank you for reading *Melt Into You*!

I had a truly wonderful time writing about Natasha and Damon. I hope you had just as much fun reading about them! I visited several small chocolatiers who inspired me to create Torrance Chocolates (because one terrific perk of the writer's life is turning real-life experiences into fictional fun), and I loved doing all the necessary chocolate-sampling "research" that was necessary, too. But in the end, nothing is sweeter than true love. And although Damon believes *he's* the lucky one, I know it's really *me* . . . because I get to share my stories with you! Thanks again for letting me entertain you.

If you're curious about my other books, please visit my website at www.lisaplumley.com, where you can read free first-chapter excerpts from all my books, sign up for my reader newsletter or new-book reminder service, catch sneak previews of my upcoming books, request special reader freebies, and more. You can also "friend" me on Facebook or follow me @LisaPlumley on Twitter. The links are available for you on lisaplumley.com.

As always, I'd love to hear from you! You can send e-mail to lisa@lisaplumley.com or write to me c/o P.O. Box 7105, Chandler, AZ 85246-7105.

By the time you read this, I'll be hard at work on my next Zebra Books contemporary romance. It's another Kismet Christmas story, and I'm really excited about it. I hope you'll be on the lookout for *Together for Christmas*!

Best wishes,
Lisa Plumley

Keep reading for a special sneak peek at
Together for Christmas,
available in October 2012!

Babysitting wasn't usually in Casey Jackson's repertoire. Neither was snow.

Taken together, that made it pretty damn confounding that he was currently driving through a blizzard on his way to a babysitting job. But this babysitting job was special. It was, quite literally, a babysitting job he couldn't refuse.

Not if he wanted to stay gainfully employed, at least.

Which he did. It was a matter of necessity. And pride.

Squinting through the windshield of his rented four-wheel-drive Subaru, trying not to become hypnotized by the flurries of snowflakes hitting the glass, Casey reminded himself he could do this. He could babysit. *And* he could drive through a snowstorm.

Hell, he could do anything! He might not typically hang out with rug rats (a very deliberate choice) or grapple with badass subzero weather conditions (or *any* weather conditions, really)—as a top troubleshooter with one of L.A.'s premier talent agencies, he had little need to do either—but he *did* get things done. He got problems sorted, difficult divas placated, and on-set imbroglios smoothed over.

Making things right was Casey's specialty. Handling things that other people couldn't manage was his forte. He was the man who got in, got everyone back on track, and then got out . . . leaving everyone in his wake satisfied, harmonized, and improbably happy to have been "managed" by the best in the business. It was just what he did. He didn't know why he did it so well. He just . . . did.

Until Casey had joined his agency, his job hadn't even existed. One crucial averted crisis later, it had. Thanks to his first major success, now his agency paid him to go wherever he was needed to rehab star athletes' dinged public images, settle down wild rockers and rappers, and mollify demanding megastars—megastars like pop sensation Heather Miller, whose over-the-top, overbudget, wildly ambitious *Live! from the Heartland* televised Christmas special had brought him to Kismet in the first place.

His agency didn't usually pay Casey to babysit. But they *did* trust him enough to give him a very long leash. That meant that he was free to deal with crises like this one on his own terms. If Casey wanted to spend the next few weeks making like a muscle-bound, frostbitten, ridiculously overpaid man-nanny while he worked his deal-making magic with Heather Miller and her TV special, he could. So that's what he was going to do.

Even if the thought of doing it while stuck in the tiny, touristy, northwestern Michigan burg of Kismet made him want to bolt for Gerald R. Ford International Airport in Grand Rapids, some fifty miles distant, and forget he'd ever set foot in town.

Seriously. The place was like a freaking Christmas card come to life, Casey realized as the blizzard momentarily eased up. He ran his windshield wipers to push away the snow and then peered outside again, taking in the picturesque, snow-piled, lively small-town streets surrounding him. Old-fashioned holiday decorations were plastered over every inch of available space. Holiday music wafted from municipal speakers, penetrating his car's windows as he waited at a stoplight. Shoppers bustled to and fro on the surrounding sidewalks, carrying overstuffed bags and smiling at one another. A few of them even smiled at *him*.

He frowned, momentarily bewildered by their neighborliness. Then he smiled back. He lifted his gloved hand in a brief wave.

The passersby waved back, then kept going. Still flummoxed, Casey watched as they made their way into a nearby sweetshop, stamping their booted feet and adjusting their woolly scarves.

L.A. was friendly enough—hell, just about everyone everywhere was friendly to Casey—but this bucolic, over-the-top holiday jollity was . . . different. It was totally inexplicable.

Somehow, he realized, his newest assignment had taken him to *The Twilight Zone 2.0: The Hallmark Channel Edition*.

Most of the year, as Casey had learned before leaving L.A., Kismet was a resort town full of lakeside B&Bs, busy bait-and-tackle shops, dusty antique stores, and rundown mom-and-pop restaurants. Thanks to in-state daytrippers and out-of-state vacationers who were willing to pay for its kitschy ambiance, the town had done all right for itself, even in a shaky economy.

What he *hadn't* uncovered beforehand—what everyone at his agency had undoubtedly hidden from him (with good reason)—was that, in December, the whole damn place turned into Christmas Central. It was, Casey thought as he surveyed the scene anew, like a Norman Rockwell painting crossed with a Bing Crosby song dosed with a big handful of silvery tinsel and hung with candy canes, then broadcast in surround sound and Technicolor. It was idyllic and authentic and damnably jolly.

It smelled like gingerbread, too. *All over town*. He'd noticed that as he'd gotten out of his car on location to meet Heather Miller. The fragrance still lingered here, miles away. How was that even possible? Who ate gingerbread, anyway? Elves?

The upshot was, Kismet was everything Casey typically avoided. Times ten. Wrapped in a bow. With chaser lights on top and a garland of mistletoe on the side and *way* too much ho-ho-ho-ing going on in the background. Because, to put it bluntly, Casey was not a "Christmas" kind of guy. As a matter of principle, he dodged all things green and red and sparkly and heartwarming. As a matter of necessity, he didn't "do" the holidays. As a matter of fact, he'd never even been tempted to.

Nothing short of a catastrophe on the scale of Heather Miller's problem-plagued holiday special—and the lucrative bonus Casey stood to earn if he brought it in on budget and on time—could have made him spend more than an hour in a town like Kismet: a place that promised candlelit ice-skating sessions, an official Christmas parade, a fanciful holiday-light house tour, sleigh rides with genuine jingle bells, a Santa Claus-lookalike contest (in the town square, right next to the community's fifty-foot decorated Noble fir tree), *and* a weekly cookie-decorating get-together and jamboree.

It was all so flipping wholesome. Casey thought he might be breaking out in freckles and naiveté already. It was possible he felt an "aw-shucks" coming on. He'd only been in town an hour—long enough to meet Heather Miller, hear her initial demands, and start laying the groundwork for the two of them to come to terms. At this rate, he'd morph into Gomer Pyle by lunchtime.

Muttering a swearword, Casey set his Subaru in motion again. He suddenly craved a cigarette, a shot of tequila, and a week's worth of irresponsible behavior—not necessarily in that order.

Boundaries made him itchy. Coziness made him cranky. And the holidays . . . well, they sent him straight into Scrooge mode.

While Casey realized that that character quirk was part of what made him ideal for this job—because his antipathy toward the holidays gave him a necessary clarity about Heather Miller's TV special and all its escalating complications—he still wasn't ready for . . . *this*.

He hadn't been ready for Heather Miller's opening salvo in their negotiations, either. Probably because she'd caught him off guard.

The problem is my little sister, the pop star had told Casey bluntly and confidentially, giving him an *almost* credible dose of blue-eyed solemnity in the process. *I haven't been back home to Kismet for a while*, Heather had confided, *and frankly, I think she's a little starstruck. I need someone to keep her . . . occupied for a while, so I can focus on performing*.

Casey had been dubious. He'd pushed Heather a little more, relying on his ability to establish an almost instant rapport.

But *People* magazine's pick for "sexiest songstress" had remained adamant. However unlikely her story, she'd stuck to it.

If you can keep Kristen busy for a while, I'm sure I can make fabulous progress on my special! Heather had insisted. She'd tossed back her long, famously blond hair (there was a shade of Garnier hair color named after her), offered him a professionally whitened smile, and added, *Kristen is a great girl. Just a little . . . unsophisticated. She's never left Kismet. She doesn't "get" show business the way you and I do*.

By the time the former *Rolling Stone*, *Vanity Fair*, and *Vogue* cover girl had quit describing her "tomboyish" younger sibling, Casey had formed a pretty clear picture of the braces-wearing, cell phone-toting, gawky girl with Bieber Fever and a wardrobe of Converse sneakers whom he was expected to babysit.

He'd decided to agree to do it, too. To babysit. *Him*.

Or at least, if not technically *babysit*—because Heather hadn't actually used that particular word—then *entertain* the kid long enough to allow Heather to get down to work.

It wouldn't be so bad, Casey figured. He'd probably trail little Kristen Miller to the mall, listen to her squee over the latest *Twilight* movie with her bubblegum-chewing friends, and watch her check in to Facebook a zillion times a day. Maybe he'd help her with her homework or something. Maybe he'd take her to the zoo. If the zoo was open in December. Whatever it took to keep her out of her older sister's way until the TV special was in the can, that's what Casey was prepared to do.

Frankly, he'd agreed to do worse a few times in his life.

As a gambit meant to earn some goodwill with Heather while encouraging her to fulfill her contractual obligations to the network, it wasn't ideal. It was time consuming and inefficient and oblique. He didn't like the idea of keeping the younger Miller sister "out of the way," either. It seemed heartless. As far as Casey was concerned, Heather should have worked out her differences with her kid sister herself, straightforwardly and reasonably, the way a regular person would have done.

But in this scenario, as in all others, Heather was "the talent." That meant she was exempt from normal human behavior and normal human expectations. Casey had logged plenty of hours pacifying performers like her. He knew the score by now. More than likely, Heather's little sister did, too.

If Kristen Miller was wreaking havoc on the TV special, causing delays for America's sweetheart, she'd have to be dealt with. Casey would have to be the one to do it. The sooner, the better. Once he'd assessed the situation more closely, he'd reevaluate things, he promised himself. For now, he planned to meet Kristen, figure out her angle, and see what happened from there. It wasn't a perfect beginning, but it was a start. And Casey believed, above all else, in moving forward.

Because nothing ever lasted forever.

Except maybe fruitcake.

And that persistent gingerbread aroma all over town.

It was actually starting to smell good to him. Spicy and sweet and full of down-home goodness, with just a *hint* of—

Ugh. Screw this, Casey decided as he noticed the unbelievably sappy direction his thoughts had just taken. He was jonesing for old-timey gingerbread, daydreaming about its flavor profile like a wine aficionado anticipating a limited-run Napa Valley merlot, *craving* its Christmassy qualities most of all. *I need a detour from Christmasville before I do something stupid*.

So he wrenched his steering wheel sideways, floored the gas, and pulled into his destination fifteen minutes ahead of schedule. He might not find the Teenaged Terror of TV Specials in the first place Heather had suggested he look, but anything was better than giving in to Christmas . . . and all the syrupy, sentimental, *deceitful* promises that came right along with it.